The Route To All Evil

The Route To All Evil

Frank Warburton

Printed in the United States of America

ISBN:	Softcover	978-1-63871-674-7
	eBook	978-1-63871-685-3

Republished by: PageTurner Press and Media LLC
Publication Date: 11/04/2021

To order copies of this book, contact:
PageTurner Press and Media
Phone: 1-888-447-9651
info@pageturner.us
www.pageturner.us

Previous titles by author
Timeless Revenge

With Thanks

To my family who have given me the need to complete this goal. A special thank you to my closest friends John & Liz who have stood by me for over forty years never abandoning me.

To all my past colleagues and friends who I have served with it is important that we have the trust we have built over the years together. That trust is special and will never be destroyed no matter what the circumstances. It is our driving force.

To the many men and women around the world who have served or are still serving your efforts are never in vain and will always be cherished by the Nations for which you protect.

Quote from the Bible

1 Timothy 6:10

For the love of money is a root of all sorts of injurious things.

PROLOGUE

Basra September 2006
Al Jameat Police Complex, Iraq.

Just sitting alone in this damp, cold, tiny 6x6 cell Tom Warburton pondered what had happened to him over the past six months or so. The bruises that he had sustained in the initial arrest he had been pulled in on were now old issues and covered by the resounding amount of new ones administered by his captors over the past few months. First they start blue then with repeated treatment they go black. They were sore, the skin so tender and sensitive.

The walls around him were cold and musky following the unprecedented rains that had plagued the area over the last two days. Global warming was the only answer Tom could think of to this change in climate in such a dry country. It had been the opposite in the weeks preceding where temperatures outside were in their 50 centigrade levels and the humidity was low, the winds that blew were dry and fierce against the face if you left it uncovered.

He knew though that this particular cell was way below the ground level as it took them quite a time to get him down to it with his head in a hooded sack when he first arrived which was, bugger, he couldn't even think how long he had been in custody.

Tom's skin was beginning to tingle as if it wanted to remove itself from the rest of him. Being unable to wash properly was a burden for him and it was this discomfort that irritated him most. Even though he couldn't see himself in any light as it was constantly dark he feared he might suffer from lice under the skin. The thought even was enough to get the itching going.

Now the weather was starting to turn back to normal for this time of year was what he had heard through his captor's gossip when he could hear them. The rain that came was in all one downward torrent and the temperatures had dropped dramatically. It was now cold due to the damp and the cold night air and Tom craved to be able to have a hot bath and shave the growth from his face that had built up on his once clean, smooth face but he knew that would be farthest from his captive's thoughts.

There was a bucket in the corner when he needed it and when he could find it in the dark, as it was he sometimes fell over the damn thing and then the stink would make him wretch. It reminded him of the stories he had read at school about the old Victorian prisons in the UK. He thought that he was just missing the rats here though, but then again sometimes he could hear plenty of scurrying and scratching around him.

This room or excuse for one did have a light, a bright light like a spot lamp that burned his eyes, when it was turned on only at times to annoy him or just to keep him awake. Usually it happens when he was trying to get sleep after a day of angry exchanges with the guards that persistently came in to question him.

Tom didn't know the difference between day or night at the present as he hadn't even got a window because of the depth of his cell underground to indicate either. There were no voices anywhere around him till the time came to interrogate him once again and then the speaker on the ceiling comes into operation and blasts his ears with what might be the latest hit songs in the desert. If only it was accompanied by belly dancers, now that would help him through this. Was he the only prisoner here or were there others spread through this place of disrepute, he just couldn't tell.

He had read so much about the prisons in Iraq, if that's where he was, he was unsure, whether they be US based or local he had no pleasant thoughts about them.

Tom had to endure daily torture and beatings but his youthful mental strength was still in the positive mode. Why, was the question he often wondered to himself? Tom would just sit thinking about his parents and what would they do if they were placed in similar circumstances to what he had found himself.

Tom's father used to often tease him about water boarding and how they used to comply to the laws in his days but the Iraqis were as good as anyone with this type of torture from what he could gather as to the effects of the water treatment he received. He had to admit if he had been hiding anything he would have given it all away to get free from their sick methods. Dad had always told him that you never were to be a hero when captured just show them you are just a normal man and cry if you have to and beg for mercy. You can give some to lighten your load without compromising your colleagues. But Tom had no secrets that had to be protected but the bastards still persisted in asking for things he had no idea about.

Stuff the movies and the tough guys that just hung on till rescue came, who the fuck was Audie Murphy anyway? Rescue was never coming for Tom he knew and he felt the Government for which he served was not even showing any awareness in the public arena that he was even missing in action. Deniability, dad used to say, was a favourite of Government Departments but Tom was a serving member of Her Majesties Forces not in any special ops or units, just an everyday officer in the Royal Electrical and Mechanical Engineers attached to a joint command of peace keepers which were left to advise and train the Iraqi Army. Some thanks you get for your efforts.

Tom just wanted to scream out at times but just couldn't give the Squaddies guarding him the pleasure of a broken man, the old man's stubbornness was coming out in him as he got older at times. Oh to have Mel Gibson or Sylvestor Stallone here to help him he thought. I'm sure the three of them could defeat and rectify the wrongs that have taken place here in this God forsaken country. Damn Tony Blair for ever getting us mixed up in it with the war hungry Yanks.

"What the hell is happening to me?" Tom thought numerous times to himself. Nearly six months he had been locked away. No visits from the Embassy and no co-operation from his so called allies in the area he was serving with. He had been abandoned and often wondered why he hadn't gone mad but then again had he? "Shit I long for justice but it never seems to be able to find me." Went through his mind.

Name, rank and number is all well and good to repeat like the films tell us but if the people asking the questions are sick of hearing it they usually tend to beat the crap out of you for your honest answers. Keep thinking James Bond what would he do in this spot. Perhaps Tom could undo the door hinges with his now long nails and proceed down the corridors of this unkempt excuse for a prison till he find a way out through the walls to freedom.

"Sod it" He thought "I would be better off being Dr Bloody Who when it comes to trying to get out of this place." He couldn't bring himself to think escape from here at the moment and that had been his sorry saga for the past six months. Just sit and hope and pray till there is some kind of resolve or some angel comes through that damn door and says "Sorry we got the wrong guy, you can go now." "I bet that will never happen." Tom thought shaking his head.

His mind keeps playing the MASH theme through and through, but when he thinks hard about it he suddenly remembers the real name of that theme, Suicide, something he cannot fully grasp no matter what his mind thinks at times.

Tom's parents probably think he's dead, lost in action or something as he had not written to them since his imprisonment or come to think of it anyone else since his incarceration here. No mail came in either or if it did it probably gave the rag heads something funny to laugh about.

Tom kept playing the same old tapes through his head to keep his sanity. "He was named after his father Tom who is English and a Londoner at that. His sense of humour is something else, believe me. However, I do wonder how his humour would have got him through this 'tits up' situation. He had served his country and got a bit of a bum deal while doing so but in the end he came out of it ok. Mums Vietnamese and lived in Malaya for most of her life under secrecy which is where I was born. She was in something like witness protection but worked in the BKN, Malaya's notorious Secret Intelligence Service."

Tom's Mum and Dad's story was a long one but it all turned out happy in the end and they are now settled in Padstow in the West of England. They are the happiest couple he had ever seen in his short life and they are so full of love for each other and Tom as well. Dad was a bit unsure when he told him he wanted to enter the British Army with Tom senior making him make one promise and that was never to try out for selection for the SAS. His own experience was the cause of many years of anguish. It is the thoughts of his parents and their affection for each other that keeps Tom driving onwards and hopeful for a future freedom. These thoughts were the ones that kept him positive.

Tom used every spare moment to keep his body in peek form. His past martial arts training which he had undertaken since the age of 10 was a blessing in some ways, it gave him the confidence to keep sane and to keep his reactions and actions in some kind of order. Patience was a word he had heard so much about and now he was learning the true meaning of it. The only thing he doubted was the word trust, whom he could trust now were very few.

Other thoughts that kept him occupied were about the country he was in now. Something he often repeated to himself when he was expecting his hosts to come knocking:

Subject matter he played in his mind nearly everyday:
Is there any truth in this following thought?

1. The Garden of Eden was in Iraq.
2. Mesopotamia, which is now Iraq, was the cradle of civilization!
3. Noah built the ark in Iraq.
4. The Tower of Babel was in Iraq.
5. Abraham was from Ur, which is in Southern Iraq.
6. Isaac's wife Rebekah is from Nahor, which is in Iraq.
7. Jacob met Rachel in Iraq.
8. Jonah preached in Nineveh—which is in Iraq.
9. Assyria, which is in Iraq, conquered the ten tribes of Israel.
10. Amos cried out in Iraq.
11. Babylon, which is in Iraq, destroyed Jerusalem.
12. Daniel was in the lion's den in Iraq!
13. The three Hebrew children were in the fire in Iraq. (Jesus was in Iraq also as the fourth person in the fiery furnace!)
14. Belshazzar, the King of Babylon saw the 'writing on the wall' in Iraq.
15. Nebuchadnezzar, King of Babylon, carried the Jews captive into Iraq.
16. Ezekiel preached in Iraq.
17. The wise men were from Iraq.
18. Peter preached in Iraq.
19. The 'Empire of Man' described in Revelation is called Babylon, which was a city in Iraq.

And you have probably also seen this statement before now.

Israel is the nation most often mentioned in the Bible. But do you know which nation is second? Under translations to today's geographical terms it is Iraq!

The names used in the Bible for Iraq are Babylon, Land of Shinar, and Mesopotamia. The word Mesopotamia means between the two rivers, more exactly between the Tigris and Euphrates Rivers. The name Iraq, means country with deep roots.

Indeed Iraq is a country with deep roots and is a very significant country in the Bible.

No other nation, except Israel, has more history and prophecy associated with it than Iraq.

And also . . . This is something to think about!

Since America is typically represented by an eagle. Saddam should have read up on his Muslim passages . . .

The following verse is from the Koran (the Islamic equivalent to the Bible) Koran (9:11)—For it is written that a son of Arabia would awaken a fearsome Eagle. The wrath of the Eagle would be felt throughout the lands of Allah and lo, while some of the people trembled in despair still more rejoiced; for the wrath of the Eagle cleansed the lands of Allah; and there was peace.

Note the verse number! Hmmmmm?! God Bless you all. Amen!

Did it really matter about that promise he had made not to try for Selection to the SAS as he felt he had got himself into just as much shit, if not more as a regular officer serving in a service Corps of all things.

Tom always remembered the Sergeant Major in Sandhurst, officer training, when one day one of his colleagues said he joined the Army to be an officer in the Engineers and not as a soldier.

The voice that thundered out of such a small man as the Sergeant Major was heard as far away as France he was sure.

"Boy, you have a lot to learn and now is the time to start." He yelled two inches from the man's nose. "When you join this man's Army you have just two things to remember. One you are a soldier first, and two you're a tradesman second. Remember that son and you may survive what is thrown at you during your time in that uniform."

He was blasted alright. Soldier first, that is what I was when this unwelcomed holiday started. Just a junior officer who got roped into a so called helping investigative arrangement with the Royal Military Police.

The arrangement to assist the RMP had seemed a simple one at first. Their objective was to investigate a so called fraud that had taken place during the end of violence that preceded the British Army's tour of duty to educate and train the Iraqis, when a cache of gold and currency had been mislaid, so they said. Some ridiculous amount of 70 million dollars. Why me though Tom had asked himself many times? But as per usual you never got answers to your questions from yourself just further confusion to comply with.

Their response, Tom's illustrious commanders, to this was the fact that the men they were looking at were the Royal Engineers tasked with the transportation and who better to understand an engineer than another one. What a load of bollocks that was to be.

Tom remembered their names well, the men in the red caps. A Captain by the name of Peter Caulfield and his trusty sidearm, a gruesome looking Corporal named John Dickson. Both men were from the North of England and Tom had major problems trying at times to understand them when they started rabbiting on in their Northern slang. Also with them was a young Intelligence officer, about Tom's age, a good looking chick Lieutenant Sandra Crisp. Boy she was something to look at even in her combat gear. Tom could see now why the old man said he never liked the idea of women serving in the front line. Boy she definitely took your mind off the job in hand.

The first day Tom met these guys would stick in his mind for eternity. This was the start of his first operation outside his normal job responsibilities. One which would lead him into unknown territory.

When will it stop? ***To the End*** [Classic for suicide]
Laying in the dark
I search for answers
My pain gathers in me
How long must this last?
What has caused all this anguish?

The dark room drifts through my mind
I understand so little
This is what it's like to be blind
Time to think and reflect
Time to concentrate
When will it end?
Tablets and medicine blend
Relief somewhat
Is this the way it is?

Darkness looms around me
No light to be seen
To take myself is it mean?
An option to consider
To ponder and sort
My decision alone
My family so distraught

Is it brave to make this choice?
Or selfish to bear thought
Can I leave all this?
What will I miss?
Is torment to befriend me?

Oh to live forever
And be with those you love
To suffer never again
A dream or possible reality
If only it were possible

Still the mind wonders
Evading what is at hand
Do I or don't I
Will I make this stand?
Those that have in the past
Escape their suffering
Brave or cowardice, it does not matter
Their choice removed the strain
For now, I cannot take such a decision so vast
Because of love then my choice now
Happiness from memories of past

Live life, love life, be life
My time is not yet right

CHAPTER 1

Outskirts of Basra July 2005
0800hrs

The warehouse was large, virtually empty other than the three four ton Bedford trucks displaying British Royal Engineer signage supplied by 32 Combat Engineers. This vast complex of what once was a vibrant Industrial area of Basra before the invasion of the Coalition forces was now a deserted and abandoned wasteland awaiting some kind of reinvention from its new leaders. It stunk of decomposing matter which was hard to explain without trying to actually find the source.

Al Hartha power station shed its giant shadow over this particular place and was miraculously partially back in production after the Royal Engineers had spent hundreds of man hours repairing it and trying to their hardest to get the majority of Basra back on line as some semblance of normality for the local population.

This warehouse was now the assembly point for a secret British mission to return Gold bullion, US and Sterling currency that had been discovered hidden away in one of the numerous Palaces which were spread around this desert nation, back to the coffers in Baghdad after serious negotiations between Britain and its equals now installed in Baghdad.

A lone forklift had just loaded the last of the cargo onto two of the trucks lined up within the shed. The third truck being a spare to follow in case there were any faults on the two loaded ones.

"Ok that's the last." Said Major Welsh RE to his men now assembled in a line in front of him. "Remember guys this all depends on you men for the security of this operation. Good luck."

There seemed to be smiles all round from the men, all were badged Royal Engineers. This was to be an adventure for the junior ones of whom two had only been in theatre about a month or so namely Sappers Waldon and Covertle. The third Sapper Reed was an old hand and had been with the present Regiment for its past six months and was looking forward to returning to their base back in Germany along with Staff sergeant Saxby who had completed two tours within Iraq. Two other sergeants, Broad and Smythe, both having been alongside Saxby on previous tours. Along with Reed the senior ranks had formed a formidable team together led by their illustrious Major Welsh.

"I'll leave you guys to prepare to move out." Continued Welsh. "you know the route and the format for communications so there is no need to go over them again."

"Sir." S/Sgt Saxby answered with complete understanding. "We are ready and keen to get underway."

"Your escort should be here any moment. Take care men and I'll see you on your return."

That statement was a bit of a porky as there had been some scheming going on between the old hands prior to this convoy being confirmed. These men had formed a plan that would definitely blow the British Command out of its nice little comfort zone into one of the most embarrassing scenarios experienced by the Brits in this theatre of operations.

Welsh left the men as they circled their respective vehicles and carried out final service checks. He headed for the small door at the western end of the warehouse where on opening it was met by a Landrover and driver. The driver was not the normal one for Welsh, as he was a Redcap, a Captain.

"All ready Tony." The redcap said to Welsh as he got into the passenger seat and shut the door.

"Looks pretty good at the moment, Peter. The men are ready and raring to go, just hope our little plan goes well and we have no upsets eh?" Welsh grinned at his partner. "You sure about your part at the graveyard Peter?"

"No worries. With the outcome we are hoping for it is worth it. What about the set up at the graveyard with the vehicles has that been organized?"

"Saxby has it all in hand."

"Shame about the new boys though Tony."

"Collateral Damage Peter, collateral damage. We must not get a conscience about anyone at this stage or we'll never succeed with our little retirement project." Welsh continued on in such a toffee nosed attitude "Have you sorted the clear way back for the trucks return through your Iraqi police mates."

"Sure have, they were only too keen with what I managed to get them through the NAAFI stores. And of course our friend Ashid has been more than obliging."

"Good, now let's get out of here. I need to be at the command centre before the radio chatter starts."

As the Landrover took off towards the highway and turned south towards the British Command centre near Uwaysan a small convoy, comprising of two Landrovers and two Scimitars tank killers, turned off the highway towards the warehouse.

"There goes the first escort Tony. They should be ready to move in about half hour or so." Peter Caulfield said to Welsh with an evil smirk to his face. He had all of fifteen minutes to drop off Welsh and get himself in front of the convoy before they moved. He was banking on Saxby to ensure that worked in his favour.

Back in the warehouse the men had fired up their trucks filling the upper reaches of the warehouse with diesel fumes. A couple of the men were having a smoke to the side of the complex while the drivers sat and revved their engines building up the air pressure in the brake tanks ready to depart.

Within the next fifteen minutes the arrival of the escort built up the excitement within the group and the opening of the warehouse doors letting in the two Scimitars finally setting up the final preparations.

The two track vehicles pulled up alongside the trucks and the crews quickly dismounted form them. The six men here were from the Blues and Royals and were made up of a lieutenant and sergeant accompanied by four other troopers, three men in each vehicle. This was a first escort and was officially to escort the three Bedford's to the outer British area around Nasiriyah before handing over to a second escort to go the next stage.

The lieutenant and sergeant introduced themselves to Saxby and went through the plan for the transportation of the cargo to their changeover point which would entail a unit of American marines continuing the escort to Baghdad. After twenty minutes they were all agreed to what route was to be taken and all the requirements needed for communications.

The Blues and Royals Landrover escort had handed over their responsibilities of the two track vehicles and had left the warehouse area to return to their own base. Therefore they had left the remaining men and vehicles as the ones to be on the convoy to Baghdad alongside the Engineers.

At 0930 hrs the convoy was ready to depart with two members of the Engineers in each of the Bedford cabs. The two new boys were split between the rear two Bedford's. The leading Scimitar edged itself out of the warehouse and lined up along the roadside outside waiting for the three trucks to follow on behind.

The commander was ready equipped with his GPMG loaded and ready for any action that might have been needed. Out came the three Bedford trucks and followed closely behind by the second Scimitar similarly equipped as the first. A crewman of the second Scimitar shut off the door of the warehouse and then scrambled up on top of the scimitar alongside his commander.

"Golf Oscar to Charlie Oscar, over" the young lieutenant spoke into his mike.

"Charlie Oscar receiving." A returned comment came over the radio.

"Golf Oscar, advancing over."

"Rodger Golf Oscar. Good luck, out."

All was now a go for the convoy as they started moving slowly forward. The next contact which was pre arranged with base would be in 4 hours at 1330 hrs. The sun was blazing down now, a most inhospitable climate for most things including sitting up top of a vehicle with the engine's warm air blowing onto you. The day was virtually perfect for their drive to Baghdad. All the men were smiling and looking forward to what was ahead, or some were and the others, the two newbies, had no real clue to what was going to happen ahead of them. Their thoughts was what they could get up to in Baghdad at the end of the drive before they had to return to their normal duties in Basra.

The convoy headed west out of the Industrial area till it reached Route 6 where they turned to the north and headed to the northern outskirts of Basra. The roads were clear in comparison to other city areas that these guys had been through earlier in the day. Most of the route was cleared by the local Police under instructions not to interfere with the convoy for any reasons.

The route took them through areas of urban sprawl, Iraqi style, finally at the outer ring of Basra where they came face to face with their first chicane roadblock manned by the Iraqi Police. This was the area of Al Qurnah where they would turn to the west and head out towards Nasiriyah through territory bordered by the River Euphrates and massive lakes to the north and south. This was a desolate open area as far as people were concerned with few inhabitants to worry about.

The lieutenant in the lead vehicle spoke a few words towards the guard commander at the roadside who then turned and indicated that his men should wave the convoy through unheeded. These chicanes were very effective at filtering down the traffic flow but also they were a preferred target to get at the Allies that drove through them regularly. A good operator could take out any vehicle he chose to with a rocket propelled grenade which was the weapon of choice for those who wanted to disrupt so called progress.

Out past the road block the road ahead was a dusty, deserted raised mound more in the form of a track than main highway. The original highway had been so damaged during the conflict to oust Saddam that the Engineers who had responsibility for the roads had forged a track alongside the bomb cratered highway until they had time to train and organize local workman to relay the concrete sheets that had formed the original roadway.

The dust stirred up by the lead vehicle nearly hid the following trucks under a blanket cloud. It would have been hard to recognise the origin of the vehicles other than the obvious following Scimitar with all crewmen covered completely against the dust ball that flew towards them. They had wrapped their faces with local scarves they had purchased from the local markets. Thankful for the ease they could cover themselves to protect from the dust thrown up against them.

As they approached the area where the machinery/equipment cemetery come graveyard had been established over the past years they slowed down. This whole area was a place that had been used to house not only the Iraqi scrap from the original war between Allies and Iraq Forces but also British vehicles that had succumbed to IED attacks and the many infiltrators that were frequently pondering this area close to the Iranian border about 50 kms from their last Iraqi Police stop.

The lead Scimitar slowed as they neared the main area on the road where vehicles would normally turn into the vehicle cemetery. There in front of them stood a Landrover with a blue flashing light and a redcap standing to one side waving them in to the side.

The lead Scimitar pulled in alongside the redcap and the lieutenant lent over the side while pulling down his mouth guard and lifting his goggles to speak to the redcap.

"What's the problem?" The Lieutenant spoke loudly above the sound of his own idling engine.

"There's been a bit of a skirmish just further down the road and I was ordered by Comcen to get back here and hold you till the area is cleared." The redcap spoke with such a convincing tone it received no surprise exchange from the young Leutenant.

"How long do you think it will take Sir?" the lieutenant asked suddenly noticing the Captain insignia on the redcaps combats.

"They were just tidying things up as I left but I am waiting for their go ahead now, but as we wait I need to get you out of sight due to the cargo you are carrying. Please follow me Lieutenant and we'll get you out of eye shot."

The redcap turned and walked to his Landrover, jumped into the driver's side and slowly pulled forward leading the convoy into the cemetery dust bowl. The convoy moved off the main road and into the midst of the cemetery till it came to a halt by what looked like two identical trucks to what were in their own convoy. The difference was that the two Bedford trucks already there were remains of an IED some months before and were not easily recognisable to most.

The time was now creeping on to 1045 hrs and no one in the convoy suspected anything being wrong with what was just happening. The redcap indicated to the leading crew to dismount and take a break. They did other than the gunner atop who stayed on alert waiting in case anything untoward happened. These men were trained well with plenty of operational experience in their team.

The redcap deliberately moved the convoy into positions that gave them fifty metres between each other and the Scimitars placed at such an angle that they could not be seen from the rest of the convoy especially the redcap's Landrover. This deliberate placement was well planned by the redcap to effect what he was looking forward to carrying out a little later.

In the back of the Landrover were soft drinks in an esky and also a couple of large flasks with the same old stewed tea that the Army was famous for. The two Blues men of the first Scimitar helped themselves to the drinks as the redcap went to the first truck and spoke to Staff sergeant Saxby.

"Hi there, drinks in the back of the Landie for you and your men. Can you go down the line, Staff, and get the others to come forward and refresh? Including the end escort scimitar." Caulfield smiled at Saxby as if giving him a signal of some kind.

"Sure thing Sir. I'll ensure the guys come forward and I'll deal with the rear." Saxby replied with a nod.

As the redcap turned and walked back to his vehicle Saxby dismounted from his truck and got his driver Sapper Covertle to dismount out of the cab and to follow the redcap. On leaving his vehicle

Saxby, on the hidden side of the vehicle, pulled out his service pistol and out of one of the pockets of his protection vest he took out what looked like a silencer and proceeded to screw it into place. Once done he placed the completed weapon into the body armour so it was hidden from view. He was also carrying his SA80 rifle strapped and slung over the front of his body armour. He started to come around his truck and began walking to the next vehicle. No one else had dismounted as per their instructions at the main briefing where they were told not to dismount unless told by Saxby or a senior officer to do so.

The next truck held Sgt Broad and Sapper Reed who had also readied themselves with silencers and pistols. Saxby spoke to Broad and Reed direct at the side of the truck. "Drinks down the front end guys. We've been delayed for a short while, some trouble up ahead." Winking towards both as he spoke.

Broad nodded grabbed his rifle and waved his head to Reed for them to both head down to the Landrover. Both Reed and Broad started chatting to each other as they came around the front of the truck.

"You two right?" Saxby asked.

"Yep we're ready when you are." Broad returned.

"Get yourself switched on and get up front, the time starts now. We have just half an hour to get this whole thing completed."

Broad and Reed had their service pistols and silencers slide under their body armour, grabbed their SA80s from the truck, and then strapped them to their fronts. They both nodded to Saxby and headed to the rear of the truck where they checked that it was still strapped down securely.

Broad and Reed together set off towards the front of the convoy where the Landrover with the drinks was a pleasant welcome for them.

Saxby now had only the last Bedford and then the last escort to deal with. As he approached the Bedford Sergeant Smythe dismounted from the passenger side and did exactly what his other pals had done, screwed on a silencer to his pistol and slide it behind his body armour. Sapper

Waldon waited till Saxby told him to exit the cab at which time he told both Smythe and Waldon that there was refreshments at the front end of the convoy in the Redcap Landrover. Both Bedford occupants pulled out their SA80s and strapped them into position.

Smythe winked towards Saxby and then set off slapping Waldon on the shoulder as a form of encouragement which soon would mean absolutely nothing to him.

Saxby now alone started to walk towards the last vehicle and what was to be the start of the master deception. He approached the Scimitar and was met by the Sgt commanding it who had dismounted wondering what was going on. He stood and greeted Saxby as he came forward.

"You know you're not to dismount before I or a senior officer requests it. We must stick by the rules laid out at the main briefing me old mate." Saxby said rather sternly.

"Yes I know but with him up there covering all angles I thought it would be alright at this stage." Replied the Sgt.

"Rules are rules mate. Our boss is a stickler for em you know." "Sorry, it won't happen again. What's going on anyway?" the Blues

Sgt asked feeling a bit of a jerk.

"Just a small hold up down the road from some kind of insurgents. Some redcap has pulled us over to keep us out of any trouble, he has drinks up front for us if you would like to go and get some. I'll see what your mate wants on top and arrange to have it brought back for him."

"Great thanks for that." Said the Sergeant and continued "What about the driver does he stay or can he come forward."

"Take him forward with you, that's Ok."

The sergeant yelled back at the driver who shut down his engine and lifted himself out of his seat and proceeded to slide off the track vehicle. He was just as keen to get his legs moving as being in the seat of the Scimitar for long periods was uncomfortable at the best.

The two Blues crewmen headed off towards the front of the convoy and Saxby once he was sure they were out of earshot turned and walked towards the Scimitar. He held up his hand in a form of friendship and proceeded to pull himself up onto the vehicle.

"How do you put up with these poxy mini tanks?" He said to the lone Blues trooper on top, who had just eased himself back a touch in relaxation.

As the trooper started up into explaining how they loved these little tank killers, Saxby jumping up on top of the Scimitar had stood with his back to him while looking around the back of the vehicle and sliding his handgun out of his vest. The trooper was too busy trying to praise the little tank that he never noticed the pistol as Saxby turned and let off a thud into the side of his neck. That thud was all that was heard as the trooper slumped forward and slide down into the turret area with his gear hanging him up on the protrusions around the cupola ring.

Saxby quickly pulled the body up slightly and propped it so as it looked as if the dead sod was still watching out for the convoy. He then quickly jumped down and walked speedily to the front of the convoy. Here he was met with the remaining personnel numbering four Blues and Royals and the remainder of his own group of Royal Engineers.

The lead vehicle gunner had been taken a drink of tea by his driver and was enjoying it while screening the outer limits of their location. The Landrover was about a hundred metres away parked in the shade of a wrecked Warrior Armoured Car just out of sight of the trooper gunner.

On seeing Saxby return the redcap, Captain Caulfield looked towards him then nodded at him. The nod was returned which was his signal to get the remainder of their little tryst up and running.

Caulfield looked at Smythe and nodded which set Smythe off in the direction around the Warrior out of sight of the rest of the men. He came around the other side of the Warrior acting as if he had just had a pee, by pulling up his zipper on his combat trousers. He closed in on the lead Scimitar as the trooper looked down on him with a broad smile on his face.

"Got to have a leak when you can eh son?" Smythe said to the trooper as he came up alongside.

"No doubt about that mate." Replied the trooper still watching outwards over the area.

Smythe was now below the trooper's position on the side of the Scimitar and was sliding his gun out of his body armour holding it closely to the side of the Scimitar and out of the trooper's sight. He now had to find a way of getting a shot off without any noise or yells which may alert the others.

Smythe with one hand shoved a cigarette into his mouth then looked up and asked "Have you got a light, mate?"

"Yeh sure." Was the welcomed reply from the trooper and you heard him fumble a bit as he rummaged his pouches for his lighter. He sighed as he found what he was looking for, then turned towards the side and began to lean down towards Smythe much to Smyth's relief. Smythe seized his opportunity and quickly pulled up his weapon letting go a thud into the side of the trooper's neck. The trooper's eyes lit up and went lifeless as he slumped over the side of the tank blood streaming from the wound in the neck.

Smythe slid his weapon back into his body armour and jumped up on top of the Scimitar lifting the body back into some form of position that would not alert anyone from a distance.

He jumped down scratching around on the ground with his boot where a pool of blood was sitting to cover it and then retraced his steps back around the Warrior again acting as if he had just had a pee round the back of it as he had done just minutes earlier.

Caulfield on seeing Smythe return went to the front of the Landrover where he had a silenced pistol down alongside his seat hidden under some rags. He removed it and slide it between a folded map he had sitting on the front seat.

Meanwhile Broad had seen what was happening and had gone around the opposite side of the wrecked Warrior where he started to slide out his weapon ready.

The group of killers were now all ready for the final act. As Broad came back around the Warrior skeleton Caulfield saw him and started to walk to the back of the Landrover. On the opposite side of the Landrover stood the four remaining Blues and Royals men relaxed and enjoying their break with Smythe and Reed just to the side. At the rear of the Landrover stood two unaware newbies in the two new Sappers and alongside them was Staff Saxby.

As Caulfield cleared the rear of the Landrover he pulled his pistol from its cover prompting at the same time the other four pulling theirs. The Blues and Royals men looked shocked, very startled, they just managed to drop what they were holding but it was too late for them as Broad, Caulfield, Smythe and Reed plastered them with numerous thuds. The four being sandwiched together hit the deck without so much as a shout of surprise. Blood began to pool around their bodies.

The two new Sappers just stood, stunned mouths open catching flies and frozen in their boots. They knew or hoped they would see some action after all that's what that had joined up for wasn't it, but this wasn't at all what they expected. The obvious new part of their experience showed as they just stared at the action going on in front of their eyes.

Their moment of action was short lived as Saxby lifted his gun and planted two quick thuds one into each of their heads. Both dropped like stones losing life far too early.

"OK guys let's get these Blues men into their little tanks and place them nearer the wrecked trucks there.

Reed get the empty Bedford and place our two sappers in the cab, then bring it to the rear of the other two wrecks." Caulfield pointed to the two trucks they had parked near. It took them less than ten minutes to get the tanks into position and the bodies into the tanks and the truck. All the men worked frantically to get it done as speedily as possible.

After positioning the Scimitars themselves they placed one body into each of the mini tank driver's seat and one unceremoniously into the turret head first on both tanks.

By the time fifteen minutes had passed the two dead sappers were dumped into the Bedford which was now positioned close to the two old wrecks of two of the trucks already laying there. The two gold and currency carrying trucks then moved away from the wreckage area and lined up facing back towards Basra.

Saxby and Smythe quickly got to work sliding blocks of C4, they had brought out secretly in the third Bedford, around the Scimitars, Bedford and wrecked trucks. A timer was added to blow in an hour and twenty minutes. Saxby went over to Caulfield and spoke to him. "All explosives are in place and should go off by 1245hrs but in case you have unexpected company here is a remote detonation switch to guarantee the explosion sooner if required." He handed Caulfield the remote box no bigger than a Malteeser chocolate box

Caulfield looked at the Engineers. "Ok you guys get a shift on then and get yourselves out through the other side of Basra before the bang goes off. I'll hang around here to ensure anyone coming near won't twig what's going on. I will leave five minutes before the main bang. By the time they realize something is wrong and get a team on route to check you should be well out of the way and hidden down south." Caulfield had a bit of a smile on his face at this point as things were just going along quite swimmingly in his mind.

"Good luck Pete. See you in retirement money land." Saxby held out his hand and the two of them shook feverishly.

The two trucks started to move off alone this time and headed back towards Basra on the same route they had come out on. The road was deserted and no sign of any dust cloud in any direction just the cloud they were making.

They were to take a detour to the south over a bridge some thirty kilometres back towards Basra then head south around to the west of Basra and skirt around the city hopefully unnoticed. The time had clicked on and stood at 1125hrs. There was still some one hour and twenty minutes to wait for the bang.

Caulfield sat back in his Landrover and sighed. He was on his way to an enriched retirement and knew if all went well he would be able to exit the Army in about six months when his time was up and slip out of sight away somewhere nice in the world. The remainder, the engineers would be posted as killed in action and would be hopefully out of the country and settled down somewhere taking care of the nest egg they had in their grasp.

Welsh was himself within two months of retirement and he was due to leave Iraq within the next two weeks to return to UK prior to his decommission.

Peter Caulfield sat, relaxed sipping at a cup of sweet tea he had mixed up in his mug from the rear of the wagon. Dreaming wasn't normally part of his regime but today he was doing it and enjoying what he was visualising on. Beaches, sun, sand, cool drinks and of course the usual girls, bikini clad of course. What would his share of the money buy; his thoughts were endless at the moment.

Caulfield was suddenly shook into reality as he heard a rumble and looking around the front of his vehicle saw a large dust cloud coming from the highway towards where the Scimitars and trucks were now set up. He quickly looked at his watch and saw he still had fifteen minutes before the timer would set off the explosion. He had the remote though just in case which he quickly grabbed for and sat patiently watching the dust cloud come ever nearer.

The cloud started to clear a bit as whatever vehicle it was creating it slowed to a crawl. Then as it closed in on the area of the trucks he caught sight of the vehicles. Two Toyota Hi Lux utes carrying about four or five young Arab men in each of their trays were looking around to see what they could steal from the vehicles that lay here.

This was common event here every little piece of reusable material was worth its weight in gold to the locals. Be it engines or parts there of or even electrical stuff they could use on some of their own gear. The old saying 'one man's rubbish is another man's treasure'.

The vehicles stopped and Caulfield placed himself behind cover but able to see clearly what the new arrivals were doing. He watched hesitantly with his finger near the detonator switch waiting for an opportune moment if he needed it.

The two utes pulled closer to the Scimitar at the front as it was obvious that the Arab boys had seen them noting their condition was undamaged. They approached slowly as it looked as if there was a soldier on top with a machine gun. As they neared even further and there was no reaction from the little tank they edged even closer still.

It became apparent that they were not going to be stopped and they pulled right to the side of the Scimitar. One of the Arab boys jumped onto the little track vehicle and started yelling at his buddies waving his arms high in the air rejoicing. He had found a dead Allied soldier which he quickly kicked and spat on. His buddies started jumping on the Scimitar from one of the utes while the other turned and headed down the line to the last Scimitar.

Once there the men in the tray jumped onto the track and repeated the same as their buddies up front. They had found treasure in weapons that were left there by the Engineers.

Caulfield looked in disgust as the Arabs set about kicking the dead ones and trying to lift the bodies out of the little tanks. There was still eight minutes before the bang and his finger was becoming ever more fidgety.

He was disgusted at what he was seeing yet in his mind he knew he was no better than those committing the atrocious acts against the dead compared with what he had done some hour or so earlier.

His finger twitched on the button but he waited just a short while more as the two utes stayed alongside each mini tank and the men on top were climbing in and out of the tanks raising firearms and screaming with joy. They obviously had not noticed the explosives spread around the vehicles thankfully and as Caulfield waited for his moment he smiled to himself.

Explosion time was still five minutes away for the blast but Caulfield could not risk any of his new spectators being able to get away and spreading rumours of what they had found. He looked and made sure the Arabs were all engrossed in what they thought was a fortunate moment for them.

A wide smile spread across his face and he said out loud. "May Allah praise you all and lead you to Paradise to meet your virgin reward." And with that he pushed down on the button which was greeted with a rather larger than usual flash and bang that reverberated around the area followed by three to four other large explosions. The air became mixed with the smell of rubber burning and hot metal.

Bits flew and dust erupted around the area on a greater scale than Caulfield thought it would be that his colleagues had set up. Caulfield had ducked his head down to avoid being struck by any flying objects from the explosions. He lifted his head up and surveyed the area around. There was no evidence of any other vehicles whether nosey or otherwise. As he turned to look in the direction of the convoy as the dust clouds settled, he could slowly see that there were bits of metal spread around everywhere with small fires sending the occasional live round exploding into the air.

Caulfield could not recognise any of the vehicles that now lay in front of him, his colleagues had done a brilliant job. Not even any evidence of the Toyota utes was to be seen. He stood, shook himself down and returned to his Landrover satisfied with the outcome. It took him only a few minutes to smash the remote unit and dispose of it amongst some nearby wrecks then he jumped into the driver's seat and set off driving past the newly created wrecks checking that no living persons were there.

Caulfield felt relieved at the efforts of the day, setting off back to Basra through the checkpoint area the convoy had first come out through. He was within minutes of his final destination of Command HQ and satisfied all was going well.

He heard very little on the radio till he was informed of some attack on the convoy when he finally got to his base.

CHAPTER 2

British Army Compound-Uwaysan
Six months later February 2006

So this was Basra in all its glory, the city where Sinbad the Sailor reputedly set off for all his adventures. He would be so disappointed now seeing the ruins left from the war that had been going on between the Iraqis, Allies and the insurgents. Block upon block of buildings destroyed what was once a living, thriving city now with rubbish strewn over nearly every road within the city area. It was not a positive type of welcome for anyone just arriving here.

Tom had been in town for about two months on attachment to the British command HQ where he was responsible for the training of local Iraqi Soldiers or what Tom felt was an excuse for a soldier as they were so disrespectful and slovenly in their appearance, actions and attitude.

The British Army command area here after the majority of the troops had left was basically two very large prefabricated offices each containing three separate rooms and a hall which once housed the local Mahdi Army followers. Around the outer inside area of the compound were various workshops where instruction for the locals was carried out on a daily basis. The Compound itself was situated in what was one of Saddam's old Palaces surrounded by razor wire and now protected by a troop of US Marines rather than British personnel. The compound was situated to the South-East of the City.

As a force the British troops were not a fighting unit any more in this precinct, just a training unit. There were a few REME guys to help train local Iraqi soldiers on how to fix their own vehicles and maintain their armaments. These were Tom's responsibility in this theatre of operations.

The strain for the REME guys was whether they could eventually teach these local troops the best way to carry out repairs as half the time they ignored their instructors anyway. There was a sense of contempt between the Iraqi and the Allies in this compound not unlike any other compound in this devastated country.

A contingent of fifteen Royal Engineers to help with the re-establishment of local services and utilities within the city boundaries. A small group of Canadian electronics technicians along with a handful of German Bundeswehr personnel numbering about twenty who the rest had no idea what they were even there for.

This made up unit had had a pretty quiet time so far but for Tom who had been in theatre about two months things were about to change when he was summoned to the Colonels Office for a meeting. The Colonel was a thick set Yankee Marine and an obvious fighter waiting to have a go anytime it seemed.

It was a dusty, dry day about 1000 hrs when Tom received the invitation to attend his beloved Colonel's air conditioned pad. The walk across the compound was for him slow in the heat of the morning. His brain was going through the filing system that he called a brain to try to fathom what was the reason why on this day he had been summoned.

It was rare that he was ever included in the frequent chats that happened in the gold wing office of the Colonel. The Colonel didn't much like Tom being he was a bit of a mongrel in his eyes having an English father and Asian mother. He was a racist through and through never once showing otherwise.

Tom slowly strolled to the Colonel's door and knocked waiting for the usual gruff "ENTER" grunt to flow through the thick door. It came as it always did.

On opening the door he was greeted by a group of people, namely two Red Caps and a quite delicious looking Intelligence officer. Lieutenant Sandra Crisp, a 5'8" tall blonde. Hair bound up at the back and a face that Barby doll would be jealous of. That's where Tom's looking stopped but there were more, a couple of suits from the Firm and the Commandant from the British contingent still remaining in Iraq, Lt Col Fred Peterson of the Blues and Royals. Also in the room was a couple of locals at least they looked that way, from Baghdad dressed in their usual tea towels and blankets. Tom couldn't quite get his head around the local language as yet and the names of things to that day.

"Come on in lieutenant." Bellowed the Colonel as Tom stood still staring at Barby.

"Sir" was all Tom got out at this stage still wondering what was going down here. Tom still couldn't take his eyes off the girl. Boy he thought to himself I've only been away from the UK for two months as it was, I would hate to think what six will be like.

Someone back home once said the camels begin to look quite attractive after six months alone with men and Tom was, for sure not really wanting to experience that.

"I'll keep this as brief as possible but what I will point out is that nothing we talk about in here is to leave this room unless we are talking to each other is that understood?" the colonel went on glaring his eyes at everyone in the room.

There was a flurry of nods all around the room as they all began to find a chair to sit on. Hard as he tried Tom couldn't get close enough to the Intelligence Barby doll so ended up sitting between Capt Caulfield head of the RMP SIB unit in Basra and a suit from 6.

The Colonel pushed his chair back a few inches and breathed out heavily. He opened a file on his desk and started to prepare himself to speak with a couple of sharp coughs to clear his throat.

"What we have is a situation that none of us like which could be very damaging to our relationship with the Government of Iraq and extremely embarrassing for the Government of the United Kingdom." he began with a concerned voice. "Over the past few months or so the British Military Police have in co-operation with MI6 been investigating a possible fraudulent action by British personnel and it is now at a point where we need to take action."

Looking around the room Tom noticed a couple of smiles from the red caps and Intelligence officer and a serious defined scowl from our Iraqi visitors. The two suits just sat serious faced and non responsive but definitely their brains were shifting through the faces around them and sizing up all of those to what they could or could not do to assist them.

"I'll hand you over to Captain Caulfield of the RMP Special Investigation Branch who will fill in the blanks hopefully for you. Captain."

"Thank you Colonel." Answered Caulfield, as he stood proceeding to place himself in front of the whole group. "Some six months ago a consignment of gold bullion including US and UK currency that had been discretely shepherded away in a warehouse here in Basra by our Bathist friends from Baghdad went astray."

There was a look of disbelief as he stopped to let us take in what was said.

"The consignment of some seventy Million US dollars was to be taken by road from Basra to Baghdad to be returned to the coffers of the Iraqi Government. This task was assigned to the Royal Engineers already stationed here instead of just the Logistics people on hand."

"Why the Royal Engineers?" Tom piped up taking on a serious flow of heads towards his interruption.

"Because, young man, they were the most senior and combat experienced personnel on the base at the time without bringing in any others, such as strictly combat troops, that could have caused a bit of a stir. We did not want that to happen at any costs as the Madhi Army was still at loggerheads with us and insurgents were still causing disruptions around the area. It was felt as it was our responsibility in this area we would take the consignment under some discreet disguise and shift it to its final destination before anyone had any idea of what was going on.

For us, The British, we thought that we need not tell anyone of our plans as we were currently negotiating with the Madhi in creating a ceasefire where we could be effectually laying down some peace move creating a possible further reduction in our troops here on the ground." He stopped again to let that piece of information sink in and also gave himself time to unfold on a whiteboard all sorts of maps and information on it.

On the whiteboard there were a couple of maps, names and photographs of figures which Tom could not quite work out from the distant position he was sitting in.

"This" Caulfield continued pointing to the first map "is the route that the convoy was supposed to have taken." He turned back towards us with a queried look upon his face. "But that wasn't the route that they eventually took. We suspect that they actually took this route here but we are not absolutely certain of the facts.

The radio information being sent back was misleading not being picked out as odd till it was too late." Again he turned to his whiteboard and pointed to the second map. "From what I could work out the wedgeheads had gone on Route six till they turned off towards Nasiriyah where we lost them about fifty kilometres past the turn off from the checkpoint. For me I was confused as to how a convoy could disappear in such a position but on seeing the area up close for myself it is obvious it is isolated from normal people movement here.

I want to go over the maps with you all more closely later but for now I need to get the crux of the story over first so you understand what we are proposing to do.

It seemed at the time we had no action against us on any front and the convoy was kept to a bare minimum of 3 by four tonners with an escort of two Scimitars supplied by the Blues and Royals. That was not going to throw up any questions as the Engineers were moving suppliers back and forth from here to Baghdad on a three daily basis anyway including escorts.

It seems that there was a skirmish somewhere between Nasariyah and their last checkpoint. But the Map reference they gave was on the original route, when an armoured unit from the Blues sped out to the target all they found was an area pasted with wrecks from both ours and opposition forces which had been accumulated there over the past few years. It was a clever position to say they had been hijacked as we found so many similar trucks destroyed, Scorpions and Warriors in a mechanical cemetery off the main road.

There was also evidence of a recent explosion in this area {He pointed to it on the map including some photographs that had been taken} which had Vehicles close to the identity of those that had left the warehouse originally.

The number of personnel that went on this convoy was kept to a bare minimum as well. Six Engineers from 32 Combat Engineers, including three senior ranks and three Sappers all from the same unit with an escort of two Scimitars with six members of the Blues and Royals. Total of twelve personnel in the convoy, names and ranks I will go through later.

The whole convoy disappeared off the radar the same day as leaving the warehouse. The Scimitars were found in the vehicle cemetery along with the dead bodies of the crew. Five of the Engineers bodies were also found at the graveyard and also some Arab bodies which signalled to us that the group had been hijacked.

At least that was what we assumed at the start. The consignment they carried was nowhere to be seen and there was no evidence of it being destroyed during the hijack.

This part of the operation had us baffled at first but after closer inspection of the bodies we found evidence that British firearms had been used against our own men. The evidence didn't get back to us for a couple of weeks because we had sent all the deceased remains back to UK to be checked by our own forensics scientists.

The weird thing is we did not find any forensic DNA evidence of the senior Engineers being part of the catastrophe we initially found. By the time we heard the final evidence report we were way behind the eight ball. It was at this point that we were called in to investigate fully and why we also included MI6 in those investigations.

There is some discrepancy as to whether there are remaining Engineers which we have not heard from since. Personally I have asked to remain on the case to avoid having to bring in another officer. I was due to retire this month but I think I had better try and sort this fiasco out first.

The other problem we have had to face is that we in the RMP lost our senior investigator last October under mysterious circumstances after a raid on the Basra Al Jameat police complex by our troops to free two SAS soldiers who we feared were to be executed by their captors, our so called allies.

The loss of course has left the RMP short staffed as far as senior investigators go. So you may understand why I have extended my time here but want to resolve this matter speedily and get the hell out of here to take up a peaceful retirement.

That is one of the reasons I have asked for assistance from this Command post."

Silence was over all those in the room as they thought of what had gone before in this operation and what their role would be in this whole affair.

"My men were murdered along with some of the Engineers which I find quite sickening." Thundered out the voice of the Lt Col from the Blues. "This cannot go unfinished as far as we are concerned."

Caulfield lifted his hand and said "Lt Crisp can you now fill in the blanks we have.

Gentlemen Lt Sandra Crisp is Army Intelligence and has been on the case for the past two months under instructions from GCHQ. Lieutenant"

"Thank you Captain Caulfield." Lt Crisp spoke in a broad West Country accent which had Tom mesmerized. He was just staring at the beauty before him and hoped he would also be able to analyse anything that she said. "As the Captain has just pointed out we were taken aback at first but we now have the final reports from Forensics which have really put the cat amongst the pigeons. After analysis of the bodies sent back, parts included, we have only been able to ascertain the authenticity of the following personnel.

They include all six Blues and Royals accounted for but out of the six Engineers only two matches could be found, that of Sappers Waldon and Covertle. There is no evidence whatsoever of any remains of Staff sergeant Saxby or Sgts Broad, Smythe, or Sapper Reed." Crisp paused to search the room for any queries to her comments that may have shown on their faces. No questions were asked from the transfixed collection, so she carried on. "We have not seen or heard any information regarding these four men since the convoy was organized and left, which seems to point to the fact they were a part of what seems to be a very clever cover-up, an inside job.

What really has baffled us all is the fact that the shipment has disappeared out of sight and so have the men involved. Something of this nature would have had to have been well organized and had the co-operation of some locals to carry it out but we have unfortunately come to a bit of a blind alley.

Saying that though we have however received a little intelligence from our friends at Six which gives us an area to the south near Um Qasr where we might be able to find evidence we are looking for. Any questions so far." Lt Crisp closed and started to return to her seat.

"Why am I needed on this subject, may I ask?" said Tom bewildered by his own presence here.

"You're an Engineer are you not?" interjected Caulfield.

"Not a Royal Engineer, Sir. Just a REME one." Tom continued

"We thought that you being an Engineer may give us an insight as to how these guys may think."

"I doubt anyone could have that sort of insight, Sir" Tom said still baffled at being here. "Perhaps Sinbad has been at it again." Tom sarcastically whispered to himself.

"I'm sure your input will be helpful Lieutenant thank you. But as I said previous we are short of officers on our side so you have been volunteered." Caulfield said virtually shutting Tom off from continuing. Tom just sat and kept quiet from then on. Volunteered was the old question, you can be so volunteered even if you yourself do not request it in this man's modern Army.

Coffee and Tea were sent for and while they were all waiting the two suits passed around files referring to the missing personnel all Royal Engineers including photos.

Staff Sergeant Chris Saxby—Royal Engineers.

Age 40 served twenty one years in the Corps and was due to retire in a years' time with full pension.

Been with 32 Combat Engineers most of his service time and was well regarded by all his commanding officers as an upright and loyal soldier.

Sergeant David Broad-RE

Age 44 a late sign up to the Army but had progressed well in his 15 years of service. Been with 32 for ten years and prior to that had been with Armoured Engineers for five. Clean and exemplary records. Sergeant Mark Smythe-RE

Age 36 signed on at 20 and progressed speedily to the rank of sergeant with sixteen years service and had turned down further promotion to avoid being transferred out of 32. Sapper Steven Reed-RE

Age 38 had 18 years of service and had been up and down on the promotion ride for many years. Promoted up to Corporal at one stage only to lose it due to a drinking and gambling problem he had gotten into while serving in Germany.

These files were a good read for the people sitting there. The soldiers listed were all above board and worthy of their rank and the respect it warranted. The file listed all the birthmarks and tattoos known to the Army Records office.

The entire group read the files and all they could think of, was why such a group would be involved in what seemed such a bizarre and daring con job.

Tom couldn't believe that guys of this calibre were able to carry out this type of disloyalty in any shape or form.

After about fifteen minutes or so the Colonel called the group back into line and continued to give out orders that would be accepted without question and got on with.

"Gentlemen I would like to introduce our two guests here today. Mr Jamal Ashid and Mr Mahmoud Brefti both from the Ministry of Interior in Baghdad. Mr Ashid is a senior Minister in the Council of Ministers and is purely observing our response to this tragic occurrence. Mr Brefti, however is an agent within the Ministry and will be attached to the investigation till further notice or resolved.

I don't need to remind you the sensitivity of this case and the need to keep it totally in house till we can resolve it.

Captain Caulfield is taking the lead of the investigation and he plus Corporal Dickson accompanied by Lieutenant Warburton will be following up on the intelligence we have received so far. I will hand you over now to Gary Warlock of MI6 who will give you a brief of the intelligence thus far. Gary."

Tom rolled his eyes and just wanted to get up and remove himself from this charade. No way was he even experienced enough to be involved in this type of investigation; he knew but why was he. He lent close to the second suit seated next to him.

"What the hell am I being involved for?' He asked in a whisper.

"The captain there" the suit said nodding towards Caulfield "asked for you personally."

Tom just stared at the back of Caulfield's head hoping to burn a hole in it and find out why. He was becoming really concerned as to being involved at such short notice with so little time on station as he had. He had only been out of Sandhurst for about a year and had this as his first overseas posting which his Commanding Officer had told him was a bit of a cushy one even though it was in Iraq.

His CO had indicated he knew the record of his father feeling that the same qualities would lie within the son and give him a step up faster than normally expected within the Corps. Tom only hoped it did as far as his father's abilities went. Oh well he thought just sit and take it all in and perhaps this will all be over pretty quickly.

"Ok" Gary said raising his voice to stop the whispering that not only Tom was into but some of the others were also throwing back and forth questions about various points to each other. "Let's get down to brass tacks then eh!

Can you all see this map clearly?" he carried on pointing to a larger map alongside the faces on the whiteboard. He never waited for anyone to answer though just barrelled on. "We suspected that the trucks involved came back South rather than travel anywhere else. We also know that they have not crossed the Iranian side of the border as the news would have been displayed as a major triumph for the Iranians and of course the trophy would have been too great to have hidden taken their relations with ourselves and the US.

We got a report of movement of trucks matching the description of the Bedford ones travelling down towards Um Qasr on route 26 but we lost them about 30 kms North of Um Qasr.

There is a village there which had been badly devastated during the past conflict as you can imagine so near the Kuwaiti border. It was part of the route we took to forge North in the original invasion so the population has dwindled somewhat.

Our suspicion led us to this area shown." He pointed with a pencil he had been fiddling with in his hand before continuing. "We couldn't find anything with our satellite monitoring but speaking to local tribesmen there we were led to a large building capable of possibly housing the trucks. It is one of the few buildings still standing in the area.

This information we got only yesterday and we do not want to go blazing in for fear of the media finding out, highlighting our actions and embarrassing us totally. The information could of course be a possibility that we are being lead a bit of a dog's tail. That is why we have asked Captain Caulfield and a small team to just get eyes on without seeming to be out of place to any locals.

There are no threats we are aware of in this area so the risk is minimal to such a small group."

Tom again rolled his eyes thinking about some of the things his father had told him about the Firm that he had experienced and the way they avoided telling you the full story if it suited them. Tom's mind was growing ever more suspicious of this investigation. In his mind he felt that the Army had the capability of sending seasoned troops even Special Forces to sort this so called embarrassing situation out without anyone, including the media, ever finding out anyway. The whole set up so far seemed rather strange to him.

"Captain Caulfield and his team will leave first thing tomorrow morning so be ready at 0600. We will be monitoring your movements by radio and will only bring in addition resources when we have positive ID on the trucks or any of the personnel that may still be in the area.

Our only hope is that the consignment has not been already shipped out of the country through the docks between here and Um Qasr. Gentlemen the target building is this one." He pointed to a spot on the map "and the file here" he handed it over to Caulfield. "is to be kept out of anyone's reach not involved with this operation. Is that clear?

"Are there any questions?" Gary put up for the group. No one responded and Tom just looked around at the faces about him and saw just a blank expression on all.

"Gentlemen, that seems to be all then at this stage so we'll close this off now. I wish Captain Caulfield and his team every success for tomorrow. You can get yourselves set up and ready to move at first light." The Colonel closed the meeting down abruptly with the two suits stepping to one side as if they were to remain to talk to the Colonel.

The delightful Lt Crisp stepped over towards Captain Caulfield and started to chat to him briefly and then after just a couple of minutes departed out the door. Tom excused himself as quickly as he could to try to catch up with her but she was not to be seen in any direction.

As if by magic Sandra Crisp had disappeared into the dust that blew around the compound constantly. Tom wondered whether he would see her again and was disappointed at her sudden disappearance so just strolled slowly over to his billet and started to prepare himself for what seemed a pointless exercise the following day.

The rest of the day Tom spent getting kit ready to last for up to four days or so, casually he went over to the armourer retrieving his weapons from the Armoury and checking them out. He was to carry a side arm of a Sig Sauer, a pistol his father was familiar with and one he recommended once before which Tom used as his favourite when at the ranges back home. Together with the standard SA 80 rifle he was ready by tea returning back to his billet to jot down some words of comfort to his parents without mentioning anything about the task ahead. He did not even get to tea that night because he was so anxious about what lay ahead he played everything through his mind so much he ended up exhausted eventually dozing off to awake in the early hours of the following morning.

The main thing that kept nagging at Tom was the statement about Caulfield asking for him personally. After all he had not been in Iraq when this convoy had gone astray so why he as a new boy in town was being asked for specifically by an RMP Captain he had no idea. It just didn't make any sense.

CHAPTER 3

14 February 2006

What a way to spend Valentine's Day Tom thought to himself as he climbed from his bunk and began dressing in his combats. Then again he had no Valentine as such at the moment, the girl he was seeing back in UK gave him a broad girth when she found out he was destined to be shipped out to Iraq for six months. There's loyalty for you Tom laughed to himself.

Still going through his mind was that delectable little Lieutenant Crisp but she had disappeared in a flash the previous day, oh the power of Sinbad. He wondered if he could find out where she was stationed through Caulfield perhaps. Well that could be a topic of conversation either at breakfast or while they drove through this God forsaken country towards Um Qasr.

Tom sealed his letter to his parents and got one of his roommates to get it posted for him. Questions had been asked the previous evening by his subordinates as to what was happening but true to form and orders Tom evaded the truth and just told the boys he was off to do some checks for the RMP at some remote police depot they had down South.

At breakfast he sat with the two RMPs and Mahmoud Brefti.

"Captain Caulfield." Tom started.

"Peter, please. If we are to be working together let's keep it short and friendly." Caulfield sat opposite Tom and watched as Tom got stuck into his breakfast.

Tom stopped cutting and continued. "Peter, why was I requested for this investigation, surely there are others in this Compound with much more experience for this sort of thing than I."

"There probably is, Tom, but they are all either foreign or Royal Engineers and we don't want anyone tipping off any we are suspect of do we? The rest of the RE contingent are suspect believe me."

"What about their OC, Pete."

"He is a new boy here like you. He arrived after the last OC Major Tony Welsh retired." Caulfield continued.

"Is he a suspect in this?" asked Tom not lifting his head from looking at his plate.

Caulfield laughed loudly. "Tony is my cousin and I would take great offence at anyone accusing him of this little crime my friend." His face turned serious as he finished.

"I didn't mean to offend anyone but surely anyone in the scheme of things must be investigated." Tom looked up and stared at Caulfield still suspicious as to why he was included in this exercise.

"Let's have no more silly statements Tom eh! Tony is a well respected officer and had been highly decorated while he was here in Iraq. He has now retired setting up a highly successful Investment Company in the UK which is doing rather well I believe. He has some serious foreign partners who have great confidence in his abilities." Caulfield finished then stood and turned to leave the table. "See you all in fifteen minutes. Corporal you're with me and Tom and Mahmoud will follow in the second vehicle." He quickly sped off towards the exit to the canteen.

Tom sat puzzled and turned to Mahmoud. "Didn't mean to upset the bloke." He said.

"Throwing suspicion onto one's relatives is a great insult in my culture as I expect it is for yours my friend." Mahmoud said finishing off his coffee with a smile.

"I expect you are right. I think I will apologise to Peter when we leave." Tom's voice showed signs of remorse to his previous statements made to Caulfield.

"Don't worry about the boss Sir." Dickson pronounced. "He gets cranky quickly just lately when someone gets personal with him. He's due to retire soon himself and join his cousin in the business he mentioned. He'll get over it so let's not get too het up on it. See you out front, sirs." Dickson stood and departed the same way his boss had done.

Tom sat and continued his breakfast while his new partner Mahmoud Brefti downed yet another cup of thick dark coffee.

They both left the canteen together and went their separate ways to retrieve their gear before getting back to the main office where two Landrovers were sitting.

Tom threw his gear into the back of the second Rover and clipped his SA 80 between the seats before climbing into the driver's seat. The one thing he hated most was the helmet he had to wear which in this climate was uncomfortable at the best.

His new best friend, Mahmoud was walking towards him from his temporary billet. He was about 180 cm tall and large framed, not fat. He walked with his head up as a proud man would do. His stride was long and faster than most. Arriving at the Rover he smiled towards Tom going around the rear of the vehicle to throw his gear into the back.

After placing his gear in the back of the rover, Mahmoud moved to the front taking his place in the passenger seat, he was not carrying any rifle just a side arm. He was dressed in combat greens, shirt and wearing his shemagh {a traditional scarf to protect the head and face from severe desert conditions}.

"What do you think of the situation Mahmoud?" Tom asked as they both sat and waited for Caulfield and Dickson to arrive.

"I have no thoughts as such at this point, my friend, just a concern that we will never recover what has been lost and I do not mean just the money side of things."

"The quicker we can sort this then the better for all."

As Tom finished the other two came out of the offices and walked to the front Rover. Caulfield looked around giving a thumbs up to Tom who returned the expression. The lead rover began to move out with Tom following about twenty metres behind.

The journey South towards Um Qasr was slow and not without many stops to clear the thirst that all members of the team felt except for Mahmoud. During the drive Tom and Mahmoud exchanged many comments between themselves laughing at times at some of the things that they had both gotten up to during their teenage and younger adult years. It seemed to both that they were striking up a pretty good friendship between their respective cultures.

The forty or so kilometres the team travelled took them over two hours to complete. The day was hot and dry and the clear sky allowed the sun to blast down onto them. It was about 0930 when they pulled off Route 26 and headed into a small town area to the west of the highway.

Caulfield pulled up just short of what looked like habitation getting out of his Rover then walking back to Tom and Mahmoud with a folder under his arm. Unfolding his package he summoned both the occupants to exit their vehicle then laid his papers on their bonnet.

"Gentlemen, this is the area we are in, just south of Az Zabbayr. The point of our interest is this area here in the northern side of this little place." Caulfield pointed to a mark on his map which looked like a bit of a dead end to Tom.

"What's there that makes it of interest to us?" asked Tom.

"Just about there." Caulfield placed his finger. "Is a large covered area like a warehouse. This end of town used to be the industrial area of the town till us lot blew the shit out of the place chasing the regular army out." Caulfield gave a bit of a snigger as if he was the one who drove out the opposition.

"And you believe that the vehicles are there along with the loot?" queried Tom.

"The vehicles possibly, the loot I doubt much is left if any at all now."

"Why don't we just walk in and check?" inexperience was showing on Tom now.

"Information we got from a local source told us that there was still a lot of movement in and out of the place therefore what we want young man is to try and catch someone who may lead us to the rest. OK"

"Sounds Ok I suppose but it's been a while since the trucks went missing so why would there be anything there for us now."

"Look, to move such large amount of cash and gold would take a fair while avoiding notice from the thieves around here. Anything of interest in this fucking country just brings out all the Ali Babas in the vicinity.

Now what I need you two to do is take this area which is the front. Park your vehicle in this street here away from view. Dickson and I will go around the rear area of the buildings. We will stay in touch with constant radio checks.

The information we have is that movement seems to happen during the dark hours so keep your eyes open at all times, take turns in watching. We have radio contact so if you see or hear anything that seems suspicious at all get on the blower to me. Is that understood?" Both Tom and Mahmoud nodded their heads. Mahmoud never said a word but just stared at the map and just burned his eyes into it as if trying to get something more out from it.

Caulfield folded his map and placed it under his arm then walked slowly to his vehicle got in it and drove away. Both Mahmoud and Tom climbed back into their Rover and set off for the position they had been shown by Caulfield.

The roads once off the main were just rubble and there was so much rubbish spread around Tom had to manoeuvre the Rover around piles that had been literally thrown in the roadway. It seemed that the fighting had only just stopped not been over for months.

As they drove the smells started to get thicker and thicker. The stench of the rubbish was accompanied by the putrid stench of sewage waste. This area had been forgotten about for any sewage repairs was all Tom could think. He hoped they would not have to remain there for too long as he felt that the smell would soak into his cloths and skin and be too difficult to remove.

Mahmoud never even showed any signs of smelling anything at all; he just sat and stared in front at the devastation that had befallen his once glorious country. How did it all come down to this he thought to himself?

As they turned near to their contact area there were suddenly people around, just a few, Tom's senses caught the aroma of strong coffee which was a welcoming smell from the other ones he had been subjected to. What used to be markets was now a battered remains of the thriving past.

Pulling into the street that Caulfield had indicated to them he found a nice little bombed out house where he could park the Rover out of sight. From here both men took their packs and weapons moving to within eyeshot of the suspect buildings.

Flat roofs all of them and large enough to house vehicles Tom thought. There was a substantial amount of damage from light weapons but no major destruction. Seems the house took the battering and the large warehouses survived. Perhaps the spoils the victors were expecting held them back from blasting the shit out of them when they were coming through.

Both men settled down agreeing that during the dark hours they would take turns of 2 hours on each to watch the buildings. Tom had become quite comfortable with being with Mahmoud now, trusting him to be a worthy partner. All his mates ever said to him prior to coming here was never trust an Arab, he would steal the bedding from you while you are asleep and you wouldn't know till you woke up the next morning freezing your nuts off.

Sitting there Tom could smell the putrid stench of the sewer again and the rubbish around them. He had good sight of the buildings through breaks in the piles of crap that littered the frontage. With the heat of the day the stench got worse making his stomach turn over at times. He never had any want for food at all till darkness fell.

Neither heard a thing till about 1800 hrs when all of a sudden there was a clicking noise that approached their position. Tom got hold of his rifle preparing himself for any eventuality and waited. Mahmoud just sat there and looked in the direction of the tapping noise that kept growing louder.

Tom raised his weapon just as a shadow came around the corner of their little hideout and stopped. Propped there was a young Arab man about five six, shemagh/keffiyeh neatly upon his head and across his face. Propped was the word as Tom suddenly realized what the clicking noise was now, it was the crutches the young man was using. He had a leg missing possibly from the fighting that had taken place in this area during the conflict.

Mahmoud raised himself up and slowly approached the young man. "As salaam alaikum." Mahmoud spoke to the young man meaning

Peace be upon you.

"Wa alaikum assalaam." The young Arab returned and nodded to Mahmoud.

Tom understood the greeting side of the language but what transpired after that was way out of his reach. Both men rabbitted on for about ten to fifteen minutes between themselves in their guttural dialect, quite oblivious to Tom. When they had finished before biding each other fair well Mahmoud placed a hand in his combat trouser and brought out what looked like some paper, handed them to his chatting companion he turned away from him returning to where Tom was watching and waiting.

The young Arab pocketed what he was given also turning away and the click started up again as he slowly hobbled away from their position. Tom heard the crutches for quite a while in the night air till they disappeared completely.

Tom looked at Mahmoud. "Friend of yours?" He said. "A worthy ally in this neck of the woods my friend." "He obviously had information for you I take it."

"Yes. I managed to be able to get in touch with him earlier yesterday and asked him to meet me here. He had told me he had something useful for me."

"How did he know you would be in this position?" Tom asked suspiciously.

"We Arabs watch and learn so he would have had eyes on all vehicles coming in and out of this area. He would have seen or heard where I was hiding out Tom believe me. Please do not be suspicious; you English are so untrusting at times."

"Sorry Mahmoud but this is my first spell out here. Did he have anything useful for us?"

"He had some interesting pieces of information. He has noticed there were trucks coming into this area but that all stopped within a couple of days of the first ones entering just shortly after the shipment went missing."

"Does he know about the shipment?"

"Absolutely not, if he did know I would not have been able to get a thing from him as he would know a few bad men here who would pay him a lot more than I did for that sort of information.

What was interesting was that he had noticed that originally there were just four men then there were five. That included a man with a beret which was of similar colour to the old Revolutionary Guard."

"You mean Red!!" exclaimed Tom.

"Unfortunately yes. The disturbing thing is the description he gave matches our Mr Caulfield."

"You have got to be kidding me. This is getting better by the minute." Tom was trying to go through what had happened in the briefing when he was told how the convoy had left and what happened to it during its movements. This was certainly strange. It was getting just like an old Miss Marple turnaround.

Tom looked at Mahmoud and searched for an answer from him but added. "What do you propose we do here now?"

"We must just sit and wait till we get an opportune time to mention it to Peter to see his reaction. I doubt if he would be very happy but if he is involved I think I need to get some of my people to come down just in case." Mahmoud broke off as the radio stated to squelch into Tom's ear.

"Bravo 2 this is Bravo 1 do you receive over?"

"Roger Bravo one." Tom replied pressing the pretzel on his webbing strap.

"Anything your side?" Bravo one came over.

Tom looked at Mahmoud and answered lying. "Nothing yet and you?"

"Seen some movement just to one side but will wait till certain. Stay alert Two One out."

"Roger one, Two out."

Tom looked at Mahmoud "Wonder what that prick is up to. You sure the description your man gave was Caulfield?"

"Positive. He was very precise and also gave me the registration number of his vehicle, the one he uses back at command with his blue lights atop."

"Fuck." Said Tom in panic. "What the fuck are we going to do?"

"Be patient my friend we will see what transpires from our mischievous friend later eh!"

"Can you get a message to your people?"

"Not just yet as I would have to leave here to do so. Let's just wait and see what happens."

Both Tom and Mahmoud sat and watched their objective, both hoping that a mistake had been made. A big mistake at that if the truth was known. Neither was prepared to sleep and neither had food or made a drink, they just waited and hoped.

Two hours later the radio squelched again in Tom's ear. "Bravo 2 Bravo1 over."

"Roger Bravo 1." Tom quickly got on the air. Both he and Mahmoud were staring at each other wondering what was to transpire from here.

"Bravo 2 send Mahmoud to the warehouse to enter through the side door. We will be entering through the rear. Tom you stay on watch and alert any movement. Over."

"Roger that 1. Mahmoud on his way. Out" Tom answered looking quizzical at Mahmoud.

Tom released the pretzel and repeated the request to Mahmoud from Caulfield. "What do you think?"

"If he is entering the warehouse there may be something there for me to look at. I will be rather careful at this stage I think." Said Mahmoud, who had stood readying himself to move off.

"Don't take any chances, Mahmoud. You have no radio contact with me so I will watch the door closely and if there is anything suspicious Mahmoud just throw the door open as a signal then I will come straight down."

"No worries my friend. I wish we all had radio connection instead of just Caulfield and yourself."

"I agree it does seem stupid not having everyone linked up."

Mahmoud withdrew his pistol. He was not going to go in without it at the ready that was for sure. He pulled back on the top placing a round up the spout, he was ready now.

Tom brought his SA 80 up to sight on the door Mahmoud would be entering through while nodding to his new mate. Mahmoud crept out from his cover and slowly, crouching, made his way towards the door on the side of the warehouse. There were three steps up to the door with no handrails.

Mahmoud stopped at the base of the short steps and looked back towards Tom. Both men nodded at each other and Mahmoud slowly, one step at a time made his way to the door. He stood at the top of the steps to the side of the door and moved his hand to the handle. Surely he thought it would be locked but as he tightened his grip on it and turned it turned with ease for him.

There was a click as the door lock released itself from the door catch and Mahmoud pulled at the handle to open it fully. He knelt down and moved across the open doorway and stared inside. Nothing suspicious at this stage he thought as he spanned the area inside.

There in front of him to his left were two large camouflaged vehicles. Mahmoud was unsure as to their origin but they looked like the right size for the four tonners of the type the Engineers had used for their convoy.

He slowly wandered inside with the door closing behind him on its spring. He stopped just inside, again spanning the area. The skylights above were damaged making the stars visible through the broken glass that had once been there. His vision improved each move he made as his eyes adapted to the moonlight that filtered in through the damaged roof.

As he moved forward he found he was standing on a platform of some description with another set of steps just off to his left that led to the floor of the warehouse. His sight had improved heaps since he had come into the building.

He cautiously stepped forward but as he approached the steps he noticed a body sprawled out on the floor below with a crutch lying beside it. Mahmoud immediately thought of his contact only hours earlier and the comment he had made to Tom about the highest payer wins the right information but it was too late. At that moment Mahmoud's brain blacked out as a large piece of 4x2 crashed down on the top of his skull. He fell to the floor not knowing what had hit him. For Mahmoud he would never again wake to the rising sun to see his beloved country struggle out from its oppression.

The body was dragged and dumped beside the other corpse that lay near the bottom of the internal steps. With one swift movement the person who had moved him sliced his throat

"Bravo 2, come in." Caulfield was sounding in total control.

"2 over" Tom responded. He was feeling mighty nervous. This was his first experience at this form of work since joining the Army.

"Get in here quick we have a problem."

Tom never even answered just lifted himself from his rest place he moved quickly towards the door Mahmoud had gone through moments earlier. Tom's weapon was at the ready as he made it to the base of the steps. He turned both ways as he arrived scanning the area.

Nothing. He made his way to the top of the steps and waited to the side of the door just as Mahmoud had done before him.

Slowly Tom turned the handle with his right hand and pulled at the door once it was free of the catch. As the door swung open Tom moved into the space with raised weapon scanning right, then left. He moved to the left of the door as the door reasserted itself in the closed position.

Hugging the wall and moving slowly further along what seemed like a loading platform he saw what looked like another set of stairs just beyond. Further from that he could make out the outlines of two Bedford four tons just sitting in the middle of the warehouse.

Tom's heart was racing like mad as he closed in on the stair wondering where the hell was Caulfield or Mahmoud. There had been no noise and there was no chatter anywhere, yet he had called him in here. Where the fuck was he?

Tom came to the edge of the loading platform and there just below him lay two bodies. Shit he thought, quickly looking around before going down the steps to check on the bodies. In his mind's eye there were shadows everywhere and he felt he could feel many eyes upon him as the hairs on the back of his neck stood out like pins.

Weapon still in raised position with his right hand holding it in the firing position so it could be used if necessary he went down the steps looking all around him as he stepped onward. At the base of the steps he saw what looked like Mahmoud, recognising his Shemagh now with the ends lying in a pool of blood.

Tom bent down extending his left hand to feel the neck of Mahmoud. There was no movement and he felt no life in the form of any pulse but there wouldn't have been as Tom suddenly realised that Mahmoud's throat was wide open.

"Fuck" was all Tom could come out with as he spanned the area about him. As he lifted his arm away from Mahmoud moving it to the other body lying alongside. The body Tom recognised was the man who had been Mahmoud's contact earlier but right to form he was lifeless and without breath or pulse as well.

Tom quickly pulled his arm away placing it back onto his SA 80 with the other but as he did darkness fell upon him as his brain felt like he had been placed inside Big Ben and all the bloody bells were ringing. He staggered forward wondering what the hell had hit him on the helmet but as he did so another blow came down on it harder than the first. The bells stopped and darkness fell as he hit the floor of the warehouse.

CHAPTER 4

Tom's head was throbbing like crazy as he started to come round from what seemed like a long sleep. He somehow knew he wasn't dead but felt like he had been run over by a double decker bus. It wasn't only his head that was hurting now but his whole body seemed to ache. His back, his stomach, legs, arms and his family jewels all throbbed, hurt and appeared swollen.

As Tom slowly opened his eyes wider he found his sight was also affected, it was pitch black. He tried to see through his left eye but saw only its eyelid from the inside. Oh hell not dead but seems as near as damn it, he thought to himself.

He tried hard to remember what had happened before he had lost consciousness but only saw blood around two bodies lying there on the floor. He tried to move and stand but that was not going to happen as he suddenly found he had been trussed up hands and feet with zip ties.

He lay still trying to listen to anything that could give him a clue as to where he was and who had him but there was no sound just the rustling of the wind around him. He was in the dirt not on a concrete floor as he thought and the dust was getting into his mouth, nose and eyes.

Suddenly lights appeared and the rumble of vehicles. Tom's only thought was that he had been taken by insurgents and now he would be facing a quick execution after a film presentation swearing his anger at his own Government. Fuck you Caulfield, you got me into this.

A boot found its way into Tom' side which made him exhale loudly in pain causing him to begin spitting some blood out his mouth that had collected there from some previous smacks to the face.

Tom rolled to try and get away from the assailant but it just brought in more boots wherever he rolled to. He passed out again and the pain stopped.

Slowly the sounds around him were becoming clearer in between the aches that racked his body and the noise of bells in his head. Everything was sore.

All Tom could hear was ranting in Arabic all around him. Darkness had overcome him but it was just a hood over his head. He felt for the floor below him and this time it felt like wood. All of a sudden the whole world moved and Tom's head went sixty to the dozen trying to work out what was happening. Suddenly he realised he was in the rear of a truck and the wood was its floor. The movement was a welcoming feeling as it didn't come with size nine boots this time.

The journey he had felt must have taken about an hour or so and it was on fairly good roads as he felt no large bumps or bouncing. He was entering into some kind of town or hopefully city as the noises around him seemed like a bustling area. The voices around him were still all Arabic which he could make neither hide nor hare of its meaning. All he could do was hope he was still in Iraq and his own people would be out there looking for him, perhaps coming to rescue him.

But what of Caulfield and Dickson, where were they? Had they been captured also? His mind was telling him that Mahmoud was dead and he was now a captive of someone or other, were Caulfield and Dickson here as well. They weren't in his present limousine that was for sure, he felt he was alone here albeit with a couple of angry voiced Arabs for company.

The truck stopped suddenly, then he heard gates being rattled, creaking open then the truck moved again going forward in a bit of a semi circle before it stopped. It was then that the real commotion began of people yelling and shouting, doors being opened and slammed shut again, running bodies showing signs of urgency. He tried hard to figure out at least some of the words that were going around him but he was so ignorant of this language that it completely went over his head.

He heard the tailgate drop then the men in the rear jumping out. Tom wondered what was next which was answered with someone grabbing his feet and dragging him to the edge of the tailgate.

Surely they would . . . bollocks, he came down hard onto the road surface. They dropped him to the floor on his side sending all the wind rushing from his lungs. The hood was quickly checked to ensure it was still secure over his head so he could not even look around and see where he was or who had him. Dragged to his feet with an arm under each of his armpits he was unceremoniously dragged backwards to a door followed by being bounced down steps. Tom tried to count how many steps he felt but lost it after fifteen when they threw him down another half a dozen to what seemed like the bottom of a pit. The men must have got tired of dragging him so they threw him down the remainder.

It didn't stop there as two more strong armed thugs grabbed him again and dragged him further, more steps. The smells around him were becoming muskier and muskier. How deep was he going? Possibly as far as hell he felt at the moment.

The final push came as he was thrown in through a door hitting the floor, as he went the hood slipped up a bit to his mouth but remained over his eyes. Darkness as he heard the door shut behind him. That sound was scary as it sounded like a large solid bloody thing to Tom. Shit don't panic, keep calm, assess the surroundings, it all came back to him what he had learnt months earlier on a course in Kent for possible captured or kidnapped men.

Tom lay exhausted, aching and very battered. He had no idea of time or whether it was day or night. He had no idea how long he had been out to it all earlier. All he could do now was wait and see what happens. He was not the sort to pray but if there was a God he hoped to all the heavens above he was going to be on his side today.

It seemed ages later that he heard echoing footsteps approaching the door that was between him and the outside world. There was a clatter of keys, locks being opened and then a squeak of the door as it came ajar. Some Arabic entered his ears yet again as someone lent down and snipped the zip tie on his ankles. This was replaced with a couple of metal ankle cuffs complimented with a joined chain. He was lifted to his feet and led out of the cell shuffling as best he could with the chain length that was between his ankles.

Nothing had ever felt as uncomfortable for him as he tried endlessly to not fall flat on his face. The guards either side kept him upright but not seeing where you were heading and not being able to walk properly was the worst thing at the moment.

It ended as soon as it started to Tom as he was turned, guided to a chair where he was dumped and his hands were released from the zip tie replaced by two hand cuffs again complimented with a chain between which was followed by the chain being connected to the ankle one dropping from the front of his waist. Tom's brain was trying to fathom out what was going on here and why he was attached to chains as if he was a bloody wild animal. The hood was left in place for a further few minutes while he heard the movement of people going out and entering into the new room where he was now sitting.

The hood was finally lifted throwing the sudden bright light into his eyes which seemed to shut them both automatically. His left eye remained partially closed when he decided to try to open them slowly. In front of him was an empty steel table which the chain on his hands was now attached to.

He turned his head slowly to be greeted by a slap in the head which sent his head back to the forward looking position. Tom remained still from then on just sitting wanting to prevent any further attraction of someone else's hands or feet on his body.

Voices suddenly erupted behind him giving him the feeling of a senior person of this crowd of degenerates entering the room. People were moving about quickly as one of the new entrants started to throw about orders it seemed for Tom.

Suddenly in front of him a large Arab dressed in military attire appeared sitting across the table from him. This man looked like one of Saddam's cousins with his thick black curly hair, large round head, deep coloured bulging eyes and the distinctive moustache noted in the old regime.

He stared down at Tom from his seating position which indicated to Tom that either he had a chair lower than his friend Saddam or Saddam was a huge fucker that towered above 99% of the Iraqi population.

"Welcome My young lieutenant friend. I hope you have been looked after well." The smirk on his face gave nothing away. "My name is Colonel Kasim Rahman of the Iraqi National Guard. I need to ask you some questions regarding the death of my dear friend Mahmoud Brefti and the unfortunate loss of funds from my Government by your people."

Tom listened thankful that at least he was still in Iraq and hopefully in the custody of who they said they were. He expected his own people would be here soon to get him out. But he suddenly thought about the treatment he had been getting, suddenly thinking that these men must think he had killed Mahmoud. Tom held his breath determined not to say a word other than his name, rank and number with the express request for him to speak to the British commander.

The answers he gave did not impress them too much as he copped a smack in the back of the head from someone with a birch type of stick. Tom unrepentant just sat and repeated his request to the Colonel. Again he copped another whack in the back of the head.

"Please Lieutenant Warburton we do not need to waste ours or your time. The quicker we have the answers we seek the quicker this will all be over."

Tom again answered as he did before, this time being punched hard in the side of the face. Tom shook his head, spat more blood out from his mouth then looked down.

"Well the British are still a stubborn race I see." Piped in the Colonel laughing. "Perhaps I should go through what we already have given to me by those that caught you young man.

Two days ago you were sent to a suspected warehouse where your commanders suspected there was a stolen consignment that they had originally sent to us. When you arrived you were placed with our Mr Brefti as part of the team. Your instructions as I can see from the Captain in charge were quite clear to remain at your post.

You were seen, however, following Mr Brefti into the warehouse after being told to remain outside. You then proceeded to cut Mr Brefti's throat and then when your own commanding officer came in you shot him also.

Since then we now have the understanding that you were a plant on this exercise being a part of the original crooks that stole the currency convoy. We know you were not in the country when it took place but you were brought in to distract us during the investigation. Just a pawn I believe. Your people have uncovered a bank transfer to your UK account of £50,000 sterling.

What do you have to say about that young man?"

Tom thought through what had been said to him so far making the conclusion from what was said that Caulfield had been injured but was still alive. What about Dickson he thought to himself.

"Well!" the Colonel said angrily banging his fist on the table which shook Tom sending vibrations throughout the room.

Tom repeated his name, rank, number and a request for British officer to be present.

No smacks that time but just the hood going back over his head and the removal of the chain from the table followed by two strong guys lifting him high enough to lift his feet off the ground and moved speedily out of the room with Tom frantically walking on air.

The next thing Tom was confronted with was being flung onto a hardboard floor and the hood went suddenly wet and then a gush of water poured through the hood material and flowed over his face, down his throat causing him to fight for his breath.

Tom had never experienced this before but remembered his father telling him about water boarding and how it causes your brain to react.

Drowning was frightening enough to hear about let alone experience it. But that was the inevitable reaction from the victim's brain, I am drowning. What was it they really wanted from him?

Tom knew nothing about the consignment that had gone missing. He had no idea what was the purpose of this classic set-up. He was puzzled about the money that they reckoned was in his account nice as it might be though.

The water treatment went on for a further few bucket loads with Tom's brain was trying to say drowning was the in thing. He tried his hardest to control his mind but he just wet himself which was the signal for the torturers to stop because of the smell that followed. They then set about hosing him down to remove the smell.

If Tom had known anything he would certainly have disclosed it after the first bucket load. Trying to keep the secrets after that sort of treatment is ridiculously idiotic.

Things weren't getting any clearer for him even after they stopped the water boarding, he was lifted then after the hose treatment the thugs dragged him back to the interrogation room.

"All we want is your confession and the whereabouts of the rest of the thieves in your group you are part of." The Colonel was showing some anger now and Tom was just about ready for what came next after again repeating his name, rank etc. The floor became his next port of call followed by a casual kicking from all directions. Tom curled himself up in the foetal position as best he could to avoid too much damage to his body parts. He stayed put, still apart from the movement created by the kicks.

"We will persist till we get the truth from you my friend." The Colonel added between the casual boot kisses.

Tom laid dormant still just taking the boots as they came in. He was getting to the point of passing out when he felt himself lifted yet again and taken away again to the water room. How much more could he take of this shit he thought to himself? After the initial dousing he spat out that he knew nothing of what had happened to the money. He had no knowledge of anything pertaining to the convoy.

Tom had no idea how many times he was removed from his cell. He had lost all sense of time. His food was never brought in on a regular time basis, his sleep was disturbed on a regular basis with bright lights glaring at him at all different times. Tom's head was constantly aching and the dizzy spells he had started to experience some time ago were gradually increasing.

Had it been days, weeks or what, Tom had no idea. His facial hair was growing with his what once was short hair was now shoulder length. Time in general had been lost to him.

How long he never knew but he was dragged again to the interrogation room after what he thought was a few days but in truth it had been nearly two weeks.

Faced with the Colonel again he sat head down and weak. Again the same questions came across to him from the big guy. Again Tom answered as he had before and yet again he was ceremoniously taken to the water room but this time he could not bear it longer than the first rush of water. He yelled out that he was willing to talk; Tom's will was finally broken.

"You are ready to give us what we want then lieutenant?" the Colonel said with a surprising glee of victory in his voice.

Tom looked up and stared into the Colonel's eyes hoping that he would see he was telling the truth to him. "I am not part of any group and have no idea why I have been singled out as a suspect. I did not kill Mahmoud, I followed him after I was called on my radio and I did not shoot Captain Caulfield. When I saw Mahmoud on the floor it was the last thing I can remember, everything after that went black." Tom was sincere in how it came out with his voice being close to breaking down.

"The evidence we have shows you were the only person in the warehouse and that it was only your gun that had used. Captain Caulfield took action quickly enough to stop you from killing him. It was he who hit you hard as you fired at him.

What about the money in your bank?" the Colonel continued.

"I have no idea about any damn money. My account only had a few hundred pounds in it when I left the UK. Please let me speak to my people there has been a misunderstanding, someone has made a mistake." Tom was beginning to plead now.

The Colonel said no more, just nodded his head which prompted someone to replace the hood on his head and Tom was lifted yet again being dragged. He feared he was going back to the water room but to his surprise the next thing he knew the hood was removed and he was thrown onto his cell floor.

CHAPTER 5

April 2006 London, UK

Tom's father had been trying to find out about his son's whereabouts after not receiving anything from Iraq for months. The regular correspondence he and his wife were used to had stopped suddenly which sent Tom Snr off to London after endless telephone calls to young Tom's unit without getting a satisfactory answer.

When he arrived at the Ministry of Defence it was a cold and bleak day outside which was not what he hoped to get from inside this great building. Once inside it took forty five minutes or so for him to be directed to the third floor finally seated in front of a Brigadier Fulsome.

"Mr Warburton welcome, my name is Fulsome and I am responsible for the investigation into your missing son."

"Brigadier I am not going to beat about the bush. I need to know where my son is or what has happened to him. He was on a training mission which as far as I am concerned there is no secrecy attached to the type of operation he was on." Tom Snr was adamant about the facts he knew as he displayed to the Brigadier his anguish.

"Yes I am aware of his REME attachment in Basra but we have unfortunately, because of a shortage of personnel, had to use some of our people there in other missions. Your son was attached to an RMP investigation about a month ago."

"Well what the hell has happened to prevent communication and the way everyone seems to be passing the buck on it." Tom Snr just kept his cool but felt like leaning across the table to this smug so and so and smacking him round the head.

"You know full well sir that I cannot disclose anything about current investigations or missions. You of all people should understand that with your experience."

"Cut the crap Fulsome, all we want to know is whether he's all right or not, not the details of the damn mission."

"Look sir, I am fully aware of your history in the service, I know you have had a rough time in the past but I am unable to help you with your queries at this stage." Fulsome was trying to backtrack somewhat and take the pressure off.

"Bollocks about me, this is about my son and if you can't give me any information now then I will take the matter further perhaps call in the media. Those bastards seem to get their way with you people." Tom was fishing here knowing to mention the media would rattle too many cages.

"Please sir that would not be of any benefit to anyone. Can you give me a few minutes while I check upstairs, I will see if I can get any further information for you. Can I get you some tea or coffee?"

"No thanks. I just need some news, that's all."

Fulsome stood, excused himself from the room and left. He was gone for about five minutes or so returning with a broad smile on his face. "It seems your son is ok but he is involved in a current investigation at present which is tying him up somewhat."

"Why couldn't someone tell us that before? The stress that has been placed on us by the Department's silence is unbelievable. When can we hope to hear from him then if that is the case? You have to forgive my suspicious attitude of your statements after my own experiences with you people years ago."

"We should have some kind of clearance within the next month and then things will be back to normal." Fulsome was a diplomatic man and his statement was accepted within reason.

"Be prepared for me calling again in a few weeks brigadier. Meanwhile I will be trying to get some kind of communication with my son through contacts I have within the Contracting businesses that are now rampant within Iraq."

"That is your prerogative sir but please be patient we will have some kind of answer soon for you that's a promise."

"I'm afraid I don't have much faith in your damn promises."

With that Tom Snr thanked the Brigadier, stood and left the premises vowing to try and find some other way in which to get information about his son.

Over the coming weeks Tom Snr called in favours from people who had remained in the Contracting business in Iraq whom he knew of from his Regiment days of old.

It took more time than he thought but by the middle of July Tom Snr had gained some knowledge which was a major cause of concern for him. He had found out that his son was imprisoned in Al Jameat for crimes against the Iraqi State. He had also found out that Tom had been charged with killing an Iraqi agent and also had shot an RMP officer.

Another twist to his information was that there was some kind of association between Tom and a group of British servicemen that had stolen some secret material from the British Mission there. Tom Snr was totally dumbfounded, there must be some mistake. Now he was about to get himself involved if he had to, to get to the bottom of it. He made another call to MOD asking for Brigadier Fulsome.

"Mr Warburton, believe me we have no more information now than when you were here some weeks back. The investigations are still ongoing."

"I know that's crap Fulsome. Would you like me to tell you what information I have been able to get from within Iraq or would you prefer to be honest with me now.

If not then I would be willing to share it with the media if I have to, to protect my son." Tom Snr was glowing with anger after experiencing the palming off actions of the military whenever they chose to.

"Mr Warburton can you please give me a few moments and I will try and get some clear facts for you." Fulsome was showing a nervous hesitation in his voice as he tried desperately to calm the situation down.

"You've got just half an hour and then the shit will hit the fan Fulsome believe me, that's a promise from me." Tom Snr knew he now had the upper hand over the Brigadier.

It didn't take any longer than fifteen minutes and Tom Snr's phone rang. Picking it up quickly after the first ring he answered blisteringly. "Warburton!"

"Ah Tom." A politer voice came over Tom Snr's ear. "I have spoken to our people and we would like to be able to meet with you at 1000hrs tomorrow morning if that suits." A request for a meet was what Tom Snr was expecting; whether it was to bullshit to him or just shut him down before he caused embarrassment he was prepared to go in a bit gung ho for this meeting.

"Ok. Where?" Tom Snr was short and sharp to respond.

"Vauxhall Cross, 1000 hrs tomorrow. I believe you are familiar with the place we will have a meeting with one of their people there who has details of what has transpired in Iraq." Fulsome was showing some confidence now knowing that a higher authority was about to take over this rather impatient and annoying parent.

"Spook Central it is. I'll be there but I'll tell you this much the last time I dealt with those pricks at 6 they tried to shaft me so I do not trust much of anything they say or do either." Tom Snr's thoughts of the past since 1972, were coming back to haunt him.

"We'll see you then." Fulsome quickly hung up the phone and began preparing himself with what lay ahead.

The following morning Tom Snr was at the Vauxhall Cross building a good fifteen minutes before his appointment waiting by the reception to be called. As he waited he expected to see Fulsome come in but unbeknown to him, Fulsome had arrived even earlier in the morning to hopefully get a step ahead of this irate man in Tom.

Vauxhall Cross was a hive of traffic, comings and goings as busy as one of the main railway stations in London. Tom Snr noticed that most of the people going through the place were so young these days. He felt that the present batches of employees were just fresh from school. They looked that young to him but he was now getting on a bit he thought to himself, everyone seems young to me these days.

He knew that there was no way he could compete with these young pups today and thankfully he hoped he wouldn't have to. But the more he looked the more he wondered how these people would be able to defend the British public feeling they had little to no life experience.

His wondering mind was suddenly startled back to reality. "Sir, someone is coming down for you now." The receptionist interrupted his chain of thought.

Tom Snr nodded taking his eyes to the elevators that sat to one side of his position. A bell dinged the arrival of one of the elevators then as the doors opened standing there with a broad smile on his face was Brigadier Fulsome.

"Glad you could make it. Please come with me, I have someone who has all the facts on your son you need."

Tom Snr rose following Fulsome into the open elevator. Neither said another word as the button for floor number 3 was pressed with both seeming to stare at the floor indicators above the door not wanting to break the silence that was between them both.

When the doors opened Fulsome exited the elevator stepping to the left with Tom Snr close to his side. Just a short walk down the corridor they stopped in front of a glass door that led to what looked like a large style board room. As they entered Tom could see only one person was inside seated at the end of the huge table that adorned the vast room. Behind him was a 50" TV screen and to one side of that was an even larger screen which had the appearance of a computer home page displayed.

Introductions were made immediately the two men stepped into the room for the benefit of Tom Snr.

"Gary Warlock, Middle East desk, Tom Warburton Senior." Fulsome made the intro between the two as he sat down opposite Gary while indicating for Tom Snr to sit alongside him. Tom shook Gary's hand and sat down.

"Tom, I know you have a history with 6 in the past so you know how we work." Gary began to try and break the ice that had obviously formed and indicated on Tom Snr's face.

"Not a very nice part of history I'm afraid as you lot gave me up to your cousins over the Pond if you have the file." Tom Snr showed his total dislike for this Department.

"That was rather unfortunate I must admit but things have generally improved over the years. Now let's see if we can resolve your concerns about your son shall we."

Tom Snr just sat back and looked at Gary as he fiddled with a file that lay before him. He went through the details briefly which told Tom Snr nothing new than he had got from his own source in Iraq.

Gary finished and looked up towards Tom Snr. "So you see we have a rather delicate situation on our hands."

"Seems that you have abandoned him from what you have just told me, which sounds all too familiar with you lot. You haven't given him any legal representation at all; you have kept both myself and his mother out of the loop which I find damn arrogant of you.

Perhaps it's to do with the fiasco from last year when you rescued the SAS guys from the same prison. Perhaps the National Guard doesn't want to talk to you guys anymore after the shit you stirred up then eh!"

"As I said this is a delicate situation. The facts are that a considerable amount of currency and gold has gone missing complicated even further with the problem of one of Iraq's own agents being murdered and also one of our RMP's shot.

After analysing the case we found it is rather cut and dried as far as we are concerned. We have therefore left the whole thing in the hands of the New Iraqi Government."

"Usual shit from you isn't it. Gets too hard and you throw the lamb to the slaughter. Those pricks have already built a reputation of failure including deceit yet you bow to their every need."

"That's not the case, Sir."

"Don't Sir me. You pack of arseholes are too quick at taking the easy way out. You seem to forget I have the past experience of you people to refer back to."

"Let me show you what the Iraqi police found when they got to the warehouse." Gary opened up the file and started to pull out photos and lay them out on the table. "These were taken on arrival. You can see the Iraqi agent here has his throat cut from behind and is lying alongside another body that was a contact of his. That man has a broken neck.

These photos show the injury to the RMP Captain who was in charge of the warehouse task.

Just as he finished there was a knock at the door which stopped further discussion, entering the room was a young good looking girl who turned everyone's head including Tom Snr.

"Lieutenant Sandra Crisp, Military Intelligence. Tom Warburton Snr." Gary introduced Tom Snr.

"What about this so called money my son is said to have received?" Tom Snr asked after just nodding to Sandra in recognition.

"That was disclosed by me to Captain Caulfield a few days before the team were put together for the warehouse task. It was information sent to me from GCHQ for which I then informed Captain Caulfield of it and he took control of the situation from then asking for Lieutenant Warburton to be attached to his team so he could get close to him." Sandra Crisp was precise and never faltered once in her speech.

"You say some £50,000 was placed into my son's account two weeks after his arrival in Iraq." Tom Snr enquired.

"Correct sir" Sandra responded.

"Were you able to trace where it came from?"

"The only clue we have is that it originated from the Cayman Islands. We do not seem to be able to get names out of the place or even a Company directive. It has been frustrating but the evidence is clear, it went direct to your son's account."

"Doesn't make sense. If that was a bribe or anything the like he would have tried to hide it not allow it to be seen in his obvious bank account." Tom Snr was starting his own probe now.

"Some people do make mistakes Tom that is what leaves them high and dry." Gary said still fiddling with the file in his hands.

"But there has been no movement on that account at all in the time since it was deposited. He has never approached it in any way whether through email or through any other source. It just doesn't tally to me. This is questionable for sure. I know my son and this is totally out of character for him. He is an honest, loyal team player."

Tom Snr lent forward starting to peruse the photos lying on the table. He kept looking at the ones that were of Mahmoud Brefti before he finally spoke.

"What evidence have you got to indicate that my son committed this murder in the first place?"

Gary continued "We have these photos from the Iraqi police alongside our own forensics people who have looked through them to make sure they are genuine and they have analysed them. See this one." He pulled one out of the group of Mahmoud lying on a slab in the morgue with markers and pointers near the throat wound. "This has been confirmed that it was carried out from behind the victim with a cut that went from right to left. T . . ."

"Whoa." Interrupted Tom Snr immediately stopping Gary in his tracks. "You said that the cut went from right to left." Gary looked at him nodding his agreement. "That would indicate that the perpetrator would have to have a strong arm with that kind of depth and he would have to have been a left hander, correct?"

"Yes that's correct." Gary said without hesitation.

"You dick heads. My son is right handed, not left handed. You should have known that if you had truly investigated it you would have found out that he could not do that kind of damage as a left hander.

Typical of you lot, as I said find the easy way out and give the lamb to the slaughter."

"This was investigated not only by the Iraqi Police but also by our own RMP unit, it was Captain Caulfield's report that highlighted your son being left handed. Also the fact that your son shot him with his pistol when he confronted him in the warehouse." Gary was now on the defensive.

"Let me look at those photos there. The ones showing my son sprawled out on the floor." Gary handed them over and Tom Snr again pondered over the photos when his face started to light up and a smile came over it.

"You lot are truly a bunch of amateurs I'm sure. Look at this." Tom Snr pointed to one of the photos. "He is lying by the side of his rifle while holding his pistol in his left hand. Don't you think that strange for a man with a rifle nearby would pull his pistol when he could quite easily have lifted his rifle and blown the other guy totally away?

Also people look at where his thigh holster is, on his right thigh not the left. What is wrong with you people? You seem to be just a bunch of fuckwits in this case."

The three others looked at the photos that Tom Snr had questioned and then started to look at each other before Sandra Crisp finally broke the stalemate. "I have Captain Caulfield's report here. He was the Commanding Officer of SIB at the time of this case." She spoke up as she punched some keys into a keyboard lying on the table. The big screen on the wall burst into action and within an instant up came a written report headed with the RMP logo and names clearly marked on it.

"Here it clearly says that your son being a left hander showed he was the perpetrator of Mr Brefti as there were no other persons within or near the warehouse at the time.

When Caulfield came within close range of your son he noticed the bodies on the floor then moved quickly to defend himself. The reason he did this is because he had been made aware of the money transfer to your son's account earlier therefore suspecting that your son may have some kind of planned deception to delay the investigation.

He was hoping to be able to catch your son out and expose him thereby allowing him to perhaps shop the remaining members of the group.

He says here that he just wasn't quick enough and as he moved forward to disarm him, your son drew his pistol and fired at him as he tried to swing his weapon around.

He says after the pistol went off he realised he had connected with your son's helmet with his SA80 making him unstable while himself sustaining a minor hit from the pistol. He took another swipe at him which made him immobile till the Iraqi police arrived at which point they took over the scene and he was taken to medical aid.

Captain Caulfield was then removed from theatre of operations for treatment and subsequently retired as planned." Sandra Crisp was reading it out as Tom Snr was also working his eyes over the report in front of them all.

"Why did Caulfield assume my son was left handed?" Tom Snr asked. "He had been observing him days before the team went out to the warehouse."

"Well he was wrong. My son is right handed and there is no way he would have tried to fire his pistol with his left. He has a perfect score if you'd like to check with his gun club as a right hander.

I think that someone has set this whole conspiracy up and my son was the stool pigeon.

I would like you to make arrangements for me to go to Iraq, see my son and I would also like you to review the so called facts you have as you are definitely up the garden path with them.

This Captain Caulfield, can I speak to him?"

"Unfortunately Captain Caulfield has since left the army, retired and has gone overseas." Gary chirped in looking rather embarrassed.

"Conveniently I bet. I would like to be able to contact him if possible."

"Sorry Tom we cannot allow that, we need to check these details against the light of your comments."

"I want action now. If my son is in prison in Iraq then I doubt very much as if he is being treated with any kind of respect being as they think he killed one of their own. Of course the memory of the great British Army release last year from the same prison would not be making matters any better either."

"Tom, please leave it with us and we will get back to you. The last thing I want is having to deal with a vigilante type parent. Please leave it to us and I will promise we will have answers within a couple of days."

"You've got two days total, that's your lot. You bastards never change do you? Assume this, assume that. It's about time you realised what the word Assume really means. Makes an ASS out of U and ME." Tom Snr stood and shook his head. "Don't even think about trying to cover this shit up now will you or I'll be on your case, that's my promise. Two days people, two bloody days" He turned, started for the door where he was quickly caught up with by Fulsome who shepherded him to the elevator then escorted him out of the building. Neither spoke to each other as Tom Snr exited Vauxhall Cross hoping to never see the place again.

Back up in the meeting room three bodies were busily trying to recover what decency the Department might still have left. How did they miss these facts? How did they fuck up so badly? Why did the RMP

Captain lead them astray? This whole affair was beginning to stink of deception from the inside.

The three worked round the clock over the coming couple of days to try and find answers to their questions but the only conclusion they came up with was the one that the man in the cell in Iraq was really innocent not guilty. How were they going to get him out was the other question, they had let the Iraqis have the case now. It was going to create a diplomatic nightmare.

Tom Snr was kept in the loop now with calls on a daily basis to stop him from throwing this all out to the press making things ever more difficult. Even the threat of the Official Secrets Act did not deter Tom Snr from perhaps uncovering one of the biggest balls ups the Country had seen since the original so called Weapons of Mass destruction call.

GCHQ and Vauxhall Cross worked incessantly to try to avoid anything leaking to the press. They made endless promises to the Warburtons to keep them from blowing the whole saga up in the air even to the point of using high level diplomats to organise some kind of negotiation of the facts. They worked hard to get Tom Jnr freed from his Iraqi prison but each time they tried they came up against the usual argument that the British were just trying to protect their own regardless of the offences caused.

It wasn't till the end of September that The Firm finally called Tom Snr and his wife to confirm they were trying to get their son freed from the jail and returned to the UK at the first opportune moment. Unfortunately they were hitting brick walls with every turn they made and had to reassure Tom Snr they would get him released no matter what.

CHAPTER 6

25 December 2006
Al Jameat Police complex

After weeks of stalled negotiations between London, Baghdad and Basra British Army commanders encouraged by 6 used an excuse to again raid the Al Jameat Police Complex in Basra.

The operation order came from the Brigade HQ with reasons for it under the guise of the fact that Shia militias were in control of the complex and there were prisoners there being inhumanely tortured with fears that many would be facing unwarranted execution within days. There was no mention of a British soldier being held in the Complex and that all information relevant to the operation was completely kept away from the media to prevent the kind of protests that they had faced the previous year.

After initially surrounding the building with Challenger tanks, including getting into a fire fight with the militia inside, British troops stormed the building killing seven gunmen and capturing many others.

One team in particular was assigned to make their way directly to the cells. Making their first and most important part of the mission was to find and release Tom from his cell. Four SAS troopers were given this task of the operation making their way in their normal controlled manner through the complex, then down to the cells in the basement till they came across the cell they needed.

Tom heard the commotion outside the cell door but was unsure whether to smile or worry after hearing gunfire at a distance before their arrival. Whether or not it was the National Guard or then there was a possibility that he might have to face an irate Iraqi group who wanted his blood as an offering.

He had no idea how long he had been incarcerated here but knew his own looks of long hair and scruffy beard that it must have been quite a while. His clothes were hanging on him now baggy, oversized and they were even in tatters on the legs and body of the shirt. One thing was for sure his captors were not into keeping their prisoners in good looking attire or even being well fed.

The noise grew louder as he held his ear to the door. It was dark inside this cell still. There had been no flashing bright lights like he had experienced over nearly every day he had been locked in here.

Noises increased followed by yells in Arabic then Tom thought he heard an English accent out there. He strained to get a better listen but was none the better. He pulled back from the door as the noise grew even louder then virtually stopped just outside his door. Trying to get away from the door he tripped on his bucket knocking it over in his fall and was covered with the past 24 hrs of his own urine. He now stank worse than he did earlier.

As he backed himself up to the opposite wall placing his back firmly against it there was a short blast followed by another and then the door was pushed off its hinges and light streamed into his cell causing him discomfort in the eye department. He held his hands to his face to protect his eyes from the light. He started to shake as he thought that his time had come, it was time to face his maker.

"Tom Warburton?" a voice called out.

"Yep" Tom answered hesitantly.

"Your vacation is over mate and it's time to go home." Said the first trooper moving closer to Tom reassuring him they were friends.

"Christ, look at the state of him." Came forth another voice just to the side of the first. "What the fuck have they been doing to him?"

"Cutters." Yelled the first trooper. "Get these fucking things off him." Tom blew a sigh of relief as the trooper stood to one side holding his arm in support as one of his team mates lent down and cut the cuffs off Tom's ankles and then the wrists.

Thank God for that thought Tom, freedom at last. He had made up his mind days or weeks ago that he was sure he was never going to see the light of day again. He was shaking violently now with either excitement or shock, he could not work it out. Two of the troopers grabbed him by the arms and assisted him to the door.

"You OK to walk mate?" asked one of the troopers.

"Mate I'll fucking run to get out of here given half the chance." Tom laughed back at him.

There was still some gunfire happening around but it was not too large a scale as when they had first gone in. On the exit from the cells Tom had at times had to step over dead men that had got in the way of the rescuers. As he came out into the compound Tom breathed a sigh of great relief

Two troopers took the front steering Tom who had another trooper helping him out the endless corridors with the last Trooper coming up the rear to cover. Upstairs they trudged to finally get their man out of the building and into a Landrover waiting just outside surrounded by other British troops from the local Infantry unit.

The Landrover took off with all the men aboard with Tom just squinting to get his eyes adapted to sunlight, something he hadn't seen for many months now. As they cleared the complex Tom could just make out a stream of Arab prisoners being led out of the complex being released to the freedom of the streets by the Squaddies.

Just a few minutes later Tom heard a loud explosion coming from their last location at which Tom just stared at the Section leader just crouched to his side.

"What the hell was that?" He asked.

"Those bastards won't be using that Police station for a while without some major repairs." The leader said with a beaming smile to his face.

Tom was taken directly to the military base hospital where he was to be checked over and readied for transport home. He said very little and did not even try to shave or get a haircut. He was just happy to shower and change into some comfortable, clean and non-smelly clothing.

By nightfall he had been cleared by the medics, gorged himself with food and was on a flight out of Basra International aboard a military transport that was flying direct to Brize Norton in the UK.

Internally Tom was ecstatic but showed little enthusiasm to anyone around him staying quiet during the entire trip back to the UK. Two or three on board tried to talk to him but he just closed his eyes as if to just sleep off the past few months. He was shutting himself off to civilization just as the Iraqi Guards had shut him off from humanity in Basra.

After landing at Brize Norton Tom was whisked away towards Epsom in Surrey. He had no idea where he was heading just told he would be staying some place called the Defence Services Medical Rehabilitation Unit for a short while where he would be assessed for his health. It was the early hours of the morning when they arrived; the sun was not due to shine for another few hours. The weather was cold with snow lying on the ground, a far cry from the place he had just come from.

As the vehicle pulled into the DMRC Tom could see the vastness of this establishment. The main structure of this large three storey red bricked building stood tall and proud amongst the snow covered trees that surrounded it. On the roof of the building was a glistening white cover, perhaps there was some truth in Father Christmas after all.

This was, Tom had heard during his training, the main centre for service personnel suffering from PTSD and other disabilities that needed rehabilitation in depth before being let out to the normal population. It was one of the finest Institutions in the country and possibly the world for the treatments it undertook. The centre had the best medical staff and facilities which put the NHS to shame, but then again the way conflict was now tending to go it was needed by the Armed Forces for sure.

He was greeted by a nurse at the reception being shown to what was a comfortable single room on the ground floor in the western wing of the hospital. He dropped himself onto the bed that sat in the corner by the window slipping off into a deep sleep. The mattress was unbelievably comfortable pulling him into the depths of warm, soft heaven felt sleep.

CHAPTER 7

Friday January 19, 2007
DMRC Headley Court.

After two weeks or so of being grilled by psychiatrists, having visits from spooks from the Firm much to Tom's annoyance. He was still perceived by the medical staff to be stuck in some kind of limbo. The assessment that was thrown around by the medical staff was one of withdrawn complex association, social isolation. Tom did not talk much in his sessions which as far as the spooks went he showed them how distasteful he thought their line of work really was.

During his time here he had seen so much pain on the faces of the other residents, amputees and those suffering what used to be called shell shock now designated PTSD. He knew that he had been placed in the box of PTSD category but was unfazed by it. It frustrated him every day he looked at his fellow patients seeing their anguish wondering how many of them had been betrayed in their theatre of operations by their own.

His one major problem which the boffins could not resolve quickly was the fact that Tom had placed himself in his own little box that had a message inside saying 'Do not trust anybody'. He never realized that this would cause him more than enough heartaches during his lifetime than he really knew.

Tom only thought of what had gone before him still having nightmares of the face of Mahmoud staring up at him after turning his body when he went into that warehouse in Iraq. The nightmares were haunting him nightly not only of Mahmoud but also of the treatment he received while in prison. Constant nightly sweats and bodily shudders shook him awake numerous times during the night.

Screams for mercy not knowing where the hell he was most of the time. He felt he was going insane.

His only way out he thought was to shut himself away from people in general as he did not even trust those close around him now. Why? Well perhaps the fact that he knew that somehow someone had set him up back in Iraq for some ungodly reason which he was determined in his own mind to get to the bottom of it. Trust, there was none as far as the Army went and definitely none as far as the Firm went, the old man had sorted that out for him many times before.

Tom's only communication from the outside was a phone call each week from his father which lasted only minutes as he couldn't bring himself to even talk to him about what had happened in Iraq. His mother he was told had been ill but was recovering from surgery in hospital. Tom couldn't even bring himself to ask to visit her. His father had told him that the past year had caused his mother some anxiety and she suddenly fell sick while he was in prison which had led to her being diagnosed with stomach cancer. Tom knew his mother as the strong woman who never let anything get on top of her but now she had become vulnerable, depressed about her son and with the pressure of her son's predicament it did not help her at all to fight what she was going through. An operation to remove part of the stomach had at the time given her a double whammy of loss as she also thought at the time that her son was also lost.

Tom's thoughts were just trained on finding out who had set him up and he was not going to allow anything else to distract him. Through his mind went the names of the men who he had seen information on that were suspect. The only female name was Lt Sandra Crisp the dishy looking Intelligence officer at the briefing, but surely she was not part of the plot. The sly chat she had had with Caulfield before she left the meeting that day was strange. She would be the first one that he would eliminate from the plot or if guilty take his own revenge on her.

This Friday as he was just settling back to relax and read a book he had got from the Hospital Library there was a knock at his door followed by a young QARANC nurse who poked her head around the door smiling at Tom announcing. "You have a couple of visitors, Tom." She finished her sentence standing back allowing two men to enter the room as Tom began to rise from his relaxed mode on his bed. The first man in he recognised as one of the suits that had been at the briefing in Iraq and the second man in was his father.

"Dad, you should have said you were coming."

"You probably would have told me not today son eh."

"Yeh, your right as usual. What brings you to my lowly pad?"

'Tom, do you remember me from the briefing we had at your base. Gary Warlock."

"Yep remember you well. You mob gave up on me if I remember it right." "No Tom we didn't give up just got led astray somewhat. At least we managed to get you out before too much damage was done." Gary was formally apologising in no uncertain terms.

"Get fucked pal. You had me done as a dog's dinner, you know it. Damage, just look at me I have lost all faith in people."

"Tom please, listen to what Gary has to say. We all want this thing sorted out as soon as possible with perhaps then you can get some closure from what he has to offer." Tom's dad spoke in a pleading manner towards him.

Gary started to explain the reasons for the delay in getting to him and the unmistakeable evidence they thought they had, that had been given by Caulfield, who now was the main suspect they wanted to talk to as soon as was possible. He explained that Caulfield had fallen off the radar very quickly after he had flown out of the UK shortly after his discharge, bound for somewhere in Eastern Europe but that is where they eventually lost him. No trace of the man has since been seen. Gary continued to ask Tom if he would be agreeable to joining the Firm and being their front man in the search.

"You've got to be kidding me. You and the rest of the establishment are to blame for what has happened to me. Trust you bastards, I don't think so. I think these conversations are over pal."

"Tom, all we have is Caulfield along with the names of those who were not identified in the remains retrieved at the initial convoy scam. We need someone who they do not expect to surface. Your extraction from Al Jameat was not confirmed as we hid it under the guise of us stopping a local militia from executing and torturing local Shia men. As far as the Iraqi Government is concerned you perished in the destruction of the complex." Gary spoke looking into Tom's eyes hoping to get some kind of acceptance.

"So I don't exist to many anymore then?"

"To the important ones you do. You can stay as part of the military if you choose or you can join us as one of ours under covert conditions. It was hard enough for us to ask your Dad here as he has experienced us at our worst.

Tom we really need someone we can trust to carry on as we also have some distrust in some of our own. It seems money corrupts the best of us at times."

"I have already resigned my commission after what has happened. This place seems to think I am suffering from PTSD so I don't see me getting any clearance from here anytime soon."

"We can handle that side of things if you think you are up to it." Gary was getting hopeful now he thought he had Tom on side.

"I'll give it some thought Gary. If I do choose to go with what you are offering I'll tell you now any double cross or dealing and I will have no qualms about exposing whatever I find out, is that clear?"

"Crystal. Look here's my card. Give me a call in the next week perhaps we can sort things out and get you up and running. Just as soon as you think you are ready though, not before."

With that Tom asked Gary if he could have time with his father, nodding to him then shaking his hand Gary left the room leaving the two Toms to chat.

Tom looked at his father and asked about his mother. What he received was a disappointing response that she was not recovering well. He told his father that he would like to go and visit which pleased the old man greatly. He said he would arrange it with the staff to get him out for the coming weekend to see her.

That cleared, he then said. "What do you think dad, do I trust them?" "Son, the only one you can trust when working in that kind of scenario is yourself. But be assured there are some that are genuine, some are loyal to the cause whatever it may be."

"Then I suppose I should give it a go using them eh. I was going to go after Caulfield myself but I might as well use the Governments resources instead of my own. The cheeky blighters took the 50 grand from my account anyway which left me with stuff all."

"Easy come, easy go son. Just don't take too many chances, you know where to contact me remember I still have some contacts around the place."

"You're getting too old for this shit I think you'd say."

"Bloody right I am. I love you son and don't want to lose you so whatever you do take care."

"I love you too Dad. Try and arrange for me to go to see Mum this weekend and we can relax again as a family."

"Sure will but get a bloody shave and a haircut eh you scruffy git, your mother would be so disappointed with your current appearance, I don't think she would recognise you." A few faux punches were exchanged followed by a hug before the two men separated with Tom going back to his book and his dad wondering down to the car to

Gary where he never let on that his son was going to comply with Gary's request.

Over the weekend Tom was able to visit his mother in her hospice where they spent two days, just the three of them being close. It would be the last time Tom saw his mother as he found out as he left that she was deteriorating rapidly, the cancer had gone into her bones and she was sinking fast. She had only a couple of months to go before peace would be upon her but they did not give that part of the information to Tom.

Over the following week Tom got himself energised to take on his new role. He began working out in the hospital gym, refreshing himself with his martial arts by contacting another like person in the hospital.

He had phoned Gary and was waiting to be cleared from the head shrinks at the hospital. It was not as simple as he wanted it to be as at the last minute the hospital shrinks had assigned a nurse to him who would be on call located in London. The nurse had been cleared by the hospital after consulting with MI6. He would have to meet her to organise a few things prior to his meeting with Gary and his new role when he got to London.

Tom left a poem he had written on his bed as he left the room the following week hoping it would give some comfort to his disabled comrades that remained behind.

Oh to be a squaddie

For those that follow me
Through this peaceful room
Hope I'll try to give unto thee
Your work is done, your suffering doth loom.

It may seem like a daunting time
Whether it be limbs we miss
As we wait for healing to begin
Or our minds remove the stress

Time will tell for us most
As we remain alive on earth
Some without feeling of things lost
Some without friends of worth

The loss is ours only to bear
What we leave behind in our past
We must face the future together
Building new friendships to forever last

We may feel we are poor
Of feelings or love gone astray
Can we face the future that comes?
Or do we hide ourselves away

We've done our job well
Followed orders to the letter
Sometimes it felt like hell
But really we should feel better

We pray to who we believe in
The answers are there somewhere
Not always coming
We just need faith in our prayer

A protection of our souls
A critic of our actions
Who are we to judge our flaws?
Someone else has that transaction

Build our spirit
Build our soul
Build our trust
Rebuild our bodies oh Lord

When we meet our maker
He alone will decide our fate
Sooner rather than later
Our usefulness in this world to debate

Our orders have been given
We've served them to our best
The support must now be driven
We need to take our rest
Pray if you must
Plead your case
We will find ease
And peace will be ours alone

But when we meet our God
He will judge us fairly
A loving God for all
To lead us in peace for ever

As quoted by Private Fred Carmicheal in his poem The Soldier The soldier waited for the judgement of his God. 'Step forward now you soldier
you've borne your burdens well
Walk peacefully in heaven's streets
you've done your time in Hell.'

May you all that follow me find your peace in this world.

He looked back into the room before he closed the door with what was a faint glimmer of a smile upon his now cleanly shaved face.

His stride was now more confident than when he had arrived here, knowing he was now on the way to redemption of any blame being he was even more determined now to find those responsible for his incarceration. The names slowly went through his mind as had done many times before.

Lieutenant Sandra Crisp, Major Tony Welsh {these were question marks at this stage though}

Captain Peter Caulfield, S.Sgt. Chris Saxby, Sgt. Dave Broad, Sgt. Mark Smythe,

Sapper Steve Reed, these were the ones he really wanted to talk to. This list just kept playing over and over again through his mind. He often wondered if there were any more involved but just knew that once he got hold of one or two of these arseholes he would then find out the truth.

CHAPTER 8

February 12 2007
Albert Serviced Apartments SW8

Tom was collected from the centre at Epsom then driven to London by a driver supplied from Vauxhall Cross. The drive took longer than normal because of the atrocious weather conditions with snow still falling in places around the country. He was eventually dropped at the Albert Serviced apartments complete with an envelope which contained key pads and security numbers that allowed his access.

The weather was still bleak as Tom exited the car causing him to shudder at the wind chill that seemed to go straight through him. He pulled up the collar of his overcoat and walked briskly to the main door punching in the code number he had been given in the envelope. He was met by a wave of warmth inside the foyer of this grand looking building once through the door. Heading for the elevator he entered after pressing the button to go up but had to press his code number into the key pad to enable the elevator to burst into action.

As elevators go this one was fairly fast but didn't quite leave his stomach behind like some of the others he had experienced during his travels. The twelfth floor came up quickly; being the last stop and when the doors opened Tom was met with an outstanding view of the local precincts covered now in a white glow from the snow still driving down on them.

London seemed still wrapped in the Christmas card look that he always imagined it had been at this time of the year. Stepping out into the vastness of this penthouse suite with its 700 sqft of roof terrace

Tom felt some relief of his previous weeks he had spent being grilled by shrinks.

"Hello you must be Tom." An Australian accent met him that startled Tom to spin around.

Right in front of him stood a 160 cm brunette about 26 years old with a figure that would be more pleasing to view in a bikini, even though the dark trouser suit she was wearing made her figure stand out nicely. But this was winter so no hope of that thought Tom, well not just yet anyway.

"You gave me a fright." Tom said looking directly into what were brown eyes in a tanned face.

'I'm Victoria Robson your Phsyc nurse, you can call me Vicki." She smiled at him.

"Well hello Vicki. They told me there would be a nurse but I don't really need one, perhaps you are wasting your time looking after me." Tom said regretting the statement as he said it while thinking that this sweet looking thing would be a nice companion for him while he was in London.

"The big boys assigned me to you to assess your re-entry to civilization so to speak. I won't be wasting my time. I am being paid well so it is just for a few weeks anyway, till they review you." She replied still with the smile from ear to ear.

"Well you had better show me around then eh."

Vicki took hold of Tom's arm and started to introduce him to the wonders of the penthouse suite. The stylish living area with designer furnishings and floor to ceiling windows gave amazing views around them. The bedrooms although small were contemporary looking very comfortable.

"This is your room, Tom." Vicki led him into the main bedroom where there was an ensuite. "Your people have put your clothes in the wardrobe; over there is a mobile phone on the side they left for your use. As well there is also a laptop for your internet use as well."

"They have thought of nearly everything." Tom said wondering whether the laptop and mobile had some kind of GPS tracking or the like so they knew his every move. That was something he would serious think about changing if it became necessary.

"My rooms next door, so I won't be too far away." Vicki added to be met with astonishment from Tom.

"You're staying here as well." The shock was all too obvious from Tom. "The powers that be felt that speeding up your recovery meant I needed to be on call 24/7." Vicki stood back from Tom still brandishing her smile adding. "Coffee, Tea or something to eat, perhaps?"

"Just tea thanks; this is going to take some getting used to after my isolation."

"It will be OK. By the way there is a message for you on your phone. Damn thing kept beeping overnight. I can't open it as there is a security pin on it which I hope you know."

As Tom thanked her, Vicki left to go to the kitchen to make the tea. Tom took hold of the phone and checked his envelope finding the pin number to open it which he punched in. Up popped the message in text:

'*Welcome to London. I hope the clothes fit ok. You've met Vicki by now and she will be with you till we are confident of your fitness. We can meet at 1000hrs tomorrow at the Brunswick House Cafe just down the road. Better than in the Cross eh! Talk then. Rest and relax. Gary*'

Short and sweet Tom thought. Thoughtful as well as he did not really want to go into the Cross building if he could help it. He still did not trust them at all.

Sitting drinking his tea he chatted to Vicki which was about the biggest thing he had done with another person, especially of the opposite sex, since his incarceration in Iraq. He found out she was here in the UK on a temporary work visor because she was originally from Perth in Western Australia. She had a younger brother and sister. Her parents were owners of a small shop in the heart of Perth. He shared with her his own thoughts of Australia he had been told of by his parents a few years ago, just the good bits of course.

Tom didn't realize how easy it was to get someone talking as once she started; Vicki wanted to tell him her life story. She had once been engaged to a guy back home, encouraged by her parents because like them he was a Jehovah's Witnesses, but she found it too demanding with all the rules and things you have to follow. She had broken off the engagement to be able to travel when she completed her nurse's qualifications. Vicki wasn't following her religious commitments at the present focusing more on her career first.

The remainder of the day Tom spent listing questions he had for Gary during the meeting the next day. He wrote down the names he was about to place on his very own most wanted list.

The evening became a virtual session with Vicki. These would be frequent over the coming days, weeks and enabled Vicki to be able to report back to the Defence Services Rehab Centre.

“The most important aspects or objectives of this treatment for PTSD are 1. Rediscover sense of purpose and 2. Rebuild trust.” Vicki said to him as she finished her little session.

“Number two is always going to be my nemesis I’m afraid after what has happened to me this past year or so.” Tom said placing his hand upon hers for some kind of reassurance.

“We will get through this Tom, I’m sure. Your symptoms aren’t as bad as they led me to believe or those I have had to help before.”

“Well I wasn’t the best patient for them unfortunately. I wanted to just be alone and think and not be part of their program.”

“It’s ok we are all here to help you.”

“Trust, remember. That’s the problem I will have for a while.” “Ok but try and trust me that’s a start for now.”

With that they parted for their individual rooms and settled down for the night. This night was not without drama as at 0230 Tom was tossing and turning, screaming out to what seemed like he was breaking someone’s neck. Vicki raced into his room to calm him down to find Tom’s arms flailing around so she just wrapped her arms around him which had the effect of instant success in calming him down. Tom eased down returning to his slumber. Vicki remained in the room till morning still cuddling Tom but with the doona between them. She awoke before Tom leaving him asleep while she rustled up breakfast for the two of them. This was to become a common thing during the coming weeks for Vicki and one which brought the two of them even more closer together.

Next morning when Tom awoke Vicki explained what she had seen during the night and also what she had to do to him to calm him down. He apologised to her but she brushed that off saying that was one of the reasons she had agreed to stay in the same apartment to speed up the process. Trust was starting to be rebuilt for Tom; even he could feel it now at this early stage.

CHAPTER 9

Tuesday and the weather had deteriorated even more overnight. The cold wind that met Tom as he exited the building brought tears to his eyes. The snow was falling in larger flakes than the day before. On the roads the slush created by the vehicles driving through the salt splattered bitumen was black against the new falls.

He turned to his right and headed down the road towards the Brunswick House cafe which took him all of five minutes to get to. Inside he ordered the largest coffee he could get sitting near what seemed like an old heater system for warmth. It seemed the most welcoming seat in the place.

He didn't have to wait long before Gary appeared at the door making his way to Tom's table where he greeted him with a firm handshake.

"Great to see you again, Tom. How are things going? Hope you have everything in the apartment for your needs."

"Feel quite good thanks Gary. You did well with the clothes they were spot on. Also thanks for the nurse she's great even though I don't think I really need her."

"The nurse wasn't our idea just the shrinks from DMRC. We have vetted her of course and she is clear but is kept out of our loop for obvious reasons. She has no idea who you are working with and we need to keep it that way."

"I have a list of questions before I get started mate." "Fire away Tom."

"Crisp, is she clear or has she connections with Caulfield?" Tom asked. "Captain Crisp is GCHQ and she was assigned to Caulfield as a young Lieutenant after the convoy incident. She had worked with

Caulfield's last CO Capt Ken Masters who unfortunately died under mysterious circumstances in Iraq back in Oct 2005. She was intelligence officer covering that incident and transferred over to the convoy investigation to assist Caulfield. We don't suspect anything with her loyalty as well we haven't seen anything in her movements to query that either."

"So I can cross her off my suspect list then? How about Major Welsh?" Tom busily looked at his list now getting smaller with Crisp knocked off of it.

"Welsh was in charge of the Engineers being personally responsible in selecting the men to actually go on the convoy. After the disappearance he was questioned but we found nothing untoward. He seemed genuinely upset at the fact that his men had been killed but turned down a request to stay while we investigated as he had made arrangements to start up a company with some overseas partners on leaving the army with that date being upon him two weeks after the convoy was arranged and departed.

He returned to the UK and was decommissioned within the month. As far as our information goes he heads up some kind of a Loan and Investment Company based out of Melbourne, Australia. I have the details here for you if you want to check it yourself." Gary had a file with him which he lifted some paper from while finishing his sentence. "All of it seems above board, it has connections in the Bahamas and Europe. All the information is in the file."

"Any suspicions of how he got up and running with this company?"
"None at all; his wife's family were fairly well off in the financial sector some years ago in the City and she had inherited their estate since their demise two years ago. She herself passed away a year back and of course Welsh was the final benefactor."

"What about Caulfield; any new leads on him?"

"None unfortunately; we have pulled out all our plugs to find him but with no success. Crisp is actually trying to find trace of him in Eastern Europe but as yet zilch. If you want I can have Crisp call on you and give you the run down on what she has so far."

"That would be good. I did have her on my suspect list but she seems, by what you say, genuine enough." Tom was still thinking about the blonde bombshell that had been at the briefing but he still had a vision of her which he gathered was highly unhealthy and disrespectful without being unprofessional.

"No Tom she is one of the good guys. I'll arrange for her to visit the apartment in a couple of days. I don't want to rush you. Look through this stuff on Welsh and be clear of what is there, you may have questions after your own research. Any questions please just text me so we can meet here as per today anytime you require. OK?"

"Great; at least I have something to get my teeth into now but I'm keener to track that prick down and find out what he knows." Indicating to the picture of Caulfield that was in the file now in front of him.

With that the two men shook hands and departed the cafe in different directions. Tom wondered why the different tracks as Gary's office was in the direction he was heading. Oh well thought Tom try not to understand the spook's head or your head will get dizzy.

That afternoon Tom spent hours on the computer trying to locate and get information on Welsh's new Company. He went far into the evening finally stopping when Vicki approached him about another little session she needed with him, boy she was keen.

Yet another restless night for Tom with again Vicki finding herself in his room comforting him without him knowing. This was becoming a habit for her but she wasn't adverse to it as she felt some kind of warmth in Tom's body. The warmth of a great personality and kindness.

The following day and night were much of the same with Tom Googling everything he could on Asia Pac Loan and Finance based in Melbourne Australia. Only the name Welsh was recognizable as all other names were not on his list.

He was keen to see Crisp again which had been arranged for the next day in the hope she had further information for him. That night was a repeat for both he and Vicki but this time Tom awoke during the night to find Vicki snuggling into him, he just smiled at her with the way she had placed the doona between them and went back to sleep.

Friday approached rapidly with Tom getting used to waking during the night to find Vicki lying beside him. He felt thankful that she was here as it helped him tremendously to overcome the demons that rose in his sleep shaking him awake. This morning it was Tom who rose first who started the day with tea and toast served in bed.

"Oh, that's nice Tom. Thank you." Vicki looked at Tom rubbing the sleep from her eyes.

"Pleasure, you have done wonders for me in such a short time. I am the thankful one." Tom smiled back at her.

Just as they had risen and dressed there was a buzz at the phone that indicated that someone was requesting entry to visit. Vicki answered to be met with a quivering female voice announcing herself as Sandra Crisp for Tom.

"Girlfriend?" enquired Vicki.

"No chance of that. She's from the Military with some information for me." Tom answered not wanting to give too much away as security was foremost in his mind at the present as Gary had told him.

Vicki buzzed Sandra in punching a code into the phone at the same time that would allow Sandra to come to the penthouse suite via the elevator.

The lift opened and there in front of Tom was that Barby doll girl he had seen at the briefing in Basra. After coming into the warm apartment she placed her briefcase down taking off her coat revealing a tight fitting trouser suit that really emphasized her curvy features, the ones Tom could not get out of his mind. "Nice to see you again, Lt Crisp." Tom said offering his hand to greet her.

"Captain now, thank you. How are you after your ordeal, Lieutenant?" Sandra shook Tom's hand smiling at him.

"Mr, please. I'm out of it all now. Congratulations on your promotion though. Feeling great now especially with help from Vicki here I'm making magnificent progress I think."

"That's great, can we get on with the information I have for you. Gary Warlock asked me to get all the relevant files for you to have a look at." Sandra continued lifting the briefcase and heading for a table in the dining area.

Tom followed asking Vicki to get some coffee on brew after confirming Sandra would like some.

"These files are for your eyes only at this stage." "Sounds like a passage out of James Bond."

"Let's be serious Tom. This is still a delicate situation for all of causing us, the Government, and the Iraqis a considerable amount of embarrassment."

Sandra started opening the files, with the first one a large one detailing information on a company titled Asia Pac Loan & Finance.

"This is the company Welsh set up with the help of some overseas investors who we are having problems even now in identifying. But we have a name of a person that has recommended the Company to many of our senior bureaucrats here. That man is Mr Reginald Aspalson who is the Under Secretary for Foreign Affairs. The link we see between them has been there since before either Welsh left the Army and also before Aspalson was promoted to his present position.

That in itself indicates to us that it is a genuine Company that the Government have looked at as a preferred partner."

"Any chance of Aspalson being bent or corrupt?" Tom asked.

"No indications of that at the moment, but what we know are that all Government ministers and senior bureaucrats are being monitored from all directions to avoid any future Government embarrassment. This is a monitoring situation controlled by 5.

The company is doing well by the reports we have. Since the start of this so called global financial crisis everyone's screaming about, the Company has profited on some of the unfortunates that had gone too deep into debt and got caught by the investment bubble. Companies that it has dealt with are large and varied, it has taken over or bought out directly many small businesses then profited by selling off their assets to other competitors in the marketplace. It has offices in Melbourne, Australia; Athens; Greece, and Nassau in the Bahamas."

"Nothing in the UK?"

"No, its head office is Melbourne. The only thing I can see that appears weird for such a successful Company is that the majority of all transactions are dealt with through Melbourne, there is very little comes out of Athens or Nassau, but that may be the way this mob works close to its heart, the head office.

I can see you think that is strange but Welsh has relatives that live in Australia having no close relatives in the UK. That was probably the reason for his move there coupled also with the mining boom on down under at the moment. And of course the other big thing about their location is the fact that Australia has weathered thus far in the global crisis better than most.

These other files are all about the men who we have lost trace on. Going through them, one noticeable thing was that all the men in question are either bachelors or divorcees." "What about Welsh? Is he the same?"

"Widower of course, never remarried and his two children live in Australia with their own families, so that enables him to be able to see his children and grandchildren on a more frequent basis. Another reason for the company being headed up in Australia I think."

"That gives me something to think about with all these people virtually in the same boat. No attachments too close to the heart." Tom rubbed his chin taking notes at the same time. "Has there been any trace of any of them anywhere?"

"None whatsoever I'm afraid. We have tried facial recognition in many areas including airport security etc but just like Caulfield they have disappeared off the face of the earth. Caulfield we know flew out to Eastern Europe but we have tried everything to find him but keep coming up blank."

"Whereabouts in Europe was he last seen or noticed, Sandra?" "Sofia, Bulgaria."

"That's where I will have to start then. Any contact that he may have had there, including any friends?"

"We know he actually stayed at the Grand Hotel Sofia on the General Yosif V. Gurko. Our contact there told us he visited a place in the district called Angel Kanchev and on checking that out we found that there is forger located there by the name of Grigor Karavelov who we know from past experience. The address is there for you." She pointed. "Third floor flat, number seven above a place known as Jimmy's."

"Great, at least I can now start looking; it's a starting point that perhaps will get me a lead on him."

"Hope you have better luck than our man did, he was politely told to bog off by the local authorities there even though he was in no means unpersuasive. Seems this guy Grigor is like a Doctor and treats everything and every contact as confidential. We were unable to get anything from him because he has contacts with the once State secret police which makes it all the more difficult for us.

Even now with Bulgaria in NATO etc we have still seen over the past few years of so called democracy that things are still influenced by the ex-operatives of the Secret Police who now are closely linked to the political and business establishments.

You'll need to be very careful there as the underworld is pretty thick with the old masters of deception."

"That's where I'll start from though. At least it is some kind of lead." Tom was beginning to get more confidence in the ability to find this Caulfield fellow. He owed him one that was for sure.

The two talked for a couple of hours before Sandra excused herself saying she had to meet her fiancé over the river. That blew Tom's dream apart as she said it, the Barby doll was attached, what shear bad luck he thought. Tom offered to walk her out as he wanted to go over to the Station to grab a newspaper.

Sandra wrapped herself up in her coat ready to face the bitter cold outside while Tom threw on a short thick coat with a fur collar to keep his neck warm. There was silence as they descended in the lift with still no words spoken as they exited the building and turned left towards the Cross. The snow had stopped now leaving everything around them wet and slushy which seemed to soak into whatever shoes or boots you had on freezing the toes.

As they approached the traffic lights where they had to cross the road a black 7 series BMW pulled up to the red light just as Tom and Sandra were walking along the pavement to the crossing area where they stood for a while waiting for the little green man to light up allowing them to cross without jay walking.

The BMW rear window opened about 100 mm exposing an olive face peering out of it towards them both. Tom looked to his right getting that horrible feeling on his neck with the hairs standing on end because someone was looking at him and saw the window down slightly through which he saw the face peering at him with its distinctive hooked type nose. He instantly recognised the face and turned his head as if he didn't notice it.

The green light came on and he grabbed Sandra's arm to walk across the road.

"What the hell?" Sandra said surprisingly.

"Keep walking. Don't look around but that BMW behind, the rear passenger I recognised him from the briefing back in Basra. The man from the Ministry of Interior."

"You've got to be kidding me. This is winter in London, what would an Arab be doing here in this freezing pathetic weather."

"Don't know, don't care but it was him and he noticed us I'm sure."
"You mean Ashid, from the Interior Ministry."

"That's the man and my problem is that the Iraqis think I died in the Al Jameat raid which may well blow my cover right out of the water."

"I think you may be getting a bit paranoid Tom."

As they got to the other side and headed for the bus terminal Tom turned as if to be saying goodbye which gave him the opportunity to see behind them. Sure enough just about the kerbside where they had walked from stood two tall Arab men looking in their direction. As the car moved off leaving the men there he noticed the CD plates that were on the rear.

"Sure thing. The car is CD plated and now there are two Arabs looking our way."

Sandra looked into Tom's eyes and saw an element of fear creep into them. She leant forward and kissed his cheek then turned to head off to the bus noticing also what Tom had seen. She looked back at Tom and said "I'll get in touch with Gary as soon as I am on the bus. Take care going back eh Tom."

"No problems Sandra, thank you." Tom turned and headed for the newsagents where he got the early edition of the Evening Standard and came out of the shop looking at it while scanning the area. Sure enough just by the bus terminal were the two Arab men checking him out. Tom took his time to get back across the road and when he had he decided to walk around the block along the Riverwalk to make sure if he was being followed.

It took him at least half an hour to walk around but he was certain that the two men were close by. They were good. He only caught a glimpse of them a couple of times when he turned before he eventually turned back on himself. The old man had taught him well when he had told him some of the old tricks to check upon possible watchers.

Tom felt certain he had lost them by the time he had come back around to the Apartments so when he went in he scanned the pedestrian walkway either side to see if they were in sight. He couldn't see them but unfortunately for Tom one of them had already clocked him and noted the way he had entered the apartment block.

Tom took the lift up to the penthouse unaware that his entry to the apartments was being watched by one of the Arab men that had followed him.

When he entered the penthouse Vicki could see he was concerned.

"What's wrong Tom?' She asked.

"Nothing just thought I had seen someone I knew from a while ago." He turned towards his room and entered shutting the door behind him so he could send a text to Gary straight away.

Within minutes a return text appeared on his phone.

'Stay in the apartment, have received call from Crisp. Will check situation before getting into contact with you. Don't answer door or phone to anyone till you hear from me. Gary.'

Tom sat back on his bed taking hold of his newspaper and started to read it but all the time his mind was going over the face he had seen peering out of the window of the BMW thinking what the consequences might be if it was who he thought it was. He was not going to say anything to Vicki as it might spook her and anyway she was not a part of this so he did not want her to be in any type of danger. Just sit tight and wait, patience, he had plenty of experience in that field, for sure.

The following day Tom got a call from Gary.

"Tom, you were right I'm afraid. The man who you saw was Jamal Ashid, he is visiting here from Iraq on the subject of the lost millions. They obviously aren't going to let it slide any time soon. He was here with the big boys upstairs and I was summoned late yesterday to face them."

"What are they after, Gary?"

"It seems there are only a few of us who know what happened to you and that is being covered by Section 20 along with the rest of the Military link. Unfortunately Ashid is in talks with The Foreign Secretary this weekend at his country residence and the subject of the possibility that a murderer was rescued from an Iraqi prison is now on the top of his list. He was sure that he saw you and the young Ms Crisp in Vauxhall near our building."

"Look, Gary I think it's time I moved on. Sandra gave me some useful information which is better than anything that we have so far so I think it is time I went on my way to find Caulfield before this other problem blows up in our faces.

Can you arrange my cover and documents for me to travel to Bulgaria next week? The sooner the better mate."

"I'll see what I can sort out by Monday for you Tom. You sure you are ready?"

"As sure as I'll ever be, Gary."

"OK, stay safe and we'll be in touch Monday."

With that the phone line bleeped and dropped out. These modern mobiles with their source of scramblers were getting better and better in their technology. Tom relaxed in the lounge for a while before he made a decision to tell Vicki he was on the move next week.

"Are you sure you are up to it Tom?" Vicki looked sad rather than concerned.

"Positive thanks to you I have a better understanding of the demons that have been plaguing me this last year. Look, I would like to thank you for all your help and perhaps take you out tomorrow for lunch at a riverside place I have fond memories of."

"That would be nice. It's a date." Vicki smiled walking over to Tom and kissed him firmly on the lips. Tom responded and gave her one huge cuddle.

"After next week you won't lose touch with me will you?" she questioned. "No, I think we will be in touch more than you think. You have become one hell of a special person to me Vicki."

They sat down together, talked about various bits of their lives and at the end of the afternoon Vicki confirmed that she would return to her native Perth which was something her parents had been hoping for a long time.

That night Tom slept better and he woke disappointed that Vicki was not lying beside him. Tom wasn't the type to take advantage of a woman, he was a gentleman and proud of it. He always tried to keep his moral ethics at the highest, but that was going to change one day.

CHAPTER 10

Sunday 18 February 2007

The sky outside was as blue as this morning. This was a strange type of winter morning for London to experience. It was still damn cold though as Tom found out opening up the sliding door to the outer terrace area. He quickly shut it behind him as he stepped through the open door to keep that warmth in the apartment.

Strolling to the handrail of the terrace he looked out over this great metropolis taking in the sights of what he was always told was a City in love with its people. It always had something going on within its area and he loved it as his father had also done as a boy.

Vicki was up and ready by 0900 with both of them tucking into a hearty breakfast before leaving the apartment then heading for the bus terminal at the base of the bridge. All the while Tom kept looking about to see if there was anyone following them. He saw no one showing any suspicious tendencies so began to relax as they boarded a #77 bus that took them along the embankment Southside to Waterloo where they got off heading towards the embankment walkway near the Festival Hall.

Tom was hoping to take Vicki up on the London Eye but when he saw what seemed like the mile long queue he just kept walking towards the east side past the Hall and under the Hungerford railway bridge.

Vicki showed she was enjoying this special time with Tom. She told him she had been on the Eye some time back so was not too disappointed at not going up it again.

The rumbling of trains going over their head across the River Thames via the Hungerford Bridge was deafening so they broke into a run to clear the bridge as quick as they could. Laughing as well as breathing heavily by the time they eventually stopped on the other side of the bridge.

Tom turned around looking at Vicki while his breath was billowing out what looked like steam from his mouth. His face was red which was not from running but from the cold wind that pierced into him. Vicki also blew vapour from her mouth also showing that same red complexion that Tom had.

They stared at each other for what looked like an eternity then suddenly Tom leant down and took her in his arms and planted his lips firmly onto hers. She responded returning the action willingly placing her arms around him and holding on like there was no tomorrow.

"I'll miss you when you leave." She said with tears welling up in her eyes.

"I'll miss you too my love, but when I have finished what I have to do I'll come looking for you and we can be together." Tom had fallen totally head over heels for Vicki for sure wanting this relationship to be the one he had always hoped for. He was unlike his fellow males at this age who just wanted the quick shag then run.

"I'll look forward to that." She replied cuddling him again holding her cheek tightly against his.

They released themselves from the lover's grasp they had on each other and resumed their walk towards the Shakespeare Globe Theatre. Vicki expressed her love of this building she had passed so often in the past but never had had the time to find out more about it. Tom seized on this opportunity to show his knowledge of this wonderful replica of the old Globe that had been constructed and opened to the public in 1997.

Tom explained that it was an academic approximation of the original design based on the evidence they had at hand of the original buildings of 1599 and 1614. He was proud to be able to reflect on the history of his father's native London. He was proud of his father and also had fallen in love with London when he first came here a few years earlier. Some say it is a dirty old town but under the grime the history of the place far outweighs any negative comments people can make about it.

It was while he explained to Vicki that the building now standing is about 230 meters from the main footings of the original theatre that he noticed a face in the crowd watching him. A man of Middle Eastern appearance was definitely more interested in Tom and Vicki than he was with the building let alone the guide that was in front of him showing a group of Japanese tourists around.

Tom did not react but took the opportunity to go inside the building showing Vicki the stage area. Once inside he steered her unknowingly to the side telling her to visualize being in an audience of the era. While she did this he watched her as she closed her eyes giving him the opportunity from where he stood to be in a position to be able to see the main doorway in.

Sure enough the guy, about Tom's height but thicker set and sporting a beard, came into the theatre area scanned around locking his focus onto Tom but at the same time realizing Tom was looking back towards him so turned his head away quickly and moved in the opposite direction.

Tom cuddled Vicki from the rear and asked her how she found it all. She remarked how wonderful it all was and the whole experience was burned into her memory for ever.

Tom moved her around gave her a quick kiss leading her out of the door keeping his eyes firmly on the watcher. Outside the main door he continued to lead them around the building strolling towards Gabriel's Wharf where he would treat her to lunch.

As Tom entered the short Mall that led to the restaurant at Gabriel's Wharf he noticed at the end of the road a black BMW just sitting with all the windows full of faces. Faces of which he could not quite make out at the distance they were parked. Tom continued to enter the Mall which had stalls either side with bustling crowds of people throbbing through it. With so many people he felt quite safe so continued up the stairs to the first floor restaurant where he chose a corner table which had been just vacated which gave him a clear view of anyone coming into the room and also gave him a good vision out onto the Mall below.

As he sat he gazed out of the window, sure enough there was their man following. The man took a spot just below the stairs which would, Tom knew, give him perfect view of their departure. Tom knew then that he would have to pick the right time to leave using the people in the market area as a way of losing the keen watcher.

After a good lunch accompanied by a couple of wines Tom began to gaze again out the window finding the man who had followed them there.

"What's wrong Tom?" asked Vicki seeing the concern on his face. Tom couldn't not tell her now, as he would need her to move and be focused on their escape from the shadow. "Just someone that has been following us for a while, don't worry though. When we leave we will lose him along the way somewhere.

"This sounds so exciting just like the movies. Should I be scared?"

"Not just yet anyway. Let's see what develops eh!" Tom held her hand and squeezed it lovingly. He was not about to endanger her life, not now.

He nodded to her that they were about to move after he had looked out the window to ensure there was plenty of movement from the bodies below. This area was getting busier from the thriving tourist crowds. He had a couple of options open to him, but thinking about it he thought he would return to the roadway where he had seen the Beemer to check if that was still there or was even a part of this. He also planned to try and place his shadow man out of step somehow.

As they left the restaurant Vicki followed with what felt like an excitement in her belly. She was obviously inexperienced at this form of life. Tom got to the base of the stairs looking directly at the man that had been shadowing them. The man instantly turned away making it all the more obvious. Tom turned to his right walking towards the road holding Vicki's hand tightly in his. As they got to the road he looked to his left and saw the Beemer still parked where he had seen it previously. Still the faces were there behind its windows unchanged which meant that no one had got out as yet.

Tom turned to his right knowing that the road led to a dead end just up to the right corner. He glimpsed behind seeing their shadow follow as if connected by some kind of string line. This guy was looking so obvious about his actions Tom thought to himself. He appeared very clumsy about his moves to the point of embarrassment. The tradecraft this man was displaying was far inferior to those practised in the Western world. His father had taught him many tricks that he had been taught during his service. Tom had also taken some minor tradecraft courses while he was at Sandhurst during his training.

At the top corner the crowds had started to filter out to just a few. As they turned the corner Tom placed Vicki gently against the wall and waited. Just a few moments later the Middle Eastern man came around the corner at a speedy pace stopping dead facing Tom. He had fucked up badly he knew it but before he could do anything about it Tom gave a one handed fist to the man's gut which made him curl up sending him down on his knees. Tom brought his left hand across in a chop to the side of the man's neck that hit the point so hard he collapsed on the pavement closing his eyes.

Tom peered around the corner noticing the Beemer was still where he had first seen it. He pulled back to see Vicki aghast at what had just happened. A few passersby had also come over to nose in on the action.

A group of teenagers who had seen Tom's moves were cheering him on shouting 'Another Muslim prick bites the dust'. This to them was the kind of fun they looked for on a trip out for the day.

Tom grabbed Vicki's hand and began to head off to the green of a small park near the dead end of the road. As they got to the grass Tom had started to pick up pace virtually running by the time they hit the green stuff. Both of them were in step with each other as they headed towards the old OXO Tower and Barge House Street. Tom knew he needed to head that way preferably getting to Blackfriars Road at the foot of the Bridge by the same name to hail a taxi as part of their get away.

As they got to the OXO Tower Tom slowed and turned, seeing the Beemer stopped at the road where he had just dropped their friend. Two others had got out the car and were now in the chase, making a hasty run across towards them. Their buddy was still sprawled out on the deck with the teenage group chanting their abuse at the men in the car.

Tom sped up still clutching Vicki's hand. She was keeping up with him being as fit as Tom was which was good for them so far. A further two hundred or so meters at full pace for Vicki got them near to Blackfriars Road. With Vicki puffing and panting fairly heavily but not conceding the challenge they made it to Blackfriars Road where Tom turned them north towards the bridge while looking for a vacant taxi that would hopefully come along. He never turned around to look behind as there were plenty of sightseers on the bridge. That made it hard to manoeuvrer along the pavement so Tom made the decision to go to the edge of the road taking a chance of not being upended by a vehicle motoring up the bridge.

They were near to the centre of the bridge when Tom saw a taxi with it's for hire sign alight. He raised his hand but still carried on running. The taxi turned on the bridge creating a flurry of horns and verbal abuse. London Taxis are used to that treatment so the driver would have taken absolutely no notice at all. He pulled up alongside the pair with Tom immediately stopping he opened the door and virtually threw Vicki onto the back seat while climbing in himself.

"Houses of Parliament please." He yelled at the driver.

"In a bit of a urry mate are we. Got a vote to make ave yer." The cockney accent came through the window that separated driver from passenger in a jocular fashion.

"You might say that." Tom said turning his head around checking behind for the men that were chasing them. He saw them standing holding their sides breathing very heavily at about the same spot as they had jumped into the cab. Tom blew a sigh of relief which was short lived as just at that moment the black Beemer screeched to a halt by the men and they jumped in. The chase was on again but this time in vehicles.

Tom got a couple of notes from his wallet and lent forward to speak to the driver. "Can you drop us off outside an underground station near Parliament please."

"Sure me ol mate. In a bit of a urry eh?"

"Just a tad." Tom replied letting the driver take the notes. "Won't be that much cock." The cabbie said holding the cash. "Keep the change. We need to lose someone."

"Should ave said me ol' mate. I enjoy a good chase." The driver instantly put extra pace on as he headed along Victoria Embankment towards the Houses of Parliament. You could see the smile going from ear to ear across his hardened face. He was going to enjoy this especially on a Sunday.

"I can drop you off at Charing Cross if yer like. It is busier than the others around ere." The driver raised his voice so they could hear him without him turning his head.

"That would be great, thanks." Tom was still looking behind noticing the Beemer was now about three cars adrift to their rear and gaining all the while. It was when they went under Waterloo Bridge that Tom saw the Beemer pull out nearly causing an accident with a small family car that was slower than most of the other traffic in the outside lane. The Beemer sped up coming back behind the cab within a cars length of it. Tom stared at the Beemer but all he could make out was profiles of heads with the windows darkly tinted on the sides. Even the bloody front window had some tinting on it which Tom knew was highly illegal except for Embassy cars and some Government vehicles.

The Beemer was soon tucked in right behind them. Tom could now work out the faces but didn't recognise any of them except the jerk he dropped a while ago.

The driver noticed the Beemer directly behind them immediately acknowledged the fact to Tom with a nod and a smile. He sped up again and just before coming up to Northumberland Avenue he expertly turned the cab from the left lane in between two vehicles on his right without signalling and catching the green traffic filter light, turned into Northumberland Avenue. There was a screech of brakes with horns blasting from all directions. The air was blue and faces were turning red with rage from even the most passive Sunday drivers.

The Beemer overshot the turn they made having to try and turn further along the Embankment to come back onto Northumberland Avenue. They were now behind some way. Meanwhile, the cab had sped along the road nearing the huge Trafalgar Square roundabout at the end when the driver called. "At the lights up ahead I'll pull to the right and slow. Charing Cross underground is just to the right guvner. Good luck eh!"

Tom thanked the driver and waited for him to slow at the lights. This was also going to bring some abuse as they were also green meaning the taxi was slowing much to the annoyance of those following them. He slowed to a crawl which gave Tom and Vicki the chance to alight making a run across the remainder of the road towards the underground. Tom looked down in the direction they had just come and saw the lights flashing on the front of the Beemer as it was trying to navigate through the traffic.

Nelson peered down on them as they made their way across the Strand, down the steps into the underground; things were so much quieter in his days.

Grabbing a couple of tickets to Vauxhall they got on the Northern line and headed back towards the Embankment Station where they alighted to change onto the Circle Line that took them west towards Victoria where they again changed to transfer to the Victoria Line south to take them just a couple of stations on to Vauxhall. Tom thought by the constant changes he would throw anyone following off the track easier. He never noticed any watchers and began to ease his already busy mind onto the next step of their exploits.

Neither Vicki nor Tom said much as they were still trying to get their calm selves back into order. It wasn't till Pimlico the station before theirs that Tom finally spoke.

"Sorry about that." He said holding her hand lovingly yet again.

"That's ok it was so exciting. Not often you get chased around town eh? Who the hell are they Tom?" Vicki's excitement was obvious but Tom wasn't so pleased.

It meant that the Iraqis were onto him here in London. He needed to get out of here quickly and lose them so he could continue his chase after Caulfield. He didn't need this shit happening at the moment.

"Just some people from my last posting Vick, don't worry about it we'll be OK." Tom just couldn't bring himself to tell her much as to do so would undoubtedly put her in more danger than he ever wanted to place her. He also had the horrid thought of his last girlfriend who dumped him because he had to go overseas on service. He didn't want Vicki to think he might be some kind of liability.

At Vauxhall they made their way quickly back to the apartment where Tom made a call to Gary to let him know what had transpired during their day out.

Gary told Tom he was sorting out all the necessary paperwork for him and would have it together within a couple of days. Tom wondered to himself whether he would have that long to wait.

Tom couldn't work out who or why these sudden followers he had gotten himself attached to were here. He could only think that the Iraqi Government had got a snip at the possibility of him being in the UK and that had gotten up their noses a tad.

After the fracas that had happened at the Al Jameat Police complex twice now they were perhaps not as friendly with their allies the Brits as they should be any more.

CHAPTER 11

The dark starless sky outside tonight was enough to worry Tom. He made sure that the apartment was tightly secured before he turned in for the night. Vicki had already turned in after sorting out her belongings and starting to pack to return home. Tom had packed some of his stuff as well and the two of them said very little to each other during the evening before eventually retiring.

Tom was restless lying awake for hours staring at the ceiling seeing the reflections that kept appearing across it from what little light there was from the night through his open blinds.

Down below in the street two dark clad figures were huddled by the main door of the apartments. One pulled out a small box with a swipe card connected to it by wire. The other had a small electronic box pressed up against the entry pad. He punched in a code and waited. The little machine buzzed then went through a sequence of numbers that appeared on a small LED pad on its face. It was only a matter of seconds before the pad clicked at the same time the door clicked and the two men pushed their way cleanly into the foyer.

There was no physical security in this foyer, the owners of this complex felt the security they had electronically was sufficient to protect the residents. How wrong they were.

At the elevator the second man swiped the card after switching on his little black box and sure enough the door opened enabling them to walk into elevator swiping the card again on the main console. There was a quiet ding from his little box which then prompted him to press the penthouse button, magically closing the doors and the elevator began to speed up heading for the last stop at the top of the building.

Both men returned their gadgets to their pockets, pulled out silenced handguns waiting patiently for the lift to come to a halt. Both were equipped with Glock 17s. They stood ready each side of the door as the elevator came to its destination and the doors opened.

Tom had dozed for a while when about 0230hrs he heard what was a strange sound to him. The elevator was on the move, something he had not experienced during his stay here so far at this time of night anyway. He got out of the bed, slipped on his sandshoes then as he was still dressed he made his way to the kitchen area where he had a view out over the terraced area towards the elevator doors. Tom made sure there were no lights on inside the apartment also making sure he did not disturb Vicki, she did not need to be frightened by what might be a false alarm.

The elevator light was on as it approached the penthouse which was only activated by a pickup in the cabin of human heat. The elevator came to its final stop and the doors opened. Tom saw straight away the two men slide out, guns in hand, clinging to the outer walls and moving in opposite directions around each side of the apartment's terrace.

Shit Tom thought to himself I haven't got any weapons here to counter act this. His first instinct was to grab a large knife which was lying on the draining board by the sink. He moved slowly out of the kitchen along the passage way and into the second bathroom which was right by the front door still clutching the 12" blade.

The two dark characters crept slowly towards the main door standing at either side of it listening. One indicated to the other to enter but when he tried he found the handle was locked. He slipped his hand into his pocket and pulled out what looked like a short steel ruler which he slid into the door jam. He pushed down towards the lock and flicked it hard. There was a click and the door handle was free.

Tom heard the handle free itself and froze, his back to the wall fearing the rapidly beating heart he could hear drumming in his ears could be heard by the two perps now entering.

One man entered making his way past the bathroom door to the door of the master bedroom. Tom waited as he was hoping that the two would come inside going past his hiding place giving him the advantage of surprise.

The first perp entered the master bedroom weapon raised and ready, but inside there was nothing as he scanned the room slowly making his way to the ensuite to the left. Nothing there either. He went back to the doorway and signalled to his partner to enter and go to the second bedroom expecting both Tom and the girl might be in the same bed.

The second perp entered slowly. Tom heard him go past his hidey-hole in the bathroom. He waited just cracking the door slightly just to see the second man creep around the corner followed closely by the other one.

Tom exited the bathroom slowly taking care not to make any noise. He heard a scuffle and then heard Vicki scream which then become muffled. He kept his patience avoiding any drastic moves, kept slowly making his way to the corner of the passage. As he peered around the corner he saw one of the men dragging Vicki under protest to the lounge, luckily the man had his head turned away from Tom's direction.

"Where is the man?" asked one of the perps in a distinct foreign accent.

"I don't know, we don't sleep together." Vicki's now frightened voice rang out.

The light to the lounge had now been switched on. The man holding Vicki had a gun pressed to her head speaking to his mate in what was very much like Arabic to Tom. Tom didn't understand what was said but before he even tried to work out what would be next he moved himself quickly through his bedroom hiding behind one of the alcoves by the bed opposite the door.

Was Tom lucky or was it just instinct, he wouldn't have time to find out as he had just planted his back against the wall when he heard the footsteps approaching his position. The man came into the room again with his weapon raised and ready but more tentatively this time made his way around the door to the right where the wardrobe was situated hoping that his target was hiding inside it.

Tom saw the weapon slowly appearing instantly recognising it, before he saw the man's figure show. He tuned in his martial arts training along with the training he had undergone in Sandhurst during the unarmed combat instructors sessions. Something he knew he was good at. Tom placed the knife in behind his belt on the left side in case he needed to draw on it quickly.

As the man came into view turning towards the right Tom moved slowly to the edge of the corner. The man turned towards the wardrobe but must have sensed a movement in the opposite direction, he spun around in the direction towards Tom but Tom was too fast for him. With his left hand, Tom grabbed the top slide pushing it to the rear ejecting the round up the spout, while at the same time his right hand clasped the back of the grip squashing the man's thumb and flicking the release catch for the magazine. This combined with a twist to Tom's left to push the weapon out of Tom's immediate line.

The magazine dropped out, a round flew out and the man's eyes bulged in a start of rage. While still holding the weapon top with his left hand Tom pulled back his right hand under his arm pit and quickly threw it into an upright move, using the lower palm of his hand jerked sharply up into the man's chin following through with the weight of his body.

There was a sudden crack making the man's eyes fly widely apart as his neck cracked and the head fell to one side. His body began to fall to the floor like a sack of spuds but Tom managed to grab hold lowering it down slowly. Tom quickly gathered the Glock re-inserting the magazine, pulling back on the slide to put one up the spout ready.

There was a call of Arabic from the lounge in answer to the sudden noise that had been created. Vicki was also heard to scream out yet again.

Tom went immediately to the door moving slowly towards the lounge at the other end of the passage. More verbals came from the lounge but Tom couldn't fathom any of the comments that came out, he was still blank as far as Arabic was concerned. He crept closer to the door of the lounge getting to it slowly he lent to one side to try and get a glimpse of his opponent.

As he looked into the lit room he saw what he was dreading most. The man inside was holding Vicki from the rear by the throat with his Glock squarely placed against the side of her temple. Tom entered facing the man with the Glock he had just retrieved raised and on target to the man's head. The man's head was way above Vicki's and even though he tried to use Vicki as his shield he was too tall to be able to do it properly without looking decidedly uncomfortable.

Tom's mind went through all that he had learned over the years. Does the victim survive if I take the shot to the head? Does the perp get a shot off if I hit him square between the eyes? This was a Mexican stand off for Tom; he was unsure of the consequences but knew it was either him or me, he had no other options.

Tom stood his ground and looked seriously into the man's eyes, he could only see one outcome here and that was death but for whom he was beginning to wonder. He pierced his eyes into the man hoping to get him unstable for just a second.

"Drop your weapon my friend or your little whore dies." The man was spitting out his best bad English towards Tom. Tom's anger began to well up in his mind. He knew he would have to keep his cool to be able to come out on top in this situation and also save Vicki.

"Let her go you rag head, she has nothing at all to do with this."
"How can I possibly do that when you have a weapon aimed at me, you British are so heroic but yet so stupid."

Tom had now thought through what he wanted to do and his aim was firmly in line with the middle of the man's head, fair between the eyes. Oh God he thought I hope Vicki survives what I am about to do. Tom had no other option at this stage of the game. He pulled back the trigger mechanism slowly freeing off the safety feature.

It felt like a lifetime wait before he slowly pulled back a bit more on the trigger, and then there was a thud which Tom felt in the recoil of the Glock. Before his eyes he saw the hole appear in the forehead of the man in slow motion and a large splash of red spread over the glass coffee table and sofa that was just behind him. Then the man just dropped backwards his hand frozen not being able to react to what his brain told him prior to the grey mass going blank. He crashed down through the coffee table pulling Vicki along with him. She screamed as they both went backwards.

Tom ran over to where they had crashed pulling her up away from the man's grasp. Blood covered her head from the entry point of the bullet to the man's head. She continued to just scream as Tom wrapped his arms around her trying hard to calm her down. The man's eyes were still wide open as Tom looked down he felt them burning through his brain. This was the first time he had actually shot and killed someone but it wasn't the sort of thing you wanted to write home to Mum about.

For five minutes Vicki was out of it thinking that Tom had shot her as well as the Arab. When she realized her situation she looked hard at Tom and asked. "How did you do that without him killing me? How stupid was that, you nearly killed me." Her voice was all confused as she ranted away at Tom. She beat her hands against his chest but Tom continued to keep his arms as close around her as possible till she stopped followed by silence then she cried into his shoulder.

"It's OK Vick, it's all over now. Let me call Gary, he will need to sort this mess out quickly before we have any more visitors."

Within an hour of his call to Gary there was a bunch of cleaners arrive from the Firm. They expertly cleaned out the deceased pair taking away both weapons. The room would take a bit more work for them to remove any trace of what had happened here tonight but the way they were into it it was obvious they had had plenty of practice in the past.

Gary's concern now was to get these two people out of the area away from the firing line so to speak. No one outside of his section needed to know this nights events, he would shepherd these two away before first light. He had already arranged a car to be brought into the garage below the complex and also had arranged another safe house but this time on the other side of town.

As sunrise slowly approached Tom along with Vicki were taken with their belongings down to the underground car park where a black Range Rover was waiting to spirit them away from Vauxhall. As the vehicle left the car park ramp Tom could see the beginnings of a new day start with the streets around them beginning to bustle alive in preparation for the start of the working week.

The Range Rover turned north up over Vauxhall Bridge and as it got to the centre Tom turned to look back at the building that stood dauntingly there on the Southside, SIS headquarters. Its splendour being suddenly lit by the upcoming new day's sunrise. A green and grey monolith, with its architectural squares and curves peering down over the River Thames below. The green was the large plate glass windows that were spread about the upper reaches of the building.

Tom turned to the front and the passenger in the seat to his left, Gary. "You know mate that's quite an impressive looking building back there. I don't think I want to see it again for a while at least."

"Looks like we may have to speed up your movements Tom. The DD has been asked some difficult questions from the Foreign Office about you. I should have what you need by Wednesday.

Miss Robson, we are booking your flight home to Perth to leave tonight if that's ok." Gary evaded Tom's remark expertly.

"I just want to go home thank you." Vicki was still shaking some but had forgiven Tom somewhat as she cuddled into him tightly.

"I will be in touch when I can Vicki, I promise." Tom looked down at her puffy looking eyes still showing signs of tears.

"Make sure you do Tom. Don't bring any unwanted arseholes with you next time though." She gave a little laugh and kissed him.

"That reminds me Gary, who the hell came up with placing your offices here."

"Why's that Tom?" Gary asked puzzled.

"Well I have heard that Vauxhall is the new Gay and Lesbian area of London, like a free for all village which is directly opposite your main entrance. Makes you wonder what types you have in charge there eh?" Tom laughed towards Gary.

"You're probably right, Tom, think that crowd decided to move there after we did, probably thought it would be safer for them eh. Some sort of protection in today's so called modern world."

The Range Rover weaved its way through the northern suburbs, up Ladbroke Grove and into Oxford Garden where finally it dropped the group off in front of number 68, one of the many terraced houses along this normal suburban street.

Gary got them both inside leaving a couple of his people there who had arrived earlier to ensure security was dealt with. Gary then left assuring Tom he would be in touch with him before nightfall.

Tom sat with Vicki for the rest of the day where they rarely left each other's arms. That afternoon before tea they said their good-byes with the promise they would keep in touch with Tom having to promise to get his affairs sorted, a polite way for Vicki to say get out of the job you are in before we meet again. Vicki was then whisked away to London Heathrow airport where she was placed on a Cathay Pacific flight to Hong Kong with after just an hour stopover direct to Perth.

After Vicki left Tom put all his energy into the files he had received over the past week or so and started to prepare himself with the next stage of his saga.

Gary got in touch with Tom that night and said that the shit had hit the fan. Ashid had been told two of his operatives had been killed in what seemed like an unauthorized operation on British Sovereign soil and he had been asked to remove himself from any further discussions with the Foreign Office until discussions with his Prime minister had been undertaken. He had been rather unhelpful at that point and was due to leave via an Iraqi Government jet at any time.

The Foreign Office had asked Reginald Aspalson to investigate the serious nature of events and report back to them. Gary was doing his utmost at the moment to avoid any contact with anyone till he had Tom on his way. This also meant that there were obstacles for Aspalson to overcome planted discreetly by Gary to help him delay any investigation that might have tied Tom into the deaths of the Iraqis.

As Wednesday arrived Gary showed up with the papers and passports for Tom. A false identity, credit cards and contact numbers for Tom to use when he needed. Gary insisted that Tom kept using the mobile he had been given but Tom had other ideas about that one. He knew that the Firm would have GPS tracking on it and his trust still hadn't spread as far as them at this point.

He had already bought himself another pre-paid mobile earlier and would use that when he didn't want the Firm to know what he was up to. He also had planned to remove the battery and sim on the Firm's mobile whenever he felt the trust dwindling. It would always be easy for him to put them back and reactivate the bloody thing again anyway.

Gary did mention that the two assailants had been examined by their own Medical Examiner before they were handed over to the Iraqi Embassy people. He mentioned that both had what looked like a figure eight on its side on their right wrists at the top going from side to side. Tom immediately thought that it might be some kind of group tattoo which he had not seen or heard of before.

CHAPTER 12

Thursday 22 February 2007
London Heathrow

Tom had been driven to the airport early this morning so he wouldn't be held up because of any weather conditions which might have caused traffic delays. It was still damn cold with the ground outside frozen and covered in places by fresh falls of snow. The flights so far this morning were on schedule but there had been rumours that the conditions were deteriorating that might lead to delays or even cancellations.

Tom was keen to get on his way out of the country quickly as questions were being asked that could put him in the situation where he could get delayed indefinitely.

At 0830 his flight to Sofia, Bulgaria was slowly taxiing out onto the runway and he felt some relief but he was feeling decidedly better when the metal object finally became airborne. Tom settled back to enjoy his flight of about 3 hours or so and sifted through his mind what he needed to do on arrival.

Landing at Vrazhdebna Tom cleared the normal customs and immigration counters without any problems. He was on a formal business trip which involved investigating hotels and locations for a tourist organization. He got many smiles from the uniformed people at the terminal but was pleased to be outside heading for the bus queue which he believed would be the best way into the city.

Taxis in this part of the world he knew had many cowboy operators but of most concern to Tom was the fact that many of the drivers were in the pockets of the local underworld so to stay out of their limelight Tom decided on the bus.

The terminal itself he had just left had recently been finished showing that the local authority had every sign of developing the Airport even further. The glass facades on the front were still gleaming in their newness. Being February it was not overly crowded and that made it quicker to exit the place.

Only 5km east of central Sofia Tom found the spot to pick up #84 bus which would take him to the city centre near the Sheraton Hotel, not that he was staying there but it was only a short stroll to his destination of the Sofia Grand where he knew Caulfield had stayed.

Having local currency in his pocket, care of Gary, he was un-phased when he boarded the bus with bag in tow finding a seat on its own to the rear. The heaters on the bus were working well and with the outside temperatures at around 6 centigrade it was thankfully welcome.

Bulgaria has a dynamic climate, which results from its position being at the meeting point of Mediterranean and continental air masses and the barrier effect of its Mountains.

The journey would take him nearly an hour because it was slow due to traffic through many road constructions that were going on throughout the area. Tom's impression of Sofia was not too impressive as it seemed that the buildings, even those from the early twentieth century showed signs of peeling stucco allowing them to fall into dilapidation. Sofia houses about 1/5 th the Bulgarian population, with its cryptic references to its ancient past of Roman ruins, Byzantine churches and finely decorated Mosques showing a very long yet colourful history.

Once in the centre of Sofia Tom alighted from the bus, checked his bearings then set about walking the remainder of the half kilometre to his hotel at the Grand Hotel Sofia. He finally arrived at the hotel by 1700hrs and was settled in his room, which was unexpectedly large and spacious, preparing to have dinner in the restaurant. The reception was aware of his business trip here and was making every possible gesture to him to enjoy his stay. Tom felt they were only trying to accrue Brownie Points for his fictitious report.

Next morning after breakfast Tom made enquiries as to the manager to get a full story of the hotel as part of his cover. He mentioned an associate that had stayed there some time during 2006, not wanting to say a name as Caulfield would have been under an assumed one anyway he showed a photo of him, which he had from the file, dressed in a suit.

The manager looked hard, then suddenly nodded saying he did recognise him. It was a long time ago he said but he remembered the man because he had an altercation with one of the cleaning staff while staying there. Tom had made a large step forward so early but how was he going to get the name that was his main objective.

"Oh, I am sorry to hear that. He seemed so impressed with this hotel when he returned to our office though which meant he did not take it too seriously."

"It was rather unfortunate." The manager said. "He had gone out of his room and left his case open and when he returned the cleaner had moved it to do her usual jobs. Most unfortunate, Mr Browning was rather furious about it all."

Bingo, thought Tom, Browning. At last a lead he could follow and if he chose to also send back to Crisp to follow up on. He would hold off on that till he had done his own little checks first.

Tom's next stop was to be Grigor's place on Angel Kanchev only a short walk from the hotel. He decided to walk because that way no one was talking to him or involved with him therefore keeping himself away from any prying ears. He could, during his walk also check to ensure there was no one watching him while he was in Sofia.

He chose to take the longer route out past the Central Post office then down to Ryako Daskalov Place. Why is it that the old Eastern countries had so much personal strife, Tom thought to himself. This Place was named after what was a Union leader that got sent to Czechoslovakia as a Bulgarian envoy after being relieved of his duties then was assassinated in Prague while trying to drum up support for his overthrown Government. Still Tom enjoyed the shops he went past which gave him endless opportunities to survey the route he had just come down checking for any followers. As far as he could tell he was safe at the present.

He arrived just outside Jimmy's about midday, walked up and past the same side of the street as the entrance door that he knew was going to lead him to Grigor's place. Turning at the end of the street he crossed over and returned the same way till he got to the cafe by Ryako's Place. He settled down there for a coffee accompanied by some kind of sandwich. He chose not to delve into its origins as it tasted quite nice but the name sounded quite repugnant.

He would not go any further today being a Friday and obviously busy. He would wait till Sunday to call on his friend Mr Grigor Karavelov in the hope that Sundays were a day of rest for Bulgarians as well as it was for the rest of us.

On the Saturday morning he made contact with the Firm's man in Sofia. Gerry Holdsworth a long time veteran of the Regiment but like Tom's old man now getting a bit long in the tooth for modern field work. Mid to late forties Tom thought to himself. Holdsworth just relished his contacts to help those fit enough to venture on the Firm's work.

"Heard stories about your old man, son. Good ones mind." Gerry said shaking Tom's hand. "Never met him though, unfortunately."

"So long as they were good eh? Now Gerry have you got what I need?"

"Sure have my boy and may I say don't get caught with it in this country as some of the Police still act like they're part of the old Secret Police." Gerry answered undoing his briefcase and handing Tom his favourite weapon that he had requested, a Sig Sauer complete with silencer. The Sig 226 is a tried and tested pistol used by the US military and also is a favourite amongst the Brit Special Forces.

Tom inspected the weapon, checked the magazine which to his surprise was full with 15 rounds. He stripped and checked all its working parts in front of Gerry who just sat amazed at the speed with which Tom completed it all.

"Used to that one aren't you lad." Gerry said in a form of praise. "Got to admit, Gerry, it has always been my favourite since the old man let me have a go at the ranges when I was younger."

"Younger, you're still only a baby now compared to most of us." Gerry laughed out loud. "Anyway, take care and if you need anything at all or get into any strife give me a bell. I'll say au revoir for now then and hope all goes well for you while you are here."

Gerry departed at the finish of his sentence leaving Tom to ponder what was left to do before Sunday morning. At least he was prepared this time for any fuck ups.

The rest of the day was mainly taken up with a walk into the city and further reading of the files he had brought with him.

CHAPTER 13

Sunday 25 February

It was fairly chilly this morning giving Tom the ideal cover for himself, shielding his face from prying eyes. Wrapping up in a fur lined, collared jacket he placed his Sig into a lining area especially made for a pistol, available from either an open or closed jacket. He hoped he would not have to use it though, after the last episode culminating in the death of the Arab gentleman back in London it made Tom shudder just thinking about it. He still wasn't used to taking life.

A quiet Sunday stroll was the order of the day. Tom taking a similar route to that he had previously taken a couple of days earlier but with a couple of minor changes to check if he had any tails on him. It all looked good by the time he got to Jimmy's shop front.

The air in Sofia bit harshly into his lungs this morning; the streets were fairly quiet with most residents presumably off to their local Churches. There was a change of smell also this morning; with fewer vehicles plying the streets than the other day the fumes were minimal giving fresh air a chance for once.

Tom readied himself to approach the bell box at the side of Jimmy's which after a quick glance to his right, then left, he huddled in alongside the button box. Fourth pair up was a card that read Karavelov which Tom immediately placed his finger upon. He had asked Gerry to get him some translation when back at the hotel to show him how to speak just a couple of lines of the local language just in case Grigor was non English spoken.

With a quick press he waited for just a couple of seconds before a gruff voice came over the speaker. Sounded like Tom had disturbed this guys Sunday specials.

“Koi E Toi?” the Bulgarian accent thick and decidedly grumpy. Tom gathered he was asking who it was.

“Brauning me izprati.” Tom replied in the best adaption of Bulgarian he could speak which wasn’t the best. He figured if he answered the greeting, that’s a laugh, with Browning sent me it may bring a response he was hoping for.

“Kakvo iskash?” Came next which Tom had absolutely no idea what it meant.

“Na angliiki, molya” Tom’s reply was just asking the occupant if he could talk in English. He politely put it as all tourists do, so he was told, as English please.

“What do you want?” Came the thick accent in not too bad English either. Thank God for that thought Tom.

“Browning said you could help me. I have money as he said it would cost me.” Tom’s bluffing wasn’t too bad he thought to himself.

The door buzzed as the speaker blurted out. “You had better come up then.”

Tom pushed on the door and entered into what can only be described as a landing area similar to those he had been to in the suburbs of London. Various smells wafted up to his nostrils. Cooking smells, garlic etc and then the worst type of smell you could get, that of urine. All too familiar with tenement blocks when the pitiful despots that never made it to their front door after a night on the turps relieved themselves on their own stairwells.

Tom held his breath a touch as he climbed the stairs and tackled the six flights of stairs that looked like they were used by the local sanitary department. Rubbish bags lined the inner part of the stairwells at varying points. Some of the tenants must have hoped if they threw it onto the stairwells then some idiot would remove it for them rather than fall over it.

As Tom approached the door of number seven it opened slightly and a head appeared in the crack. Grigor must have been all of five foot nothing with his face pretty drawn like someone out of a starving Biafra. The door opened wider revealing the short thin body of a man of about 40ish. On his head was a white taqiyah, or short rounded Muslim cap. Tom didn’t show any signs of surprise with what appeared before him.

Grigor waved Tom in through the door and instantly Tom was met with the over powering whiffs of incense being burnt. Throughout the passage and rooms was a smoke mist at ceiling height indicating the pollution the incense was causing? Tom thought that this guy was either a heavy smoker or he was burning his candles at both ends to create a film of pollution for any tall people to have to tackle.

Tom was shown into what was the main sitting room where carpets adorned the wall and floor. A Koran was on a table in the far corner with what looked like a prayer mat rolled up and placed beneath it in the table legs. The smell of the incense was more profound in this room. To the right was a low backed sofa set of three seats and opposite was a vast desk which had many papers scattered across it. A computer stood on the desk along with a printer.

"You say Browning has sent you here. What is your name?" Grigor looked suspiciously at Tom.

"Yes, that's correct my name is Phillips." Tom answered without faltering.

"I have had no message from our mutual friend. What are you looking for?"

"A complete change of identity is required." "Why is that my friend?" Grigor probed.

"My enemies have become many I'm afraid." Tom answered again looking around the room he had just been led into to ensure he had everything in his mind frame.

"Enemies we all have but why does Browning sends you to me?" Grigor was now standing by a desk which had many draws either side and was about to place his hand upon one of those at the top.

"He is a friend from the past in Iraq where we first met. He has helped me through many troubled times." Tom watched Grigor as he placed his hand on the drawer knob, while he made a move with his right hand to be able to free up the Sig in case it was needed.

As Grigor pulled the draw and moved his hand inside bringing out a large antiquated revolver which he immediately pointed at Tom he spoke with a warning concern. "Browning said there are no more to come through here, he was the last. Who are you my friend?"

"I've just told you, a friend of Browning." Tom showed Grigor a surprised look at the revolver that was now pointing directly at him.

"Then you need to sit down while I get some kind of authority from Browning or his associates." Grigor flicked the end of the revolver to indicate for Tom to take a seat on the sofa set. Tom obeyed sitting on the edge though as Grigor moved across the desk to where a telephone lay he picked it up with his left hand, having to lay down the receiver before he could begin dialling. This wasn't good, Tom needed to do something and fast. He moved forward quickly while releasing the grip of his Sig under the lining pulling his hand so both were free to use.

Grigor stopped dialling as he turned to see what the sudden movement was. He had while dialling moved the revolver barrel slightly away from Tom's line much to Tom's relief. Grigor was caught unaware as Tom hit the revolver to one side with his left and planted a sharp but forceful chop to Grigor's windpipe with his right. Thankfully the revolver did not discharge as Grigor fought for breath falling back onto the desk.

Grabbing the revolver from Grigor's hand Tom then held him by the throat on the top of the desk while pulling out the phone line from the wall by wrapping the cord around the revolver barrel and pulling. Grigor was fighting for breath with rapid gusts billowing from his throat. "Now my little friend, information is what I really want." Tom said with a slight smile appearing from his lips. "You mentioned Browning's associates, who are they?"

"May Allah . . . curse . . . you . . . and . . . your . . . chil . . . dren?" Grigor struggled to get out. Tom pulled him up from the desk top and thumped him heavily into a chair that was to the side. He lent down while still holding Grigor by the neck and wrenched out an electrical cable which he then used to tie Grigor's hands behind his back and to the chair. While he did this he noticed on the right hand wrist was the similar tattoo of a figure eight side to side across the top of the wrist.

Secure as he'd ever be Tom stepped back and sat facing Grigor waving the revolver at the owner. Grigor was not overly impressed and kept cursing under his breath in Bulgarian.

"Speak English you little jerk. This antique here is for the museum." Tom said throwing the revolver onto the sofa. He removed from its hiding place his own Sig watching as Grigor's eyes open wider at the sight of a silenced weapon.

"I have powerful friends, you are a dead man for this."

"I've been dead before that's nothing new to me and seeing as your friends are not here at the moment I have no concern about your threats. Now information is what I need. I need to know who Browning's so called associates are and where I can find them. Now make it snappy as I have another appointment today and do not wish to spend too much time in this shit hole of a place."

"I have nothing to say to you." Grigor spat out in a fiery way.

Tom looked at Grigor and then lent across the sofa where he found a scarf lying. He got up behind Grigor and tied the scarf across his face pulling hard onto his mouth and stopping any form of noise other than a moan from exiting it.

"Nod if you want to talk Grigor. Now are you going to answer my questions?"

Grigor's eyes blazed hatred at Tom but he just sat unmoved. Tom lifted his Sig and placed the silencer onto Grigor's left kneecap then smiled at him. Still nothing so Tom pulled at the trigger and a thud sounded sending Grigor absolutely rigid in pain. Blood streamed from Grigor's knee and his face began to be covered in sweat.

Tom lifted the silenced weapon from Grigor's left knee and moved it to the right one, Grigor was in tears and shaking his head rapidly as if to plead for mercy.

Tom asked the same question again and this time Grigor nodded. Tom removed the scarf a touch and waited. Grigor was gasping for breath, fighting back the pain that was shooting through him. The pain was an obvious problem for this little man.

"Browning was sent by a friend from Iraq." Grigor fought back the tears of pain. "He was one of five that were sent to me over a period of time."

"What were their names?" Tom asked pleased with the immediate response he had gotten.

"I have no names, they just came. Four at the start, then Browning last." "Listen you little fuckwit, how do you forge papers without names.

Now don't be a jerk just give me their names."

Grigor was crying openly now in pain, tears were flowing down his cheeks and he just nodded to a filing cabinet to the side of the desk. Tom went over to it and pulled out the top drawer. Nothing of any good in here it was all in local language and Tom had no clue. He searched through each file in the top drawer pulling out one by one and where he could not recognise any names in English he looked at Grigor waiting for a response. As he got none he threw the file onto the floor.

This charade went on throughout the top drawer and half way through the second one till at one file in particular Grigor looked away. Tom went through it slowly and found what looked like the name of Browning in Bulgarian which Gerry had showed him a couple of nights before. He pulled that file and kept going.

By the time Tom had got through all four drawers of the cabinet the apartment was looking as if a burglar had been in and tipped everything out onto the floor. There were driving licences of varying countries, passports and ID cards strewn about the floor. Tom finally had hold of five files which he would have to have translated, now what to do with Grigor.

Tom switched on the computer but it was of no use to him as he could not read or write in the script that was displayed on it.

He knew if he left Grigor then he would have his friends from the old secret police on his trail fairly quickly. There was only one option for it; Grigor was to be silenced for good. Unfortunately this fruitful little business of false identities was coming to a close. This was final sale night for Grigor.

Grigor had lapsed into silence realizing the next move that Tom looked like he was going to make. He had lost a lot of blood and was trying as hard as he could to stop falling into a coma situation.

Tom reapplied the scarf to stop any noise from Grigor's lungs. He then placed a double tap to the head, goodnight Grigor. Tom shuddered again and replaced the Sig into his lining. He felt some kind of shame as to what he had done. He checked himself over for any trace of blood splatter and was pleased by the fact that he had none splashed on him.

Before leaving Grigor's abode he went through some more areas in the bedroom and kitchen but came up with nothing. Folding the files he had and placing them in the inside pocket of his jacket. He wasn't fazed about fingerprints as he had not taken off his gloves the whole time he was in the flat.

Tom left the flat shutting the door behind him and casually went down the stairs. Lucky for him even now after about three hours with Grigor, there was no one about that would be able to report his presence there that day.

Outside in the cold daylight he again made sure he closed the outer door and then made his way in a long roundabout route back to the hotel where the first thing he did was call Gerry. Gerry was the link for him to be able to translate the files he had in his possession.

Gerry came over that evening, not staying even for a drink, leaving virtually immediately so he could get people in his team to get translation of the files underway. Tom settled down to an evening of music, hoping that no one would be missing Grigor anytime soon.

CHAPTER 14

During the night Tom heard sirens and got a glimpse of blue flashing lights through his open curtained windows. It was in the direction of Grigor's place he thought but he was determined he would sleep on through all the noise and wait to be briefed by Gerry the next day.

It was at 0900 hrs that there was a tapping on Tom's door. It was rapid and Tom sensed by its sound that there was a problem so before he opened the door he placed his Sig in the drawer of the cabinet to its side.

As he opened the door with the chain still attached he saw Gerry red faced caused from the cold outside. He pushed the door shut again, released the chain and opened it to let Gerry in.

"Shit has hit the fan my friend." Gerry said coming into the room and helping himself to coffee that was on the table by the window. "Your little friend was found during the night which has created one almighty commotion around his apartment."

"Do I need to exit stage right, Gerry?" Tom said showing signs of a sick sense of humour gained from his old man.

"As yet we don't know what the police are saying but what we do know is that the case has been handed over to the Gendarmerie under a former secret police agent by the name of Colonel Raminov. He has taken complete control of the incident and is at this moment questioning everyone within the block and close to the block personally. He must have been a friend of Grigor."

"How did you go with those files?" Tom anxiously asked.

"Our translator worked overtime during the night for us. We have some names but no way of checking who, what, where at this stage. There were no photos of course but the names are interesting.

Derek Sweetman, Mark Thorn, Peter Southwaite, Colin Phorbes and your friend John Browning are all named in the files and they have been issued various documents but we cannot fathom for which country they have them or what their original identities were.

We are holding back on any searches at the moment because of this Raminov fellow, if we start asking questions of people who have left the country or maybe still here and he is a friend of Grigor then he will be onto us and we might be in a bit of a quandary.

The other thing that has got us all puzzled is the mention of a terrorist group that has been associated with Al Qaeda, I.I.G.; Infinite Islam Group, some new group of terrorists that came to light only about a year ago. They have claimed responsibility for some minor disruptions in Iraq and the Yemen, but nothing too drastic at this stage. This is our major concern though. Were these ex-military guys part of the organization in some form or is this just a co-incidence."

"That is a bloody worry for us. If they were recruited by this mob who's to say what they have been or up to now. I think I need to move onto the next part of my journey Gerry. I need to get across the border to Greece and check out the office there of Asia Pac Loan & Finance.

This whole thing could be bigger than we expected. Can you get the information off to Mark in London for me?"

"Already done Tom. I will get you a vehicle you can use to drive to Greece, it will be CD plated so should get you some clearance when you need it and you can leave it with our people in Athens when you are finished with it. OK?"

"Great. I'll get myself sorted and get out of here tomorrow so not to look too obvious to anyone." Tom turned towards the internal phone and buzzed the reception. "I will be booking out tomorrow morning, can you please make up my invoice." There was a short conversation from the reception and Tom spoke again. "That's great. Thank you very much and I am sure we can arrange some tours to be able to use your facilities. I have to travel up through the west to Serbia, Bosnia, the coast area of Croatia and make my way through to Italy to make up a grand tour which will include your beautiful country" Tom replaced the receiver and looked back at Gerry who was just about to break out in fits of laughter.

"Tours eh, use your facilities! Grand tour to include your beautiful country!!!You smooth talking salesman. I reckon you could sell refrigerators to the Eskimos Tom."

Both men laughed as they drank more coffee. Then Gerry turned on the TV for the local news but his face turned serious.

"Well blow me down; they are looking for a connection with someone from the Middle East. It seems a Middle Eastern gentleman was seen during the course of the week visiting Mr Karavelov a number of times. That should give us a bit of a breather Tom." Gerry was cut short then and turned to face Tom. "Shit, someone saw a white male going into Grigor's block yesterday and coming out a few hours later. They have a description of him and . . . wo" There on the screen came up a photo fit picture of someone with features similar to Tom's but the face wasn't too clear with Tom's features. "Shit someone saw you mate. They even have your real name."

"That's real strange Gerry, no one knows who I am here except you. But the identikit, it's not that clear eh! I'll get rid of the coat I was wearing just in case that can identify me and pinpoint me. Hope you haven't dobbed me in Gerry?" Laughing Tom left his chair grabbing the coat, folding it and placing it into a laundry bag which he gave to Gerry. "Get rid of that for me please Gerry. I'll keep the Sig just in case it's needed on the trip."

"I'll get going Tom and organise that car for you immediately. Don't get caught with the gun though pal or you could find yourself in the Bulgarian doss house for life or even better shot. Not the best of choices here for that offence eh?"

"I'll be right Gerry. See you in the morning then."

With that the two men parted company. Gerry made off with the bagged coat which was destined for the incinerator at the Embassy and Tom started to pack his case making sure that he left nothing behind that could give anyone a clue about him.

Tom kept his ears and eyes on the news but not being in English he had no idea what was going on. He just knew that the picture of the man of interest was not a very good likeness of him at all. Let's see what tomorrow brings Tom thought settling back to relax with a stiff drink.

Across the way at Grigor's Colonel Raminov had paced the apartment where his friend Grigor had been killed. He had ideas floating in his head as to who the culprits were but was still unsure of their ultimate origin. Foreign Police agencies were always looking to shut down forgers as good as Grigor.

He had already called his friend in Iraq, Jamal Ashid and was telling him of the professional execution of his best forger. That alone had caused Ashid a few problems of his own which would have to be dealt with soon.

"Colonel, you say no one saw anything. No one coming or going at all just one of my men was noticed during the week." Ashid swore in Arabic as he hesitated a while. He had wondered after London what had happened to Warburton but now was a chance he might be able to lay more blame upon him. Perhaps flush him out if he was actually in Sofia.

"A favour Colonel if you please. I have a description of a man I want you to put on an identikit on your TV. He is someone who has caused me some concern of late and I have lost track of him. The name of the man is Warburton and he is a British soldier who killed one of our men during an investigation over stolen artefacts here some time back. Perhaps we may be able to flush him out with your help. Don't be too precise with the description as if it is him I do not want to frighten him off totally. I will however send you a perfect photograph we have of him for your personal checks."

"I see no problem with that; I will get it underway immediately. What about all the papers here, we do not want anyone checking on them do we? I suggest we have them all collected up and destroyed so there is no trace to either you or I."

"Excellent idea Colonel. We will meet soon I am sure and I will thank you personally for your call."

The Colonel ended the call and turned to his offsider instructing him to collect all the paperwork lying around and have it transported back to his office in sealed boxes. The old incinerator at Gendarmerie Headquarters was about to be worked overtime tonight.

The next step for Raminov was to get the identikit picture sorted out from the description Jamal had given him. Along with the name he would get it onto the National TV as soon as possible.

All outlets covered, Colonel Raminov left the scene and returned to his office to try and trace anyone coming into the country over the past few weeks from the UK with the assistance of the actually true photograph he would personally use.

Unfortunately for Tom he would have a list by next morning of only a dozen names of people entering the country from the UK including the places where they were staying. Also he would have Tom's photograph to be able to use to visit the hotels where the arrivals were staying. Raminov felt confident he would have this Warburton man in his custody by lunchtime.

CHAPTER 15

Tuesday 27 February 2007
Sofia

It was very early this morning when Gerry phoned Tom's mobile to let him know he was ready downstairs with the vehicle he had promised. Tom hurriedly left the room taking his luggage down in the lift with him calling in at the reception to clear his bill with them.

Outside the early morning air stung his lungs as he breathed it in. Gerry was standing besides an idling dark blue Land Rover Discovery bouncing up and down from one leg to another to keep his circulation going.

"You pick the best times Gerry, couldn't you sleep?" Tom smiled at his old contact.

"Thought I would get you going before the days traffic got up and running my boy." Gerry said opening up the rear door for Tom to throw his luggage into. "There is a box hidden under the driver's seat for your know what to hide. She's full and it also has GPS that may be of help. There is a satellite phone in there in case either you need me or I need to get something to you."

"You think of everything mate. Thanks for the help and keep yourself safe eh!"

"Bon Voyage my friend and good hunting."

Both men shook hands as Tom pulled the driver's door closed and selected drive. He turned his head as a final farewell smile to Gerry, flicking the indicator and pulled away from the curb side heading off towards the centre of town again while watching carefully in the rear view mirror for any suspicious tag-a-longs behind him.

It was 0530hrs which meant the roads were quiet as. Tom went through the city centre for the last time then headed off towards Route one which would take him directly down to the Greek Border.

There was snow on the ground but the roads were pretty clear. There was little traffic on the main highway which gave Tom some relief as he could push along in the vehicle uninterrupted. He reached Blagoevgrad in about 2 hours and had a quick coffee at one of the service centres. Time was creeping on for Tom but he was hoping to be able to cross into Greece before 1000 hrs. Unfortunately we all know that the best laid plans of mice and men don't always fall into place as we would like.

Tom was thankful at having a 4 x 4 to navigate the roads with the ice and snow. Along the route he had seen many rolled and smashed vehicles just left lying by the side of the highway. Seems their tow companies aren't as efficient as the rest of Europe.

Across the high points, the narrowing of the roads at times didn't delay Tom much at all; he made Kapatovo about 10 kms from the border by 0930 when he also received a message on the satellite phone from Gerry.

"Where are you mate?" Gerry asked with a concerned voice. "About ten kms from the border, what's up?"

"Just got a bulletin that the Gendarmerie are looking for a westerner with the description given on TV. They have singled it down to about 12 at the present so it won't be long before they pin point you.

Raminov is leading all investigations and hotel checks personally so you may be able to cross before they can actually cotton on. Just be aware that Raminov may have also alerted his boys at the border."

"I'll put on a bit of a rush then to get across. I'll let you know when I have got over the border Gerry."

Tom started to speed up hoping to be able to get to the crossing before anyone could be alerted. Unfortunately for Tom just ahead of him one of the many juggernauts that frequented this road had just side swiped a couple of cars and the debris was all over the road causing the inevitable that had shut down the highway.

As Tom approached what looked like a back up of traffic he noticed the sign to his right telling him that it was only 3 kms to the Greek border. So near yet so far Tom thought starting to look around for a break somewhere that could assist him. It was quickly upon him just up from a fuel station with barriers either side which stopped him from going off road till he was up to the fuel stop.

Here he turned into the left and surveyed the countryside along the left of the road he had to get through. The accident was about 300 metres in front of his position but the road was a mess with damage from the vehicles involved spread from arsehole to breakfast. Tom had to make a quick decision, eventually deciding he would attempt to navigate off road then come around back onto the road after the accident scene if he could.

Tom left the road just before the fuel stop and headed for what looked like a farmers cottage about half a km away through the fields. It was chancy but the ground seemed hard enough in the frozen climate and the Land Rover handled it without a problem. The looks he got were of amazement as people waiting at the fuel stop patiently waited with steaming cups in hand for the road to be re-opened and they could get on their way.

Nearing the cottage Tom turned and headed virtually parallel to the highway circumnavigating the accident scene. Just as he was parallel with the accident he felt the vehicle suddenly slide coming to a sudden halt as his front left wheel sank in what seemed like a mud pool.

Tom's heart jumped into his throat and started beating rapidly. He was not a defeatist, got out of the car to look at the situation. Sure enough the left wheel had put itself up to the axle into a bit of a bog. Tom was amazed that with the cold snap they were experiencing that the pool was not frozen. He jumped back into the driver's seat moving the vehicle between forward reverse till he got the rocking motion he was looking for. Placing the vehicle finally into reverse he drove the vehicle out slowly from its precarious position. It seemed like a struggle but with low range and a bit of revving he had it back onto solid ground for all four wheels within minutes.

Tom's move now was to venture closer to the accident area through the field. He just hoped the farmer wasn't watching as he tore up the freshly cultivated whatever it was in the field. He doubted whether anything was growing due to the wintery conditions. He half expected to be shot at for doing what he was doing but it proved pointless worrying as he came within 200 metres of the road again and was able to drive back up onto it. The problem now was the traffic was so built up going in the opposite direction it blocked him from getting onto the side of the road he wanted to drive on.

He drove alongside the jam that had built up heading in the direction from whence he had come till he found a break between two trucks which gave him the opportunity to cross to the correct side and continue on his way. Two kms to go, time was clocking on to 1030 hrs, Tom thought and the road was clear ahead now, foot down and don't spare the horses.

Back in Sofia Colonel Raminov had received his list of suspects and along with the photo Ashid had sent he went off at great pace to visit each arrival on his list. By 1030 he had gotten down the list to number 5 and was just about to go into the Sofia Grand Hotel to question reception.

At that point Tom had pulled up at the Border post waiting in the queue to cross. The Gendarmerie had been given instructions by Raminov to be on the lookout for a murder suspect but Raminov had issued only the photo kit picture he had placed on the TV. Tom was not suspected and along with the Diplomatic plates was waved through without question. Tom's relief at seeing the Blue and White Greek flag got him to start humming Zorba the Greek out loud.

Coincidences apart, the two of them crossed as one at the same time. Tom crossed the border and sped off towards Thessalonica and Colonel Raminov got what he was chasing a perfect identification of his suspect from reception at the Sofia Grand hotel. The Colonel immediately ran from the hotel and radioed the border area to the west where he had been told by reception that that was where Tom was heading. He wasn't a fool by any means though so he also alerted the border guards at the Greek border crossing.

Within the few minutes of his communication he received what he was really dreading and that was the confirmation that a vehicle with CD plates aligned to the British Consulate had crossed just minutes earlier and had been cleared to pass. The Colonel was furious and yelled at the radio telling the idiots to get off after him even though it meant entering Greek sovereign territory. His men argued with him over the radio the consequences to actions he was requesting of them.

Colonel Raminov's pride sunk to a new low at that point and he retreated back to his office so he could inform Ashid as to what had happened. Ashid on hearing the news cursed politely and told the Colonel he would deal with it from there. At least he said he had a firm lead knowing where the man was and where he would be heading to.

Tom was unaware of the turmoil in the Gendarmerie office that he had created for Raminov when he contacted Gerry to let him know he was over the border. Gerry did caution Tom not to get complacent as there was a treaty of co-operation between Bulgaria and Greece now since Bulgaria had entered into NATO.

Gerry was quick to tell Tom that he had already dispatched a man from the Embassy in Athens to meet with Tom half way to be able to give him fresh documents and also exchange cars in case the one he was in had been identified from Sofia.

Tom continued his journey towards Athens in the hope that no one would be after him just yet. He knew he had about six hours of driving to go before he finally arrived in Athens.

Unknown to Tom was the verbal traffic that was now going down between Iraq, Greece and Australia to cover as many tracks as they could. Tom was completely unaware of the disruption he had caused the Asia-Pac group.

CHAPTER 16

446 Collins Street, Melbourne
1900hrs 27 February

On the tenth floor of the Collins Street building were about six various business offices all of varying natures. One in particular had a plaque on the door that stated Asia-Pac Loan & Finance. Inside this office stood just a reception along with two separate rooms behind used as personal offices. One large one which housed the CEO of the Company which was lushy furnished and had all the bling that would impress some of the best brokers in the world. The other office was smaller and housed a couple of desks in which only one was currently used.

Tony Welsh CEO extraordinaire was just about to leave his desk in the larger office this evening when one of the phones on his desk started to buzz. It wasn't your ordinary type of phone but a rather technological one that had its own inbuilt scrambler unit. Tony shrugged his shoulders knowing that it would have to be important, possibly one of his clients wanting to expedite funds to somewhere strange around the world has had been the case since he started up this business after leaving the Army.

"Hello." He answered waiting for the interconnection to kick in.

"Tony, Jamal. How are you my friend?" the sound of the Middle

Eastern accent always gave Tony the shivers. He often wondered why he had ever got involved with these people as he had no real positive feelings towards them at all. Their objectives in the world were undoubtedly questionable. Anyway the money was great to have and the bonuses he had acquired over the last year or so far outstripped the current salaries of any CEO in any business in the western world let alone in Australia. He had closed his mind off to the possible outcomes that existed due to his financial prowess and directions to assist them.

"Jamal. I'm good and as you I hope. What can I do for you at such an ungodly hour?" Tony sat himself back in the comfy chair that he occupied for up to ten hours a day hoping that this would not be too long a conversation.

"You remember the Engineer that was supposed to take the heat out of our little enterprise last year? Warburton, well he has surfaced both in London and again in Sofia just recently."

"Bollocks, I thought you said he had died in the raid on the prison by the Brits." Tony suddenly sat himself bolt upright looking decidedly shocked.

"We were mistaken my friend. He showed up in London near to your SIS headquarters in Vauxhall and we tried to terminate him then but failed." "I thought you guys were good. He wasn't even a Special Forces man. What the fuck has been going on, Jamal? Why leave it so long to let me know?" Tony's anger started to grow and his face started to colour in red as he placed his left hand across his forehead to wipe away the sweat that was starting to form.

"Calm my friend. We will deal with him, before he can delve into our affairs. Unfortunately it seems he has terminated our friend Grigor in Sofia and is now heading for Athens. I suspect he has gained some information on your people located there. We must take alternative actions immediately Tony to avoid any disclosure of our business.

I propose that you get your two people out of the Athens office sending one to your Melbourne office and the other I suggest you send to Nassau. We then have to cover our tracks somewhat to confuse anything being uncovered."

"How close is he to Athens, Jamal?"

"He could be there within the next five hours or so by the information I have received from my people in Bulgaria. I have despatched a couple of my people to the Athens area to deal with him but I need to make sure so will your people help before you send them on the other travel arrangements."

"Yes, of course, most certainly. He doesn't know the guys there, he has never seen them in their earlier form or even been in touch with them prior or after our little lottery win. I'll get right on to it for you from this end."

"I propose we try and eliminate him before he actually gets to Athens but in case I also propose we terminate our connections in Greece for the time being to be on the safe side."

"What are you suggesting there?"

"Well it is so convenient that the office is right beside the Offices of your own British SIS in Athens so I intend to get our people to blow it up and cause as much disruption to the city centre as we can. We owe our Greek cousins a bit of a blast anyway to get them aware."

"I really don't want that under my wings, why do we need to do that, Jamal? The people there have all been great in their co-operation and Oh fuck; I suppose we have to do something to stop anyone finding out what we have got intended for the area ultimately anyway eh?"

"So right my friend. It has been a most pleasing and profitable association between us so why spoil something that works well. The Imperial powers are now faltering in their endeavours and we need to take advantage of it all anyway. Leave it with me my friend; just get your men ready.

Also the man that you send to Nassau, we need him to make sure that there is no trace there either to connect us. The Cosmetic surgeon we used, Dr Rheingold, the little Jew, he must also disappear from the scene. He has served his purpose and we have got no further need for his expert hands. All your men, except you of course, have been changed in some way. You understand we need to close any avenues that remain open. I'd hate to think what Rheingold would do if he found out he was helping his enemies to destroy his own homeland."

"Consider it all done." Tony was frustrated. He had long ago thought his own Government were going in the wrong direction and serving in its army just accentuated the problem for him with orders that he felt were not really military but political objectives. He knew the men he had used in his little group were all disgruntled members of the British Army who were seeking ways of getting one up on them.

"Then I will leave you with the changes we have agreed on and hope we will see the end of our annoying little man Warburton. Goodbye for now Tony, I will speak to you soon."

Tony answered him with a quick farewell which wasn't that convincing. He banged the phone receiver down and swore again to himself. This wasn't how it was meant to be he thought. He was just going to handle the money with the others were going to recruit and train some of the Jamal's men. Why had it gone so Tits Up now?

Tony picked up the receiver and dialled the Athens number getting an immediate response from Peter Southwaite, aka Mark Smythe. After a few welcoming gestures he explained the plan that had been discussed with Jamal. It took all of fifteen minutes to formulate the talks agreeing who and why would travel where. The conversation closed with both men wishing each other good fortune with the prospect of being able to have a drink together not too far in the distant future.

It had been an hour and a half now since that damn phone buzzed and the next call he made was to Nassau to get them up to scratch on the events that had progressed during the last few days in Europe.

Again there were wishes of good fortune including the parting notes of a drink together in the not too distant future.

It was 2100hrs when he made his last call which was to his cousin John Schofield, aka Browning, aka Peter Caulfield.

"John!" Tony said still having some difficulty in saying the name as he had always known his cousin as Peter. "Your little scapegoat has reared his ugly head in the UK I'm afraid causing our Iraqi friends some angst."

"Little scapegoat, you mean Warburton? Thought the little arsehole was dead, killed in the prison blunder by Basra Garrison."

"Seems we were either mistaken or misled mate. He has been getting up Jamal's skin for the past few weeks and has killed our little Bulgarian friend Grigor." Tony then went on to explain what had happened in London and Sofia.

"So you see we have little options but to close our Athens operation and tighten our control in Nassau and here."

"I wouldn't have thought that prick was anything like his father, Tony. He was such a quiet introverted man on the base. How wrong can you be?"

"Look we will have to just sit tight and monitor the situation at this stage. I've got Southwaite going to Nassau and Mark Thorn, aka Steve Reed coming here at this point after they get rid of this Warburton fellow in Greece.

As far as the office explosion goes in Athens, well that should shake up the Greek Government a bit and make them think about their association with the Yanks and Brits in the future. Unfortunate I know but it seems we have to do it to stop any possible links with what we are doing there, here and on the Bahamas.

How about we get together in the morning out at Westgate Golf Club and hit a few while we think about our next moves."

"Ok, Tony, see you there about 8 then."

They both closed their conversation down and went about their evening chores. Tony was late for his dinner engagement which he had to cancel meaning he would have to buy something on the way home but for John it meant he could carry on screwing the young barmaid he had befriended earlier in the week. Life was good, John thought but there are always speed humps on the way.

CHAPTER 17

It was about 1600hrs when Tom turned off the main Thessalonica to Athens highway and headed into the township of Larissa. Gerry had instructed him to stay on Route One that went past the airport. Once past the airport he would go over a bridge over the Pinios Potamos at which point he was to take a right onto the E65. Gerry gave instructions to punch in to the GPS Geniko Kratiko Nosokomio which was the main hospital. That was to be his meeting point with his man from Athens.

As Tom pulled into the car park of the hospital grounds the sky was starting to darken over from heavy clouds overhead but the night was also starting to creep in urgently wanting to shut off the day. A day Tom was pleased to see end.

He pulled up at a quiet point of the car park where only about a dozen cars were located. He stopped the Land Rover getting out to stretch his legs hoping the wait wouldn't be too long before his contact arrived from Athens. He was lucky for not ten minutes later a black Jaguar sedan pulled up alongside him. What was it with black, Tom thought to himself? These diplomats have absolutely no colour in their lives at all.

Out of the Jag jumped a six foot tall bronzed Brit. Looked like he had spent too much time on the beaches rather than working. His short jet black hair and olive skin could easily have mistaken him for a local till he spoke.

"Way eye man." He said in a strong Newcastle accent. A bloody Geordie, how misleading it was. "Gerry sent me and I was to give you this envelope while we change vehicles."

"No worries mate." Said Tom grinning to himself at the appearance of this young man who was about the same age as himself. "I'll just get my gear out of the back so you can get going eh."

The young man didn't say his name nor made any other gesture as who he was at the Embassy. He kept everything to the point he had been instructed to, handed the envelope to Tom while still smiling broadly. Tom threw the envelope into the passenger seat of the Jag, went to the Discovery where he removed his weapon from its hiding place without the young guy seeing what he had done. He then removed his case, throwing that into the boot of the Jag which his new friend had just opened for him.

"Thanks mate." Tom said lifting his hand in a formal wave. He got into the new car checking the fuel gauge. Well it was just under half so Tom would have to top up before he tackled his final leg to Athens. He opened the envelope and emptied the contents onto the seat next to him. Shuffling through it all he exchanged what he had with the new placing the old documents and cards into the envelope giving it back to the guy who was standing next to his driver's door.

With the exchange done Tom checked that the young guy was driving directly back to Athens that night which he was; as he acknowledged. Tom thought that it would be too dangerous to travel both Diplomatic plated vehicles along the same road at the same time so decided he would pull up overnight here in Larissa after refuelling.

It was getting darker by the time Tom had fuelled at the nearest garage and found a small Bed and breakfast style place just on the outskirts of the town. He settled for the night early hoping he would be fresh enough early tomorrow to venture to the office he had written on a note in the file he was carrying. His Sig was securely placed inside his case in the room and would remain handy. The last thing he wanted was any more shocks like he had had in London.

What was the old Scout motto, Be Prepared.

Next morning Tom awoke at seven and when he went downstairs he was greeted with a large American style breakfast which filled him to the brim before he finally set off towards Athens. This would keep him going for the rest of the morning meaning fewer stops on the way.

Over the next three hours Tom was working through his mind what he wanted to actually do when he arrived in Athens. His priority was to get to the office pronto and check it out.

Driving in to Athens from the North was a real spectacle for Tom as he came closer to the city from the high points North he could see a polluted cloud layer that lay above the city, seemingly strangling it from on high. It was a strange sight but for a city like Athens it showed just how the pollution was kept above the city by the climate it occupied.

The views Tom saw from his arrival point were spectacular. The Acropolis standing grand on its high plateau, looking down on the land below showing off all its glory. This was supposedly where the beginning of our civilized world had begun. Tom was to realize that even here the troubles of far off places can take its toll without warning.

Tom got closer to the city and was just about ten kilometres out when he was suddenly caught in one of the worse traffic jams he had seen in any capital city. As far as he could see was a line of cars, buses, trucks and bikes. He had never thought it could get this bad here. All the vehicles were idling over which wouldn't do much for the pollution in the sky above their heads, just add to it all.

The traffic was going along at a crawling pace as it slowly crept forward inch by inch. It wasn't till an hour later that he actually saw what was causing it. Still smoking was a large tangle of vehicle metal strewn across the roadway. The police were directing the traffic around it as best they could through some of the very small side roads. How the buses and trucks faired was beyond even thinking about.

It was a shock as Tom got closer to the tangled mess he saw what looked like the remains of a Discovery. He couldn't work out a number plate or anything just the partial rear section of what seemed like a similar vehicle to what he had driven the day before.

He seized an opportunity to pull over into one of the back streets and park. Walking back towards the direction of the smouldering mess he was visualizing the face of the young Geordie who had taken the Land Rover the night before hoping he was totally wrong in what he was now thinking.

As he came around the corner of the road where the explosion, as that was what it seemed to be, stood he suddenly realized the shape was a Discovery the same model as he had used. He walked as close as he could towards the wreckage trying to see if there was anything of recognition on the vehicle for him.

The shock wave hit him as he then noticed the number plate that was lying on the road beside the pile of what was three to four vehicles. It was the plate on the Discovery he had been driving.

The ghouls of any accident stir around the devastation in the hope of seeing body parts it seemed. He joined many others staring, trying to see what a normal person would try to avoid. There were signs of blood but no actual bodies. Most of the wreckage had been pulled to one side with signs there was evidence that many cuts had been made to possibly free what poor souls were inside these once objects, cars.

As he came close behind one of the patrol officers who were holding back the ghouls he lent forward and asked in English. "What happened here?"

The officer slightly startled by the English accent turned and looked at Tom. "There was some kind of an explosion here last night. Many people have died including children. We don't yet know the full story."

Tom thanked the officer, slapped him lightly on the arm and turned around fighting his way out of the throng of people now collecting and returned to his car. Inside he dialled Gerry's number.

"Tom, where are you?" Gerry asked instantly. "I have some bad news from Athens."

"I know, Gerry, I have just seen it. What the hell happened?"

"We had reports from our friends in the Greek Interior Ministry that there was some kind of a flash of some kind that was witnessed coming from a van parked on the side of the road and then there was one almighty explosion. I don't think I need to tell you our friend was killed instantly."

"It is sickening to look at it and the poor bastard was so young and refreshing." Tom felt sick in the stomach as he spoke knowing in his mind that it was possibly meant for him.

"It was meant for you I think Tom. It seems someone doesn't like you poking around. Look the office you are going to, I meant to let you know it is right by the side of the Firm's local office. They have done some checks on the office you are to visit but have come up blank as we originally suspected. There are three people that work there, two men whose names are on your list, a Peter Southwaite and a Mark Thorn. Neither flagged any red markers for us but both work for Tony Welsh's company. The other person is a local girl, 26, who is their receptionist.

I think the best thing you could do is call into our office first and link up with our man there. He works out of the office alone having just a couple of analysts at hand in the office to assist him, one of those you met yesterday poor sod. His name is John Thomlinson, nice enough guy and ex Regiment. I have told him you are on your way so he is expecting you sometime this afternoon. Take care Tom, this thing is beginning to give me the shits. I've been in touch with London where Mark really is concerned about your wellbeing also."

With that Tom hung up and started the Jaguar engine but he hesitated before selecting drive. He felt utterly sick at what had happened to the young Geordie last night. He pushed the selector to drive saying to himself "I'll get you bastards for this." The wheels screeched and he took off towards the area of the office for Asia-Pac.

Turning into Ploutarchou Street Tom looked around for a parking spot. He had to stop himself from parking close to the office he was looking for as with the CD plates it would have looked too obvious. He eventually parked two streets away and walked back towards the office with his sig firmly inside his jacket pocket less the silencer. He didn't care how much noise he made as now these bastards were really pissing him off big time.

Finding the block of offices he scanned the area for anyone who may be watching for him to arrive. He walked past the frontage a couple of times and also stood opposite to view the area around. Satisfied that he was ok, he entered the building making his way via the stairs to the fourth floor. As he got to the landing he turned away from the door directly facing him which had the plaque on it to indicate that of Asia-Pac Loan & Finance and went in through the door next to it which just had a plaque showing some Company name he did not recognise and its mapping services.

As he entered the office a receptionist looked up from her place behind a reception desk and smiled at him. "Can I help you Sir?" she asked in perfect English. Her facial features and skin tone looked as though she was a local lass but then again so did Geordie's till he opened his mouth.

"Yes. John Thomlinson please." Tom smiled back at her.

"Have you an appointment sir?" she asked.

"No but he is expecting me. Stan Richards." Another alias Tom had to get used to he thought.

Before he had even finished talking a man came around the corner of the reception, he was about 175 cm, in his mid to late thirties who had shoulders the size Sampson would have been proud of. An obvious weightlifter type who took great care in looking after himself and his appearance. Arnold Schwarzenegger in miniature Tom thought to himself.

"It's Ok Ethie I have it thanks." He said as he made his way towards Tom. He held out his hand shaking it fiercely nearly pulling Tom's arm out of its socket. "Glad you got here safe Stan." He said pulling Tom in the direction of his office. Once inside he sat down in a swing office chair next to another which he indicated Tom to take. Tom sat down and looked at John.

"Unfortunate event last night eh?" John said trying to get the conversation going.

"I just can't believe it. Poor sod had no chance by the sound of it."
"Some kind of rocket launcher from a van we believe. No trace and not

eyewitnesses who could give a description of any kind. Sometimes this can be a shit of a job Stan but someone has to do it."

"What can you tell me about our friends next door?" Tom asked wanting to get into the action immediately.

"Apart from there are two men, Southwaite and Thorn, and there is also a receptionist there, nothing. Local girl like ours in there as a receptionist. There is nothing out of the ordinary we have been able to uncover. The Company is actively involved in the local stock market and has been known to buy up struggling companies before then selling them off in parts to others that are interested. They make quite a bit of money from their exploits like that.

There's been some activity this morning with a courier bringing in a number of packages to their office. They were all marked stationary, we haven't been able to contact the company that sent them as yet so we have no suspicions on their contents. The delivery company checked out OK though."

"Are the two men in there at the moment?"

"I believe they are, have been since mid morning."

"Then I think it is time I went in and tackled them with what I have so far."

"I'll come in with you just in case you need a hand. Are you carrying?" John asked putting his hand inside his jacket and pulling out a Glock which he checked making sure one was up the spout. "Can't be too careful, can we?"

"Yes." Tom confirmed.

They both stood, Tom checked his Sig as he was trained to before they both stood to leave with John opening up the door and Tom followed him out.

John smiled across at Ethie, the receptionist telling her he was heading next door to their neighbours for a chat. She returned his smile and put her head back down to continue whatever she was doing in front of her.

As the two of them went out the office both had a hand inside their jackets gripping their weapons in readiness. They turned towards Asia— Pac with Tom taking the lead pushing on the door and entering.

The time was now creeping on to 1430 hrs with the office seeming to be a buzz of activity. Tom went straight towards the receptionist asking for the manager. He was met with a puzzled face at first but after some quick pressing of buttons she finally got one of the guys to come out to them.

"Hi there, I'm Peter Southwaite, how can I help you?" he said coming around the counter and shaking hands with Tom.

"A friend of mine asked me to look you up when I got into town, John Browning." Tom stared at the man's eyes for any recognition of the name. Nothing not even a quick look of shock.

"Come on in, Marie coffee please." He said as he turned then passed the receptionist leading the two men to an office just behind the partition.

"What can I do for you then gentlemen?" Southwaite said as he came around his desk. The office was awash with graphs and pie charts spread all over the wall space. Looked quite impressive Tom thought to himself as he and John sat down opposite them trying to quickly fathom them out.

"John gave me a contact back in Sofia that I was able to use with great success." Tom continued.

Still no recognizable sign from Southwaite's face, this guy was good and had a face like ice. It showed no surprise or any trace of unease.

"Perhaps," Southwaite said rising from his seat. "You may like to speak with my associate next door. He is the one who has contact over the border, I believe he may be able to help you."

Tom got up and started to follow him just as Marie entered the office with a tray with the coffee mugs on. Thomlinson stayed seated, looked up at Tom to indicate he would remain and perhaps check out what he could from this office. Tom moved out the door with Southwaite closing it behind him.

As they walked a short way down to the next door, Tom started to get a little uncomfortable. He readied himself for anything that looked suspicious. His hand inside his jacket he followed stopping just short of the door.

On the door was a sign, Mark Thorn, Tom recognized it as another one of the names he had obtained from Grigor. The door opened and Southwaite walked straight into the room which prevented Tom from seeing what was in front of him. By the time Tom was inside the room no matter how much martial arts training a man has there was no defence against a length of four by two placed rather heavily between your shoulder blades.

Tom's head went black as he dropped to the carpet covered floor. He was out for the count as the man who had administered the blow came forward and started to tie his hands and feet up. A gag was applied and Tom was lifted into a soft leather chair that had been moved away from the wall where it usually stood. Thorn had removed his Sig from his jacket after frisking him and stuck it into his own pocket. Tom was then gaffer taped to the chair.

Southwaite quickly went to the desk and pulled out a 9mm Beretta complete with a silencer. He exited the office holding the handgun behind his back. As he opened the door of his own office he found Thomlinson standing by the window with his handgun firmly placed in line with the entering body.

"What the fuck is this?" asked Southwaite not moving from the door keeping his hand still held behind it holding his handgun.

"I think you know full well what this is. I think you had better come in and sit down while we wait for my friend to come back."

"I don't know what you are after but we do not keep any cash here."
"It's not the cash we are after just some information."

Behind Southwaite Mark Thorn had been hearing what was going down and had come close to his partner to be able to take the handgun from him without Thomlinson seeing him. He leant back against the wall out of sight from the doorway as Southwaite brought his hand forward and started to walk slowly into the room going to the sofa to his left. He deliberately left the door wide open and when he sat kept his eyes firmly upon the gun pointing directly at him. He shuffled himself as far along the sofa as he could forcing Thomlinson to move his eyes away from the door to be able to keep them onto him.

As Southwaite settled himself down satisfied that he had gotten the full attention of his assailant he barked. "What the fuck do you really want?"

"We just want some answers regarding a little forger my friend saw in Sofia."

"I haven't got a clue what you are talking about. What would I need a forger for anyway?"

"I think it goes way back beyond that anyway. Perhaps take your . . ." Thomlinson suddenly stopped as a shadow caught his peripheral vision and he spun around towards the door but it was just a tad too late for him as before he could cite the man in the doorway a thud rang in his ears followed by total darkness as he fell forward with a hole suddenly appearing in his left eye. His head exploded as he fell forward and his sentence remained unfinished.

"Thank God for that Mark." Southwaite breathed a sigh of relief. "These bastards obviously know a lot more than what they are letting on. The other one is the one that should have been blown to smithereens last night by Jamal's men. How is he getting away from them so easily. I suppose we will have to deal with him now."

"He's out of it at the moment but we had better get the rest of our gear ready for this afternoon as instructed." Mark continued forcing away the gun from Thomlinson's fingers. "We haven't got a lot of time left. Do we take the other one with us and find out all that he knows or do we just leave him to dissolve here with the rest next door?"

"I don't really give a shit at the moment, let's just get our stuff sorted and get the fuck out of here."

The two men quickly closed the office door and locked it behind them. Mark walked to reception and checked to make sure Maria was still there and none the wiser for the events back in the offices behind her. They then carried on to the rear office where Tom was still out of it, trussed up in the leather chair.

Behind the door and along the wall were built in cupboards that went from floor to ceiling. Mark started opening the doors of the cupboards revealing drums full of petrol with small packages of what looked like Semtex along the tops on them. There must have been at least two to three pounds in each of the four cupboards.

Tom had started to come around a touch but hadn't moved from his now taped position. His eyes were squinting and fixed at what the two guys were up to in the cupboard. His head was aching with his vision still a bit blurry.

He could see inside the cupboards and saw the fuel containers. His eyes couldn't believe the amount of what looked like Semtex above each drum of fuel. There would have been enough explosive there to bring down a six storey building.

This was serious stuff. These jerks were going to demolish this whole building and possibly take down half the remainder of the block along with it.

Tom relaxed his hands and felt the ties of wire coming loose a touch around his wrists. He was not about to make any sudden moves from the position he was in as he knew he would not be able to take both these men down at once anyway but the question of his feet being trussed was another headache for him.

The men worked feverishly at what they were doing, occasionally looking over at Tom, seeing him unchanged continued on their merry way. Once they were satisfied that they were ready Southwaite pulled out a mobile from the desk and proceeded to wire and tape it to the middle batch of Semtex which was interconnected with the others.

Tom kept watching but in his mind he could do little about it all as he had had no explosives training whatsoever just the occasional use of explosive to remove seized track pins on tanks. He would not be able to do a thing to disarm this little lot. His worry was when were they going to blow it all, he listened intently not moving a muscle. He began to pray that he would have time to get out of his present predicament. Where the fuck was Thomlinson?

"That's the last Mark my man." Southwaite said with a sick looking grin on his face.

"This will bring down the whole building plus half the block causing that much devastation that the authorities will be sifting through it all for days before finding out anything." Mark looked pleased with his workmanship, rubbing his hands sadistically.

"Four o'clock. Time for us to disappear then. Marie will be here to lock up or not." Southwaite sniggered. "We will be well away by the time I dial into this little beauty. Five o'clock should see the whole going home thing seem like a doddle."

"Pete, I'll get off home then and get my gear together then destroy whatever I have that can be traced."

"I will be right behind you Mark. We will catch up at the old Hellenic Shipyards Wharf near my home about seven eh? From there we can take our bloody time getting across to Brindisi. Don't be late eh. Ring if you get delayed as I will if I am. This little lot will go off at five so the City is going to be in absolute chaos and ferries out will get delayed. You, coming in from Salamina on your boat, shouldn't be held up at all from that direction."

"Seems good to me, see you then mate." Mark chanted as he left the room and walked down the passage way waving a farewell to Maria saying he would see her in the morning. He departed and hightailed towards the port where he kept his 20 foot yacht anchored during the day. His trip home was always a pleasurable one in this part of the world, pity he was having to leave it when he was just beginning to enjoy himself.

Peter Southwaite looked around at Tom after Mark had left, walked across to him to check his condition. As he approached, Tom squeezed his hands so it blew his wrists up slightly and gave the impression that the wire was still tight. Southwaite checked the wires satisfied it was tight giving Tom a nudge and without getting any reaction from him he then turned to exit the office, on the way out he locked the door.

Tom sighed with relief realizing that they could have just blown him away there and then. What had happened to his sidekick Thomlinson, he thought to himself, he must be in trouble in the other office. Never mind time was running out, he knew what time this thing was going to blow and he knew he had only about fifty minutes to get the fuck out of town before this little eruption did its thing and vaporized all in its path.

Tom worked his hands curling the fingers in as much as he could. The fingers of his right hand enabled him to pull his hand out of their wire clasp slightly. He eased back a touch as he did not want to push too hard which would cause his hands to swell up. Deep breaths he told himself, relax and then retry, suddenly his hand came free and he moved with some urgency to pull his left hand out. The tape around him didn't have too much hold by the time he had twisted a few times to stretch it out. Finally he broke free of the tape and then went down to untie his ankles.

Free but time was moving on quickly. The clock on the wall gave him about thirty five minutes left before the big bang. He had to find Thomlinson quickly so moved to the door which he tried as hard as he could to force the damn thing open but he was against its normal opening. He was forced to pound the door which was a solid as a rock. There was no response from the other side. He knew that the receptionist would not leave till five but then again the bosses had left and there was the possibility that when the cats away then off went the mice as well.

Tom continued to bang on the door for a few more minutes. He gave it away after no response was forthcoming then moved to the cupboard where the explosives were lying ready for their big hoorah. Tom was no expert in explosives but thought he might look to see if he could do anything at all to stop this shit from happening, sadly he scratched his head and turned away, hoping the others in the office were out of the range of this little boom.

He tried the telephone but when he lifted the receiver it was dead. He had no phone with him after leaving them in the car in case they were discovered and traced.

Clocks ticking, Tom had now gone to the window where he found it totally secured and solid. Some clever prick had secured all the windows shut thinking that they were saving the loss of heat or cold from the air conditioner unit from escaping.

The chair that he had been sitting on just a few minutes before he lifted up and threw straight through the glass framework. It crashed through then dropped to land beneath the office block into what looked like a small yard below. He used a wooden ruler off the desk to quickly run around the outer frame to free up any slithers that remained so he didn't get cut on.

Twenty five minutes left, sweat was now visible on Tom's brow as he leant out the open window and surveyed what he had seen from the inside. Just to his right was a fire staircase but it was at least 2 to 3 meters away from the window. He didn't stop to think about it anymore as time was running out for him fast. He pulled himself out onto the window ledge; surrounded by other buildings he placed his feet slightly apart and leant back onto the frame behind him with his feet at an awkward angle.

He would only get one chance at this he knew. There was no way to go left as there was a barbed wire frame stopping him from getting around the window to the offices of the SIS next door. The jump was the only option he had left. Twenty two minutes left, he took a deep breath and then threw himself forward as fast as he could. It all seemed to hang in the air at that moment as he set his eyes on the hand rails of the stairs ahead of him. His arms moved forward as if he wanted them to stretch them out like elastic and wrap themselves around the handrails.

Time felt like it had just stood still for a moment then with a final burst he desperately tried to grab the rail, he didn't get a good grip and lost it with one hand which made his whole weight go downwards pulling hard on the hand that had made it, the right one. The force of the downward fall pulled hard on his shoulder and he felt a sharp pain sear through his muscles in the joint. Frantically he pulled his left hand around and grabbed the rail hard to relieve some of the pressure on his right.

Tom hung for a few seconds as he swung his legs into the stairway area finding the top of the rail below which stabilized him and enabled him to finally get himself into the stairway and onto to terra firma.

Twenty minutes left, Tom just took off down the stairs two, sometimes three at a time. Reaching the base he found the gate across it was locked. There are some bright sparks about, this was supposed to be a fire exit yet it was secured. He went back up a flight and climbed over the rail jumping down the final few feet to the ground. His shoulder was aching now but he was more concerned about the time left. He checked his watch and saw he had as little as fifteen minutes. There was no time to save anyone as he would have had to run around the block to warn everyone which by then would take the time to virtually zero. He had no option but to get his arse out of there and as far away as possible.

Ten minutes to go with Tom making it to the Jag frantically racing to dial the Satellite phone. Immediately he got an answer from Gerry. "What's the score, Tom?" Gerry asked.

"Mate there is a bomb in the office next door to yours so get the people out quick." Tom said urgently and hung up.

He grabbed his bag and started to walk in the opposite direction of the office. As he walked he ran through his next move. Five minutes to the event Tom had made his way to what he saw as a safe area. It was a small park where he sat pulling out his mobile, Gary's communication, ripping off the rear cover and dropping out the battery, then the sim card. He placed the parts in a plastic bag and replaced it all back into his pocket.

He again dialled the Satellite phone, two minutes left, and called Gerry. "Yes Tom." Gerry's voice came on quickly.

"Did you get the message to them Gerry?" Tom asked in earnest. "They are vacating as we speak mate. Do you know where John was as he hadn't returned from the office you both went to?"

"Sorry I . . ." Tom's words stopped dead in their track then as one almighty bang accompanied by an enormous fire ball rose from the vicinity of the office block. It was blinding, even from this distance. Tom turned his head to shield himself as he started to feel small particles reigning down all around him. There were screams and shouts coming from all directions with the blast noise seeming to continue forever.

"Gerry, you still there?" Tom finally yelled into the phone.

"Yes mate and I heard it. How big was that bloody thing?" Gerry was sounding shocked from his position way back in Sofia.

"Mate it was big enough to take out three blocks I reckon. I'm sorry I couldn't get to you any earlier."

"Its OK Tom just stay out of the way and keep safe. What's your next move?"

"I'm going after those two bastards now. I'll be in touch when I have finished with them."

"Tom, perhaps it should be left up to the local boys in uniform now. We have their names and they can deal with them from here."

"Fuck off Gerry. I owe those pricks now, big time." And with that Tom hung up then dropping the satellite phone into a bin near the bench he was sitting on knew that now he had now become rogue. He left the park and headed for somewhere he could hang up his bag for a while and then he was going after those two boys from the office.

Behind him as he walked he heard the sound of sirens coming from all directions bearing down on the location of the office explosion. As he turned to see what was happening he saw flames billowing up high above the tops of the office blocks with smoke leaping up to join the rest of the pollution above the Greek capital.

Finding a hotel near to the ferry points Tom booked himself in going straight to his room. Here he turned on the TV and scanned the channels. He didn't need to go far as nearly every channel had on it the devastation that he nearly ended up in the middle of.

The screen was showing what looked like a building with its top blown completely off and the buildings next door to it also were obliterated with windows blown in, walls holed and there was still the sound of screams from somewhere in the vicinity of the microphone.

The gist of the saga as it was all Greek to him was something to do with a gas leak. The Government were obviously holding back till they either got firm evidence or some organization somewhere in the world wanted to claim the responsibility.

Tom was unaware of the chaos being caused in the airwaves around Europe as Gary Warlock tried desperately to get in touch with Tom, even through Gerry in Sofia and also people on the ground from the Embassy in Athens. It was useless for them, they had lost all forms of communication via mobiles and the GPS indicators showed nothing for Gary's mobile that Tom had stripped with the satellite phone being eventually recovered from a bin in an Athens park.

Gary was now deeply concerned that Tom had flipped his lid and was on a vengeance trip which would just leave corpses scattered around the place and no more answers regarding the job he was really there for. Is all they could do was wait, be patient till they hoped Tom would be in touch with them again.

CHAPTER 18

While Tom had kept his eyes fixed on the room's TV he was also trying to locate the address of Peter Southwaite somewhere near the old Hellenic Shipyards. It wasn't too difficult to trace once he got the hang of the local form of white pages he had available and was able to pinpoint the area to within a fifteen minute drive circle.

He pinpointed only one Southwaite in the area near a place called Chaidari, checking his watch which was indicating 1800hrs, he knew he had only one hour before the two men would be meeting. He quickly grabbed a jumper leaving the hotel taking a cab to the address he had got from the book, a place called Athanasiou Diakou.

The taxi ride took only fifteen minutes after hurrying the cab driver up with a generous tip to grease his palms. What he saw when he got there was a huge house situated upon a large mound with high walls surrounding it just like a castle. The road went around the property in a U turn which the taxi took slowly when Tom saw the gigantic electric gates that stood in front of the main drive. The taxi pulled in just past the gates out of sight.

Leaving the cab and sending him on his way, Tom went to the gate searching around for any cameras that may have been there as part of the security. None he could see within the gate proximity and the gate was securely locked but climbable if you were brave enough to have a go. Tom couldn't see the house from this position as the drive turned away to the left climbing upward. The only other thing Tom was worried about was if there were dogs patrolling the grounds.

He finally decided to scramble over the gate doing so pretty quickly even though his right shoulder was still giving him grief from his staircase ordeal that afternoon. Once over he listened for any signs of dogs or even security guards around.

So far so good he thought as he made his way along the side of the vast driveway under the cover of the bushes that aligned it, to a point where the house came into view. It was a vast mansion, nearly as high as the offices he had been in earlier that day. Tom could see from his position that it stood so grand with three stories of pure indulgence with a roof top that held serious walkway rail around it. This bloke would have million dollar views from this picturesque palace in the hills.

Tom crossed over the drive and headed for the rear of the building. He was carrying no weapon so he was just going to count on his own martial arts skills, which didn't do him much good against a piece of four by two earlier.

Keeping close to the wall he made his way around the building looking everywhere for any signs of cameras or guards. Tom finally came to a doorway which when he tried the handle it turned and opened easily.

Just to his right side near the door was the garage which had a large Mercedes parked in front of it. This would be Southwaite's escape vehicle he thought so he delayed his entrance into the house and went over to the vehicle looking in through the driver's window. Will wonders never cease he thought as he caught a glimpse of the vehicles keys still sitting in the ignition?

He slowly opened the door and removed the keys. Looking around for some kind of weapon he might be able to use but unfortunately luck wasn't that great. Pushing the door of the car closed without too much noise made he turned away from the car looking round the garage frontage when he saw a brace lying by the garage door. He hastily picked it up, then headed back to the house rear door he had opened.

As Tom went into the house he entered what was like a boot room through which he found the kitchen area. Stopping by every door he came to he closed his eyes, opened his mouth slightly and listened, trying to get the best from his hearing. Nothing could be heard coming from anywhere ahead so he ventured on carrying out the same procedure at each door he came to.

It wasn't till he finally got up the first flight of stairs that he heard what seemed was someone throwing things into a case on the floor above him. The top floor must be all the bedrooms and it was here that he finally caught a glimpse of Southwaite speedily throwing what looked like banknotes and a few clothes into a large case. He was alone racing around the room frantically doing what he needed to do.

Tom eased himself to the door checking that his target was totally alone. He slowly peered into the room which was larger as a bedroom than the whole bloody penthouse he had stayed in London. All clear and seeing that there was no weapon in the hands of his target, it was lying on the bed just out of his reach, he launched himself into the room towards Southwaite.

The shock on Southwaite's face was classic. His eyes bulged at the sight of Tom coming at him. He had no time to jump aside as Tom just barrelled into him knocking both of them to the floor in a heap. Tom lost grip of the brace he had picked up which went noisily sliding to the side of the room out of reach of both.

An exchange of angry blows erupted between them. Both men being trained in unarmed combat made it more the desperate for each to get away from the opposing man. A swift knee from Southwaite landed in Tom's stomach area lifting him off his opponent and away to the left of him on the floor. Southwaite immediately jumped to his feet looking around to get his bearings, the gun on the bed was all that was in his mind. Tom didn't give him any chance to get that as he jumped up planting a swift side kick which connected to Southwaite's right arm throwing him off balance and onto the bed. He hit the bed and immediately rolled to one side preventing Tom from pounding in from above onto the top of him.

As Southwaite rolled he let his feet drop to the floor and stood ready to take on Tom. Tom had come across the bed after him but Southwaite took the opportunity to take Tom's feet from him by swinging one of his legs around in a waist high kick. Tom lost his legs in that quick move and bundled onto the bed rolling himself to the opposite side of the bed. The gun had dropped to the floor with all this going on on the bed.

Southwaite had seized the moment with Tom down by running from the room and out onto the landing. Tom quickly got to his feet following as quickly as he could. Outside on the landing Southwaite had run towards a small stairway to his right that led up to the roof. Tom was in hot pursuit with his right shoulder aching badly as he ran.

Tom reached the roof area to find a glass framed walkway that went all around the top of building. He saw Southwaite head to what appeared to be another door about 180 degrees around the roof. Tom leapt over the handrail and headed across the centre of the roof hoping it was strong enough to hold his weight. He reached the doorway just before Southwaite after leaping back onto the walkway facing him as he ran towards the door. Southwaite stopped dead in his track so beginning a Mexican Stand off for Tom. Tom edged slowly forward as Southwaite stood his ground.

Tom really wanted Southwaite to make the first move to come towards where he was giving him the advantage of being able to stand firm. Tom however had to edge forward, Southwaite realising he had the advantage broke into a smile staring straight at him.

"Why can't you just die quietly you little shit?" he spat out at Tom. "Not ready for that part of life yet, are you?"

"Look Warburton how about you take the money that's downstairs and we part here as friends?" Southwaite was hoping for a bit of a reprise as he was older, puffing like an old billy goat and not at all as fit as he once was. His present lifestyle was not what it used to be and it showed around the waistline on him.

"Stuff your money; you killed many innocent people today for what? You and your cronies are worse than the terrorists we both used to hunt together."

"Times change, the powers that be don't care about people like you and me. We are expendable. It's time for us to change that scenario and look after ourselves because they won't."

"Perhaps I am young and naive but my morals are still intact not like you arseholes." With that Tom moved forward and threw a couple of quick punches to Southwaite's body. Both were shielded off by Southwaite but what he didn't expect was the follow up front kick which sent the wind out of his lungs throwing him down onto the walkway.

Tom stood frozen in his stance as Southwaite caught his breath standing up again showing he was no longer willing. He was puffed and started to throw punches wildly at Tom. Tom ducked as Southwaite came forward throwing a wild right hander. Southwaite's arm flew out through the air with such gusto it threw him off balance and he lost his footing hitting the glass barrier with such momentum that he began careering over the top. He tried in desperation to get a grip on the top of the glass as he went over but missed. Tom saw immediately that his opposition was about to fall to the ground below so leapt forward grabbing wildly at what he could get which happened to be Southwaite's left hand with his right. The pain in his shoulder tore into his brain again as he hammered himself chest first into the glass barrier as Southwaite's weight went fully onto his arm.

Tom took the strain looking hard down onto Southwaite's face. Why didn't he just let him go letting him check the windows from the outside on his fall from grace? No, that wasn't what Tom wanted just yet, there had been enough dead bodies to date. He wanted information; he wanted his ultimate goal of Caulfield.

Tom looked piercingly into the eyes of Southwaite, seeing the terror now in his mind.

"Where can I find Caulfield?" he asked the desperate man hanging by a whisker.

"Pull me up and I'll tell you." Southwaite wasn't going to give too much even in this predicament.

"I can't hold on for much longer arsehole. Tell me where I can find him." Tom had started to get his left hand over to help grab hold of Southwaite. His right arm was beginning to go numb.

Heavy breathing accompanied by the eyes of fear that were in Southwaite now were not bringing out anything. Tom pulled hard at the arm he had grip of and started to lift Southwaite up towards the top slowly.

"OK if you don't want to give Caulfield up then how about your contact in Nassau then?" Tom let him drop a bit now he had both his hands on his arm to enforce the issue.

"Shit." Southwaite yelled in terror. "Look just get me up safe and I will tell you everything."

"No deal." Tom said starting to let the man down a touch. Fear began burning out from Southwaite's eyes again.

"Alright, alright. The man in Nassau is Derek Sweetman. Now for Christ sake pull me up will you?"

"How about where you guys got the face lift while I am at it."

"Fuck you. Just pull me up."

Tom pulled then let him go down again. "I'm waiting. Name?"

"Rheingold, Rheingold. Now please get me up eh."

Tom had a bit more information now but was not prepared to kill this man for the sake of revenge so he strained every muscle he could muster pulling Southwaite back up over the top of the barrier. As he did, Southwaite collapsed onto the walkway panting like a baby, Tom bent down planting a well directed blow to the side of the neck which sent Southwaite out cold and limp.

Tom struggled for a moment to gain his strength back before he finally managed to throw his charge over his shoulder. Returning back downstairs to the ground floor from whence he had entered and where he dumped Southwaite into the boot of the Mercedes. He looked around the garage finding some zip ties which he used to immobilize Southwaite while he was locked in the boot. That may stop him warning anyone outside that he was locked in there. Slamming the boot down, he went back up to the bedroom where he picked up the items which had come second best during their little fracas. As he lifted some of the items from the floor he saw the Beretta compact handgun underneath which he scooped up and placed in the top of his trousers belt. Finally he locked the case taking it down to the car waiting for him to leave.

It was now seven and the other creep would be at the shipyard waiting patiently for his buddy to arrive. Tom started the Merc and drove down the driveway. The gate was still shut as he pulled up in front of it.

As he looked around the various spots in the cab for where someone would put a touch pad he whispered to himself. 'I don't suppose open sesame me would fucking work then.'

Finally in the centre console he found a touch pad which he pressed and the creeks at the gate started up instantly. The huge gates began to part, Tom revved the car and as the gates gave him enough room to squeeze through he slammed the thing into drive and let rip through them, the wheels squealed as he spun the steering wheel around to return to the main road and onto the shipyards about ten minutes away.

He still had no clue who these two really were from the original group even though he had the files including the cross references from Sofia but he didn't much care as his only interest was to get Caulfield the one who had killed Mahmoud and set him up.

He arrived at the shipyard wharf about quarter past seven and drove slowly along the front of the old wharf where he caught a glimpse of the boat. Sure enough there it was sitting with its motor idling over tied by one rope to the small jetty that still remained in place in this dilapidated part of the wharf. Obviously waiting for a quick getaway.

Tom stopped about fifty meters from where the boat was tied and started to get out. He was shielded from view from anyone watching as the car was left hand drive which allowed him to alight between the car and the wharf wall.

Just as Tom alighted from the car he heard a whoosh sound that seemed to come from the opposite end of the wharf road. There was a smoke trail with it as well. The next thing he saw was a flash and the boat disintegrated right in front of him. Tom hit the deck and rolled to the wall just as he heard some hurried movement then another whoosh.

By the side of him was a rather damaged wall and there was a small enough gap for him to roll through which he did urgently and kept rolling as a loud bang sent bells ringing through his ears. A flash then silence. The smell of burning and the distinct smell of tyres on fire filled his nostrils. Tom's head was ringing so loud it felt he was inside Big Ben at midnight and they were using his head as the clanger.

Tom struggled to get himself up onto his feet and ran at full speed to the end of the warehouse structure where he estimated the noises had come from. When he got to the end he could see through cracks in the ancient worn wall that there were two Middle Eastern men laughing aloud and exchanging nods of approval from each other.

Tom saw a door just out to the left side of him, so making his way to the door he mustered his senses to be able to get a clear shot at the men. He pulled the Beretta out of his waistband and pushed gently at the door. It opened slightly giving him a view down to where the two Arabs were standing. Their vehicle, a van, was further down the side of the warehouse off to one side but they were in no hurry to leave as they seemed to be making sure their targets were positive kills.

Tom eased through the door and slid himself over beside some old rusty pipe work that was running along the outside of the building. As Tom came within earshot of the men he lifted the handgun up quickly checking it. Aiming at the nearest man he pulled the trigger, it let out a bang followed by a yell of pain as the man he aimed at fell to the ground clutching his butt. The other man spun around pulling out his handgun but Tom let off another shot which caught the man in the arm. Tom's aim was all over the place; his head was still spinning from the blast at the car and the bells, those fucking bells.

The men struggled to help each other while also trying to fire at Tom which just kept Tom's head down. The injured man who had copped one in the arm ran towards the van that was parked just about ten metres from their position. Tom tried to let another shot off but it hit one of the stanchions and ricocheted around a few other metal objects before going silent. The man got to the van, started it and took off showing just how team spirited he was. Tom crept towards the man writhing around the floor gripping his arse tightly.

As Tom came up on him he held the Beretta to his head and slowly kicked away the rocket launcher by his side. Then he frisked him for anything of use while holding him on the floor with his right knee.

Finding a small handgun he took possession of it and then asked him. "Who are you working for?"

During the frisking he noticed on the right wrist the sign he had tried to work out from others before, the infinity sign. He was now associating the sign with the I.I.G. group.

The man looked blankly at him shaking his head. Tom repeated the question but again the man looked blankly at him.

"Are you I.I.G.?" Tom asked.

The man again looked blankly at him and shook his head in a gesture of not understanding him. Tom looked around knowing he had little time to carry on this charade here before the authorities were all over the scene. This had been one hell of a day for Athens and it hadn't finished yet by the looks of things.

Suddenly hearing sirens he leaned into the man placing his foot on the front of the leg where the point of bullet contact had been in his butt. The man let off an almighty scream.

"Who are you working for?" Tom asked again, placing more pressure on the wound.

"Yes, Yes . . . I.I.G . . . we were . . . sent here . . . to . . . stop men . . . from being caught."

"Thank you." Tom said but not releasing any pressure. "Who is your boss?"

Again, another blank look. There wasn't much time left. "Give me the name of your leader." Tom's brain went silly inside thinking he was at the cinemas as a kid when the Martians came and asked to be taken to your leader. All jokes aside though it brought a response along with the pain.

"Ashid. His name is Ashid."

"Thank you, now that wasn't hard was it. Your reward for that is." Tom pulled the trigger and the man's brain exited the thick skull on the opposite side spreading itself across the roadway where he and his partner had set up their assassination bid.

Tom got up and took off not looking back at the wharf. He knew he had had no option but to silence the man because if the authorities had gotten the information he had then it might have sent Ashid into hiding somewhere in this vast world.

Tom made his way back to the hotel, disposing of the handguns he had in his possession in one of the tributaries he passed on the way into the City. When he was in his room he set himself down to think about what he been told this day. Rheingold, Ashid, I.I.G., his head was still pounding so another few paracetamol were a welcome relief. He dropped asleep on the bed and didn't wake until 1000 hrs the next morning.

Turning on the TV he again had to judge for himself what was being said as the journalist was showing the remains of the boat and car and what looked like three corpses that had been placed on the waterfront in body bags ready for transport to the morgue.

The news reel ran though the office building explosion again, then back to the wharf which got Tom thinking that somehow they must be trying to link them possibly now looking at some kind of terrorism plot instead of a gas explosion. The next link would have to be poor Geordie's demise the night before in the Landrover, perhaps it does come in threes like the old wives tales says it does.

Chaos was now filling the airwaves in Athens; there wasn't a moment's break from the disasters of the past few days. Over the coming days there would be many conspiracy theories going around, giving Tom ample time to ponder his next move. He had not been in touch with anyone from back home but had been phoning Perth Australia and talking with Vicki. This relationship over the phone had been uplifting for Tom in many ways; it kept his feet firmly anchored as far as his decision process was heading. He was keener now to get this project of his finished so he could continue with the relationship he felt had come as a blessing with Vicki.

On the following Tuesday Tom decided to put the Firm's mobile back into use again, that was to get in touch with Gary. It took less than a minute after he had put it all together before the phone started ringing aloud.

"Where the fuck have you been Tom?" Gary was sounding a little furious at the lack of communication between them.

"Well good morning to you Gary and how are you?" Tom came back with rather more than the usual sarcasm. "Seems all hell has broken loose in this tiny little country the last few days. Any news for me from your end?"

"How much more devastation are you going to leave behind you Tom?" Gary started to calm hoping not to push Tom too far.

"Well Gary it's like this, someone seems to be knocking these guys off before I can get to them. It seems mighty suspicious that as soon as I get close some bastard blows the living shit out of them. Besides that the first killing, of young Geordie from the local offices here was really meant for me." Tom was laid back on his sofa and waiting for some kind of insight from the other end of the call. Trust, that word, how much it covered Gary and the bureaucracy at Vauxhall Cross.

"Tom, this whole thing is getting way out of hand. Our people and the Greeks are working overtime at the moment to try to pinpoint the source of the actions happening down there. We are no closer to an answer than anyone else and the last thing we want is the yanks to get in on the act thinking they are Knights on their white chargers. That would just turn this all into one big shit fight."

"Well I have a lead for you Gary. When I was at the wharf getting my arse nearly burnt off one of the culprits there gave the name of his boss."

"Who is it Tom, we can get straight on to it then?" Gary's excitement was breaking out.

"Ashid!" Tom replied listening hard to the response it got. There was a flutter of breathing irregularities before Gary answered.

"You're bullshitting me Tom surely. Ashid is one of our closest allies in the new Government in Iraq."

"Well Gary what about the London show after I had been seen by the same man. Then the explosive end to young Geordie, followed by the office bang and now the two ex Engineers that have been wasted away here. It doesn't make sense.

At first, yes, I could understand Ashid having the shits with me for what he thought I had done but it's just too co-incidental theses last few killings. I think we need to really have a good look at him Gary."

"I understand your concerns Tom but believe me Ashid is solid and one of ours in Iraq. The last thing I want to do is upset that pratt Aspalson by making false accusations. He's too close to Ashid at the moment.

I have put eyes on in Nassau but there seems nothing untoward coming out of there at the moment. The same is the case with Melbourne. The company Welsh has got is looking extremely squeaky clean in every aspect."

"That in itself is questionable Gary. I am going to leave here in the next couple of days and make my way to the Bahamas and check it out myself. Any chance you can get DNA through our friends here in Athens for the two Caucasian bodies they had from the wharf to verify who's who.

Oh by the way Gary, one of the guys I took out had that tattoo on his right wrist."

"Interesting Tom seems we have some kind of link of sorts. The other stuff is already underway but don't hold your breath, the Greeks are slow at the present, a little inundated you may say, with that stuff and with all the shit that has happened they have put all their resources on border security and checks of non locals and their movements. NATO bases are under full alert and protests are building at their very existence within the country.

I am surprised you haven't been interviewed yet Tom."

"Haven't seen or been approached by anybody as yet. I will make my move as I said in the coming days."

"Ok mate but for Christ's sake leave the damn mobile alight so we can track you." Gary sounded off in a pleading voice as Tom pressed the disconnect button again stripping down the phone. Trust had to be earned he knew and with what was happening he trusted no one, except Vicki of course.

CHAPTER 19

Wednesday 7 March 2007

Tom waited a further couple of days in the hope that the authorities in Greece would have eased up on their searches of foreign nationals but they had increased their presence around the place rather than decreased it.

Troops had been placed at all the main ports and airports carrying machine pistols, looking decidedly serious about things. This was really not the time to be trying to leave the country but Tom had no other option. With what had already happened it was obvious to him that the others would be on their guard now thinking that he was after them and eliminating them as he went.

Car hire here wasn't the easiest thing to do at the present. There were so many questions to be answered now when filling in the forms. The Government had issued more forms to all companies to check all movements in and out of Greece of anyone even their own. It took Tom a couple of hours to get clearance for the hire he had requested so he was relieved as hell when he finally got into a small Citroen hatch back and drove away from the car hire offices.

Sometimes people wanted to know too much which caused Tom to have to think of names of family members he had never met and worse still that did not even exist with the name he was using travelling under.

The journey out of Athens was not the clearest of paths he was hoping for as at nearly very intersection there were armed police with troops checking all papers before they let you pass. Instead of taking just an hour to get to the Corinth Canal it took Tom close to four hours.

Stopping at the Canal to grab a bite to eat, with plenty of coffee for his caffeine fix, he stretched his legs to get a glimpse of the famous cut through the rocks. To his delight as he stopped in the middle of the bridge and looked down, there below him was one of those big cruise ships slowly making its way through the Canal. How he wished he was on board that cruise ship having not a care in the world.

The Corinth Canal connects the Gulf of Corinth with the Saronic Gulf in the Aegean Sea cutting through the narrow Isthmus of Corinth separating the Peloponnesian peninsular from the Greek mainland. It was dug at sea level therefore needing no locks; it measured 6.4kms long and just 21.4 metres wide. Impassable for most modern ships it is a tourist thing these days and there they were right beneath him, all feet up and enjoying the slow ride through the Canal relaxing with their cocktails all topped up.

Tom's destination was a little more mundane, the port of Patra where he hoped to be able to get on a ferry to Brindisi in Italy. He had tried to get a flight out but they had been delayed so drastically that it was not possible to get one out of the country for at least the next week. This was his easiest route but as he found out there were many others trying the same route as he. It took him another five hours to get through to Patra with roadblocks placed in the most ridiculous of places.

It was dark when Tom eventually arrived in Patra going straight to the port offices to try and book his passage out. He had just missed the ferry leaving that night but was successful in getting booked on the Grimaldi ferry the following day at 1700hrs.

Tom had to kill time now, he had difficulty in getting any accommodation in town so decided to tough it out in the Citroen overnight. It would be uncomfortable but at least he was ready to get out of Greece.

Melbourne that same day.

Tony Welsh had been watching the news reels for the past couple of days depicting the devastation in the Greek capital. He was frustrated by the fact that he could not get hold of his men that were located in Athens but just put it down to mobile coverage as he knew they would be afloat heading to Brindisi in Mark Thorn's, aka Reed's, Yacht.

The phone rang as another news report was sequencing the events in the Greek capital. "Hello!" Welsh said sharply into the mouthpiece.

"Tony, my friend." Came the accented Arabic voice of Ashid. "Have you managed to deal with the matter in Nassau yet?"

"Nassau. I'm just trying getting to grips with the shit we have created in Athens. Who were the three bodies at the wharf, have you any idea?" Welsh was hopefully praying at trying to avoid the thought that they may include his two boys.

"Unfortunately no, I have no idea." Ashid lied directly over the phone keeping a straight face at his end. "I had men there to take out this Warburton fellow which was I believe quite successful. You people did a wonderful job at the office and I was just taking the opportunity in phoning to congratulate you on it. It seems that the actions that have taken place have given us a few more important alliances there in Greece for the future including our hopefully eventual plan to bring about the removal of NATO bases for the Americans and the British."

"Well I haven't heard from my boys since the explosion which is a worry. They should be in Italy by now and on their way to their respective destinations. I'll give them another couple of days before I can do anything in Nassau.

We have our finger on the pulse I assure you which includes the fact we are keeping a close eye on our friend Rheingold."

"Splendid then, I will wish your men God speed, as you say and look forward to hearing from you in the near future."

Ashid hung up and turned to his deputy standing beside him. "Make sure you have all the information for the bank accounts before we commit to our final elimination of the British stool pigeons. Malik."

The young man beside him nodded with a brilliant smile across his face magnified by the brilliant white of his teeth, he knew he was a good hacker knowing full well he could outwit the British men who thought they were Ashid's allies.

Ashid continued with, "You must fly to Nassau and upset the flow of money to Melbourne. There you will need to ensure all supplies held there are placed in containers and shipped out to the UK and Australia as we had arranged. The money in Nassau must then be transferred from their accounts to our own in the Cayman Islands.

I will make sure the men there are dealt with, you will not have any worries about that side of things."

Malik was a computer whiz kid about twenty five who had been educated in the USA at MIT. He was slowly processing a way to bring all the various accounts, that had been set up by Welsh in Australia through his connections in the Cayman Islands, together into the one controlled by his boss Ashid.

Malik nodded with approval and left his employers presence to prepare for his trip to the Bahamas.

For Welsh his worries were the two in Athens. He knew they would have been in touch if anything had gone wrong so with not a thing heard he had doubts of his own leading him to call his cousin to try and get some sense out of it all.

"It's all right Tony. Give the guys a couple of more days before we start to worry. The accounts held out of Athens are all in your control so bring them all home and close the doorway to any prying eyes."

"You're right mate. I'll give them till Monday to touch base then I will have to use the guys in Nassau to do Ashid's dirty work for him. I just hope he was right when he said that kid Warburton has been dealt with at last."

"Looked quite convincing on the TV and we haven't heard anything contrary from anywhere else have we."

"No, London is quiet though Athens have released no names whatsoever. I expect I am worrying for nothing eh? Getting too old for this shit I think."

"Need a holiday Tony. Get all this all out the way and we can take a break and go catch some fish, sun and crumpet."

"Is that all you think about you dirty old sod?"

"Mate you've got to go one day and my way is buried up to the groin in some young chick. Couldn't think of a better way to end such a complex life as mine." Caulfield laughed aloud which irritated Tony's ear.

They farewelled each other with Tony going back to his work shuffling more paperwork around trying to hide trace of his actions through the company. He had just been successful in acquiring yet another Mining company out of the Bowen basin in Queensland and was preparing to dismantle it and sell it off to its competitors in the area as going concerns to boost their own operations. He was good at this little scheme but if any of the employees he had sent to the dole queue ever got hold of him they would be pulling him limb from limb as he sacrificed them in the process.

His next task was to bring all accounts back from Athens and hide them amongst the rest he had spread around the world. This was going to cause him some frustration as Malik was already scrambling to take control of finances in Greece. By the time this day ended he was to have a large headache caused by the frustrations he was encountering. In the end he would give up today and try again tomorrow.

8 March 2007

The ferry had just pulled away from the Patra port area and was sailing on to its destination of Brindisi. Tom had got himself one of the comfy seats up top instead of a cabin after first getting fed and watered in the large cafeteria. He settled himself down to the voyage which would put him into Brindisi at about mid day on the following day. He had made sure he hadn't been followed scrutinizing nearly every Middle Eastern looking person around including the women twice as much as his own kind. He was sure he was alone and relaxed to sleep.

Tom would get a clear run to Rome where he was going to book his flight to the Caribbean.

CHAPTER 20

The Alitalia flight took off on time at 1325 hrs on the Sunday but he was no sooner relaxed and nodding off when it arrived at London Heathrow 2 hrs later. He only had an hour and half stopover here but that seemed like a lifetime as he was constantly on the alert in case someone had flagged him on one of the high level computers they used at GCHQ. His relief was fairly noticeable, if someone had been watching him, when the flight for the next stage of the journey was called when he boarded the Virgin Atlantic plane taking his business class seat hoping to get some shut eye. The route he had chosen would be complicated for the average traveller but for Tom it threw in a few curve balls for anyone trying to locate him on route.

Arriving at JFK Airport made Tom a little nervous. His impressions of the yanks were none too favourable due to his father's experiences with them. He was just thankful to get through immigration. He would have to go in a transit bus as he had his ticket to continue through to the Bahamas.

A bus collected him and others heading through to the Bahamas. They were transported across to the other Side of Queens via the Van Wyck Expressway and the Grand central Parkway to La Guardia Airport where they had about twelve hours wait to kill. Tom remained in the airport complex deciding not to expose himself to any of the authorities in this Country by being flagged leaving the airport complex.

Sleeping in an airport departure lounge is not the most comfortable but for Tom it appeared the safest option for him, anyway it was more comfortable than the Citroen he had recently slept in.

Delta Airlines called his flight the following day Monday at 1045 when he again breathed a sigh of relief as the flight lifted off. He caught a view of the city in all its glory as the plane banked around out of La Guardia heading south towards the Caribbean. New York City was vast living up to its name of the city that never sleeps. The whole place was a buzz of excitement or terror depending what your current emotional status is in this world. Tom could just make out the area where the Twin Towers used to be before the catastrophe in 2001

There was yet another stop on the way at Atlanta but it wasn't long before Tom was flying across the clear blue seas around the Caribbean. It was 1700 hrs when the plane banked around and he caught a glimpse of the colours of the Ocean. The bright blues and varying shades of green that completed this paradisiacal looking island of New Providence.

Landing at Nassau International Airport was as smooth as silk. When alighting from the plane and getting past the customs people with what seemed like the greatest of ease Tom immediately hailed one of the many cabs outside the terminal asking for the Red Carpet Inn on E Bay Street which was opposite the Atlantis resort on Paradise Island.

Tom knew that there was no British Consulate here in The Bahamas, all consular duties were dealt with by an Honorary Consul or through the British consulate in Jamaica. That would at least give him some free space unless Gary Warlock had had someone come over from one of the other Islands in the region to track him down. Trust, that word again rang through Tom's brain, could he trust Gary, he was still sceptical about it all after what had transpired recently on his travels.

The motel he had chosen was nestled in a semi residential area about ten minutes from downtown Nassau as well as ten minutes from the beach and Paradise Island. It is set on about 1½ acres of land, with tropical tranquil gardens throughout and set up as a typical American style motel in its appearance and layout. With 40 rooms in all, Tom was sure he could blend in with other tourists that occupied the other rooms around him. Amenities in the rooms were good so Tom was happy especially when he looked out of his room's window down onto the tropical gardens below.

Time now was for Tom to put his plan in Nassau into action. His first port of call was to try and find the Cosmetic surgeon whose name he had got from Southwaite. That was the priority as he could then start to pin together the faces with the names of the original sinners. Cosmetic surgeons always kept before and after shots, at least the legal ones do.

Again the local white type pages came in pretty handy when it came to finding people here as well as everywhere else in the world.

Rheingold was not a popular name and after a quick search Tom only found the one in the whole district of Nassau and that was in a suburb called Indigo. That was the starting point for tomorrow morning for Tom because for now he needed to rest, recoup from his long ordeal and think.

Offices of Asia-Pac, Nassau.

Early on Tuesday morning in the office of Asia Pac, Nassau located on Woodes Rodgers walk in Festival Place there was stirring amongst the natives. Inside the offices there were two men and one female. The female was just the receptionist who had just received a call from Melbourne putting it through to the main office of Derek Sweetman, aka Chris Saxby, at the rear of the complex.

"Sweetman here." Derek answered the ringing implement with some anxious look upon his face.

"Derek, Tony, is it good time to talk." Welsh was sounding a bit nervous from his seat in Melbourne. With no complicated telephone systems in place here there was a need for being extra cautious.

"You're Ok, Tony. What's the problem?"

"Look Derek we have had no response from either Peter or Mark in Greece since the closure of the office the other day. All hell has broken loose there as you can imagine since last week which is what we all expected. I am getting a bit concerned that the boys have been hijacked either by the authorities or that Warburton character." Tony was being talkative more so than he usually was.

"Hold on a bit, Tony let me switch on the speaker, I have Colin here with me so you can speak to both." Derek leant forward touched the speaker button then replaced the receiver on its cradle. "Carry on Tony."

"Messages out of Athens are mixed but it is possible that the boat that was blown up at the wharf could have been Mark's. I have no firm evidence yet but being I haven't heard from either of them I am assuming the worst.

Our friend from Iraq wants us to tie up loose ends in Nassau, I think you know what that entails. Our friend Rheingold has to be removed from our contacts list unfortunately with no further contact to him."

Both Derek and Colin looked at each other knowing exactly what the statement meant. They were to eliminate Rheingold and make sure there was nothing to implicate the company from his side.

"I understand, Tony. When does this need to be completed by?"

"ASAP, lads. Our friend is watching and if we do not complete the task he will using his resources."

More concerned looks between the two lads in the Bahamas office. What does Ashid think he's doing pushing the buttons on what was their operation? He was supposed to be the silent partner and sit tight till he needed something from them not dish out the orders. Seems like the leadership of their little group was about to change with neither of these two boys liking that very much.

"OK, Tony, consider it done. We will get straight onto it."

"Take care lads and give me a bell if you encounter any problems or when the jobs done, bye for now." And with that Tony hung up his end leaving the two lads still staring dumbstruck at each other.

"What's going on here Derek?"

"Haven't got a clue mate but I know Ashid is supposed to be out of sight and out of mind. Seems he has grandeurs of power. I just hope he doesn't want to run the whole show because if it wasn't for us he would have nothing anywhere. Bloody rag head wants his head pulling in."

"We'll have to do this job carefully because of the security in Rheingold's community area. I'll get some gear ready and we can get it out of the way by tonight.

Bye the way there is a shipment coming in from Freeport this afternoon and we have to be there to off load it and put in the warehouse. About 1600 I think they will be docking."

"No sweat. We will be able to get that done before we go and see the doc.

This shipment coming in, is it the weapons or the explosive gear first?"

"Explosives first, the rest will follow next week I believe. I understand they have taken consignment of that stuff on the mainland and are trying to ship it out of Fort Lauderdale under the US Federal noses. Hope they don't get caught else they could be spending their days in Guantanamo."

Both turned away from each other going their separate ways. Derek sat at his desk holding his head with an impending headache coming while Colin moved out to the warehouse out back to ensure he had enough room for the consignment that was coming in.

While this was going on Tom, who did not have a clue where the office was for Asia Pac at this point had unknowingly driven past the office area where it was in a beat up old Chevy, a relic from the States. He had turned west towards the Orange Hill area. The receptionist at the motel had got him a good deal for the car, Tom just thought he could have got a more inconspicuous one if he had done it himself. This bloody great thing was as big as a tank.

Driving down past the gated community of Indigo, where Tom could see there were about 20 or so houses within, he looked at the entrance from both angles driving back around after stopping for coffee then coming back on himself. Nothing seemed untoward so he mustered his courage to ring the entrance bell for Rheingold and try and get into see him.

Pulling into the gate area and alongside the bell push he had to swing himself across the front seats of the left hand drive vehicle to get to the bell. Pushing the number he had got from the local telephone directory he waited till someone answered. It didn't take too long before a female voice came over the speaker.

"Hello, what can I do for you?" a distinctive American drawl was heard through the speaker.

"Hi there. My name is Stevens and I was given Dr Rheingold's name in the hope of getting some repairs done." Tom hoped he would be able to fool the person on the line.

"Who was it who recommended you to us?" she asked.

"Guy I knew in Europe by the name of Southwaite." Tom gave that name knowing full well any inquiries wouldn't produce much unless the guy had contacts through the Ouija board.

"Just a moment. Please." The speaker went off and there were a few moments where Tom was beginning to think he had trod on the wrong notes for this guy. It seemed like a lifetime but just a moment later the speaker sparked up again but this time there was a man's voice there, American with a touch of a Yiddish accent to it.

"How is moy friend Mark?" came a question which caught Tom straight off as a trap to catch him out.

"Peter Southwaite Dr, Mark was his partner at the office."

"Sorry moy boy so it is. Come on in eh." He finished as Tom heard the buzzer pressed and then the gates began to open up. "Right at de end of the road on the right."

"Thank you." Tom just managed to get out before the speaker died in the arse and he shuffled back across the seat to the driver's side accelerating into the community complex. As he drove down the road slowly Tom took a mental note of all he saw. How close the nearest neighbour was and any possible escape routes if he became compromised.

As Tom pulled up at the front of the two storey house which was situated at the highest point of the area with a neighbour just across from the front porch way about 150 meters a short bespectacled elderly man came out the front door. He would have been about 150 cm tall but unbelievably thin in comparison to other men his height. A broad smile lit up his face. The house with its white balustrades stood in Grand splendour and showed no signs of any weathering considering it were so near the sea.

Tom got out of the vehicle stretching his legs then walked up onto the porch where he held out his hand to shake the man's in front of him. They exchanged handshakes, then looks and the Dr led Tom in through the front door to the lounge area which overlooked the swimming pool surrounded by palm trees that separated it from the beach about twenty meters away.

"How is my friend Peter?" Asked the old man as he plonked himself down on the lounge. "Please, have a seat."

"Peter is taking a short break at the moment. I believe he's on the move out of Greece shortly." Tom said hoping that nothing had been heard from where he had come from.

"Well, well, that is good. Now what can I do for you young man?" as he finished an old lady sauntered into the lounge with what looked like a tray of coffee and cakes. "My wife Sharon, Mr Stevens." The old lady nodded at Tom and placed the tray between them before leaving the way she had entered leaving the two of them to it. "Please, Mr Stevens help yourself." The Dr said waving his hand across the tray.

Tom acknowledged his invite and proceeded to fill a cup with the strong mix of coffee adding some cream to it. He didn't take any cake as he was feeling a tad full from the breakfast he had had back at the motel.

"Dr my main aim is to change my appearance a touch to remove obvious recognition points such as nose and cheek form."

"Not in any trouble are you?" the Dr laughed. "Don't want to get into strife at this point of my life do I?"

"Unfortunately Doc I was blamed for something that I have since been cleared of but I am fed up with the implications every time I go about my neighbourhood. Thought perhaps a change of some of the looks I have would do the trick and people might then accept me more." Tom suddenly thought to himself that that sounded complete and utter bullshit and quite rightly so as the Dr looked at him and shook his head.

"What do you really want moy boy?"

"OK Dr no fooling you I can see. The reason I am here is to trace a man who set me up for a murder charge. That is out of the window now but it is causing some bad feelings around the place and for me to end it I need to bring the man home to face the music. That's the truth of it."

"And what is the name of this fellow?"

"Originally Peter Caulfield, then I believe he was known as John Browning"

"Name doesn't ring any bells, I'm afraid."

Tom pulled out from his jacket pocket pictures he had of the men in question. He lifted the one on Caulfield. "This is the man as I knew him." Instantly Tom could see there was recognition there from the Doctors eyes.

"Sorry no, I do not recognise him at all." The Dr lied starting to flush up a touch.

"Come on Dr, I can see you recognise him, now don't let's have any crap eh."

"Just a moment let me get my other spectacles and then I will have another look." The old man raised himself up from the lounge walking over to the opposite door from where the kitchen was. Tom followed with his eyes but as soon as the man went through the door Tom got up going directly to the door placing his ear as close as he could to it.

He heard the man pick up what sounded like a telephone and heard the familiar beeps you get from the touch pad on it. Tom threw the door open and pounced at the Dr tearing the phone from his grasp slamming it down onto the cradle. He leant over and ripped the cord from the wall then spun around and faced the man who now was standing open mouthed and ashen faced.

"No good calling your friends Doc. I want answers and you are going to give them to me now." It was then that Tom noticed where he had come into. The whole room was white floor to ceiling with white tiles across the floor and in the centre stood a table, an operating style table with all the instruments you may need for most surgery just sitting there under a light cover.

As Tom went to grab the old man the Doc turned sharply making a grab for one of the instruments on the table. He missed his footing stumbling over. Tom leant down extending his hand to lift him up.

"Look no one needs to get hurt here Doc. I just want the name and whereabouts of the man who set me up and you must have a photograph of your finished work. Isn't that what you guys do?"

"Confidentiality, you know the score."

"But you were willing to phone your friends and tell them I was here weren't you?"

"I was phoning the Police young man."

"Cut the crap Doc and let's sort this out sensibly eh?" Tom said taking hold of the Doc's shoulders then placing him into a chair in the corner by a desk that held a computer, printer and small filing trays.

Tom went back to the door closing it, wedging a chair under the handle making sure it couldn't be opened with any ease from the other side. Returning to the red faced little Jew he bent down taking all the old man's private space and said "Did you know that an Arab is in league with these men?"

"Impossible, they are British and have served in Iraq fighting the Iraqis. There is no way they would work with them after their experiences. They are my friends."

"They are also in league with one of the Iraqis and I need to get to the bottom of it very quickly. There have already been too many deaths from these men as it is."

"I cannot believe what you are saying. These men are reputable business men."

"They certainly have you fooled that's for sure. The Arab I told you about is going by the name of Jamal Ashid and I think he is linked to some terrorist group called I.I.G. now please help me then you and your wife can go your own way and be left alone."

"I am sorry young man but I have no recollection of those Arab or terrorist names whatsoever. Now who do you work for?" The old man kept his cool rather well while just sitting now watching Tom as he went through what was on the desk in front of him. "I don't think you will find anything of interest there." He continued.

"I am with British Intelligence trying to piece together a major crime committed some time ago." Tom was reluctant to have to tell someone he was intelligence but he saw no other option at the moment. He liked this little fellow feeling that he had also been dealt a dud hand in the whole episode.

Midday arrived and apart from a few knocks at the door from Sharon to see if her husband wanted anything there was nothing else, no phone calls or callers. Sharon was easily fended off by her husband who just said he was busy and would be out shortly. However, it was another two hours before there was any movement.

Tom assembled his mobile yet again to get hold of Gary. He had come to a dead end with the Doc but felt confident enough to let Gary have the name and see what comes out of it.

"Gary, I have a Dr Rheingold here who was the surgeon for the group after their disappearance from Iraq. Can you give me any information on him, he is being rather stubborn at present but if we can shake the skeletons from his cupboard perhaps he will see how serious we really are."

"Leave it with me Tom, I'll see what I can do. I wish you had told me about him before you left for Nassau, I could have it all laid out by now. Still building trust issues eh Tom?"

"You got that right, sorry Gary, it will take time for me to open up to people you have to understand that after what I've been through."

"It's ok Tom I do understand. I'll get back to you soon." Gary ended the conversation and set about his own task of finding out all he could on Dr Rheingold.

The Doc just sat hoping in his mind that not too much would be uncovered on his chequered past life. Meanwhile Tom tried his best to get the Doc to co-operate with him but each time he felt he was banging his head against the wall.

It was three o'clock when Gary called Tom back, at which point on answering Tom told him he was putting the call on speaker.

"Well Doctor Aaron Rheingold has had some past that someone has tried to cover up a bit over the years. He graduated in Israel at twenty two in 1967 as Benjamin Neeve and immigrated to the US where he worked in the Walter Reed Military Hospital for 20 years before he set up a private practice in Fort Lauderdale Miami.

Those twenty years are a bit sketchy because of our cousins cautiousness, naturally, but they have told me he did some excellent work in repairing some of the damaged personnel who were returned from various war zones.

His practice in Miami went on for about eleven years till it was unearthed that he was involved with some of the Mafia bosses, cosmetically that is, from up the East coast. He was arrested by the FBI and charged but turned State's evidence, opening his files to the Feds which saw many of his old clients being sent to the penitentiary for rather extended periods. He was put into witness protection, set up in The Bahamas and was given the identity you have now. He was also told not to continue to practice in his past profession.

Seems the Doc has broken all the rules Tom. I'll leave it with you mate and will eagerly await your call."

"Just a moment Gary, tell this old guy who the men we are looking for are working for."

"Well if he'll listen I can only say that the men who he has treated as patients are considered enemy combatants of both the British and United States Governments. What he needs to remember is that he was instructed not to continue to practice any cosmetic surgery and therefore he has violated his protection conditions by so doing. Therefore, if he treasures his safety he needs to come clean with you and open up or you may well let the Feds know in the US that he has crossed their line leaving him on the edge of being hunted by the men he once betrayed. I'll text you the number of a pal of mine in the FBI who would be keen to save the US a few dollars by cutting the doctor off the payroll."

"Thanks Gary, I'll get back to you."

Tom left the phone assembled this time; trust was slowly building for him with Gary. The Doc was now leaning forward with his head buried in his hands. He started to hum words as if in prayer but Tom just tapped him on the shoulder just as his phone beeped to let him know he'd received a text message.

"Well Doc seems you have been a naughty boy. Now either you come clean with me or I am going to phone this number which means your life starts to fall apart. Your choice doc." Tom waited but still the Doc sat murmuring to himself weighing up his options. Tom took hold of the mobile and started to dial the number he had received. "Last chance Doc." He said as he went to press the send button.

"Stop. Stop. Please my wife, our lives, please give me a chance here, please." The pleading went on as Tom cut off the number he had dialled and waited patiently for the doc to come clean.

"Doc, look I haven't much time. Everywhere I have been these last few months I have had to deal with people trying to blow me up or the ones I have spoken with so I don't think we have as much time as you think.

I am not concerned as to what you have been doing since your arrival here providing you help me. I will do the best I can to make sure you are safe again."

"OK. OK. Let me get to the computer." The Doc moved closer to the desk. Tom watched closely hoping that the old fool didn't try and delete everything before he could stop him but he was soon convinced the Doc was going to help him so as to stop his own live falling apart.

As the Doc brought up list after list of patients he had treated in this new life he turned to Tom and asked. "What of these men, will they try to eliminate me once I betray them?"

"I can't promise anything Doc but what I will say is I will do my best to get you away from here till the men are removed and back in our custody. That's all I can promise you."

"Then young man I trust this will suffice your requests." He pressed a key and up flowed pictures of six men, they were before and after shots but one of the men had only a before shot. Tom recognised his shot from the file on Asia Pac, that of Tony Welsh. He scanned the other five, two he recognised as the two in Athens. He knew they were no longer current in this world. The other three were interesting though and the one he was sure he would not forget was the one under the name of John Scholfield, which was the one he knew as Peter Caulfield. The before shot of the man made him shudder somewhat.

Tom had everything he wanted now getting the Doc to print up the three men who were still alive, both the before and after shots. His next move was to try and get the Doc and his wife to some kind of safe house before he removed the two men from Asia Pac in Nassau. Inside his gut he felt some kind of joy and satisfaction at getting closer to the man who had set him up, the one that had been the one that killed Mahmoud, Caulfield.

The time was now closing near five o'clock when Tom removed the chair allowing the Doc to let his wife know the full story about what had happened and what was going to eventuate from here. She was calmer than her husband was going directly to the kitchen boiling up some more coffee and with cakes on the tray alongside returned to the room for them all to enjoy, something like a last supper.

CHAPTER 21

Back at the dock near the Asia Pac offices at around 1615 hrs a cruising Yacht about thirty foot long had pulled into place alongside the jetty and was met by Sweetman and Phorbes. Hurried exchanges of words between the men on the boat and those on the shore before both groups of men joined forces in unloading boxes of explosives from the Yacht. The boxes were taken to the warehouse behind the offices of Asia Pac and stored there under the listing of tools.

Within half an hour the consignment was completely unloaded with the yacht preparing itself to leave the docks and head back out to sea.

"OK Man, we'll catch up den on the next shipment. Next week then man." The captain waved to the two men on the shore as he put his motor into reverse to remove the tautness in the ropes holding him to the jetty.

"No worries, safe trip back, till next week then." Sweetman said as he undid the rope and threw it to the man on the aft of the yacht.

"Time to finish our other job then Derek." Colin Phorbes turned and headed back to the offices where they had their weapons secretly stored inside Derek's safe.

"Better get a move on then eh?" Derek said striding off after his pal. In the office they prepared for their last job of the day still wondering how they would finish up that evening. Derek told Colin to get some incendiary devices from the store to use so they could get the house burnt to the ground leaving nothing for the authorities to be able to trace. A fire with a couple of oldies in it was sometimes easier to explain these days. That done Derek picked up the phone and dialled the Doc.

"Hey Mrs Rheingold, how are you? Derek Sweetman here, look we need to speak to the Doc rather urgently, is he available this evening if we call around now, can be there in fifteen minutes?"

Sharon told Derek to hold the line as she held the receiver to her shoulder while whispering to Tom and the Doc what had been said by Derek. Tom looked at her whispering she should try and put them off till the next day but when she went back on the phone Derek brushed it aside and told her it was really urgent and they would be there shortly.

Tom immediately swore under his breath telling both the oldies that they should get whatever they could together quickly so they could then leave. Ten minutes later they were about ready to get into the Chevy when the buzzer went letting them know that the two men had already arrived at the gate.

Tom had no way of getting the two oldies out as they would have to go the same way as Sweetman and Phorbes were now sitting.

The buzzer went again causing the three of them to quickly look at each other, the two older ones were now looking decidedly scared.

"Look Doc, get back inside with Sharon and go to your surgery room." Tom looked around at what he could use as weapons but it was so spic and span around this house it was unbelievable. Going in through the front door he opened all the doors, surveyed the rooms he looked in and coming up blank. Nothing of any use he thought to himself, closing all the doors he bolted the front door and headed to the surgery room.

"Have you got a tool kit, especially a large hammer Doc?" Tom asked as he came into the surgery shutting the door behind him.

"Yes, I need to go into the garage out the side here though." Doc indicated to a large French window that was to the side of the room. Tom nodded at him and the Doc shot off out the doors disappearing around the rear of the house. He was only gone a couple of minutes, meanwhile the buzzer was going berserk. On his return the Doc was carrying a toolbox in his arms and was puffing like an old horse. Tom instantly relieved him of his burden and told them both to sit down and try to stay calm.

"Try to relax Doc." Tom said above the noise of the buzzer which must by now be infuriating the boys at the gate. Their patience must be lagging by now which Tom hoped would give him the advantage to prepare. The biggest concern he had was if someone was going in or out of the complex they might let the two men in.

Looking around the room he saw two oxygen bottles sitting near the door. They were an 'F' size about a meter in height with a screwed cover at the top to protect the valve mechanism. Tom pulled both over to the side of the room directly opposite the door. With both bottles feeling full he lifted one of them up onto the bench cupboard that split the room in the middle. The bench was conveniently pointing out from the wall opposite the door towards the door about two metres in length.

Turning the valve covers he removed both covers from their respective bottles. He then gathered sheets, towels and other linen he could find and propped the sides of the bottle he had placed on the bench. Searching into the toolbox he came up trumps with what looked like a lump hammer, a small square headed heavy, short handled hammer. This he placed by the valve at the ready. He just hoped there was enough force inside the bottle to allow it to become a missile.

Both the Doc and his wife looked at what Tom was doing with question marks clearly in their eyes. What was this young man up to?

"OK Doc. Is there any way you can get to the beach then out along past this complex?" Tom asked as they both clutched each other's hands.

"The beach yes, but we cannot go either side as it is private both sides. There are fences restricting access." The Doc answered.

"OK then. Take Sharon to the Beach and find somewhere to hide down there till I come and get you. Don't come out till you hear from me, is that clear?"

Both the Doc and Sharon got out of their chairs nodding at Tom. Sharon was now starting to shake as the Doc led her out the French windows and off around the back of the house towards the beach.

Meanwhile both men at the gate had finally given up on waiting and had buzzed another member of the community asking to be let in. After just a few awkward questions one of the other residents eventually opened the gate as they were being disturbed by the two constantly buzzing.

Tom heard the vehicle pull up outside the house. He couldn't see their arrival as the front of the house was off to the right of the room he was in and he had all the doors shut through the house to slow them down. There was a hurried banging on the door and a couple of yells as the two men felt they were being shunned by their old friend.

Suddenly Tom heard the splintering of wood as the front door imploded by the force of Sweetman's shoulder. Tom listened at the door but could not hear a lot of what was going on in the front of the house. He opened the door slightly giving him the view of the lounge where he was first introduced to the Rheingolds. He saw little but heard the men out in the kitchen area.

"Rheingold, hello anyone home."

"Bastards must have known what we were up to." Came another voice from the kitchen.

"Fuck em, Col, go into the surgery and let off one of those canisters. We need to destroy all evidence he has on that damn computer or any records in the office. If they are anywhere here we will get them. Don't bother with upstairs as when we fire this joint up they will be the dummies on the top of the pyre."

Tom heard footsteps approaching and quickly shut the door. Going over to where he had placed the gas bottle on the cupboard he grabbed the hammer and waited. He had read somewhere that breaking off the valve of these types of bottles turned the bloody thing into a missile. He had never seen it done but hoped that it did as they said for it was all he had to use.

The door handle twisted slowly as if the person on the other side was expecting someone to be on the other side. As it turned to its fullest the door started to slowly open, a hand appeared holding what looked like a can of beans but was in fact an incendiary canister. Tom recognised it from his days in Iraq as an M14 TH3 with its colours of light red with black markings. It had a sheet metal body, filled with 26 ounces of thermate {TH3} mixture. The total weight was around 32 ounces. When ignited a portion of the thermate mixture is converted to molten iron, which burns at 4,000 degrees Fahrenheit. The grenade burns for 40 seconds and can burn through a ½-inch homogeneous steel plate. It produces its own oxygen and will even burn under water. This was serious gear they were about to use Tom knew. He looked at the hand closely as the door opened farther; the safety pin was still in place and had not been pulled.

Tom was not willing to fry without a fight as he lifted the hammer as high as he could, then bringing it down with all the force he could put behind it onto the valve mechanism of the bottle.

By this time the door had opened enough for Phorbes to see into the room. It was at this point that he caught sight of Tom but before he could do anything, even call out there was a loud bang as the hammer hit the valve unit and fractured it completely off. This was followed by a quick whoosh which Phorbes never got a chance to hear as instantly the force of the gas releasing from the valve end against the wall turned the bottle into the missile that Tom had hoped for. It had already hit Phorbes in the stomach propelling him directly across the lounge room plummeting him into the wall at the far end before Tom could get the second bottle up and ready. There was a great cloud of red as Phorbe's stomach exploded under the force of the pressure of the bottle against the wall. The bottle buried itself into the wall by about half its length before it ran out of propellant gas. Phorbes never knew what had hit him yet alone been able to scream out anything in either pain or warning.

The noise that had been let out by the eventual crash into the far wall of the lounge brought Sweetman rapidly into the room where he saw the carnage of his pal spreadeagled against the wall. He started firing his hand gun in the direction of the surgery.

Tom dropped behind the cupboard avoiding any ricochet from the rounds as they hit various elements within the room. Tom waited only a couple of seconds then stood quickly repeating what he had done with the first bottle. It too took off sending Sweetman ducking for cover as it swept across the lounge and barrelled into the wall directly into the other bottle which then sent it off course over to one side of the room where it hit the wall and again buried itself like the first into the wall. This gave Tom the chance he needed to get out the French windows and he took off towards them.

Behind him Sweetman had recovered himself removing the pin from a grenade he held in his hand. He lobbed it into the room through the open door while at the same time retreating back to the kitchen area.

There was an almighty explosion behind him at the same time as Tom hit the dirt outside the French windows. Glass and debris rained down on him followed by flames quickly behind. It took all Tom's energy to roll and continue to roll till he couldn't feel the heat that had chased after him.

Back in the kitchen Sweetman pulled another canister from his pocket and while exiting the house lobbed it behind him running towards his car. Another explosion shook the air leaving the house with flames front and rear. The flames caught on the rubber gas pipes in the kitchen that led to the cooker which started yet another explosion followed by a roar of flames billowing upward to the second floor. The surgery was burning rapidly with all the cleaning fluids that were stored there it just fed the flames created by the canister, the whole room was engulfed licking up into the upstairs rooms.

Tom recovered and stood up turning around to see what was happening behind him. As he did so he heard the screeching wheels of Sweetman's car take off from the front. Standing there he saw the car, a large black suburban come into view with the driver pointing his handgun towards Tom which he started to let rip. Tom dived for cover over a small edge which was the border area of the swimming pool. Unable to stop the motion he had created for himself he plunged into the deep end of the pool going straight under the water. A couple of rounds hit the water behind him but then there was nothing just the glow of the fire that was now engulfing the whole house.

Tom got to the side of the pool and lifted himself slowly out to just see the arse end of the suburban disappear towards the exit gate. He sat on the side of the pool surveying the damage making sure he had not been hit by any of the rounds. Then he realized the printouts he had got the Doc to do for him were in his pocket, slowly pulling them out they were already dripping with water and as he opened them the ink was starting to run. Ruined, now he has nothing to help him look for Caulfield. The two faces he now had in his mind, as he had written one of the men off in the house were now sketchy. Was the other man there Caulfield he was unsure, he was about the same build?

Tom went down towards the beach as dozens of the residents came racing out from their homes to look at what was happening. As he got down to the beach his clothes were becoming uncomfortable and his shoes were starting to squelch as he walked.

Tom called out. "Doc, it's Ok you can come out now." There was no response so he yelled again hoping that the Doc recognized his voice.

Just off to the right of him were some upturned rowing boats lying in the sand. As he was about to call again there was a movement when one of the boats lifted on one side and out from under it came two scared looking faces. They peered out at Tom before they stared off to one side looking at the billowing smoke and the flames that had once been their beautiful home.

Tom collected the both of them up quickly, then slowly walked them back towards the house where he hoped the Chevy was still there untouched by the flames. The crowds had gathered by the time they turned around the front of the house. Some of the people were beginning to stare and point especially at Tom in his bedraggled look. Unfazed Tom got calmly into the Chevy, waited for the Doc and Sharon to get on board before he started it up, steering them all away from the burning mess behind them, out of the main gate and down towards the motel where Tom was staying. All the way back Tom surveyed the area around him ensuring that he had no eyes on him.

Giving the car back to its owner he took Aaron and Sharon to his room at the hotel, all the time not one word was spoken between the three of them till they got to the security of the room. Both Aaron and Sharon were still shaking when they entered the room. Tom secured the door as they entered.

Going to the shower Tom refreshed himself removing his wet clothes and getting on some dry ones. In his pocket was his two mobiles, both had had a dunking. He got both out and binned his prepaid one after removing the sim card. Taking hold of the mobile from Gary he stripped it and laid the parts out on a dry towel.

On re-entering the room he found both his guests still sitting in the same position unmoved and still shaking.

"It's Ok. Relax, as soon as I can get hold of my boss I will get you off the island and to safety." Tom sounded convincing but the two shaking elders were still unmoved, unpersuaded.

Tom's concern now was to get these two people away from any harm as soon as possible. It was all too obvious that their previous so called patients and friends had now become their adversaries.

"Why oh why are they trying to kill us?" Aaron asked Tom with tears appearing in his eyes. "Didn't I do enough for them when they came to me?"

"You probably have served your purpose and they want to tie up any loose ends. That's how these people work in this crazy world." Tom replied as he went over and put the kettle on. If in doubt he thought make a cup of tea or coffee, which might calm them down some.

The night would be altogether quite crowded as Tom offered up his bed for the two oldies seeking his own rest on the couch which was just a tad smaller than his height. The night went off without any trouble but Tom awoke with the stiffest of backs.

CHAPTER 22

Next morning a quick check of the mobile showed it was still somewhat damp from its swimming experience the day before. Tom wasn't going to risk blowing the guts out of it so chose to leave it on the window sill in the direct sunlight in the hope it would dry enough for him to use it again.

A trip to the shopping mall saw him purchase yet another prepaid mobile in which he put his sim card in. He wanted to keep the number somehow because he used this one especially for calling Vicki when he needed to. A quick shop in the supermarket getting some food which was a welcomed sight for the two back at the room when he returned.

"What is going to happen now?" asked Aaron positively calmer than the previous night.

"As soon as I can use my mobile over there." Tom pointed to the sunbaking model on the sill. "I'll be able to arrange for you two to get away from here. I won't leave you here too long alone, believe me."

"Thank you young man." Aaron said wiping his hand across his forehead.

"I will go and see if I can get another vehicle to use, after all the last one really stood out like dogs balls. Elvis must have been in town with that one I think." This brought a smile on the faces of his guests. "Just don't use the room phone or open the curtains. When I return I will knock three times and wait then knock twice more, so don't answer the door till then. I should only be about ten to fifteen minutes." With that Tom looked first out through the break in the curtains to check the area below then went to the door cracked it open peered out and disappeared out of it closing it firmly behind him.

Where he had hired the car the previous day was about a five minute walk and all the time Tom looked around checking those in the near vicinity. At the car hire counter the guy behind the counter smiled from ear to ear as Tom came in.

"Hey mon how goes it then? Need another trendy car today eh boss?" he rattled off in that familiar West Indian Rastafarian accent which Tom had come to like.

"Yes if I can but not one that stands out too much eh." Tom looked around the yard behind him to see if there were any standard ones there. All he could see were yank tanks decorated in all colours of the rainbow. Well the name above the door did say 'Stand Out Cars' which really summed it all up.

"Well mon I ave a small one out the back, it's mine own personal transport my man but I am sure you will be ok to use it. Oh bye the way mon there was someone in earlier asking if I knew who had the car you had yesterday."

"What did he look like?" Asked Tom showing some unwanted concern.

"White honkey type. Know wot I mean mon. Business geek type. Told him I's not the only one wiv these cars on the Island. Friend of yours or not I am confidential mon."

"Thanks for that. There are some unwanted friends of mine here who I just do not want to see this trip if I can manage it."

"No probs. Come out back and see what I ave got for you."

As Tom followed the local man out through the back door he was amazed at the car that was on offer. A mini Moke stood there, bright orange and no doors as they were.

"Got anything that doesn't enable me to be spotted from the moon." Tom laughed.

"I have got one other, follow me." And they strolled over to a shed just to the rear of the yard. On opening the door an old 1970s Morris 1100 which looked like a patchwork quilt with its rust spots all over.

"Only other one I have mon. Goes like a dream though, don't let the paintwork fool you."

Tom looked at the guy, laughed and said "That will do just fine." He slapped the guy on the shoulder and handed him his credit card then went around to the driver's door where he just turned the key getting the engine to roar straight into life. Surprised as he was he felt the guy really looked after the motors of his little business well.

Tom pulled the Morris out of the shed and steered it around to the front of the shop where he met his new friend took hold of the paperwork and return of his card. Still laughing at each other Tom left the shop driving the car around to the nearest stairwell closest to his room and parked it up.

Up at the door he tapped three times, waited then tapped another two times at which point the door opened slowly and Aaron's head appeared in the gap.

While Tom had been arranging his new vehicle, just up the road at Asia Pac the young Malik had called into the office to speak to Sweetman who fortunately was not around. The receptionist had no clue as to when he would be back or where he was at the present time. She also did not know where the other partner was located either; she had tried to phone them but had got no response from their mobiles.

Malik had a letter, addressed from Melbourne Head Office asking that he be given all help in the process of auditing the business in Nassau, which he handed to the girl who then led Malik to the rear and opened up all the offices he needed to be able to check inside.

Once in to Sweetman's office Malik set about typing up the consignment requests for the two containers that were to be transported to London and Sydney. After completing all the necessary paperwork including the customs export forms he handed the completed paperwork to the receptionist so she could arrange the containers to be loaded. No questions were asked even though it would mean the warehouse would be empty after this consignment, oh well she thought they were probably upping the business and pushing more product out.

After Malik had done what he needed for the containers he headed back to Sweetman's office and plugged a USB stick into the computer starting to open up the financial files that were supposed to have been secretly hidden away from all prying eyes except of course for Sweetman and Phorbes. This young man was good at what he did because within the hour he had unencrypted all he needed to be able to download all the financial information he needed for Ashid.

At about 1400 hrs Tom excused himself again leaving Aaron and his wife alone in the room telling them he was just popping out for an hour or two. Not informing them he was about to go to Asia Pac to see what was happening there after yesterdays debacle.

By the time Tom had pulled up in front of Asia Pac it was near three. There seemed to be a mass of people working frantically out back to load two 40 foot containers that had been placed between the offices and the warehouse area. There were forklifts going to and from and the containers were being filled to their extremities.

Like worker ants milling around their termite mounds, no one got into anyone else's way and the flow of traffic went smoothly as they all set about their work.

Tom entered the offices going directly to the receptionist. "Mr Phorbes please." Tom asked knowing full well that Phorbes had been impaled the day before and wouldn't be about today.

"I'm afraid he is out, sir." The young coloured lass answered with a rather posh English accent.

"How about Mr Sweetman then?" Tom didn't really want to face him at this stage but it was worth a check to see if he was in.

"No sir I'm afraid Mr. Sweetman is also unavailable."

"Anyone else who can help me lovely." Tom asked winking at the young girl which brought the biggest of smiles to her face.

"There is a Mr Malik in from Melbourne but he is only auditing here at the moment."

"Perhaps I could just have a word with him." Tom searched his brain for the name but came up empty. Malik didn't ring any bells but hell worth a try to get some information from.

The girl tried buzzing unsuccessfully to the offices giving up in the end and excusing herself to go and look for Mr Malik. She was gone just a few minutes then returned to say he could not help Tom.

Knowing there was a door to the rear of the offices that led to the warehouse Tom politely left and strolled around to the rear of the block. Here he saw all the commotion up close as forklifts and people jostled for position around the containers. All he could see were boxes marked tools or equipment. It didn't enter his mind what they might have been hiding. The containers were near to being full now and a quick glance into the warehouse showed Tom that the whole place was near to empty. He wondered if they were moving it all out and abandoning the place after the cock up of yesterday. Still he wasn't interested in what the containers held at the present more interested in this Malik fellow in the offices.

He slowly opened the rear door that led into the office area and pushed it open. No one was around here just a couple of doors open one to his left and the other to his right. He slowly crept down the passage way until he got to the nearest door which was the one on the left. He leant forward slowly craning his head around the door jamb. There was a desk on the far side to the door with a computer sitting upon it but no one was inside. He entered the room scanning around the walls. There were pictures from fishing trips, golfing days and a couple of pictures of the two men he had come to grips with yesterday.

There was nothing else, no other pictures that could be the one important one he wanted that had got damaged yesterday, Caulfield's.

Exiting the room he again slowly peered outside before going back into the corridor. At the next door the one on the right he heard what was a man talking to himself. He couldn't make out what the words were but it sounded all too familiar as Arabic. Again he peered around the door jamb of this office seeing that it was a larger room than the other. A desk sat opposite the door with on the top a computer over to the left of the desk. Behind the computer was a young Middle Eastern man whom Tom presumed was Malik.

Tom straightened himself up and boldly turned into the room. "Mr Malik." He said startling the man at the keyboard. Malik stood, his face not quite white but decidedly paler than it had been while he was sitting.

"Who are you?" he asked in a hesitant voice.

"Stevens sir, I am a friend of Mr Phorbes, I do some work for him occasionally." Tom could see the fear suddenly creeping up into the Malik's eyes. Something wasn't quite right here.

"Phorbes is not here today; perhaps you should come back tomorrow."

"Wasted trip that would be I'm afraid as I have come from Trinidad. You may be able to help me though anyway as you are from Melbourne. I have a question regarding Head office." Tom was scratching at straws here but he could see that Malik was in an uncomfortable position and becoming very irritated. Tom turned and closed the door which brought Malik quickly around the desk towards him rapidly.

Tom turned to see Malik place his right hand inside his jacket. He was about two meters from him at that point and Tom could only guess what he might have hidden there. He strode forward giving Malik little room to pull anything from his jacket which startled him even more. He went to step back pulling at his hand slowly getting whatever it was from its hiding place.

Tom grabbed hold of his arm just as Malik exited his hand from his jacket holding a small Ruger KP94 pistol. Tom gave a swift twist bending Malik's arm sharply back. There was a sudden crack, a yell of pain from Malik and the wrist went limp dropping the Ruger from his grip. Tom caught it with ease reversing it to point back at Malik's eyes. The eyes went wide with fear as he fell back against the desk clutching at his now dislocated wrist joint.

"Who are you then?" asked Tom waving the Ruger into Malik's

face. "I am here to audit from Melbourne." Malik answered resting his butt on the desk top and holding his wrist tightly.

"Auditors with guns eh, the worst kind." Tom looked at Malik's eyes and saw the fear growing greater. "Now what are you really here for Mr Malik?"

"I am here to audit. My boss sent me to get all the current details of the business checked."

"Mr Caulfield sent you then?" asked Tom trying to trap the young man.

"Yes, yes Mr Caulfield. You know him." Malik was not the type for this sort of job that was for sure he hadn't done his homework too well. He was a brain with the computer stuff but as a spook he was a dead end.

"Lies, Mr Malik. Mr Caulfield doesn't exist as far as Melbourne goes. Now open up or you may find you won't be able to play sports that require legs in the future."

"Audit, audit." Panic had set in to Malik now as he was slowly trying to move himself around the desk to the computer screen. The last thing he wanted was for this man to see what he was up to.

Tom stopped him at the corner of the desk and planted a thump with the butt of the Ruger behind his ear which sent him crashing to the floor. Tom bent down straight away ruffled through Malik's pockets pulling out a mobile phone and also a couple of USB sticks. As he stood up again he looked at the computer noticing another USB stick placed into the front of the tower. He stepped over Malik and stood in front of the screen where he caught a glimpse of the slide that was showing 85% download complete. He waited till the 100% download complete came up and then removed the stick placing it with the others into his own pocket.

The screen on the computer was showing records of accounts indicating at the top of the page the name of a bank in the Cayman Islands, Butterfield Bank located in Georgetown. Tom quickly scrolled the list and saw to his amazement the total monies were up and over the forty million mark. He blew out a short breath then switched off the computer.

Malik was stirring at his feet so he leant down to lift him up not wanting to leave another corpse in his path. As Tom lifted him Malik took hold of a bin with his good left hand whacking Tom hard across the head. Tom dropped Malik from his grip as he went backwards after the impact also dropping the Ruger. Feeling warmth slowly coming over the top of his head he put his hand up to check the point of impact and when he checked his hand there was a distinct wet patch of red blood. He could feel it was starting to flow forward, soon to be over his forehead and flowing into his eyes.

Malik had now stood and was about to make a run for the door when Tom leapt forward grabbing his shoulders firmly by jumping up virtually getting upon him in piggy back style. Malik fell forward and smashed down onto the floor again clutching the broken wrist to prevent it getting caught up anywhere.

Tom landed on top of Malik's back leant forward, grabbed his chin with his right hand and the right side of the back of his head with his left and pulling to the right with his right and pushing left with the left sharply he heard the crack as Malik's neck separated from the rest of his spin. There was complete silence as Tom breathed out a sigh of relief.

Fuck another corpse, Tom said to himself as he lifted the man up dragging him around to the seat behind the desk. He propped Malik up in the chair turning him as if he appeared he was still studying the computer. He switched the unit back on and picked up the Ruger. It may come in handy the way everything was starting to pan out yet again for Tom.

Searching around the room he checked every draw he could see. The top right of the desk was locked but it was not a problem for the letter opener that lay atop the desk. Pulling it open he found under a pile of paper a passport and photos of a world away. The photos were of a group of Royal Engineers who were huddled together alongside an armoured vehicle smiling and laughing at each other. On the rear were the names of Saxby, Broad, Smythe, and Reed but just to the left of the names was a little passage saying taken by OC Tony Welsh after entry to Basra April 2003.

Tom quickly collected up all the papers of interest and photos including the passport as that would put the kybosh on Sweetman getting out of the country unless he got a lift on one of the many boats that were used to smuggle in contraband. Still for Tom it was one less exit Sweetman could take to get away.

Opening the office door slightly he peered through, still quiet out in the passage so he opened it fully, went through shutting it after his exit. Exiting by the back door he noticed that the containers were now secured shut with what appeared to be seals on the handles as security for the customs. All the men involved in the loading had disappeared and just as he closed the door behind him he turned to see a large container straddle carrier pull over one of the containers clamp down lifting it then taking it from its place at the warehouse towards the dockside where it would undoubtedly be placed aboard one of the many ships that call into Nassau.

Tom jumped into the old Morris and drove off towards the motel again picking up more food for the evening. Here he placed his usual knocks on the door to gain entry and after going inside placed all that he had removed from Asia Pac into his case for security. He never mentioned anything about his exploits that afternoon to his guests who by now were settled to being in this small room trusting the man who undoubtedly had saved them from certain death.

Tom was still unsure whether to fire up the mobile yet so decided to leave it till the following morning. That evening about 1800 hrs he heard sirens which could have been the realization of the receptionist at Asia Pac that her visitor from Melbourne was in actual fact dead not mesmerized in front of the computer he was sat before. Tom had the TV on the news and sure enough there was a news flash telling the viewers that there had been a murder at Asia Pac of a visiting executive who had been found dead in the office with his neck and wrist broken. There was no mention of someone of Tom's appearance calling in to see the regulars at Asia Pac thank goodness.

Tom was relieved at the news report knowing full well that Gary would be on his case when next he spoke to him next.

CHAPTER 23

Nassau
Wednesday 14 March

"What the Fucks going on Tony?" Sweetman was calling from his mobile at his apartment in Bayroc.

"Slow down Derek and start again, slowly eh." Tony Welsh had only caught a small part of the outburst that had come down his phone line.

"Someone was at Rheingold's place when we arrived. Whoever it was took out Phorbes and then got the two Jews out of there.

We managed to fire the place up but I don't know where the hell those two are now. They need to be dealt with I know but I can't do it alone if they have help as I don't know how many there are.

The other thing is this afternoon I found out someone presenting with something from you had been given right of way to the business and has expedited two containers that are now on the docks bound for London and Sydney. What's going on Tony?" Sweetman had calmed down slightly but his voice was very hesitant as he spoke. You could hear the sound of fear and distrust coming through.

"Derek, I have no idea what it is that has happened. Nobody was sent from here to Nassau.

Can you find out what he was up to in the offices, Derek?"

"Not now I can't because he's dead, someone must have followed him or they are part of the protection detail for the Rheingold's."

"Dead you say? Any idea what he was up to?"

"No, the only thing I know is that he organized two 40' containers to be shipped out and that left nothing in the warehouse. I also know he was of Middle Eastern origin so is Ashid getting involved in the day to day running of us now?"

"Certainly not. I have had conversations with Ashid and he assures me he is leaving everything to us to deal with. Did you recognise the ones at Rheingold's, Derek?"

"No way, it went off too quickly. All I saw was a large Chevy parked at the front of the house and I have checked but have come up blank with anyone who may have hired it or even own it. There's no one on the Island who owns one the colour we saw so obviously someone is paying to keep mouths shut."

"Look mate see what you can find out. There must be something we can find, person or persons coming in recently etc. Be careful and stay clear of the office for now till we know what is happening just in case it is under observation."

"Righto Tony but I am on my own here now. I'll give it a couple of days and be back to you by the end of the week."

The phone call finished and Sweetman sat and pondered who he could trust on the Island. He had some contacts at the airport and thought that would be his best bet at this stage so he started dialling his mates at the airport.

Iraqi Interior Ministry

Thursday 15 March.

Frustration was showing on the face of Jamal Ashid. He had waited up all night to hear from his little protégé Malik but nothing came. There must be something wrong as Malik had promised a call whether or not he had gained entry to the offices at Asia Pac or not.

It was late by the time he had summoned two of his top operatives to his private office and given them both orders to immediately fly to the Bahamas and find out what had possibly happened to Malik.

It was as he was giving these orders that a messenger came to his door knocked aloud and after being called in dropped a printed message on Ashid's desk and hurriedly left. Ashid quickly stopped his instructions to his two agents picked up the paper and looked at the message.

The message had been sent from the Nassau police headquarters to the Interior Minister after the discovery of Malik's body in the offices of Asia Pac. It read:

Royal Bahamas Police Headquarters
East Street Hill
Nassau
New Providence

Dear Minister,

After the discovery of a person in a Nassau business area we need to clarify the identity of the victim one Ibrahim Malik. The papers on the victim gave these details with his current employer of the Interior Ministry.

We have attached a photograph in the hope that you will give a positive identification by return fax.

Commissioner Phillip Edwards. OBE

Ashid's face dropped and he started to glow a brighter shade than normal. Angrily he thumped the table in front of himself a number of times swearing under his breath.

"You two will get to Nassau immediately. Find out who killed Malik and deal with the two men who are listed on this file.

I also need to know if the containers mentioned are safely on their way out of Nassau." Ashid had no knowledge of what had happened in Nassau earlier as there had been no communication between him and Melbourne. He threw the file at them as if it was their fault and both men dropped their heads in embarrassment while slowly backing out of the room.

"When you find whoever did this I want them to suffer is that understood?"

Nods came from both agents agreeing in their task ahead. They placed what they needed into their jackets and left Ashid to his own temper.

Ashid was furious. He wanted the money train to end up in his line rather than through Melbourne but now he was unsure what had been done by Malik while he was in Nassau, whether he had succeeded or whether he had been caught out.

He swore again in his native tongue and dialled Melbourne.

By the time Tony Welsh had answered his mobile Ashid was calmed down, playing his normal cool role.

"Tony, my friend have you heard from your men in Nassau yet?"

"Not as yet Ashid. They were dealing with Rheingold today so I should hear within the next twenty four hours."

"Can you make sure you keep me informed my friend?"

"Certainly Ashid. How's things your end, anything going on we need to know about?"

"Nothing at all. Everyone is quiet in this neck of the woods." Ashid gave out no surprises even though his capital, Baghdad, was dealing with car bombs on a daily basis. Part of life as far as he was concerned and nothing that could put him off his eventual goal plan.

Both men wished each other the best and the line went dead. Ashid turned away from his desk and called it quits for a while mentally going through what he could send to Nassau police in relation to Malik. He felt a little depressed as he saw young Malik as an up and coming young man he could trust within his organization. He had plans for that young man, plans that would have placed him in the senior echelon of his network.

Back in Melbourne Welsh breathed a sigh of relief as he thought about the trust he had had with Ashid previously but now was beginning to doubt it all. That was the reasoning behind him not letting on what had happened to his men in Nassau.

Back in Nassau Tom had the confidence now to put his mobile together so he could get in touch with Gary and try and get the Rheingold's to safety.

Slowly piecing it together making sure he couldn't see any corrosion or wet areas he finally got the mobile assembled looked skywards, as if that was going to help, and switched on.

The light came on the screen and the pretty tune it usually played when he had done this before started up. Tom smiled and just hoped it worked both to send and receive.

Before Tom could touch any of the keys the bloody thing started to ring putting him off guard for an instant.

"Hello Gary." Tom said immediately into the phone.

"Mate you certainly are building a reputation around the world. You've been out of contact for days then wherever you are there seems to be an imminent supply of dead people left behind. What happened over there?"

"Well firstly my mobile doesn't take too kindly to swimming so had to dry it out a touch. Secondly as I was getting the Rheingold's out of their house when the two Asia Pac guys landed on the doorstep and tried to fry us all using incendiary devices. However the Rheingold's are safe at the moment and are with me."

"Ok. I have heard there was a body of Middle Eastern origin found dead in Asia Pac offices, did you have anything to do with that little fracas as well?"

"Tried to get some information at the offices but when I approached the shit he pulled a gun on me. What was I supposed to do Gary?"

"Couldn't leave him breathing at all eh?" Gary was laughing down the phone now. "Anyway we have information that he was working for Ashid, his name was Ibrahim Malik. Seems that Ashid is seeking out our REs as well. Possible retribution for the cash out of Iraq."

"Gary, I am sure Ashid has his finger located somewhere in this whole damn set up."

"Let's not jump too high Tom, see how things go. What is your next move?"

"I need you to get the Rheingolds out of here to safety somewhere. What happened was definitely a possible hit on them and they are not at all safe being left here on the island. How quick can you move them Gary?"

"Can you give me a couple of hours; I might throw this one over to our American Cousins being they put them there initially. Tell the Rheingolds not to worry I won't give their little game away just bend the truth a bit. I have a contact in Langley who owes me one."

"Sounds good, but can you get a hurry on as I want to try and pin down Sweetman before he gets out of this place. I have his passport but I know through the many smugglers in this region he could quite easily get on a boat out of here."

"Roger that Tom I will be as quick as I can. Anything else."

"I don't know if this is of any use but when I was at the offices of Asia Pac they were loading a couple of 40 footers which they had filled from the emptied warehouse there. Don't know if they are pulling out or just sending supplies to somewhere else. Leave it with you mate."

"Sounds normal for an Import export mob but yes I will look into it for you. Speak soon Tom."

Gary hung up and Tom placed the mobile into his jacket pocket. He would need to try and locate the residence of the two ex RE guys quickly to see if he could pick up more information for the cash hijack investigation.

Thumbing again through the equivalent of the white pages he came across a couple of Phorbes which he wrote down their numbers to try. With Sweetman he had four to choose from, two were on the Southside of the Island in areas of some disrepute from what Aaron Rheingold indicated. The other two were located on the north side one in a place called Bayroc not far from where the Rheingolds lived and the other in a place called West Shores vacation homes.

Aaron said that Sweetman had called once before and had only taken a few minutes from the time of his call to arriving. Tom thought that Bayroc would be the most likely but decided to call the West Shores place first to check.

He dialled the number in the book determined that if he got an English voice he would hang up and try the other to see if he could eliminate either. As the phone rang he closed his eyes and tried to visualize the face he had seen in the car that had flown the coup at Rheingold's place.

All of a sudden the phone clicked and a male American accent said hello at the other end. Tom asked if Derek was there but just got a few questions as to who the hell was Derek. Just one short minute and Tom had finally filtered the address down to the one for Sweetman. He ticked it off at Bayroc.

Next was to try and isolate Phorbes address and again he was ringing a number to see if there was any response. The first number produced no answer so Tom tried the second one at which he got a female voice to answer and Tom asked for Colin. Instantly the answer was no Colin here and the phone quickly hung up.

Unless someone was on to him then he had the two addresses and the first one he would attempt to get to would be Phorbes as he knew he couldn't stop him. First and foremost was to get the Rheingolds out of the Bahamas quickly as.

An hour or so later his mobile burst into life and on the screen was the name Gary lit up nicely. "Gary what have you got?"

"Right, we have success in some form or another. Our friends in Langley are keen to get the couple back to the States then off to some other faraway place to hide. I told them they assisted us and they ended up placing themselves in danger because of that.

The problem I have is getting them out of there. Langley cannot get there for a couple of days, but if I can arrange transport from Nassau to Miami they will be taken in under the protection of Southern Command.

Tom the earliest I can get a plane to you is tomorrow morning at 0700. It will be leaving Jamaica and is a Company jet. It is a Lear jet call sign November 367 Golf Charlie. Be at the Air Ambulance Centre at the Southside of the airport. You can get to it from Coral Harbour Road.

Give me a bell when they are airborne Tom so I can warn our cousins of their arrival time."

"Thanks Gary, much appreciated. I have got some USBs and other information I need to get to you, what's the best way for me to pass it on to you."

"Give it directly to the pilot Tom. Make sure it is all sealed in an envelope; I should get it in a couple of days. Take care Tom and please no more corpses."

Tom closed the mobile down and looked around the room to see what he could use as an envelope. Obviously, he thought, no one writes in this neck of the world, nothing. Off he would have to go to get a good quality envelope.

By nightfall the Rheingolds were beginning to relax knowing they had only to wait another twelve hours before they were up and away from the Bahamas. Shame Aaron thought to himself as he had viewed their living here as a slice of paradise. Nonetheless, when you delve into anything that is suspiciously outside the box of legality then you can always expect it to come back and bite you on the arse.

The morning of the sixteenth at 0600 Tom and his guests were ready for their final trip across Nassau. They all squeezed into the little Morris and trundled off towards the city where Tom would soon see if there was anyone on his tail. Turning in and out of streets he needn't have gone down gave him the feeling of safety as he could not see any other vehicle following them. He finally came onto John F. Kennedy Drive which took him round to Coral harbour Street and by 0645 he was parked up outside the Air Ambulance centre.

Directly on the dot of 0700 a jet landed across the airport taxiing itself to the Centre where they stood. Tom waited till it was stationary checking the call sign on its engine cowl. All good, as soon as the steps were lowered he got the Rheingolds out of the Morris and walked them over to the plane. At the base of the steps stood a familiar face, a guy who had been responsible for flights in and out of Iraq when he had arrived on station there.

"Well I never. Thought you had been locked up somewhere from what the newspapers said." Phil Ryder was the co-pilot of this jet and he smiled as he saw Tom approach.

"Don't believe all you read in the press. You know they make up stories just to sell a few editions." Tom was reluctant to get talking too much with this guy as he did not know him too well. He always thought him a bit weird when he first met him back in Iraq.

As Tom came to the steps he introduced Aaron and Sharon then followed them up the steps of the aircraft. Phil looked at Tom in a suspicious way which made Tom react. "It's alright I just have to give the pilot something for my boss to deal with in London."

Phil turned on another smile and continued to show the old couple to their seats. Tom entered the cockpit. Inside the cockpit there were dials everywhere confirming to Tom that in no way would he ever take up flying. Having to look at all these damn dials, when would you find time to see where the hell you were going?

The pilot turned in his seat and nodded to Tom. "Believe you have something for me?" he said holding out his hand.

"For Gary Warlock in London. Pretty urgent." Tom smiled at the pilot seeing how much the same age as himself he was. On his flight jacket was the RAF emblem and on his shoulders were the markings of a Flight Lieutenant, two bars.

"Pleased to be of assistance." The pilot continued securing the envelope into a flight folder he kept under his seat. "Just need to top up to get all the way to Miami and we are off."

Just as he spoke a fuel tender was pulling up, one man jumped out and attached the crucial earth strap to prevent any static sparks from igniting any fumes. The second man, from the driver's seat was out the cab as soon as his mate shouted clear he had the cap down and the nozzle in place ready to pump in the avgas.

Tom left the jet and turned to see Ryder pull the steps up and lock the door. Within a few minutes the fuel tender had done its job, removed itself from the jet and was returning to the main side of the airport. The jet was now ready to depart, fired up it taxied to the main runway where it sat to wait for a passenger jet to land. Tom waited in earnest as he watched the tiny jet push forward onto the runway and instantly its revs were up as it began to scream down the runway becoming airborne within a few seconds Tom watched as the Lear jet banked over and headed out in the direction of the US. They were out of his hands now thankfully so he returned to the Morris phoning Gary immediately to let him know the jet had left complete with its cargo.

CHAPTER 24

Tom sat in the Morris, checked his map and located where the Phorbes address was that had not answered his earlier phone call. It was within a gated community, as most top executives chose in this country for their security, called Love Beach Walk. About 9 kms from where he was which took only a matter of 15 minutes to reach.

Drawing up outside the gates he had a good look at the set up there. Situated on a secluded white sandy beach which was about one mile long the four, four storey blocks stood in splendour surrounded by their lush tropical gardens. Just off to the side in the area was a large swimming pool. Tom thought of the last episode he had at Rheingold's with the pool and shook his head with a laugh.

It was now mid morning and there was plenty of movement in and out the main gates. People off to their daily chores for a Friday at the end of a pleasant week or just going to work late. Tom watched with caution in case any of Phorbes allies were in or out of this complex, especially Sweetman. He saw little opportunity to be able to enter as when a vehicle came out it was only a matter of seconds after it passed the outer sensor that the gates closed directly behind them. It left no time for anyone to be able to drive in undetected.

Tom saw a young woman with a pushchair heading for the gates at about 1030hrs, thinking this to be the best opportunity. He leapt out of the old Morris and ran over towards the single gate where pedestrians entered and exited the community. As the mother with her young child approached the gate Tom lent forward as if he was to punch in the number code for entry. As he did so the woman opposite pressed on the exit button. The gate opened and Tom stood to one side to allow her through then wishing her a good morning ducked quickly into the complex.

The block he was looking for was positioned at the end of the short road and overlooked the beach area. He strolled around the swimming pool area and onto the block. Now the difficult part thought Tom as he surveyed the speaker box at the door entrance. Tom fumbled for a while looking as if he had lost his key or had dropped something. While he was bent down searching for fuck all he noticed a man walking slowly towards him dressed in overalls and carrying a ladder.

"Hi there, lost something?" asked the worker as he neared Tom. "Certainly have, but never mind I will have to get it again. It was a phone number of a mate of mine." Tom stood up and faced the worker as he placed his ladder on the road way in front of the building. "I was about to call him in actual of fact to surprise him."

"Lives here does he?" asked the local man with a curious look to his face as if he was sussing Tom out wondering if he had permission to be in the community area at all. "Someone let you in the gate did they?"

"Yes a lovely lady with her little one just let me in when I mentioned my friend's name. Colin Phorbes, he lives in the penthouse here in this block."

"Oh, Mr Phorbes, yes really nice guy, not expecting you then?" more sodding questions from the overalls man.

"No, wanted to surprise him as I have just arrived in Nassau and wanted to look him up. We go back a long way."

"Love surprises I do, just hold on and I'll let you in eh."

"Thanks a lot. My names Stevens, Joel." Tom was getting good at coming up with weird names in an instance and they seemed to work for him so well.

"OK Mr Stevens." The guy moved forward pulling on a set of keys he had connected by some kind of retractable string to his belt. "There you go sir. Have a great day." He said turning, picking up his ladder and walking towards the other block to the side of them. He was chuckling away to himself as he wandered off to his chores.

Tom entered the block going straight to the stairwell where he pulled on some thin surgical gloves before he opened the fire door and started up the stairs to the rooftop apartment. As he went he thought to himself how these REs had certainly looked after themselves with their accommodation.

At the top he came across the door to the penthouse, having a quick look at the lock then holding his ear to the door to check if anyone was on the other side he set about trying to enter. Out of his pocket he pulled a six inch steel rule placing it in the door jamb near the lock then pushing it as far in as he could. Once in place he then worked it up to the lock assembly. He had had great success in doing this before in the UK but it took him a number of goes to get it to connect on the lock here before he flicked it harder and the door cracked open.

What met him was one of the most immaculately furnished apartments he had seen. Through the welcoming foyer he eased slowly with its neutral coloured tile floor which spread throughout the whole place. The ceilings were shaped into the form of the roof which gave it a roomy feel. To his left was a wide window with sliding doors leading onto a spacious veranda. He guessed you could have held a family BBQ there for about twenty people without getting into each other's way. The wall in front of him was vibrantly coloured, with the ceilings styled as they were it gave the whole room some feel of exquisiteness.

The fully equipped kitchen completed with its stainless steel appliances and a large breakfast counter was immaculate. Tom doubted that this area would have been used very much by Phorbes at all.

Tom worked his way through the apartment with caution, finding first what looked like a guest bedroom which on closer inspection was empty of everything except the bed linen on the queen size bed. The next room he came to was what looked like another bedroom which had been turned into an office area. This was going to be the main room for Tom to search but firstly he wanted to check the remainder of the place out before starting to search the office.

The last room he came to was the master bedroom again with a vibrant coloured accent wall paired with exquisite decor that transformed this master space leading to its own private balcony. The master bathroom had his and hers basins, a Jacuzzi bathtub and separate shower.

Sifting through the wardrobe Tom came across clothes fit for a king. Style had been no problem for Phorbes that was for sure. He had more pairs of shoes than Imelda Marcos ever had which took up over half the space of the whole bloody robe. Pity his shoe size was different or else Tom would have lent a couple of pairs. After a few minutes of pulling aside clothes, checking pockets Tom came up blank and decided to go back to the office.

In here he found a laptop which he opened and switched on. He was unable to enter it due to the password protection on it so just shut it up again determined he would take it with him when he left to have checked. Through the desk drawers he shuffled through heaps of paperwork also finding Phorbes passport which he placed with the computer.

An hour later he was getting frustrated at not finding anything useful so he went out into the main living area and started to go through the drawers etc that were in numerous furniture spread around the room. All he came up with was a box of 9mm shells and a silencer which he had absolutely no use for without the weapon it fitted. Still having hold of the Ruger he had confiscated from Malik he knew it was full therefore short of coming under heaps of fire he wouldn't need to load himself too much.

By 1330 Tom had exhausted his search, he went to the fridge opened it and scanned the contents. A few soft drink cans stood in the door along with bottles of beer, there were plates with pies, cakes and chocolate biscuits. Phorbes must have been on an obscene type of diet, there were no vegetables and no fruit. Tom grabbed a handful of biscuits along with a coke then after nourishing on that he gathered what he wanted to take after finding a bag suitable and placed the items in

Time to leave he thought to himself as he started walking out of the apartment he closed the door behind him and then took the stairs the same way as he had entered. Outside there was no one around, he could not see the guy who had let him in so just started a leisurely stroll to the exit. Reaching the gate he pressed the button allowing the gate to open at which he strolled through getting back into the Morris and driving back towards his motel. He wanted to have a play with the computer to see if he could open the files that lay inside.

Driving past the Asia Pac offices there was still a police presence there and blue and white tape was strewn across the entrance and around the side of the building. It had been a couple of days since his bout with Malik there and the police were still trying to piece the whole thing together. Perhaps they were being hampered by Gary and his cronies at Vauxhall Cross.

Back in the safety of his room he stuck the kettle on and fired up the laptop. Tom's university days had been of great help in the past to hack into computers providing they didn't have complex firewalls. Within an hour he was into the main document section and sifting through each file as it appeared.

What he found wasn't overly exciting, just references to Phorbes old army days something like an auto biography. To Tom it looked like he was putting together some kind of draft for a book. There were about three hundred pages in total of which there were some interesting reading. The period when the stolen consignment happened had little to no references to any untoward behaviour though.

What Tom did notice however was the tendency of the writer to criticize his own command structure including the Government of the day. The main thought coming out of the writing for Tom was that the writer was so pissed off with his load and the orders he had had to bear he was turning against the system that had trained him so well. He even had patches in there that showed great empathy towards the Islamic people but not one mention of any terrorism antics.

One file showed him a banking spreadsheet that had over seven figures in its balance with the name of the bank on the top as the Canadian Bank located in the Caymans. After hours of sifting, reading, analysing Tom closed the laptop and marked it as having to go to Gary in London to be checked over.

That night Tom made plans that he would go to Sweetman's place next day to see if he was still around but first he would have to call London to tell them what he had found so far. He also wanted to check with Gary to see if the information he had sent previously had arrived there.

CHAPTER 25

Saturday 17 March

There was no early rise for Tom this morning, he felt utterly exhausted after the past few days. Sitting on the computer for hours the night before just drained him totally. After his breakfast he decided to give Gary a call to see what had transpired from the information he had sent to him.

"You'll be pleased to know that the Rheingolds arrived safely and are now in the secure company of our cousins. They have assured me that the two of them will be relocated within the next few days somewhere nice hopefully to live their lives in peace."

"That's a relief Gary I was a little concerned they may have been duped by Langley. Seems they can be humane at times eh?" Tom chuckled to himself. He was beginning to get the hang of all the Spook society now but as he was told earlier in the piece don't get too complacent with it as it can go tits up at any time with the majority of who you could call allies ducking for cover. "How about the envelope I sent on to you any chance to have a look at it?" Tom continued as he hurriedly drank his second cup of coffee to try and spark himself back into life.

"Haven't got it yet because the jet hasn't arrived back in town. I am expecting it to return on Monday so will have a look then and get back to you as soon as I can.

Have you had a chance to see if Sweetman is still in town? We have not heard anything at this end about him; anyway news from where you are seems to take forever like the old jungle drums. I know the Foreign Office has been able to put the block on some of the events that have taken place there to assist us. That's the worse with not having our own office there I suppose."

"No sweat Gary. Look I was able to get into Phorbes place located his computer which I have had a look at. Just a few diary notes like an autobiography list but there was also plenty of bank statements. They may tie the information together that I have already sent you. What do you want me to do with it?"

"Keep it safe while I arrange some kind of pickup in the coming days. It's pretty quiet in the Caribbean at present apart from you depositing dead bodies around the place. Still it keeps the authorities on their toes Tom."

"I think that's about it. I am hoping to get into Sweetman's place today if possible. Either way somehow I will find out if he's still about or not."

"Mate, try not to leave him lying around if you can. You're building quite a reputation here I'm afraid. The way you are going they may well christen you the Grim Reaper. Stay safe Tom."

Tom just laughed as he hung up the phone. So far in his travels he had left numerous corpses lying around the place, but knew that the majority were bad guys. He thought he must also be getting a reputation for his way of leaving vehicles damaged or wrecked just like the bodies he had come across.

About the same time as Tom was having his conversation with Gary the two agents sent by Ashid had just landed at the main airport in Nassau and were on their way to Sweetman's apartment. The advantage they had was his mobile number that Ashid had given them to use to locate him for the purpose of finding out what happened to Malik. Sweetman was blind to what they were really up to when he invited them to meet him at his apartment.

Tom remained in his room till after lunch before he readied himself to drive out to Bayroc. Saturday was a leisurely day here in paradise, more so than the other days of the week, as he drove past the many beach fronts covered with exposed skin and even some white pointers to his surprise. Seemed every man and his dog were out to the pleasures of beach and babes today. Boy some of these babes he saw well as far as Tom was concerned it left absolutely nothing to the imagination the way they were dressed. Oh to relax on the beach.

Trying to clear his head from the degenerate thoughts he was starting to build up he drove the car around the main road past the Wyndham resort which was huge compared to other resorts he had seen on the island. Just minutes further on he pulled into what was now a familiar sight, a gated community.

Seems all the modern buildings had this type of gated security. Either it was a way of just keeping the noise away or the crime rate here in Nassau was diabolical. The later was the real reason.

Tom knew that the building he was looking for was a seven storey building housing what was described as Beachfront Executive Condos. Tom needed patience now as he waited to see the coming and going of people resident in the complex. There seemed to be a constant flow of traffic today as he sat with a newspaper in his hand as his disguise for just sitting there. Quite a few families lived in this gated community and much of the traffic looked like it was for the normal Saturday soccer or cricket outings with mum as the chauffeur.

Tom remained in place for about two hours before something caught his eye. There at the gate was a large car, a Cadillac, exiting with what appeared to be two Middle Eastern men sitting inside. Tom lifted the paper to avoid direct sight between him and them as they drove through the open gate turned to their left heading towards the main part of town. Tom looked at them as they drove past to make sure they were alone. He couldn't see anyone else in the car as they sped past him taking no notice of him at all.

Tom's mind churned over the possibilities, after Athens with the rocket launcher episode and now these two coming out of the complex. Was it just a coincidence after all Middle Eastern men and women travelled quite freely around the world in this day and age. Must not be prejudiced must we thought Tom.

He waited a further half hour just in case his mate Sweetman appeared, but nothing just the constant stream of mums and their kids. Tom got out the old Morris, walked slowly over to the gate just as a car was pulling out. He went to walk to the pedestrian gate but then when he saw the main gate open he waved to the occupants and strolled through. They probably thought he was a resident who couldn't be bothered with using the other smaller gate.

The block Tom needed was the one nearest to the beachfront so his stroll took him through lush landscaped gardens yet again. They certainly knew how to tart up the place for the higher class here that was obvious.

He soon came to the block with its portico structure at the centre of the front. Sweetman's unit was a second floor condo and as luck would have it just as he got to the main door which needed a security pass key a couple was exiting. As they came out they held the door open for Tom, while still chatting to each other, which he thought was very considerate of them, if only they knew. He went through thanking them politely.

Whenever needing to enter premises like this preventing discovery Tom always took to the stairs. He slipped on his thin CSI style gloves as he ascended. By the time he had climbed the stairs it was past three. On the landing there were only two doors showing Tom just how large these condos were in size.

Tom crept over to the opposite door from the one he wanted and listened, coming out from the condo was what sounded like a baseball game going on. Whoever was in there had his sound system turned up full which was fine for Tom as if there was any noise made it may not be heard straight away at least not by this resident.

Going over to Sweetman's door he knocked at it fairly hard. The doors were large double styled doors with no peep hole. No answer so Tom wrapped his knuckles again on the door. Looking around to check that no one had heard anything he got out his trusted steel rule. Sliding it slowly into the door section between the two doors he pushed it down towards the locking mechanism. He just hoped that it was not double locked.

Coming against the barrel resistance he stopped and again looked around towards the opposite door. All clear so he quickly flicked the rule and aye presto the door opened. He held onto the door tightly as he slowly parted the two units.

Going in he pulled out the Ruger from his pocket. As he went through the doors closing them directly behind him he scanned the area in front of him. Inside the condo it was quiet, a bit too quiet Tom thought. The condo opened out to a spacious living and dining area, it was bigger by about three times than his room back at the motel. Again like Phorbes the decor was exquisite; neither of these men had been frugal with their needs.

To his right was the kitchen with passage way going down to what must be the bedrooms. Still no sounds coming from anywhere inside. It felt uncanny to Tom because of the sight of the Arabs leaving he thought they must be visiting Sweetman. Perhaps he was wrong, there was always that possibility. The veranda doors were closed as were all the windows. Nine foot ceilings adorned this condo with windows Tom noticed that were hurricane proof.

Firstly he would sneak down to the rear area of the condo listening all the while for any sign of life. Nothing, absolutely deserted. Damn, he thought to himself perhaps the bastard has already flown the coup. He came back up the passageway still holding the Ruger in readiness for any event that could throw its ugly head into the equation.

Re-entering the lounge/dining area he made his way to the door on his left. This must be the master bedroom. Slowly peeking around the open door he saw the bed as big as a dance floor, something that a party of people could have fun on. It was empty though so he made his way through the door where directly to his left he got the shock of his life. Directly through the door and to the left was what is normally the walk in robe but this one was a mess with all the clothes strewn over to one side and there dangling high above the floor was Sweetman in what Tom recognised as being known as the Palestinian suspension torture.

Its formal name is **Strappado** and it is a form of torture in which the victim's hands are first tied behind his or her back then the victim is suspended in the air by means of a rope attached to wrists, which most likely dislocates both arms at the shoulders. Weights have been known to be added to the lower body or feet to intensify the effect and increase the pain.

Here was Sweetman hanging stripped to the waist. Tom looked at how he was secured and noticed that someone had wedged a wooden beam, which was part of the shelving unit of the robe, between pipes that were services fed around this part of the condo out of sight.

Sweetman's shoulders were bright red and Tom could see that with the cases that had been tied to his legs the force had pulled both his arms completely out of their sockets. When this type of torture is used it usually leaves the victim alive but without the use of his arms the technique typically causes brachial plexus injury, leading to paralysis or loss of sensation in the arms. Tom pulled off the cases and tried to rip the ropes from where they were tied. As he did so he noticed that Sweetman had a puncture wound in his neck. Feeling for any pulse proved difficult in this position. He felt nothing. Sweetman wasn't breathing at all. Looking at the poor sod Tom cut the ropes letting the body down slowly. The arms were loose as totally disconnected from their normal sockets. Laying him down Tom felt again for a pulse but it was useless there was none. The neck puncture mark showed signs of a redness that measured about the size of a two bob coin about twenty millimetres. On Sweetman's forehead there was blood and once Tom had wiped it he immediately recognized the sign that had been carved into his forehead. The infinitely sign about fifty millimetres across.

Tom just knew that the two men he had seen were visiting Sweetman, what were they up to. First London with him, then Athens with the two men there, now Nassau and Sweetman. Ashid was behind this he knew for sure, he had to be. What was he doing he wondered? Was he getting revenge for the money or was there something else more sinister involved, this was something he would have to sort out sooner rather than later.

Searching every area of the condo Tom came up blank. It was clean as. He had spent long enough here so decided to get out before anyone managed to see him. There was nothing he could do for Sweetman. It meant there were only two originals left now, Welsh and Caulfield. He had to somehow get to them before anyone else did. He wanted to find out the full story, the reason why he was set up. That was his ultimate goal; the Government investigation was second to it.

Exiting the condo he slipped quietly down the stairs and out into the early evening air. Strolling as casually as he could towards the gate he exited the secure complex.

Back in the old Morris he cursed the way things had gone so far. Why couldn't he just sort something out without dead bodies coming into play? Tom sat there for a few minutes trying to think hard, was there someone in his immediate contacts who was double dipping on both sides. Who was it that he had to look at to distrust. Just as he was about to start up he noticed in his rear view mirror the car behind with its two Arab passengers sitting there intently watching him.

How the fuck did they know he was here? What now he thought this old tub would probably be swallowed up by their vehicle no problems. He kicked the old Morris 1100 into motion selecting first and slowly pulling away from his parking spot. The Cadillac started off behind him.

Tom took his time initially as there were a few other cars sharing the road this time of the day. He drove along the foreshore in the opposite direction of his motel past the Marina Village into Western Road. Further along the road he passed Old Fort marina where he swung a left into South Ocean Road, not taking too long before he finally came to the southern coastline of the island. He threw another left into Adelaide Road where a building sat in the centre island which reminded him of one of the old Toll houses that were used in the eighteenth century back home.

Trees to his right he saw on the left another road running parallel to the road he was on. He was unsure about the roads on this neck of the island and just prayed he would be able to escape the clutches of the two following closely behind. They had held back a touch at the start of the drive but now they were inching closer to Tom's back end as other traffic became less frequent. Tom's thoughts went back to what the guy had said about the Morris being a get up and go car. He hoped he was right as he was about to try it out.

Again Tom swung the car to the left with yet again passing another road island style house. This road had nothing ahead for him as he stared into the rear view mirror to see the Cadillac swerve around the corner after him sideways. They were starting to get serious now.

Suddenly Tom looked forward noticing the road just stopped in front of him in about 20 meters. Time to test the old Morris he thought as he pulled hard on the handbrake which slammed on the rear brakes but he kept accelerating as the car was a front wheel drive. Pulling the steering wheel hard to the right the Morris started to slide and completed a 180 degree turn where Tom finally halted facing the way he had come from. The Cadillac had also stopped seeing the dust stirred up by what Tom had done. They stood just 30 metres from him facing him down like one of those Fast and Furious films.

Tom selected first again, waited a few seconds while he got the Ruger out and placed it under his right thigh. He opened his window, looked keenly at the vehicle facing. It was a left hand drive so Tom's first thought was try to pass it on its left giving the passenger little aim if he was carrying.

The clutch came up and the front wheels spun throwing dirt, dust and stones up in a cloud. The Morris started off towards the Cadillac aiming to its left. The Cadillac moved forwards eventually swinging itself to its left and blocking the road, giving the passenger clear sight of Tom as he came towards them. The chicken run had begun.

Tom saw their manoeuvre and quickly spun to the right where he could see the shoulder of the road just with enough room for him to pass. He aimed sharply onto the hard shoulder and before anyone could see what was coming next Tom was past their boot racing back up the road in the original direction. Another hundred metres or so Tom saw what looked like a track on his left which he took in third still accelerating. He just hoped that it wasn't another dead end or he would be stuffed.

The Cadillac had to take a couple of moves to be able to turn around, a multi point turn for this tank, but once they had gotten around they made great haste to catch up with Tom. Nearly taking out a tree as they turned to follow Tom on the track they bounced the back end of their car against one of the largest trees on the plantation and that created a terrific bang leaving a massive dent in the back right quarter of the car. Their deposit had just become the property of the hirer.

Tom had made some considerable distance between him and the pursuers, so far the track was still open to the front of him. At the speed he was going he knew that if it stopped sharply he would definitely be in trouble as speeding cars and dirt tracks give little traction to stop short.

Trees were on the right and the left as he sped along. The track was rough as guts jolting every bone in his body as the old Morris bounced along, the room between the trees was just enough for the Morris to clear both sides by a minimal distance. The Cadillac would have been scratching both sides of its body to be able to penetrate the foliage here, slowing the two Arabs down somewhat.

After a couple of minutes Tom saw a break in the trees and swung the Morris into it at the same time swerving with the handbrake applied again to swing him around to face the track.

He alighted from his trusty steed covered in dust making his way to the tree line to his left. He took the keys with him to make sure the two behind didn't take them thereby shutting off any exit strategy he had. He could hear the Cadillac screaming up the track and could also see the dust cloud it was leaving behind itself.

Tom crouched down about two lines of trees back being able to sight the track but also being able to keep his eye on the Morris. With twilight slowly creeping in he strained his ears to listen with his eyes shut. The noise of the Cadillac came closer and closer as did the dust. Scratching noises could be heard as the sides of the lumbering tank scrapped along the trees either side of it. It sped past him still throttling hard when all of a sudden it slammed on its anchors as it had passed the open area where Tom had parked the Morris and they had obviously seen the old Morris parked there.

As the Cadillac slide to a halt it caught the left hand wheels in the soft verge that had begun in the clearing. This caused the wheels to dig in hard and the whole car started to lift as if it was about to roll over. Unfortunately for Tom it didn't, coming down hard back onto all four wheels but the action did cause the unbelted passenger to fall over across the driver losing his weapon onto the floor of the car leaving both men entangled together and shaken for a moment. The dust cloud they had created finally enveloped the Cadillac making it unseeable to the human eye.

Tom seized his opportunity and leapt out of his hiding place racing towards the Cadillac under cover of the dust cloud that had been following. The men didn't see him coming as they started to get their composure together again. Tom slide alongside the driver's side as the door came open exposing a dark head of hair and a bearded face. Tom instantly slammed the Ruger into the side of the man's head sending him crashing into the dirt alongside the car leaving his legs tangled behind him in the car.

There was a scurrying in the passenger side as the passenger opened his door and tried to race around the car to where Tom was. As he came around the front of the vehicle he came face to face with the Ruger stopping dead in his own path.

Tom waved the Ruger as if telling his opponent to face the car with his hands spread. He stood still not wanting to do anything for this young man who had blindsided them.

Tom waved the Ruger once again stepping forward one step alongside the driver's door. The man threw his arms up to show he had no weapon. Tom again waved the gun which this time brought the man in front to obey the command he had given. He turned and leant forward onto the bonnet with his legs still together but his hands spread apart on the bonnet.

Tom walked to his rear pressing the gun into the man's back then placed his foot between the man's legs forcing them apart which threw the man off balance and therefore away from any thought of trying to outwit Tom.

Frisking someone with one hand while holding a gun to their back is not as easy as it seems but Tom managed to be able to get every pocket and possible hiding place for guns checked. He removed ID cards and passport from the inside pocket of the man's jacket. Tom again pushed his foot in between the man's legs forcing them further out from the car.

"Now what can I do for you two?" Tom sarcastically said to the spreadeagled figure.

"Nothing." Was the only reply Tom was to get from the frustrated foreigner.

"Who do you work for?"

"No one."

There was a groan from the car as the driver started to come around. Tom lifted his right foot slamming it against the door which produced a blood curdling scream from the trapped driver. As he did that the spreadeagled man suddenly jumped his feet forward and rolled to the side.

Tom spun around onto him but he had started to take off across the open ground. Tom lifted the Ruger and let off one shot which copped the man in his right calf. He went down like a sack of shit screaming out in pain.

Tom went around the door and pulled the driver from his compromising pose. Dragging him out onto the dirt it took only a few seconds to frisk him finding nothing but ID cards and passport, the same as the other man. These he took and quickly placed them into his own pocket along with the others. The driver was still out cold and his mate was just writhing around on the floor, blood dribbling out of his pants trouser leg getting baked with mud as he trailed it in the dirt. He wasn't going anywhere fast.

Tom removed the driver's shoes and his leather belt. The belt was a handy thing to use if; long enough which it was. Tom tied the driver's wrists together behind his back with the belt using a figure eight configuration but while doing that he again noticed the same tattoo of infinity on the right wrist.

Making his way over to the injured one where he did the same thing while two red glaring eyes were pondering whether he was destined for Paradise and his many Virgins within seconds. Both these guys are from the same group, this Infinity thing was beginning to stir up questions. Going back over to the Cadillac, Tom let down all four tyres after removing the valves using the caps that were on them. He checked the inside of the car finding a Gyurza Russian Army pistol lying on the floor. He slid out the magazine depositing the weapon in one direction in the trees and the magazine in the other direction in the trees.

Back to the Morris he threw the two pairs of shoes into the back seat and started the car moving off slowly around the Cadillac. The driver was still out cold with his passenger still rolling around in the dirt in obvious pain. Tom thought this was a better conclusion as he hadn't left any dead bodies this time. Gary would be pleased. He was getting a bit of a stigma with all the trouble he had gone through in recent weeks.

By dark he was back in the area of the motel where he dropped off the Morris telling his new mate, Vivian { his dad must have been a cricket fan}, the car was as good as he said it would be. He made sure that his new mate wouldn't tell anyone checking up on him would know where to find him by greasing his palm with a few crisp dollars. He also gave him the shoes saying they were well tried and would last for a few years yet. With that he laughed and sauntered out of the hire shop returning back to his room at the motel.

CHAPTER 26

Back in the safety of his motel room with the four walls around him, Tom sat wondering how the hell he was being outflanked by the men from the Middle East. He went through all the names he could to try and identify who might be the root of the problem and feeding someone with information about his whereabouts. Gary was the only one he had spoken to who could pin point his location so does he trust him or does he pull the plug on their association, he was willing to give it one last try. He dialled in the mobile to get Gary who answered almost immediately.

"How did you go Tom?" Gary came on sounding overly keen even excited.

"You won't believe it mate; there was someone who beat me to Sweetman. I was being observed by a couple of Mid East guys who were probably with Sweetman before I got there leaving me with the find of a lifetime. The poor bastard was trussed up Palestinian torture style dead as a dodo. It seems, Gary, someone has got the edge on my movements and I don't like it. I still think it is Ashid going by who and what seems to be there when I arrive. Sweetman also had the infinity sign craved into his forehead."

"Look Tom, Ashid is closer than you might want to think to Aspalson. I can't imagine he would be able to get anything from that one, believe me. Were you able to find anything useful at Sweetman's place?"

"Absolutely sweet fuck all. The two Arabs followed me when I left and tried to get the better of me on some remote roads but I have slowed their campaign down a touch now."

"Oh Christ, Tom, not more bodies for me to explain away, please."
"Not when I left them, they were trussed up at the southern point of the island with no car, no shoes. The only thing is one of them has a hole

in one of his calves where he tried to flee. Otherwise they are both well and kicking. I have got their passports, IDs etc which I will get to you as soon as.

First one is a Samir Kanaan, second one is Tariq Bazzi, that's the poor bastard with a hole in his calf. I thought they would have a hell of a problem trying to leave without them without causing a few waves."

"What's your next move Tom?"

"I might go via Florida and drop the passports etc to your mate there at Fort Lauderdale if that's ok by you."

"I'll make sure he is expecting you. When do you hope to be there?"
"In the next couple of days I think Gary. Can you give me his number so I can contact him directly when I get there?" Tom thought to hold off any definite till he was sure he could actually trust Gary. This was becoming more and more difficult with people after his experiences in Iraq who could he really trust. The only name that came to him other than his parents was Vicki and she was in the country where he would hopefully catch up with Caulfield. Plans to be made, travel to arrange.

"Alright Tom I'll sort out the two Arabs for you, just be sure to stay safe eh? I'll text Jay Coyles number to you as soon as we are done here."

With that Tom hung up, waited till the number for Jay Coyles had appeared on his screen then noting it he again stripped the mobile down till next he was prepared to use the damn thing again. Who could he trust? Questions, questions, questions. Doubts, doubts, doubts.

Tom had a walk late that night to find food as well as clear his head. He had seen nothing on the TV about anyone being shot today which was strange for this place as everyday there was something or other happening in the criminal world.

Sunday 18 March.

Tom rose early, ate and then phoned the airport to get a passage on a flight to Miami. He was in luck as a direct flight was leaving at 0940 that morning. It would mean only an hour and a half before he would be in the States. He planned to get to Miami, and then drive up to Fort Lauderdale arranging a meet somewhere outside the city, somewhere he could take full advantage of if things went belly up. This was his way of testing out the trust arrangement he felt towards Gary, he just hoped he was wrong in thinking Gary was not on board.

Leaving the motel he deposited the stripped Ruger between two large garbage bins that sat at the rear of the motel. His taxi took only a few minutes before it dropped him off at the US Departures Terminal. In just a few more minutes he was seated in the terminal, waiting for his flight to be called.

Continually looking around testing his field craft he was certain he was not under any observation. Not even a suspicious look from the Yanks crew as he boarded the American Airlines flight aboard an Embraer RJ145. When he entered the cabin area he found it was almost deserted. There were less than twenty people out of a possible 50 seats on today's flight which pleased Tom no end. The flight had a few turbulent jolts but all in all it was quick and comfortable.

Flying in over the tall buildings, condos and resorts that were scattered along the Florida coastline here was an eye opener. This was America's retirement central Tom knew.

Within two and half hours Tom had landed at Miami airport was through customs looking at the many hire desks that served customers arriving at this majestic looking place. Taxis everywhere, cars blowing their horns, screeching of brakes, yes it was all alive here in this place.

Coming out of the American Airlines terminal Tom noticed the hire sign for Dollar car Rentals. He thought it might be like he had in Nassau with old and sometimes ancient cars but he was pleasantly surprised when he went into the office being dealt with immediately and in a seat of a medium compact within fifteen minutes. Service beyond reproach Tom thought hoping all that was coming before him would be as easy as this.

The drive to Fort Lauderdale was about thirty miles meaning he would be there by just after lunch. Tom decided that he would stop at a motel outside town and arrange the meet for the following day. Being a Monday he knew that there would be a lot more people around to assist if he needed more cover. The Trust thing was still playing a big part in his mind at every turn.

He was beginning to feel alone, abandoned yet he knew that there was people somewhere in the world who cared and worried about him. How would he ever shake this feeling of loneliness.

Aspalson's Country Lodge, Oxfordshire
Sunday 18 March

In the small office Aspalson had in the rear of his lodge there was complete silence as Ashid looked at the reports from Nassau he had brought with him. Both the police report in relation to Malik and a more recent one from the men that he had sent to deal with the two ex soldiers there. They had unfortunately been picked up by the local police but being without ID or passports they had one hell of a time to try to arrange their exit from the Islands.

He was not amused. His face was starting to glow red as his hands turned into tight fists. They were eventually lifted then slammed down onto the desk in front of him followed by a few swear words in Arabic.

Aspalson, sitting on the opposite side of the desk jumped in surprise.

Ashid looked around the desk at the men now assembled before him. Two Europeans sat there wondering whether Ashid was about to have a heart attack from the way he was acting.

Ashid slowed himself down a touch and lent forward towards the two European men. "Gentleman, thank you for your quick response in allowing me coming here today. I understand that your co-operation with our Government at this time is very much appreciated.

In regards to these other matters that are also important to us all is the fact that a certain murdering ex soldier of yours is still being allowed to cause us some discomfort around the world with his actions.

This Tom Warburton I thought was killed in Greece at one point but now I find by the last contact I have with my men in Nassau that he was predominant in delaying their task and now has put them in a position of holding as he stole their identification including passports. The text I received from you Mr Ryder at Nassau airport was also worrying.

What, my friends is the story behind this one man band of misery?" The better dressed man facing him lifted himself proudly in his chair and answered with a somewhat gusto. "Mr Ashid, may I say that the British Government has no idea what or who is behind this rogue soldiers plans. It seems he is on some kind of vendetta, a vigilante.

I have asked many questions at the Home Office and also have had contact with our friends at GCHQ without any response as to any form of operation regarding this man coming to our notice. He is not carrying out any operation for Her Majesties Government I have been assured of that." Aspalson looked at Ashid waiting for some kind of outburst as he had become very accustomed to from previous meetings.

"Mr Aspalson I respect your comments but obviously we have some kind of operation here that we or you do not fully understand or even comprehend. Somehow this man is being aided by your Government through one department or another." Ashid was now pointing his finger fairly at Aspalson in a threatening manner.

The second man then piped in quickly before the conversation got totally out of hand. "May I please put some clear and precise explanation on this whole affair for you, Sir? After the recent trip I had to the West Indies as a co-pilot on one of the Governments jets I was made aware that we were used by MI6 to detour to pick up two Americans from Nassau and while there I saw an old friend from the past, Tom Warburton. It seems he is working alongside Gary Warlock at six. That was the text that I sent to you."

"Mr Ryder you have been very forthcoming with your information which I surely have a high respect for. That did enable me to notify my men in Nassau but unfortunately they were not able to deal with him as I said." Ashid added as Aspalson turned his head and glared at Ryder drilling right through his head. He felt he had been bypassed with this text even though Ryder had told him of it when he originally arrived back in the UK.

Ryder continued. "The people we took out had been rescued by Warburton I believe and we were tasked with the job of getting them safely to the US in Fort Lauderdale where they were taken into custody by CIA operatives that I have also had dealings with in the past. As for their destination I could not get that information at all, unfortunately.

As for Warburton he gave the pilot a package that was to be delivered directly to Warlock at Six. What was in it I have no idea as the pilot would not confide in me about the package total. I was tasked on arrival in the UK to immediately escort Mr Aspalson here to his home."

"Thank you Mr Ryder. Gentleman it is obvious now that this fellow Warburton is working under some guise of your MI6 so let's not beat around the bush anymore. I want to know where he is now and what he is up to or the payments that you both have had in the past and are expecting in the future will be cancelled forthwith.

I need to have his exact location as soon as possible so we can deal with him permanently. Is there any chance you can put pressure on this Gary Warlock at Six?" Ashid looked directly at Aspalson waiting intently for a positive reply.

"That may be difficult as we do not want to expose our future plans to any one at Six by asking questions such as Warburton's whereabouts. I will endeavour to try and get some information from them that may be useful in you locating the man. Please give me a couple of days, I will return immediately to my London Office but firstly I will call Gary Warlock asking him for an update on anything of importance regarding Iraq." Reginald Aspalson looked at Ashid and saw a faint glimmer of a smile;

he returned it with his own smile. Money was important to him as his salary package sure wasn't enough to be able to live to the means he wanted to in the future.

As for Ryder he was just the normal opportunist type of fellow who saw a way of exploitation and ran with it. The money was always handy for him to help with his ways, strange as they may appear.

More was discussed including future co-operation from these two treasonous deviants. Their meeting lasted a total of four hours before finally they all agreed what was needed for their future success. The termination of Tom Warburton.

The meeting ended there with firm handshakes then Ryder and Aspalson escorted Ashid and his two personal guards that were also present during their little chat to a vehicle parked at the front of the Lodge supplied by Aspalson for this visit. They were driven directly to their small jet awaiting them at the Oxford airstrip nearby, from whence they took off heading back to Baghdad.

As soon as his guests had gone Aspalson made a call to Gary Warlock. "Gary, just a quick word, I wonder if you would be free to have a chat about what has been happening as far as Iraq goes. I have a few concerns in relation to that fellow Tom Warburton, he seems to be popping up at the most inopportune times and causing us some embarrassing problems."

"I can be available tomorrow morning about 1000 if that suits, perhaps at Vauxhall. I have a pretty tight schedule for the day and that is the only time I have free at present." Gary was a trite amused at the interest Reginald Aspalson was taking in Tom.

"That's fine Gary, till then." The phone went dead and Aspalson turned to Ryder.

"What do you think this Warburton character is up to Phil?" "Haven't got a clue but I know he is in deep with Warlock, Reg. Do you want me to come along tomorrow for a bit of support, I have spoken to Warlock previously and done some work for him in the past."

"I think that will be welcomed Phil, let's hope we can stop this arsehole causing Ashid any more upsets after all it's our retirement fund that's at stake."

They both burst out laughing as they sat back, relaxed on the large sofa clutching not only a large whiskey each but also holding each other's hands. That night would be a frolicking one for these two gay lovers.

The following day at Vauxhall Cross two tired looking men strolled into the building after alighting from a Foreign Affairs Office vehicle. They were met at the reception area and escorted to the third floor where Gary was holding most of his day's meetings in one of the large presentation rooms.

"Good morning gentlemen." Gary rose to greet them both, shaking their hands and indicating for them to take a seat. "Now what can I do for you, I believe you have some questions regarding Tom Warburton?"

"We certainly do, Gary. Can you tell us if he is working for you here or is he some kind of mercenary out there only we are having to answer some pretty awkward questions from our new friends in the Iraqi Government? He seems to be popping up in the most awkward of places causing some embarrassment to our Iraqi colleagues."

"I'm afraid that question I cannot answer just yet. Tom has been dealt a bit of a rough end of the pineapple since he went into Iraq and we are trying to aid his recovery to date."

"How are we able to do that and why are Six involved, not the Defence department?"

"Defence handed over to us because we were in the thick of it when we rescued him from Basra. They have asked us to continue with that task reporting to them as to his recovery." Gary was good at lying, he had learnt long ago when he left Cambridge and was recruited by Six that not all members of the Government departments played on the same field. He was determined to protect Tom at all costs in trying to solve the Money loss that had happened back in Iraq.

"Certainly does seem strange for you to take this sort of responsibility on." Aspalson looked at Gary furrowing his brow some. "What form of help have we, or sorry you, have given him. Can I ask that of you?"

"No that's OK, we have had a nurse attached to him for a while in London to help him through his problems which I must say were Gremlins I would not like to have to conquer myself. From there he showed remarkable progress so we allowed him to pursue personal goals but to still keep in touch with us on regular basis."

"You say personal goals. Can I ask what they might be?" "Unfortunately I do not know the full extent of those I'm afraid.

That's where we have let him have a free hand so far but have expressed directly to him that we are here to help him through it all."

"This nurse did she give him a clearance to be able to return to his duties?"

"She certainly did but as yet we are not giving him duties to follow up on. She showed some quite remarkable techniques which have produced a result we look forward to be able to use in the future."

"Is there any chance I can speak to this nurse to get some background from her about Tom's current mental state."

"That would be difficult as she returned to her home in Perth." "That's not too far away perhaps we could go and speak to her." "Perth, Australia, Sir. Vicki Robson returned after she finished her assigned duties with Tom." Gary suddenly stopped thinking he had let out too much information out as it was. But these men were on his side surely they were no threat to Tom.

Ryder turned towards Gary and spoke. "You say personal yet I happened to come across Warburton in Nassau where he handed over two Americans we transported to the US and also handed the pilot a package addressed to you Gary."

"Yes that was true, he was there at the time when we needed something minor to sort out so I used him to locate the two and assist them to the plane where you met him. As for the package it was addressed to me but was really for his parents. That was delivered by me as they are going through some bad personal trauma at present.

Unfortunately Tom's mother passed away two days ago from cancer. I haven't yet been able to get that information to him as he hasn't called me back." Gary was thinking this Ryder guy was a bit of a nosey bastard, not just a lowly pilot in the Air Force. He made a mental note to find out a bit more about him.

Gary knew that Ryder had been used by his Department at Six to fly covert operations at times but he was seemingly too close to Aspalson for his liking. It didn't make sense someone of his rank being attached to the Foreign Office Under Secretary.

Aspalson had got some headway with a name and place now and was rather keen to get the hell out of Vauxhall so he could relay the information to his cohort in Baghdad. He excused himself rather unexpectedly and rose to leave.

"What is Tom doing to cause the Iraqi Government any embarrassment may I ask?" Gary was now fishing himself as Aspalson hadn't come too clean about what he was really after.

"It seems he has popped up in Athens, then in Nassau when our Iraqi friends have had something on. It seems he gets in the way of their operations for some unknown reason causing delays."

"Probably coincidence Sir, I expect."

"You are probably right there but if there is anything you can keep me informed about regarding his movements it would be truly appreciated." Both men were now edging for the door. Gary nodded to them both as they left him alone in the massive conference room. Gary thought hard as to why there was so much interest in Tom by Aspalson but decided to keep it in the back of his mind for later. He had to firstly get the news to Tom about his mother which was not going to be very pleasant for either of them.

As Aspalson and Ryder left the Cross they remarked to each other that there was something else going on between Tom and Gary. Their first option was to get the name and address of the nurse to Ashid thus leaving that side of it all with him. The last thing they wanted was to be involved in anything resembling a leak to a terrorist.

The afternoon was spent chasing down addresses for Vicki Robson in Perth Australia. It was after a few tries that they actually found the one they were looking for. They did not want to go direct to the files as they would be undoubtedly monitored with the two of them then being highlighted as checking.

With the information they had gained they messaged Ashid in his Office in Baghdad with what would be the biggest heartache Tom would feel since coming home from Iraq. It would be even more devastating than finding out his mother had died because that he was prepared for, it was coming soon he knew.

CHAPTER 27

Monday 19 March

Just South of Fort Lauderdale by eight miles where Tom had the night before done a bit of a rece to the local plaza about ¾ of km away from his motel which was a good stroll in the cool of the evening.

He was comfortable with how he would approach the meet today if it could be arranged that quickly. Using his prepaid mobile he texted Jay Coyles' mobile asking for a meet this morning. It didn't take long for him to receive an answer.

After making the arrangements for 1100hrs Tom set off earlier for the Plaza to watch to see what or who was around especially anything that appeared remotely suspicious for him.

Arriving at the Beach Way Plaza he immediately went to the entrance where he had arranged to meet Jay. It was a small coffee shop located right by the exit which for convenience for Tom enabled him to have an exit strategy. Just up from the coffee shop was another cafe with two other shops between. This was to be Tom's viewing point. He had made a good evaluation of all the types of patrons in and out the night before from a seat near a handrail which separated the walking area from the cafe itself.

Tom was at the cafe an hour before the meet where reluctantly he walked around the rest of the Plaza to check it out. Being only single storey he did not have the problem of people looking down on him, except for the cameras that were spread about the place to protect shoppers from the local petty criminals.

There were few cameras in the vicinity of the coffee shop and cafe. Just at the entrance to the Plaza with the next being about half way along the walkway which would only get the back of Tom's head if anyone was actually looking for him.

Comfortable with his choice he pulled the baseball cap he was wearing down closer over his eyes and headed for the cafe. Taking a seat he waited patiently for the time of the meet. He had no idea what Jay Coyles looked like so he had asked him to purchase two large mugs of cappuccino and sit at the table closest to the main door. At this point it was still vacant but both the cafe and coffee shop were filling up fast due to the lunch period now closing in.

Tom thought his timing might be a little off but persevered till the approaching time of 1100 hrs ticked over on his watch. He was now sitting earnestly awaiting the contact with Jay still sipping on a half cup of cold coffee he had purchased to be able to sit in the cafe. He had refused the usual top ups that were normal for these establishments after the second one being fixated on the table near the door he had instructed Jay to go to.

As the clock ticked over he had noticed a group of men only coming in through the doorway. He kept his eye on some as they strolled off past him. Suspicious of everyone, this was how Tom felt at the present. Trust was a weird thing to gain for him these days. The men filtered off becoming no threat at all.

Damn, Tom thought as the table was taken by two young females dressed in no more than what could be only described as a piece of material resembling a skirt. Mini skirt would have been an understatement for what they were wearing. Just bending slightly to place their coffee cups on the table gave Tom a bird's eye view of what they had had for breakfast. Distraction, yes sir but his eyes were still fixed on that table now pleasantly. What would Jay do now the table was taken, but then again nearly every table had someone on it by this hour?

All of a sudden a stocky looking crew cut Caucasian man walked up to the table and laid two large mugs onto it apologising to the young girls sitting there. They nodded at him while he sat down opposite them legs crossed. No jacket and no sign of a handgun as could be seen on some others who wore their jackets showing the signs of holsters lay underneath as they walked around.

Tom gave it a few minutes while studying everyone near at hand to the table. Comfortable with the moment he stood and slowly walked towards the main door as if he was going to exit. Still looking about him he could see no other person even resembling a watcher so at the door he stopped lent over Jay's shoulder and spoke.

"Hi Jay nice to see you." Tom smiled at the two girls as they looked across to see such a delightful looking young man about to sit down. Tom sat as Jay acknowledged Tom with a stand and handshake. Jay then pushed one of the coffees over towards Tom.

"Great to meet you at last Tom. Gary has told me a lot about you and of course I need to thank you for the other day. Our friends are once again safe thanks to your help."

Tom sat down but the chatter between the two of them was more like talking about the local politics as they did not want the two girls getting any bad ideas about the two of them. Finishing their coffees Jay and Tom stood, farewelled the girls which got them both a warm smile from each.

"Great to be alive eh Tom." Jay said as he smiled back at the girls. Walking through the Plaza and out the opposite side Tom waited till there was no one within ear shot of them.

Placing his hand in his pocket he pulled out the ID s and passports he had seconded from his Arab mates in Nassau. "These are for Gary. How did he go with their names?" They had stopped by a small bench near the outside area not far from the bus shelter.

"He gave me their names and base. Kanaan is from Basra and his friend Bazzi is from Nasiriyah. Both are members of the elite group that are employed by the Interior Ministry. By all accounts you have stirred up a bit of a hornets' nest there." Jay chuckled as he gave the news to Tom.

"This definitely puts the finger firmly on Ashid I think or else it has to be someone close to him. What I can't understand is every time I make a move they are not too far behind me."

"Gary said he was certain it was not Ashid but he would remain open with it for now. He said also that he had a visit from Aspalson this morning London time asking questions about you. He would follow up on it as he feels uncomfortable about Aspalson and his tag along Ryder."

"Ryder you say?"

"Yep, Gary said that the pair is as bent as a nine bob note, whatever that's supposed to relate to. I can never get my head around the English sense of humour or slang."

"The pair are gay, well I never. That answers some of my worries. Ryder saw me in the Bahamas."

"Yea I guessed the gay part. Mate I have some news for you that Gary asked me to pass on. I'm sorry to be the one to tell you though, but your mother passed away a couple of days ago. Gary held off telling you because he thought it may have upset your plans in Nassau. I'm really sorry buddy."

"Its Ok Jay I knew it was close. She was suffering from cancer and it had turned very aggressive of late, we were all prepared for it to come sooner rather than later."

"Gary wondered if you wanted to return to the UK. If you do I can arrange a flight for you from Lauderdale."

"NO thanks, Jay. I need to finish what I have started. It is getting close to the end now I can feel it. I'll give my Dad a ring from my hotel tonight make sure he is ok."

It was a shock like Tom thought it might have been. He did not want to see his mother in the condition she was in as it was more upsetting watching what was once a beautiful looking woman, slender and fit reduced to a bag of bones with her eyes looking as though they were ready to fall out of her skull. Tom just wanted to be able to visualize her as she used to be. He was sad but he knew he had to carry on being able to clear his reputation fully. He knew she would be proud of him once he completed what had to be done.

The two men parted with firm handshakes both disappearing in opposite directions. Jay would report back to his friend Gary in London sending on the passports etc he had been given. Tom slowly strolled through the back streets of Dania Beach to his room at the Super 8 motel. His thoughts were firmly on his mother now. She at least was not suffering any more. He would miss her deeply. Then Dad of course, the years he waited to be together with her and now it had come to an end. He had been dealt a dummy hand that was for sure. Perhaps we Warburtons had been cursed with problems that would flow through all the generations to come.

The time had clocked over to 1700 by the time he had got back to his room which meant that it was mid day in the UK. He thought he would ring his father to say hi, let him know he was OK.

The phone beeped a couple of times when he had finished dialling before the other end answered.

"Hello." Came the familiar voice of his father. He had grown close to him since being introduced only a few years before. He often felt he wanted to be so much like him in many ways. His mother was totally smitten by this man who had saved her from a massacre in the Vietnam War.

"Dad, its Tom. I've heard the news. I'm sorry I am not there for you though."

"That's ok son so long as you are ok that is all that matters now." Senior knew this was a normal phone so did not go into any detail in case there were ears on the line somewhere.

"You Ok. What about the funeral?"

"Don't worry, it's all arranged just a few friends from here with Geordie and his family coming over. I'm keeping your mother's wishes to take her ashes back to her village in Vietnam when we can both go there together, OK."

"I'll try to get my job done soon Dad and then we can have a break together then. I really want to see where mum came from."

"It's a deal then." Senior sounded pleased but also sad at the same time. "You take care of yourself my boy. By the way Mum left you a message to keep close to yourself."

"Message? What did she say?"

"She told me to tell you to remember these three lines your grandfather told her when she was younger.

Keep your wits sharp.
Keep your heart open.
But make sure you keep your gun loaded.

Always remember them and you will stay safe. Take care son, I love you."

"Love you Dad." Tom hung up as tears started to well up in his eyes. His mother was gone but still he knew she would be there wherever he was through thick and thin. His father was still there though in body, he was a tough guy but as he got older he knew he would eventually succumb to ill health as is the future for all of us on this earth.

Tom laid back on his bed imagined the good times he had had with his parents and smiled to himself. He overcame the sadness that had overtaken him and just smiled as he knew that soon he would be back home with hopefully his dream girl on his arm to introduce to his Dad.

He picked up his mobile sending a text to Vicki that he was on his way to Perth. She replied within the hour asking for his flight number with any other details he had. She was overjoyed at the thought that he was coming to her thinking he had finally sorted the problems of Iraq out already. How wrong she was to be.

He had no way of telling her what flight number as he hadn't even checked for flights himself yet so just told her he would let her know when he was on his way. He also let her know his news of his mother which again brought tears to his eyes.

After a couple of hours Tom sat and wrote as he had done many times before a small poem to try to ease his pain. Although he had had such a distant style of relationship with both his parents the love he shared with them was above all else and he was truly saddened for his mother's passing.

Lost loved one

I see an image
So bold and fair
The features so prominent
The eyes and love within

I see a loved one
Taken so young
Vitality and good looks
Lost forever in this life

Too young to be taken
From my side she's gone
So young to leave
So alone am I

They live for us to live on
They accept to go before
Even so it is a shock
So unbearable, such a waste

Believe for a time
Far beyond where we are
A time of reunion for all
I'll see her again

Protect all you have
Life's so delicate tree
Protect each limb
Tomorrow may bring a storm
To crash our limbs to the ground

Enjoy all your loved ones
No cares of their faults
Kisses and cuddles abound
Take stock of all those around
For tomorrow
Brings new ground

He finished the little prose then folded it and placed it into his wallet.

CHAPTER 28

The following day he returned to Miami where he booked into a small motel close to the airport. He was not a big drinker but he let it all go at this point of his life. He felt cheated by God as he became angry at losing his mother. A sign of the grieving process was what any good counsellor would say. For Tom it was a time of indifference, he bought a large bottle of Southern Comfort from the corner store along the road, retreated to his room and began to look for the bottom of the bottle in the hope that it would give him the answers he was looking for.

On the Wednesday when he decided to open his eyes he realized that the world hadn't changed any. His head was a throbbing mass, his throat felt like the hairy armpit of a gorilla and his stomach was making noises similar to that of an erupting volcano. He couldn't move for hours for fear of the room around him spinning out of control. It was mid afternoon before he braved the elements and ventured out to a nearby burger bar in the hope that food would right his ills. It didn't. He just had to let the process take its course so back to the bed and rest.

Waking on the Thursday in the small hours he was angry with himself for allowing emotions to get the better of him. He was hungry now and room service was the only way he could get food without leaving the room. For Tom reality was screaming over the horizon at him. He had lost two days virtually and he knew he needed to get out of the US then onto Perth as soon as he could. There had been numerous texts to him from Vicki asking about his flight but he had not responded to them at all. This morning after a hearty breakfast he would try and answer her texts and arrange his flight schedule.

At 0700 he was at the Miami International awaiting his flight which left at 0810 taking him via Los Angeles where he would have a layover of

5 hours to kill. On arrival in LA he took the opportunity to have a look around part of the city. He was keen not to use any airports he had used previously for fear of someone pinpointing him in any way then flagging him to the security organizations.

His flight would take him from LA to Tokyo and then onto Kuala Lumpur where he would visit friends of his and also members of his family. Here it was going to be another emotional torment as he would need to tell some of his mother's closest friends that she was no longer around.

While Tom was coping with his loss as well as trying to arrange his flights from the US to Australia there was some frantic communications going between Baghdad and London in regards to the nurse Vicki Robson. Ashid needed to verify all the details before he put some of his agents on to it. He was delighted to hear that Warburton and Robson had struck up a relationship after first meeting in the apartment in London.

It didn't take Ashid's people long to be able to source the mobile number Vicki was using and being able to then put a tab on it. They were able to monitor her texts and the replies she was receiving totally without her realizing it.

Ashid was in his element now when he was told that Tom had contacted Vicki informing her he was making his way to Perth to be with her. He knew that the young man would not allow the final piece of his puzzle to go unchecked so it was to be an opportune moment for Ashid to be able to deal not only with Tom but also finish off the contacts he had struck up with the money train that had begun in Basra. It seemed to Ashid that he could kill two birds with the one stone as the British have a habit of saying.

While Tom was languishing in Los Angeles two of Ashid's agents had flown into Perth locating the residence of the Robson household. They also had located Vicki's workplace at the Royal Perth Hospital in Wellington Street.

They had just two days to be able to ascertain her normal route to work before she would be off roster for the four days following. Therefore they had to tackle her before the rest days started. They had it off to a 'T' after just those two days.

She used to leave home, take a five minute walk which would get her to a bus stop where she would take the number 100 bus taking her to the Canning Bridge Station where she would take the train which followed the Kwinana Freeway to Perth City. She would then alight at Mandurah

Station where she would walk to her place of work at the hospital, about 10 to 15 minutes.

They had decided to tackle her on her last day travelling home. They would have one follow her from the hospital and the other would wait with a car near the point where she would get off the bus before her five minute walk home. It was to be here that they would lift her, question her to find out what plans Tom had on his arrival in Perth. They already had the texts messages between them but the fear campaign was the icing on the cake as they would be one step ahead of him on his quest to find Caulfield.

The thing they most needed was to have Vicki so fearful of them that if any conversation between her and Warburton was made face to face they would get to know what was actually said.

It was Sunday afternoon when Vicki left the hospital to travel home at the end of her roster. She was getting excited at the prospect of seeing Tom soon and introducing him to her family. She was also hoping he was finished with the secret squirrel stuff that had befallen him in London. Yes, she certainly had a bigger bounce in her steps today but she was totally unaware that for the past two days she had had a secret admirer on her tail to and from work.

Another person had also joined the team of followers. An Englishman had flown in on the Saturday morning with instructions from Ashid to take control of the situation using his two top agents to finally bring Warburton to his end. Phil Ryder was full of himself wanting to prove that he was a top dog in the game but his two co-orts were not overly impressed with his personal approach and man management skills. At one point they felt it would be easier to cut his throat than listen to the idiot.

As Vicki got off the bus preparing to walk the five minutes or so to her parents home she headed for the traffic lights just ahead. On the opposite corner where she would cross stood a BP fuel station. She did not even notice the dark skinned man who had got off the bus directly after she had. He stood for a while to give her time to get ahead then followed. She stopped at the lights and hit the button waiting patiently for the little green man to glow before her on the opposite side of the road. The night had crept in but it was still one of those balmy nights with temperatures out of the ordinary being high for this time of year.

Beep, Beep, green man flashing she strode across the intersection, not a care in the world. Just a few more metres before she would turn into her street, opposite the turning was a group of shops but being Sunday they were all closed today with their lights out and no patrons about.

The street lights were none too bright with having fewer than most streets in this neighbourhood.

Turning into Downey Street alongside the low picket fence than abounded the corner house she saw a car parked against the pavement just a bit further on from the corner. She took no notice as in these side streets people parked along them whenever or wherever they needed to and anyway this might have been someone calling on the corner house residents.

What she failed to be able to see was a man standing just inside the gateway of the drive ahead. He was cleverly shielded by the trees that the corner house had growing along their frontage. From behind she hadn't heard the footsteps of her follower who had sped up a touch to be closer to her at this point. Why would she have known she had no care in the world her man was coming for her soon.

As Vicki got to the drive Ryder walked straight out causing her to stop dead in her tracks and stare perhaps in shock at the sudden appearance of him. Before she could say or do anything a hand came around her face clamping it hard onto her mouth to stop her from screaming. Her eyes bulged in fear as she suddenly remembered the night back in London in the apartment.

Phil Ryder grabbed hold of her arms and the two men lifted her up and manhandled her towards the car which just had its rear door thrown open as the girl was grabbed.

Phil stood to one side as the man at the rear pulled sideways on Vicki as he slid into the back seat pulling her along with him. As the two virtually fell into the car Phil closed the door, as he did he looked around to ensure they had not been noticed. There were no other persons around, lucky for them. Jumping into the front passenger seat the car started and slowly pulled away doing a 'U' turn heading back out onto Ley Street turning South then heading down till Patterson where it started to head west. When reaching the Kwinana Freeway it took a number of turns to get onto the opposite side of the freeway where there was a small park on the edge of the Canning River. Here the car stopped and all the lights went off. The driver got out and scanned the banks to make sure that there was no weekend fisherman on its banks near at hand to be able to recognize them.

As he returned he just lent against the car leaning down to the open driver's window and telling Ryder all was clear.

Ryder turned in his seat to be able to look at Vicki in the rear. She looked terrified with the hand of the man still clamped on her mouth. She could smell spices off the man and the taste of the man's hand was deplorable.

"Vicki, I will allow the man to remove his hand but you must promise that you will not scream. If you do then I will not be responsible for what he does. We just need to talk to you and as soon as we have we will drop you off home straight away no harm. Is that clear?" Ryder had this sick looking smile on his face wondering what this girl really saw in Tom Warburton.

Vicki tried to nod her head and Ryder could see she wanted to co-operate with them. He nodded to his mate in the rear who slowly removed his hand from her mouth.

"What do you want?" Vicki quivered out from her lips. "Who are you?"

"Let's just start with we know that Tom is coming to see you shortly and we know how he feels about you and of course you him." Ryder was beginning to enjoy this little escapade. "All we want is for you to be able to message us of his plans when he arrives. We need to know his every move." "Why would I do that? Who the hell are you?" Vicki was growing in confidence as she wanted answers from this smart arse smooth talking man in front of her.

"Look lovely I work for the British Government and our little friend Tom is doing things he shouldn't be. We need to be able to help him to stop the foolishness that has overcome him of late before he gets hurt."

"What do you mean?" Vicki was worried now Tom was in trouble with those who had helped him originally. That trust thing was still Tom's nightmare by the sound of it.

"Tom's actions are not what we need at the present time and we need to pull him back a peg or two. The thing is we need to know exactly what he proposes to do here in Australia and most essentially, also we need him not to know we are checking on him. Can we count on you to help us?"

"Why don't I speak to Tom and perhaps I can get him to pull back from whatever it is you don't want him to do. I know he will listen to me."

"We cannot warn him that we are here my dear as he has made it obvious from past attempts that he is not going to listen to us anyway.

I really regret this but it seems it may be necessary, I believe you have a younger brother and sister who attend the local high school here and I am sure you wouldn't want them to come to any harm."

Suddenly Vicki became alarmed again as she felt the cold chills going through her body. She loved her little brother and sister dearly, no way wanting anything to happen to them. Perhaps her parents could do something if she approached them but as she thought of that Ryder hit her with yet another threat.

"There is also of course your dear mum and dad. You see Vicki we know their every move from the time they go off to the Kingdom Hall for their meetings and also the business hours of their little shop they have in the city. If you want them all to stay safe and secure you need to be able to keep quiet on this little conversation and to do as you are told."

Vicki was horrified at what was happening to her. She was adamant as to the safety of her family and that nothing should ever happen to them at all. She just nodded at Ryder asking. "What do you want me to do?"

"Firstly you speak to no one about what we have discussed with you today including Tom or any family member. It is essential you keep absolutely quiet about this whole affair and then when it is all over you can go back to being a happy little family again. Am I making myself clear sweetheart?"

"Very." Was all Vicki could say in response to him.

"All we want you to do is text us when ever Tom makes any plans or tells you about anything he intends to do. That is if he tells you what he is up to. I will put my mobile number into your phone under the name of Phyllis in case he asks you any questions about the contacts on your phone. Phyllis will be your old school friend if need be. Hope he's not the jealous type."

"How long do I have to do this?" asked Vicki.

"Till I text you letting you know we are finished. Now believe me if you let him know what we are doing we will rip your family apart and you may not see any of them again. Is that clear?"

"Yes, yes." Her voice was now taking the form of panic as she spoke. She was totally terrified now, damn spooks' business she knew it would all end up in tears. Why had she got so close to Tom she asked herself? Why had she fallen so deeply for him? Damn the Governments, all of them, her Witness beliefs that God would destroy all of them one day couldn't come soon enough for her.

They sat for a short while longer while the driver finished his cigarette before he climbed back in, started the car following a nod from Phil Ryder and they drove off taking Vicki back to where they had lifted her. When they dropped her off Ryder reminded her of her obligations and the consequences if she failed to adhere to them. Vicki slowly walked the last few meters to her parents' house where all the lights were ablaze and music was coming from more than one place inside mixing into a form of tortured music.

She opened the front door walked in to the welcome of her mother who never noticed any difference in her daughter's appearance, assumed she was tired after the roster she had just completed. Excusing herself Vicki went straight up stairs to her room where she got herself undressed, slipping into the shower but staying there for a period of time which was not at all normal for her. Could she wash off the smell of those men that had touched her or the hold they had on her? How she loved Tom and craved to be able to see him again but was he bringing an unnecessary burden onto her and her family. Perhaps she may be able to convince him how pleasant it is to be part of the Witness community instead of the normal accepted ways of the world. Get him away from what he was doing. All she could hope is that he would see that there is a future in the resurrection as stated in Revelations. Please God let her be able to convince Tom to become part of her life and be a Witness as she was.

The one thing she did know was that she would not be sharing this incident with anyone when Tom actually arrived. She was totally unaware as to the technology these guys had hand to, they knew her every text and also whatever she received including phone calls. They also knew her every move.

Over the coming days she would be tormented but somehow she would try to relax so as not to alert Tom to any wrong understanding. She had to play by this fellow Ryder's rules or her family would undoubtedly be in danger.

CHAPTER 29

Tuesday 27 March 2007

There had been some upsetting days with close friends in Kuala Lumpur and Penang for Tom. He had to go through his mother's loss every time he spoke to someone new. It was too distressing at times with him just wishing it was all over and in the past. He thought he would become cold to death by now after all that had happened these past few months but needless to say he still got the pains of loss for his mother.

He had text Vicki yesterday giving details of his flight to Perth and how he was looking forward to seeing her. He knew his heart could manage anything with how he felt for Vicki, she had really taken a place inside him which he truly loved feeling. She had taken the heart from him calming it smoothly.

He had said his final farewells to everyone in Malaysia the night before then bright and early he was at the airport ready to fly to his new love. He sometimes thought that he would let the rest of his troubles be forgotten but his brain kept telling him he had to finish the final task or he would be tormented in the future.

He had had no contact with Gary even keeping the mobile disconnected so there was no GPS trace for them back in the UK. After the US meet with Coyles he was beginning to trust Gary a touch more. There had been nothing to implicate him in any wrong doing as yet. He hoped that trust would not be wasted though.

Relaxing in the business end of Malaysian Airlines flight 125 he has five hours or so before he would be landing in Perth. He was really looking forward to seeing and holding Vicki again. What he didn't know was that across the other side of the world a smug looking

Aspalson was planning his downfall in a way that he would disappear in the outback never to be found again.

Communication between Ryder and the UK was frantic after the boys in Australia got the text through that Tom was on his way. Plans were hurriedly being made to enable them to remove Tom completely from the face of the earth soon.

At three in the afternoon the plane landed at Perth Airport and taxied into its rank where the passengers started to exit through the tunnel. Tom being business class got out before the main throng of passengers which were a mix of backpackers, Malaysian holiday makers and families returning to home from a holiday. It was a bustle of activity as everyone descended on the baggage carousel to await their bags. Fortunately for Tom his was one of the first to appear out through the flap on the wall riding along the conveyor belt.

Grabbing his case he wandered off through to immigration and customs where he had no problems getting through quickly. Over that hurdle he started off to the exit of Customs into the arrival lounge and through the big automated doors where on the other side he was met with crowds of welcoming people but not for him however.

As he pulled the case along by his side he finally got to the exit point to the main terminal building area. The point where the rails stop and the people there ran and cuddled as if it was the only time they had ever met. Suddenly two hands clamped around his eyes from the rear. The hands were soft and warm to the touch. Tom knew they were the hands of Vicki and he slowly turned to see her bright smiling face with eyes glowing facing him. There was no other move left but to kiss those beautiful lips that were pursed in front of him which he did.

They were locked in each other's arms for what seemed like a lifetime. People pushed and shoved around them to get their own bags through to get out to their relatives and friends frustrated by these two lovers who didn't seem to have a care in the world.

Tom pulled away realizing that they might be in someone's way, grabbed his case and Vicki's hand then walked over out of the passenger traffic before they got trampled down. Finding a quiet area he again kissed those lips he had so desired for so long.

"Hello my love." Came the sigh from Vicki. "Have you finished with your little job?"

"Let's not talk about that now, lovely. How are you? I've missed you so much, you are the driving force that has kept me going."

"Ok, let's just get to the car park then home. My parents are so keen to meet you but they won't be home till later though."

"Then we can be alone together and I can tell you how much you really mean to me."

"You are looking well Tom, I'm sorry about your Mother though; cancer is such a cruel disease."

"I'm just sorry she couldn't have met you, you would have liked each other I know that for sure."

"We will one day, let me tell you how later."

Vicki had borrowed her Mother's car to go to the airport, she had no idea if she was being followed but didn't care. It took them a matter of minutes to get out of the airport traffic heading off to the west to Manning where Vicki's parent's home was. Arriving shortly after four thirty they were met at the door by Vicki's younger brother Troy.

Troy offered to take Tom's case for him but Tom declined saying he needed to get himself settled somewhere near not realizing that arrangements had been made for him to stay with the Robsons. Vicki quickly explained that her parents had made up the spare room for him as he was very welcome to stay. Tom was overjoyed, it meant he wouldn't have nights alone while here which was good for him at the moment. He had had far too many of those lonely nights.

The evening was spent getting to know each other again and Tom was quite taken with Vicki's parents when they finally arrived home. Although religious they were down to earth, friendly placing absolutely no pressure of their own convictions upon him. Dinner was a bit strange for Tom as they all held hands while Vicki's father gave a prayer of thanks. Tom just closed his eyes keeping quiet till they had finished the prayer then got into the food laid out on the table. Tom got to meet the younger sister, Lorna, as well. The evening was a great relief for Tom as he relaxed and sat cuddled up to Vicki on the sofa trying to forget all his misfortunes of the past.

The following few days were ones of walking, talking and loving the moments between Vicki and himself. Vicki showed Tom around the city area including King's park which he loved. It was one of the places that he had heard his father speak of many times so it was an absolute pleasure to be able to see it for himself.

It wasn't till the Thursday that Tom suddenly told Vicki he still had some stuff to sort out. He told her he would leave Perth in the next couple of days and go east to Melbourne where hopefully he would finish what he had started. She tried her hardest to dissuade him but to no avail he was determined to finish it. She had spoken to him about many of the things that her religion promoted in forgiveness, resurrection, and trust in God. The night before she had tried to persuade him to go along with the family to the Kingdom Hall but Tom had declined the offer saying perhaps in the future he might look at what was on offer.

Vicki tried once too often to talk Tom out of his goal being met with a stern reaction from him. He told her that it was commendable that she felt the way she did about the lasting peace of forgiveness but he had to find his own answers. It was too easy to take hold of perceptions of what was written in books without analysing them. After all, he told her, perceptions were one or a group of men's interpretations of something and you couldn't really see if it was the right interpretation or not till you really looked at it yourself coming up with your own conclusions.

Tom definitely had his doubts about religious connotations no matter which ones he looked at whether they were Catholic, Jewish, Muslim, Hindu, Church of England or Jehovah's Witnesses all had their good and bad points about them, something he was not prepared at present to pursue in any way. He felt if you shrouded yourself in one particular group you may miss the truth of what was actually real.

Vicki pulled back a touch after upsetting Tom hoping she could deter him another way but he was so stubborn in his mind she knew he would be difficult to stop. With this in mind she set her mind to being able to stay with him till he finished his job perhaps somehow steering him away from danger where she could. It was going to be a delicate thing to do but she was determined she wanted to keep Tom as her soul mate so anything she could do was worth the effort. Also her nemesis Phyllis had told her to tag along to keep them up to date. That warning again for her family.

Accepting that Vicki wanted to come with him he made arrangements to take the long way to Melbourne finding on the net a way of doing just that. He had found that some of the mobile home companies actually paid people to relocate some of their vehicles between major cities. Tom seized the opportunity for one of those by booking to take a six berth camper from Perth to Adelaide leaving on Monday the second of April. Vicki was overjoyed to be included although her parents were a bit wary of the point of just the two of them being alone for so long on such a long trip by road. Tom went out of his way to assure them that he would be the gentleman through and through but at the same time hoping that they could finally be alone and perhaps share each other fully as he really wanted so much.

Vicki, once she knew the plans that had been made texted to Phyllis on her phone. She hated having to do it but thought that if they could help her by stopping Tom getting into trouble she would benefit in the end. The return text just said thank you.

Receiving the text Phil Ryder read it out loud to his two co-orts. It gave him time before Tom would pick up his ride and leave Perth, time he would use to its fullest. This was the best news as it was a long drive across the Nullarbor with many a person going missing on that exact route before.

The timing was opportune for Ryder and he immediately sent a message to his friend and lover Aspalson back in the UK. Now he had to make plans for the trip making sure he and his two mates were ready somewhere on the road to finish this little soldier boy off. He didn't care about the fact that Vicki had told him she would be going along, just collateral damage for him but also she was the listening post for his endeavours.

CHAPTER 30

Sunday I April

April fool's day lingers on most peoples' lips when it arrives on the calendar. Today was no different and making it worse being a Sunday meant more practical jokes being played than ever. For the men preparing to go hunting for Tom you would have to wonder whether they or Tom were the Fools.

Ryder and his two men left Perth on this Sunday after he confirmed with Vicki that all was on course as per Tom's plan. They had changed vehicles and hired a V8 powered van which they could use to sleep in if necessary. They made it to Norseman where the Nullarbor Plains started; it was the only highway through to the Central part of Australia leading down to Adelaide then off to Melbourne.

The Nullarbor Plain which means: *nullus*, "no", and *arbor*, "tree" is part of the area of flat, almost treeless, arid or semi-arid country of southern Australia, located on the Great Australian Bight coast with the Great Victoria Desert to its north. It is the world's largest single piece of limestone, and occupies an area of about 200,000 square kilometers (77,000 sq mi).[1] At its widest point, it stretches about 1,100 kilometers (684 mi) from east to west between South Australia (SA) and Western Australia (WA). They say treeless but the start from Norseman has many small trees aligning the roadside.

The road beyond Norseman was bitumen but lonely and long. There was one particular stretch that boasted that it was a 90 mile straight nearly 150 kilometres. This was also the area where the Plain became almost treeless. This for Ryder was the favourite pick to be able to hijack Tom's trip to deal with him. With this road they could see the traffic from either side for miles giving them many opportunities to tackle the rogue. Ryder had no firearms but he saw that the three of them could and should be able to tackle Tom easily; after all he was just one young man. He had already asked Vicki if Tom was armed at all which brought a swift answer of no.

On Monday the second of April Vicki took Tom to pick up the motor home from its city depot from whence they took it back to Manning where the two of them loaded enough linen for two beds to be used and plenty of food and provisions to last them for a week or so.

They left at midday travelling through Northam then on to Southern Cross which they made their overnight stop. Next morning they were going to be making a similar length trip to Norseman where unbeknown to Tom, Ryder and co were anxiously waiting his arrival.

Tom took one detour around Kalgoorlie just to say he had been there, another mention of his father's exploits years before. They eventually pulled into the BP fuel depot at Norseman before dusk refuelling ready for the long haul across the Nullarbor the next day. Tom had checked the map finding it was nearly 2000 kilometres to Adelaide so it was not just a one day drive more a three day expedition. They booked themselves into the local caravan park to relax for the night. While Tom was off getting a shower at the camp shower block rather than trying to squeeze himself into the one in the back of the motor home Vicki was again texting Phyllis the plan for the following day. She knew Tom would rise at day break and start off as soon as possible to make the most of the light so be able to find a point to hunker down somewhere in the great unknown.

Ryder was only a couple of hundred meters away in a local motel when he received the message immediately relaying the message on to his two men. They would need to be ready as once they all started the quest across the plains there would be opportunities arise they must be ready for. His two Arab mates were not taking many chances as they had acquired a couple of baseball bats while in Perth. The stories they had heard about this Tom fellow were not at all very friendly. Unknown to Ryder though, was that one of the agents with him had also acquired a revolver from a bikie contact that was given him by one of Ashid's contacts in Perth.

The night was cool but clear, there was a slight shower during the night which kept the temperature low. Tom while he had been in Perth had had only one turn of nightmares which had caused some anxiety to Vicki's parents. They knew what Tom had gone through in Iraq and praised their daughter for being so devoted to helping people like Tom.

That night Tom had a relapse with the response that Vicki immediately jumped into bed alongside him to calm him down. As much as Tom wanted to he held, he found he wanted so much to be able to make love to Vicki. It was a strain and he felt it was for Vicki as well. Her religious convictions would have gone out of the window if Tom had placed a hand somewhere which caused some kind of tingle or electric shock effect. She knew that but sometimes prayed that he would make the move therefore relieving her from being the perpetrator religiously. Alas though the night was uneventful.

Next morning Tom was tidying everything up on the outside of their mobile home and while he did that Vicki quickly sent a text that they were about to leave. By 0700 hrs Tom was seated in the driver's seat and moving out of the caravan park heading back up to the BP where he would take a right and head out into the Nullarbor. The flat expanse of nothingness was all Tom could think of but he would be pleasantly amazed at the beauty that the Plains had to offer people travelling there. His target for today was Eucla about 700 kilometres further down the track.

Heading out from Norseman the road was good; little traffic either way made it a quiet ride. Both sides of the road had bushes and trees set back about ten meters or so either side. This was a blessing as the wildlife around this country was not your normal small rabbit but more a large one in the form of a kangaroo which could do some serious damage to the vehicle if hit. Another candidate for road kill was the emu a larger than life flightless bird.

This style of scenery went on for a few hours before the open Plains laid out in front of them with virtually no fauna about anywhere just the odd small salt bush. The sides of the road were sandy looking and not very inviting if he suddenly went off the main thoroughfare so he had to be careful about fatigue. Vicki wasn't up to having a go at driving this vehicle she reckoned it was more like a furniture truck to her.

They had stopped after about three hours for a brew at the side of the road and then set off again. It was so peaceful Tom thought to himself. Little to no traffic in either direction and the weather wasn't too bad apart from some light rain the night before. Tom hadn't seen another vehicle for ages he thought to himself rechecking his watch. The last one he had seen was a triple trailer truck that was hiking along in the opposite direction which must have been doing about 100 km per hour.

The road ahead was clear and the sun was bright above him now, a relief from the earlier hours when the sun was directly in his eyes rising from the East. This stretch of road was so long and straight he thought he may have been able to tie the steering wheel down put the engine on cruise control and go back and have a short sleep. No wonder they had so many people dozing off on the road in this vast country. This would be a hell of a problem if you were tired.

Just ahead he could see a white van to his left as if it had been pulled over for a break but was indicating as it was about to re-enter the road to continue its own journey. As Tom came closer he only saw a driver in the front thinking the poor bastard must have been off the road having a sleep. He passed the van sitting on cruise control and speeding along at about 110 km per hour, the maximum for this road.

As he passed the white van he saw in his mirror it pulled out following them along the road. No worries, thought Tom, a bit of company if anything goes wrong was all that came to mind. As the white van caught up to the rear of Tom's vehicle he peered at the reversing camera screen that was placed on the dash to his right and saw that there were now two people in the front of the van. It came very close to the rear of his vehicle with Tom thinking he was about to overtake him but it didn't, it just sat within a couple of feet of his bumper. He had heard many people talk about slip streaming to save fuel and thought this guy was possibly doing the same thing.

The van pulled out so as to overtake at one stage then went back behind. Tom couldn't work out what was going on with him as there was nothing coming towards them in the opposite direction. Then all of a sudden it pulled out into the right of his vision speeding up alongside him. As he glanced down he saw what was a dark face staring up across at him, an Arab face.

"Fuck." Tom exclaimed surprising Vicki who was dozing off in the passenger seat and jumped at the expression.

"What's wrong Tom?" She asked concernedly.

"Nothing Vic, nothing at all." He was watching the van closely now as it slowly crept to the front quarter of the mobile home. Tom tapped the brake which switched off the cruise control making the large mobile home slow under its own weight. Just as he did so the van pulled sharply in front of him and the brake lights blazed on. Tom did not hit the anchors because at the speed he was doing it would have been fatal for them both in such a large vehicle and top heavy to boot. He swerved to the van's right steering the mobile home as if to overtake the van.

This did not work out too well because as he pulled to the right the van saw what he was doing and deliberately moved back in front of him again. Tom hit the horn and brakes at the same time.

The van did the same making sure they kept the mobile home in place behind them. Their speed had declined to about 80 now and Tom was starting to consider that this deliberate act was something more than just a local type of hijack. The man he had seen was Arab looking. Perhaps again they were on his trail, but who had told them. Gary wouldn't have known as he had not lit up the mobile phone since he had left the USA. His head was trying to roll through who had known his movements. Nobody knew where the hell he was just now.

The last thing he wanted was to pull off onto the shoulder as it didn't look firm enough for the weight of this type of vehicle. The van was slowing further and Tom made numerous attempts to go around him without success.

"What's wrong Tom? Are they trying to hijack us or something?" Vicki had started to grip the handle by her side as Tom wrestled with the wheel trying in vain to get around these damn dimwits.

"Don't know Vic. Looks like another Arab on my back but I am not sure. Does this happen much out here someone getting hijacked?"

"It happens but not too often. What are you going to do?"

"Just hold on tight, I am going to try something and see what comes out of it." And with that Tom slammed the vehicle down a gear planting his foot onto the throttle. The home lurched forward smashing into the rear of the van sending it all over the road but still keeping control of the vehicle he was in. Tom gave it another go but this time he went off to the right of the rear of the van as the van pulled over he smacked it hard on the corner post which sent it careering off the road and onto the shoulder where he threw up sand, dust and stones all over the front of the mobile home as it passed by.

Tom seized the opportunity speeding forward changing up the gears and placing his foot firmly on the accelerator. The speed limit might have been 110 km per hour but by the time Tom had got momentum going on the mobile home it was plummeting along at 140 km per hour. It was driving well so Tom just kept the speed up hoping they would hit some traffic or even a roadhouse sooner rather than later. It wasn't to be just yet though.

Tom peered into the mirrors either side as well as looking at the reversing camera screen to see the van speeding after them easily catching them without any problems. Their vehicle was powered by a four cylinder turbo charged diesel but looking at the way the van was catching him it looked like they may have had petrol powered V6 or V8 under its bonnet. Within just a minute the van was again up to the bumper of the home.

Tom tried to tip the brakes to frighten the driver behind but that didn't work. This guy must be good Tom was convinced he had had training in something like surveillance techniques. He tried to keep the speed up but as he came around one of the few bends that were on this road the van slammed into the rear of him causing him to have to fight hard to keep the damn thing on the road in a straight line. Vicki screamed loud.

Tom told her to get in the back and wrap herself in the blankets on the bed at the rear then hold tight. He was hoping it wouldn't come to it but if he did turn this thing over then the body being fibre glass would just crumble around them. If Vicki was wrapped up below the window line she would have some protection if the thing did turn and crumble.

When he saw that she was well wrapped up securely he sped up yet again. He could hear her sobbing in the rear but took no notice. The van came alongside yet again before Tom could block it. He tried to push across to force it off the road but it was too powerful for him and just sped up past with one set of wheels churning up dust and shit off the shoulder of the road. The van was again firmly back in front of him again trying to control his moves.

It slowed and Tom belted it once again in the rear but the van stood firm this time. One of the rear windows had smashed on this attempt. When Tom looked up into the van he suddenly saw what looked like a baseball bat smash the rest of the window bits out which hit the front screen of Tom's vehicle. Tom accelerated smashing the rear of the van yet again just as the bat was coming out of the window. He hit it with such a force that whoever was holding the bat it let it go because he must have catapulted forward in the rear of the van. The bat came out and smashed into Tom's windscreen making it shatter before him. The bat dropped and he felt it smack something underneath. Now he was doing over a hundred kms per hour and couldn't see a blasted thing. He lent forward while allowing the vehicle to decelerate and punched out the screen as quickly as he could.

Tom's hand was bleeding by the time he had finished punching the screen out. The screen flopped and dropped hitting the road smashing even more spots under the vehicle. The wind was rushing into the vehicle now causing the speed to drop as it was like it was a big collector similar to a parachute and pushing back on the vehicle from the inside.

Tom's eyes were watering from the wind gush coming through the open front end. He looked at the rear of the van in front, saw the hire sticker and the damage he had done to it. Well he thought if I am going to lose my deposit then so are you buggers. He had dropped down to about 70km per hour now letting the van stay just ahead of him. If only he could hold them off till there was some other traffic on the road around them then there might be some sort of defence for them. There was nothing though, the road was completely clear both directions. Not a sign of life or housing anywhere. How isolated this bloody place was.

Vicki hadn't moved from where Tom had told her to hide, she was too scared to show her head at this point. Had she done the right thing? Were these guys the ones she had texted or were they some other group trying to get to Tom? She wasn't prepared to risk lifting her head above the blankets she was now firmly beneath. She felt the wind blowing through the mobile home and there were towels pillows and sheets fluttering about inside.

After a further two kms Tom was beginning to feel the mobile home starting to shake somewhat. He scanned the dials in front of him but they all seemed a blur with tears in his eyes caused by the wind still gushing in through the open front. He brought up his right hand wiping his forefinger across the eyes to clear them. Then he saw the red line of the water temperature gauge and the needle just above it sitting in the danger zone.

Shit, something, the blasted bat had hit the radiator. He had to slow further as to push on too hard would cause the whole engine to seize stopping them dead, then he would be face to face with whoever was in the van in front. He had to make a decision and fast.

Just up ahead was a wide area of just dirt and scrub either side of the road. This was going to be his last chance he knew before the engine blew. He was going to risk virtually wiping out the motor home with what he had in mind. There was no other option left for him. He slowed to about 50 km and waited a few seconds. The van slowed just ahead about fifty meters or so in front. Tom changed down a gear and slammed on the throttle for one last hoorah. The motor home leapt forward with engine screaming, the rev counter whisking away into the red zone, the temperature gauge went right to the top of its glass case looking like it might just bend the needle. Tom's speed went to just over the 80 mark as he came up close to the van. He could see that the driver was watching him closely to be able to shut off any exit Tom might think he had either right or left.

Both drivers' eyes were on each other as Tom came within the last couple of meters as he then just steered slightly to the left, as he did so the van went left. Tom took the opportunity then to slam the motor home into the middle of the van rear by steering sharply right. He hit the van bang smack in the centre of its rear doors which threw the van sideways. With the motor home still pushing hard it spun the van to its left causing the front left hand wheel to start to dig into the dirt which forced the whole vehicle to lift up on its left hand side. Tom continued to push hard with the accelerator fully planted on the floor and saw much to his pleasure the van lifted up high enough to continue its momentum over onto its right side.

The van started to barrel roll continuing away from Tom as it went allowing him to slow down. Tom's engine sounded as if it was about to come through the floor as it strained under the pressure of heat and space between the moving parts internally. He eased off the throttle slowing the whole unit down on its own steam.

The van had turned over four times and was about to bounce to a stop on its roof. Tom pulled the motor home in towards the van as it came to a standstill then rammed it hard into the rear doors pushing it along on its roof lodging it between two thick prickly bushes. Both vehicles came to a halt as Tom jumped out of the motor home and ran down towards where the passenger door was. As he pulled on the door a body fell out at his feet, blood pissing out from its head. The man who had come out obviously didn't have his seat belt on and had smacked his head around during the rolling. He was unconscious and his features and colour were Arabic.

Tom looked into the van where he saw the driver, another bloodied Arab, trying to frantically free himself from the seatbelt he had on. Leaning across the seat area while standing on the inside of the roof, now the floor Tom placed a quick karate punch to the side of the head and then another to the man's throat. It virtually paralysed him sending him completely limp. What is it with these fucking Arabs?

Looking around into the rear of the van Tom noticed the tangled mess of a man in the rear, who was face down with arms and legs tangled up in gear that was stored in the rear. Before he pulled himself out of the van he checked the driver's pockets for anything useful. Finding nothing except a passport he took that pushing it into his own pocket. Back out of the van he frisked the bloodied mess outside of the passenger door and found not only a passport but also a loaded revolver. He removed both from the man's person.

Coming around to the rear of the vehicle he had to reverse the motor home away from the doors to be able to open them. When he started the motor home it groaned and strained before it finally burst into life. He quickly reversed the vehicle away from the doors just before it finally stopped dead. The engine had finally seized and was now a fixed ornament in this wilderness.

He again jumped from the motor home and went to the doors where he opened them cautiously before peering in the back. It was a mess, there was gear everywhere and the man on the floor, once the roof, was still out cold to the world. Tom crawled into the back and grabbed the man's shoulders lifting him and turning at the same time. To his amazement he was confronted with a face he knew.

There in front of him was Phil Ryder, his face was smeared with blood but he was breathing. "What the fuck are you up to Ryder and why the Arab contingent?" He said to himself then searched around for anything of importance on him before he exited the van going to the side door of the motor home. Climbing inside he looked at where he had sent Vicki and to his amazement she was still trussed up under the blankets and had not moved an inch. Still sobbing he placed his hands on her for comfort to calm her down.

"It's alright Vic, you can come out now." Tom laughed as he said it. He didn't want to frighten her so waited till her scuffled hair began to appear and then her terrified eyes came over the blankets. She then pulled herself up into a seating position looking tentatively at Tom.

"Have they gone?" she asked looking out of the side window. "No, lovely they are all in their van at the front of us." "What do they want Tom?"

"Fuck knows. Don't care, let's just get our shit together and try and get a lift out of here. This little home is dead in the water."

Vicki asked nothing else as she and Tom got only the essential stuff they would need together. If they had to walk out of this desolate place they needed to only carry what they really needed.

As Tom exited the side door he noticed a vehicle coming towards them from the opposite direction they were travelling. He didn't want to have to go back towards Perth so he would let that one go providing they hadn't seen the mess the two vehicles were in. Walking out towards the road Tom turned around where to his amazement he saw the rear of the motor home showing no sign of the van or damage there. It looked like he had parked it up amongst the bushes for shade. The car going in the direction of Perth just slowed to check on the figure they saw. Tom waved them on and smiled. Their vehicle slowed but when they saw Tom wave them on, they accelerated, tooted the horn and waved back. Tom sighed with relief.

As Tom neared the roadside he saw what looked like a truck coming towards them in their direction of travel. He would try and wave it down to get a lift if he could. He turned to see where Vicki was. She had come out of her little hiding place with the bag she was told to put only essentials in and was walking slowly towards Tom. She did not even look at the van on its roof but as she got near to Tom she asked. "Are they dead?"

"No just a bit shook up. Don't worry about them, they will be ok." Tom assured her.

The truck was now looming up on their position and must have seen Tom waving him down from the side of the road. It was a Kenworth with a couple of trailers on its rear. He slowed and pulled up just past where Tom was standing. The driver stayed in his seat and waited for Tom to come to the passenger door, no one got out of their vehicle in these parts for fear they could be hijacked.

Tom opened up the door peered at the driver who was larger than life. He was huge from the head down. If he stood he would have resembled the largest barrel ever made. Tom smiled at the man. "Any chance of a lift mate?"

"What's wrong with your bus there?" the truckie asked.

"Damn radiator got a stone through it and it's blown the bloody engine eh." Tom looked at him shrugging his shoulders.

"Just you and the Sheila is it?"

"Yep, just the two of us. Off to Adelaide for a break." Tom hoped that this guy may be going all the way for them.

"Ok mate. Get your girl to climb in the rear here and you can run shotgun eh. I can drop you off at Ceduna as I'm hauling gypsum from there across to Perth."

"That's great. Much obliged. I can call the hire company from there and arrange pick up." Tom turned to help Vicki up into the cab and as he did so he whispered in her ear not to say anything about what had just happened. Vicki nodded relieved they had got a lift meaning she was not going to have to walk miles upon, miles.

The big Kenworth slowly moved off from the side of the road picking up speed as it went. Tom looked back towards the vehicles they had just left but there was no sign of life around it as yet.

Tom's mind was doing back flips trying to work out how Ryder knew he was there or why he was with the two Arabs. This was getting weird. He hadn't even put the mobile phone together for Gary to get a fix on him as yet. This was getting uncanny for him, who was it that knew his every move? Did they have a damn satellite on his case?

CHAPTER 31

The big rig really got up some speed as it headed for the Border between West and South Australia. It actually beat the speed limit Tom noticed as he looked over towards the driver's gauges. The actual speed this rig was doing with the two trailers on was over one hundred and thirty. These drivers have a renowned reputation for fixing their speed limiters so they could push the rigs faster even though the speed limiters were on their rigs by law.

They passed through the quarantine station at the Border Village without having to stop. Going the other way and the officers there would go through the vehicle with a fine tooth comb. It was one of those things where one State didn't want any unwelcome bugs from another one. South Australia must have been a bit more lenient but as Tom would find out one day, when he researched this country, they had a quarantine station further into the State and were just as worried about fruit and vegetables being carried as the others.

Pulling into Ceduna as the sun began to set about 1830 was a pleasant experience. The welcoming sunset as it disappeared over the horizon was something to ponder about.

During the ride Tom had asked the usual questions of is there a car hire place or even an airport. To his joy there was an airport that had two flights a day between Ceduna to Adelaide. As they got to the town centre Tom tried to get a call into the airport but unfortunately was out of luck. A recorded message told him to ring the office over in Adelaide but when he tried was unable to get an answer there this time of night, another recorded message. The truck dropped them off near town at the BP Service station because he was detouring down to the harbour side ready for another load to be put on.

After thanks between Tom and the driver the couple watched as the truck pulled out of the servo. Tom along with Vicki headed into the service station restaurant.

Tom managed to find a taxi number by the phones inside the restaurant area. It was only a matter of minutes before the taxi arrived and after a quick chat Tom decided not to take the driver's advice, as he told him the best place to hang your sack for the night was in a motel nearby. He also said there was a Caravan park that had onsite cabins which Tom favoured more so in case the trio following managed to get to Ceduna looking for them, their first checks would certainly be the motels. He hoped they would be able to get a lift past Ceduna thinking Tom was heading to Adelaide by road.

At the caravan park they managed to get a cabin where they were snugly camped down by eight o'clock. Tom had managed to get through to a booking company eventually to arrange a flight but that wouldn't be till the next morning. He would have to be on his guard till then during the night just in case the trio following actually got to Ceduna. After arranging the flight he made sure that the cabin was secure by planting a few bits of furniture by the door to give some sort of warning if anyone tried to get in. He slept with the revolver close at hand under his pillow.

Vicki was frightened the whole night, she wanted to be able to text the man of their position because she was worried about her family but Tom gave her little opportunity to be able to do it without seeing what was happening. She would have to wait now till an opportunity arose tomorrow.

Tom kept putting scenarios through his mind trying to work out how he was being followed. The other thing that was now bugging him was the fact that Ryder was one of the people after him now. This was becoming more and more confusing for him. He had lost all confidence in people yet again and refused his own idea to ring Gary.

Next morning, early, Tom got himself into the shower where he stayed longer than usual to get his head around the coming day. While he was in there Vicki took the opportunity to text Phyllis where they were including their plans for the day. She gave all the details including where they were staying and the flight they were hoping to take by nine o'clock that morning. In reply Phil had text back that he was in Port Augusta but still wanted Vicki to try and delay their departure from Ceduna till later so he could actually meet the plane in Adelaide. Vicki was completely oblivious as to Phil being part of the hijack the day before.

As they went to leave the cabin Vicki tried to put on a bit of an act saying she had a serious migraine and would like to stay in the cabin a while to try to ease the aches. She blamed the previous day's events for her condition. However, Tom wasn't going to miss the flight at any cost finally persuading Vicki to just get on board with him after he went and purchased a good pair of sunnies for her. Tom explained that they would be in Adelaide by 1030hrs and safe. She couldn't delay him at all as much as she tried so took the opportunity at the airport to use the ladies room to text Phyllis again to let him know she had had no joy in delaying their flight.

CHAPTER 32

Melbourne Thursday 5 April 2007

In the offices of Asia Pac this rare bright morning there was some order of panic organised though it may be amongst the two partners who were in at the break of dawn. Both Welsh and Caulfield had come urgently to the office after they had failed to get any response from their people in Nassau over the past few days. Both were hurriedly trying to position the Company assets they had control of into some form of order they alone could control.

"I can't believe this Peter, there should be at least twenty million in the Cayman accounts. I just cannot get into them to transfer it out."

Caulfield looked at Welsh with a suspecting gaze. "Those guys wouldn't have done the dirty on you would they. That's an awful stash of cash to not try to get."

"Peter please, those men were the most loyal people you could have on your team. You and your police mind are far too suspicious at times. You know that someone hijacked them when they went to Rheingold's place taking out Phorbes."

"Yes I know that. But why hasn't Sweetman been in touch with us." "I don't know. After speaking to the receptionist there has been absolutely no contact with him since we heard about that business with the gentleman we were supposed to have sent there being killed in the offices. Sweetman is probably holed up somewhere hiding just in case someone is after him as well."

"That doesn't answer the fact about the accounts Tony."

Welsh sat down on his computer and started to Google Nassau and the local news. He found the piece about Malik there but could not find anything else relating to Asia Pac. What he was unaware of was the fact that the authorities had put a block on the death of Sweetman after some pretty frantic chats between London and the Bahamas.

He gave it away after an hour or so and went again to Peter's office next door. "Peter there is nothing on the net of anything of importance about us or our people there."

Peter Caulfield just looked blankly with the usual look he would give to a suspect he might have pulled in when he was a Military Cop. Shaking his head he acknowledged Welsh. "Perhaps it is time to take up and run Tony. We have made more than plenty and the problem I have always had is the association we have had with that weasel, Ashid. I do not trust him, what with the feedback we got about Athens, it seems his men are popping up in all the right places and that includes this guy that popped up in the office at Nassau."

"Perhaps you're right Peter. I'll check our records here and transfer the assets over now." He turned, walked back to his office and started to punch numbers of code into his keyboard.

Peter Caulfield aka Scholfield started to empty drawer loads of papers from his filing cabinet. He dragged over a large rubbish bag and the shredding machine, slowly feeding paper after paper into it. He was determined not to leave a trace of anything for anyone.

Two hours later Caulfield had finished in his office. It was empty of any paper trail; there was no trace of anything or anyone occupying the bloody place come to that.

Welsh was virtually finished with his little task on the computer transferring what funds he could get his hands on. He was smiling broadly by the time his cousin came into the room. "Done Pete. I've managed to transfer all the monies from Athens including from here to our off shore accounts. We haven't done too badly either. Even with the loans we have placed with Ashid we have close to two hundred million which doesn't include the money that was in Nassau's accounts."

"Tidy little business we have had eh? The financial crisis sure as hell exponentially lifted our profits. You are a genius cous.

Look I've emptied my spot next door, now we should get rid of what evidence is laying around in here. I just feel that we are running out of time and those bastards in Whitehall might be gaining ground on us."

Welsh assured his cousin that they were protected via Aspalson. He had made the recommendations for a lot of transactions to go between them and the British Government. As far as they were concerned the British Government were oblivious to what had happened these past few years.

The biggest thing they now had to worry about was that if they became positively linked to Ashid too closely with what he had planned in the future then that would surely give them an extended stay at Camp Delta in Guantanamo. Although they had been assisted in the escape with the cash from Iraq by Ashid they were also fully aware that he was planning a strike against the allies at some stage of his future. Neither thought about the importance of the containers at this stage or their destinations after they had left Nassau.

By the mid afternoon Welsh had paid off the receptionist giving reasons of having to move the main office to a major seaboard city in the US to meet the demands of future trading. He wasn't lying either, they had made a packet churning over business that had defaulted in the States and there were many more to go if they so chose to continue.

Neither Welsh nor Caulfield had any intentions of continuing their business ventures however. They had enough money now to be able to live in splendour for the rest of their lives and more. After all some of their partners were no longer around to take a share of the spoils which gave these two more of it.

Welsh made some quick calls demanding that all the furniture which was on hire was to be collected immediately. Being the weekend of Easter he had to be rather firmer than normal but managed to have all the hired gear collected late that afternoon. That started during late afternoon with protests from workers collecting the items who would normally have got away from work early being Easter. With everything gone from the offices it left Welsh with just a couple of boxes and his laptop to contend with.

All documentary evidence had been destroyed through the shredder then carted off to some security company furnace. The office was completely empty by the time the two of them were ready to depart and go their separate ways as they had always agreed. Welsh would be going off to Sydney or at least near where he could live out his days close to his family. Caulfield was heading off north to Queensland, nothing permanently planned as yet but he would test the water as he went he said.

Just before they finally kicked everything into touch Welsh set up a call to Ashid's office to discuss the loans and future transfers. He was not prepared to let Ashid know the true nature of his actions as Caulfield had placed the seed of distrust in his mind about the men so far lost.

"Ashid, Welsh how are you?" Welsh was super cool on the phone for this one.

"Fine Tony and you? No problems I hope?" Ashid was concerned about the reason for this particular call as it was outside of their normal communications dates.

"All good my friend. Just wanted to touch base with you in reference to our loans with you and the future payments. I believe you are well aware of the figures?"

"Certainly Tony. I have instructed my people here to relay transfers as per our original discussions. I can say that I am close now to be able to resign from my post here and take up my other options. Our business together has been so far very profitable for the both of us."

"That's good Ashid, then we are still on the same page so to speak."

"Certainly my friend. I hope to be able to visit you in the near future to extend our dealings further."

"I'll look forward to that. Till then." Welsh had heard enough just wanting to just get away from the terrorist he had coupled with for a quick kill of the cash. He had no intentions of having any further dealings with Ashid including sending any more monies or even receiving what was a fictitious loan repayment. Ashid would twig in about a week that something was adrift when communications either from him or through his bankers were receiving returned responses from the Asia Pac business unanswered.

Ashid obviously had no updates for him about what was happening around the place. Perhaps Peter was right and he was behind the deaths of their friends and colleagues. Never mind, time was up now it was their turn to disappear. They looked around one last time at the empty office and as they left Peter Caulfield, aka Scholfield began unscrewing the signs that had adorned their personal office doors the past year or so. All that remained was the glass door signifying that Asia Pac resided here.

In the car park below the office block they shook hands telling each other they would keep in touch, after all they were family. Welsh got into his silver grey Mercedes E270 CDI and sped out the car park into the traffic away to his outer suburbs home at Mt Evelyn.

Caulfield opened the door of his deep green BMW M3, snuggled himself into the driver's seat, started it up spinning the wheels one last time to his own bemusement making a hell of a racket in the underground car park. He pulled out the car park and turned towards his own little retreat of a penthouse apartment overlooking Albert Park raceway.

Asia Pac had closed for business one last time today.

CHAPTER 33

The Regional Express plane took off on time from Ceduna Airport heading south towards Adelaide. Meanwhile Phil and his merry band of misfits were hiring yet another vehicle that was going to take them onward to Adelaide. They left Port Augusta at about 0830 and were down past Port Pirie before Tom's flight was even off the ground. By the time they had reached Two Wells just north of Adelaide the plane had landed with Tom and Vicki leaving the terminal then taking a taxi to the Tollgate Motel at the foot of the main highway to Murray Bridge. It was out of the way and not very well known. Adelaide had just started to recover from the V8 supercars that had taken over the whole of Adelaide in one way or another during the month earlier. All everyone was talking about was the weekend of 1 to 4 of March when the State had played host to the supercars.

Tom didn't want to leave anything that could trace them so did not try to get a hire car from the airport, instead choosing to phone for one from the motel when he arrived and picking it up that afternoon from another suburb alone. Tom had taken the revolver with him when he had left in order not to let Vicki find it by mistake causing her to worry even more.

He had instructed her not to answer the door to anyone except him. It was when he returned with the vehicle that as he turned into the motel car park he noticed a man with a bandaged head sitting in a car parked closely against the wall opposite the entrance door. On closer look as he turned his car around in the car park he saw that it looked like one of the men from the van.

Tom was damned if he could work out what was going on, how the fuck did they find him this time? His concern quickly went to Vicki who was up stairs in the room alone or so he thought. He backed the car to the far end of the car park under a shade cover and waited for a short while. It took all of fifteen minutes before he saw Phil and the other Arab come out of the entrance door of the motel and saunter over to the car with the bandaged head sitting there waiting. They got in and the car reversed out leaving the motel through the arches. They turned to the left and drove off.

Tom got out of the hire car running over to the exit to see which direction the guys had gone but as he got to the corner of the arches there sure enough they were just parking the car opposite the arches after turning their car around. Tom pulled back quickly and went directly up to the room where he found Vicki just sitting there quietly.

"Everything Ok sweetheart?" he said as he came into the room.

"Yes Tom. Just been watching the TV."

"No one disturbed you then?"

"No it has been quiet since you left. Why?"

"Just checking to make sure you are OK my love."

Tom wasn't sure of what was going on. Surely not he thought as he looked at Vicki. He shook his head and went to his bag where he had the Mobile that Gary had given him.

He turned to Vicki saying he was going out to get some food and would be back before she knew it. She just nodded at him. Something wasn't right, Tom thought. She hadn't come over to kiss him even; she hadn't even smiled like she usually did. She appeared unnerved but why?

He left the room assembling the mobile phone as he walked ready to get in touch with Gary. It was two o'clock in the afternoon here making it four in the morning back in Old Blighty. Oh well time to get serious and wake a few people up. Tom thought if I'm awake so can the rest of the buggers around the world should be.

Tom took a point near the roadway where he could watch over the three stooges he had seen led by Phil Ryder. He watched, concentrated for a while then dialled Gary's number. A crusty, sleepy voice answered the phone on the other side of the world. "Hello." It was an effort for one so tired and now disturbed in the early hours.

"Gary, Tom, need your help mate. It seems everywhere I go the Arabs are on my tail straight away. This time though they have Phil Ryder with them."

"Hold on Tom. Where the fuck are you? We were beginning to get worried not hearing from you for a while."

"Adelaide, Australia."

"Great. I wish you would trust me and leave that damn phone on permanently."

"Sorry Gary, I had to find out who has been setting me up since I left London."

"Thanks Mate, and?"

"The pricks found me again across the Nullarbor, of all places, tried to run me off the road in the desert but failed thankfully. I don't know how they are tracking me but I do know it isn't via this mobile."

"Have you got another one you are using?"

"Yes but I haven't called anyone on it." Suddenly a pause and then. "Hold on, yep I gave Vicki a call to let her know when I was arriving."

"There you go. You say Vicki, the nurse from here in London?"

"Yes Gary, the Nurse. She is with me at the moment. I needed someone I could trust and she was the only one who fitted the bill."

"Thanks a mint pal. Give me the number of your other mobile and while you're at it the number of Vicki's just to be sure."

Tom quickly read out the numbers of the mobiles to Gary while still keeping a close eye on the three stooges opposite. He told Gary where he was at the present but at the same time he said you probably know by now anyway with the GPS tracker. Gary said he had just received a message that gave him Tom's location.

Gary told Tom to stay put even though there was someone watching him. He instructed Tom to hold off moving just yet till he could check the numbers and find out which was the one being tracked and by whom.

"Tom if you do have to high tail out of there please leave the phone on for me to trace you. It's time you definitely trusted me I think."

"Don't let me down Gary, I'm getting mighty pissed off with the betrayal business."

Gary laughed down the phone trying to reassure Tom that he could trust him. He possibly had already done that with the way Tom had used his phones since Nassau. Tom was convinced that there were other forces that were running against him and they were responsible for these interruptions in his travels.

Tom remained where he was watching and waiting. Patience was always a strong point in his character and this was just another test for him. It wasn't long before his phone burst into life. As he answered it knowing that Gary was at the other end because Gary's name showed up on the screen for him.

"How did you go?" Tom was really keen to know where this was all going and who, was the cause of his upsets.

"Mate, can you get to a computer and down load your emails? I think what you read there will blow your mind away. I've traced the calls on both phone numbers you gave and have printed all the communications between them and others for the last seven days. The email has been sent."

"Ok Gary. I will try and get the use of the motel's computer to read it. Give me half an hour or so." Tom hung up and returned to the entrance foyer where he found the manager. He asked whether he could use the motel computer to just print out an email someone was sending him from the UK. At first the manager was a bit unsure but after a short chat Tom finally persuaded him to go to his hotmail account and just print out the one from Gary. He took all of two minutes producing the printout just two pages long. Tom thanked him and went to go upstairs to the room to read it but suddenly stopped short staring in disbelief at what was in front of him.

Right there on the pages was the number that had been communicating with someone called Phyllis. That number was Vicki's, it had all the information of where he was, the plans he had put in place and what he intended to do. There was one in particular, a passage about trying to delay the two of them from leaving Ceduna which he remembered she did try with a supposed migraine. Tom was aghast; he had been betrayed by the one and only person he had trusted since returning from Iraq. He was frozen to the spot and couldn't move either up the stairs or out the door. He felt absolutely gutted, abandoned and betrayed. This sort of betrayal was worse than what he had experienced in Iraq

Suddenly his training and his past martial arts meditation lessons kicked in, he turned leaving the building. He read through the report again slowly pondering his next move. He had trusted Vicki explicitly since London; she was the only one who had really shown him his worth since prison. She alone was the one who had been treating him with the belief he could rediscover his sense of purpose and rebuild his trust in others. He had done that trusting Vicki totally. Now though, he was at a loss where it had led him, she was the one who had put them both in danger. Why? There was no other alternative but to front her with what he now knew, he turned retracing his steps up to the room where she was patiently sitting waiting for him.

He entered the room with what must have appeared to be a frown as Vicki noticed it immediately. "What's wrong Tom?" she said noticing the paper in his hand.

"Who the fuck is Phyllis?" Tom burst out angrily.

"A friend in Perth, why?" Vicki tried her hardest to keep her words strong and firm but there was hesitation in her voice.

"Let's have no lies eh Vic. Your religious beliefs tell you not to lie. The truth will set you free they say. Phyllis or shall we say Phil."

"Why have you been going through my phone Tom? I thought you and I had a trust between us?"

"I might have believed that in London but now I'm not so sure. Just outside on the road are the three stooges that tried to run us off the road a couple of days back." Tom threw the papers down onto the bed in front of her. "Explain that shit will you. I didn't touch your phone but the spooks sure as hell can trace things when they want to thank Christ."

She picked up the papers and started to read through them. Her face went pale as she went further line for line. Then tears started to flow down her face as she looked up towards Tom.

"I'm sorry Tom but they forced me to talk to them. They threatened my family."

"What was wrong with telling me, I may have been able to sort it before it got this far."

"I was frightened Tom. Please, I love you and I don't want to lose you."

"It's a bit late for that. You've totally betrayed our trust. Looks like it is back to square one for me, not being able to trust anyone. All the time we were travelling you told me that all was ok and there you were leading those arseholes to me slowly but surely. Don't you realize you were not only getting me in the firing line but you were also putting yourself in danger? Do you really think they care what happens to you anyway?

I'm sorry but you have crossed a line I can't forgive, it's over before it starts. You can make your own way back home and don't ever get in touch with me again. You and your damn religion, the so called Truth, load of hypocritical bullshit."

"Tom please, forgive me. Please I love you."

"Forget it Vicki I need to be alone. Forgiveness is not in my nature at present unfortunately for you. I am out of here now." He grabbed his bag placing his stuff inside it. He turned to Vicki as he finished. "Perhaps Phyllis can help get you back home."

Tom walked to the door leaving a sad, crying Vicki sitting on the bed regretting all that she had done this past week. As he opened it he turned back. "Goodbye Vicki and thanks." With that he went through the door and that was the last she would ever see of him. Storming down the stairs he went straight to the car, got in the driver's seat and slammed his fists together on the steering wheel in anger. A few deep breaths before he was ready again to take on whatever lay ahead.

Slowly he drove out of the motel through the arches and turned left heading up the hill towards Murray Bridge. The three stooges didn't move as he went out but he saw that the white guy, Ryder, was busily on the mobile either texting or trying to phone a friend.

It wasn't long before his shadows were right up his jacksy staying close on the freeway. They wouldn't try too much here as there were too many cars around in both directions but Tom knew when the opportunity came they would be on his case. Being Easter weekend now every man and his dog were trying to get out of the city and hide in the country somewhere. It seems no matter where you are in this world it is always the same at Easter.

They clung to him all along the Freeway till it turned into the Dukes Highway. Here Tom took a chance overtaking a truck making sure that his shadows were caught behind it. He held there for at least twenty kilometres till they finally got around the truck and again engaged his bumper.

Tom wasn't flustered and just let the guys behind stay where they were. The afternoon was closing in fast and if they were going to make a move it would probably be then when the dark looms in. Tom was committed to let them make the first move if they dared. If not he would try and lose them somehow. The more he thought about it the more he realized that if he took out these three then that is three less in Melbourne for him to worry about.

Out through Nhill in Victoria he was staying on the main Adelaide to Melbourne route the truckies took which went down through Ballarat. He would wait till he had the advantage. The traffic was now filtering down a substantial amount as he drove further along into the countryside.

It was dark by the time he had got to Horsham, the road was still busy and the trucks were still aplenty. As he started to enter Horsham he hit the throttle overtaking a truck that was slowing down a touch. Tom completed the manoeuvre but his shadows had to remain behind the truck through the town.

He continued through the town not taking the turnoff he was supposed to take which led to Ballarat. When the truck turned the shadows car had to make a serious change of direction to continue behind Tom. Tom started to accelerate going through umpteen roundabouts with his pursuers closing in slowly. There was no time to mess around thought Tom. He just hoped the roads he was taking were not dead ends, for him that would be a fatal mistake at this stage.

Another few kilometres he arrived at the edge of the town and passing alongside what seemed to be a lake with park areas at intervals. He looked closely in his mirror seeing that his shadows were way behind after having to go through so many roundabouts. That slowed them a touch as they were forced to slow and check to make sure Tom hadn't gone off at another tangent at any of the roundabouts.

Tom switched off his lights and pulled sharply into one of the car park areas alongside the lake and waited. Engine still running and in gear ready to give chase. As he sat there the other vehicle came past without noticing Tom in the shadows. Tom quickly spun his wheels and was on their tail before they could realize what had happened. He still had his lights off.

Just ahead he saw in their headlights the edge of the road was closer to the lakeside so seized the opportunity, now or never. This was a tiny narrow road and thankfully there were no other cars on it. A few trees he knew he would have to help them miss if he was to complete what he had planned in his mind. They had by now noticed him behind and were busily conversing with each other trying to work out a plan to reverse the situation. Tom gave them no time to change as he slowed then raced forward and again gave them a taste of his training with a bash to the right corner of the car which caused it to steer violently to its left. The road was too narrow to take evasive action even though the driver tried and before they knew what was happening the car had taken full flight over the edge of the lake then into the water.

Their car launched over the footpath edge of the lake and landed some fifteen meters in to the lake. It started to sink slowly as frantically all three inside started to lower their windows to escape the water. Tom came to an abrupt halt jumping from his car holding the revolver he had taken from them on the Nullarbor.

Standing on the edge of the water line he stared at the car as it slowly went down to its window edges, water was beginning to flow in through the open spaces. Three figures started to climb out through their respective openings and climb onto the top of the car.

Tom laughed out loud as he saw the frantic efforts of the three trying to stabilize themselves on the roof of the car but the surface was wet and very slippery. It wasn't long before one of them slipped going head first into the muggy water. Tom watched as the fallen body started to swim towards the edge of the lake. It was at the point he finally got to the edge that Tom gave him one almighty bash across the skull with the revolver. He was not prepared to take any prisoners anymore. The man's skull burst open with blood pouring out. The body slipped slowly back into the water face down with just the remnants of a few bubbles before there was nothing just a floating corpse.

The other two had not seen what had actually happened and were still hesitant to move from their position of uncertainty even though the car was still going down and by now the water was half way up their calves.

They must have guessed though what had happened to their man as they both said something then together they dived into the water and swam in different directions. Tom looked at both assessing who was the weakest swimmer. He made his mind up following that swimmer for a few meters before he finally held up the revolver took aim and fired. The swimmer stopped splashing and the water showed no further signs of movement. The body in front of him showed Tom that he had hit him and his face down position was not one you could sustain for a long period without drowning. Two down, one to go.

Tom raced back in the other direction where he had seen the third man move. He couldn't see or hear him. This meant he was either out the water or further out away from sight after hearing a shot being fired. Tom strained his eyes to see what was on the water. Nothing other than the first poor soul he had hit.

He turned to move back to the car when all of a sudden a wet arm came around his neck with another arm coming behind in a neck clamp that would put him out if he wasn't quick enough to escape.

Tom grabbed the arm in front with his left hand and with the right he pushed the revolver around his body and prodded the muzzle of it into the wet material behind him.

"Stop now or die your choice." Tom managed to push from his mouth as he felt the grip getting tighter.

The arm at the rear let go and both disappeared from Tom's throat.

Tom spun around to be face to face with Phil Ryder.

"Seems you have the upper hand Tom old boy." Ryder said backing away from the muzzle of the revolver. "I think perhaps we need to talk, don't you."

"Past fucking talking with shits like you Ryder. Who sent you after me or can I guess, our friend Ashid?"

"You seem to have all the answers Tom so why ask?. Ryder was now standing about three meters from Tom his eyes clearly fixed on the revolver that had him in its sights. His mind was going through all the possibilities that were available to get out of this shit situation.

"Answer me you ponse. Is Ashid the one you are working for?"
"Now come on Tom you know I can't tell you anything."

"Then perhaps you might after this." Tom lowered the revolver and let off a round which hit Ryder in the knee. He screamed loudly and dropped at the same time. Thank goodness this place was deserted Tom thought to himself.

"Shit, there was no need to do that you arsehole. Who the fuck do you think you are, James fucking Bond?"

"Listen you little poofter just come clean with who sent you and why."

Phil Ryder was in total agony writhing around on the floor. Tom walked over to him and placed his foot near the knee. "Talk shithead."

There was another blood curdling scream as Tom applied a slight pressure to Ryder's now bleeding knee. Gasping for breath amidst the pain Ryder looked up with daggers flowing from his eyes. "Fuck you Warburton."

The foot went down even harder and the pained face turned a brighter shade of red. The noise from his mouth would have frightened off the Yeti if they were around to listen. Again Tom asked him who he was working for and yet again Ryder held off. He might be gay but he sure as hell was loyal, but to whom.

Tom didn't want to waste any more time so he just placed the revolver to Ryder's temple asking him one last time. Ryder sneered at Tom closing his eyes. There was no turning back now and with the third shot from the revolver Tom blew Ryder's brains over the lakes calm waters.

Into the waters went the revolver far out in the middle, Tom stared then decided that there was something else that could also follow. He put his hand into his pocket and pulled out the pre paid mobile he had been using. They were easy to pick up and this one had Vicki's number on it and possibly a tracking device was now set up to locate him. He took one last look at the messages that were on it, all from Vicki. Apologies, pleading and wanting her man to return to her so she could repair the damage she had done to him and live happily ever after. The phone would get a quick lesson in water affects on electronics as he threw it as far as he could going further than the landing spot of the revolver.

His next task was to float Mr Ryder out into the lake to join his friends. That took less than two minutes after which Tom just stood watching as the waters calm as they were just let the bodies drift towards the far side of the lake. Job done, now it was time to clear your head boy.

The journey must continue for me Tom thought to himself. He was nearly at the final hurdle. Tom got back onto the main highway heading to Melbourne where he lost all track of time. Yet again he was leaving a trail of bodies along the route, Gary would be pleased.

He was within thirty kilometres of Melbourne near a place called Werribee when he finally pulled into a service centre to got some food and fuel. After fuelling both the car and himself up he parked the car near to where the trucks were parked up snuggled down to get some shut eye. He was not going to call Gary just yet. He decided to wait until morning.

CHAPTER 34

Next morning was a typical Melbourne morning, cold and wet. Tom awoke from another uncomfortable night squashed in the back seat of another hire car. This was a far cry from the comfort he had had in the motor home. He started to wonder how he would be perceived now he had written that unit off as well as when he took this hire car back it would definitely mean he would lose his deposit as he had dented it as well. He would now become an insurance liability in Australia. Thank goodness he never used his real name for hiring purposes. The British Government did have some good things left in it of use to him.

Struggling to stretch working his way over the backs of the front seats so as not to have to get out and get wet. For someone in his mid twenties he felt like the old geriatrics he had seen in nursing homes. If this was how he felt now God help him when he did get older.

He needed coffee, lots of it and something to get that empty feeling out of the pit of his stomach. The rain was coming down in a drizzle, the worst kind he thought, the soaking kind. Out in that and he would be drenched through in a matter of minutes. Looking over at the kiosk area of the fuel service depot he saw that there were a few empty spaces by the pumps so he decided to drive over and be a bit cheeky. He parked at the first pump that also gave him shelter from the drizzle around. Walking into the shop area he managed to get a large cup of coffee to accompany some chocolate bars that said eat me in front of the counter. That was the fix he really wanted, an early morning sugar fix. Thicken the blood and block out the cold. Load of bollocks really but a little reverse psychology for the mind. Back into the car holding onto his coffee he drove a few yards to get clear of the pumps.

Tom savoured his hot drink like nectar as he scoffed down a couple of Boost bars for his sugar fix. Hoping the Boost lived up to its name at least.

Now refreshed he pressed the mobile phone contact for Gary. The UK being ten hours behind meant again he would probably be disturbing him in something whether it be sleep or, and he hoped it wasn't, in the middle of a passionate scene with some female liason.

"Hello Tom." Gary's voice sounded quite wide awake for what would have been about midnight back home.

"Gary, I'm just about to go into Melbourne. Have you had any luck with the information I sent you from Nassau?"

"Sure did. We have located monies to a grand total of thirty three million dollars which we have managed to freeze till we ascertain the real identity behind it all.

As for your mate Ashid we are checking on a few details that you have given us and we are under the assumption now that you were right in your suspicions about him. Your old friend Sandra Crisp is checking that all out for us as we speak.

What do you propose to do next Tom so we can cover you?"

Tom thought for a while and wondered why there had been no mention of three bodies he had left en route to Melbourne. Oh well bush telegraph will undoubtedly catch up sooner or later he was sure.

"Me, well I intend to try and get a fix on Welsh and Caulfield in the city. I'll just do some surveillance stuff till I can bc surc how many the two of them have around for protection. By the way Gary, our friend Aspalson may be a bit pissed off in the coming days."

"Why's that Tom?"

"His bum buddy went for a swim last night with a hole in his head." Tom chuckled at the thought of Ryder and the two Arabs floating along the river through the bush.

"Thanks for the warning Tom. Was he alone in that?"

"No there were two Arabs with him but they are keeping him company in the water mate, sorry."

"Is there any chance you could keep some of the people who you come up against alive?"

"Doubtful the way they approach me Gary."

"Ok Tom, leave the phone on and keep me in touch. Take care." With that Tom hung up and sat back trying to stretch his tired bones.

Time was ticking away and he knew he had to get to the last two before they had a chance to disappear. For some reason he had seen all too often the past few weeks an array of trouble encircling the men that had committed the original crime of theft. They seemed to be a target as well as he was.

The drive into Melbourne was quick being a Saturday. There were no hold ups on the Princes Highway with Tom finding himself in the city within about forty minutes. He was able to park directly outside the office block where Asia Pac was located on the tenth floor.

446 Collins Street was just one of your everyday type office blocks and as it was Saturday it was closed. On the ground floor of the block was a seven eleven store which Tom went in buying himself some needy refreshments and decent food stuff. He asked a few questions to see if Asia Pac were well known outside the office space but the staff did not have any idea who they were or what they did.

Tom left to find some accommodation that would be within a good walking distance of the offices so he could leave the car and not have to tackle the traffic. He had a close call just up from the office block when he tried to turn right and upset many of the local residents in the city because he did not understand that in Collins Street they have a strange habit of turning right from the left lane. He thought it strange but it was a foreign country to him and he had had some mighty strange experiences in others in the past. Just to stop people pulling in front of the tram lines and delaying them while turning right though was the strangest thing ever. To carry out this manoeuvre, as Tom found out with shouts at him and horns blasting, was to indicate right from the left lane staying in the left lane pulling across the intersection and waiting in the lane till the lights changed then continue on around.

If Tom wanted to stay under the radar he didn't do it this Saturday morning for sure. After circumnavigating the block without any further heckles or hassles he found Oaks on Market Street that had studio apartments available for short stays.

After booking in he was amazed at the facilities it had to offer its guests. There were premier leisure facilities include a fully equipped gymnasium that looks onto the hotel's indoor heated lap pool, sauna and spa. Guests could also choose from Oaks on Market's two licensed restaurants. The only thing here was Tom had to park his hire vehicle across the block at a public parking lot.

The beauty of this location was it was within a minutes' walk of 446 Collins and also within easy reach of the main areas of Melbourne. This part of Melbourne especially Collins Street had within its easy reach Goldman Sachs, Lazard and the Stock Exchange. Probably the main reason Welsh had picked the office space he did to be able to be close to the financial hub.

Sunday and Monday would be spent running through the local white pages for addresses in the names of Welsh, Caulfield or Scholfield. This was Easter weekend and there was little to no activity in the businesses that adorned Melbourne or then again any other Western Business sector for that matter. He also made a couple of calls to Gary at Six to see if they had uncovered better information of the residences of Welsh and Caulfield. Those calls produced little other than what he had already got from the White Pages. Tom needed to do some further research being unsure of what he might find on Tuesday morning at 446 Collins.

CHAPTER 35

Tuesday 10 April 2007
Collins Street Melbourne

This morning was again chilly and wet as the rest of the Easter Weekend had been when Tom left his accommodation and strolled up to Collins Street. It wasn't as busy as he thought it might be, but many of the workers over Easter do try to take extra days off to lengthen their stay away from work. He took his time looking at nearly every face he could, to see their inner self. Suspicious of everybody that came close to him or even looked at him was part of his natural reactions now. By the time he had made his mind up to enter the office block it was nearly 1000hrs.

Entering the foyer at the entrance he went directly to the list of companies that was hung just inside on the left. He ran his eyes up and down the list confirming what he already knew, that was that Asia Pac was on the tenth floor. He noted also the opening times of the office on this one as it was the only one that actually listed an actual time which was exactly 1000 hrs.

Looking around the foyer, seeing nothing of any suspicion he ventured to the staircase where he took two steps at a time up the flights ahead of him. The stairway was completely empty with everyone he had seen coming into the building opting for the lift.

At the tenth floor he opened the door which led him to the landing where all the offices at this level had their front entrances. He glimpsed at the first door then continuing till the third door which showed him what he was searching for. It was a full glass door with Asia Pac sign written across its top panel. The door was still locked which contradicted the start time he had seen down below. Perhaps they were taking some extra time off this long weekend.

Tom peered through the door holding his right hand up above his eyes to stop the light reflections from behind him glaring back and disturbing his view. There was no sign of any habitation at all in the reception area, in actual fact to Tom it looked quite barren. There was no one else around on this floor other than within the other offices so Tom decided to call into the office next door.

The receptionist in the neighbour's office was quite apologetic being it was not their worry anyway. She was sure that the normal for Asia Pac was that their receptionist was always on time ready to open at 1000hrs. She thought it strange that no one was there as her associate receptionist there was always quite informative of what was going on. She had seen her before Easter and nothing had been said about extra time off so she offered to phone the number she had for them to see if there was anyone in the offices at the rear behind the locked front door. Tom accepted her offer but after a couple of frustrating moments she hung up shrugging her shoulders and again apologising to him. Tom nodded his thanks and excused himself saying he would wait for a few more moments before leaving.

As Tom exited the office he saw to his left two young looking guys about his age huddled at the door. They both had olive complexions about them. The next moment without even looking at Tom, they laughed at each other as the door they were in front of clicked and opened. Tom thought they were part of the office personnel so just stood back waiting for them to enter the Asia Pac offices. After they disappeared into the offices he slowly went to the glass door to see that it hadn't been relocked after entering.

Pushing at the door it opened with ease, so he entered. He could hear a lot of swearing going on further down the corridor which was to the side of the reception counter. Tom stood by the counter and waited, taking the opportunity to listen to the two young men down the other end of the corridor. Clearly they were upset as they were cursing someone or something. They were definitely Australian accents he was listening to as they ranted and raved with the 'F' word as well as others of disrepute.

Tom stayed put patiently waiting for one of the men to come to the front counter to help him. What he had noticed was that there was nothing around which signified any business being conducted in this office space at all. No posters, no lists, no files, not even an IN tray. No pens or paper, the whole look of the reception was one of desertion.

Tom was brought back to reality as he turned to look down the counter by what was said to him from the corridor.

"What can we do for you mate?" as Tom looked towards where the voice had come from he was confronted with a six foot plus bronzed muscleman.

"I was trying to get in touch with Tony Welsh." Tom answered sizing up the man in his view.

"And what the fuck do you want with him?"

"Sorry." Tom said in response. "I did not want to upset anyone. Tony and I go back many years. I was in town so was hoping to catch up with him." Hopefully the lies would fend off this guy's obvious aggression.

"Bastards not here mate. Think they have done a runner mate on all of us." The big guy moved towards Tom as his matching friend came down the corridor still cursing but this time had a mobile pinned to his ear. "Anyway what's your name?" the man asked Tom.

Tom answered with another fictitious name while sussing out his moves as he was feeling as if he was being boxed in here slowly being pushed away from the entrance door into a corner. The other guy came around the corner pinning his eyes directly onto Tom. He started giving a description of Tom into the mobile.

Tom tried to move his angle to gain a possible access to the glass entrance door but as he moved the speaker on the phone smiled shutting the call down he was on. It didn't look good for Tom; he had put himself into the firing line once again. These guys were speaking in Aussie accents but their appearance was Mediterranean looking. Here we go again Tom thought more Middle Eastern confrontations.

Tom backed himself to the glass wall but was blocked from the door by the bigger of the two men in front of him. The man behind put his hand into his pocket pulling out a handgun complete with silencer. Tom's eyes focused on the weapon and he started to sweat some. He had no answer to what was now pointing towards him.

"Seems our boss has been looking for you for a while mate. Now he can be sure you will be out of the scene this time." He raised the weapon up and took aim.

It was at this moment that a sudden shadow appeared at the door and it started to open. As the door opened further the handgun went quickly away and a young girl's voice suddenly filled the air. "Oh you are open. Is Joy about?"

Before anyone could answer Tom had manoeuvred himself around the big guy towards the door standing beside the young girl who had tried to help him earlier. The gunman wasn't impressed and pulled the weapon out pointing it at both Tom and the young girl who let out a weak shriek as she saw what was pointing at her.

"Better come out the back you two." The man holding the gun was flicking the weapon as an indication of the direction for the two at the door to take. Tom put his arm close to the girl's to reassure her as she stood slowly draining of colour. The last thing he wanted now was for her to faint on him and therefore leave him having to carry her giving no opportunity to deal with the crisis in front of him. He placed his hand around her arm slowly leading her to the doorway that led down to the offices.

Both of the men who had broken into the offices were now between Tom and the main door. He was constantly searching for a way to counter these two big thugs. Past the first office then onto the second where the door was already open and where Tom walked slowly through to see that the room was completely bare.

Moving across to the far wall Tom turned still holding the young girl by the arm, she had by now stopped shaking. She was getting her colour back slowly and Tom could see in her eyes that she was brewing for a fight.

The two thugs looked at Tom before the armed one moved closer to him and said "Where are the men who are usually in this office?"

"Wouldn't have a sodding clue this is the first time I have been here. Seems they have done a runner on you as you said." Those comments just earning Tom a smack across the face with the butt of the handgun which sent him staggering backwards. By doing that the oppressor had riled the young girl who went for a pocket in her jacket pulling out a small spray can. She held it directly at the man's face pressing the button on the top. It sprayed what Tom thought must have been some kind of pepper spray as the man dropped his handgun and immediately put both hands up to his eyes and yelled in agony.

Opportunity thought Tom as he placed a hard well positioned kick to the man's genitals. That brought the guy to his knees struggling for breath. As he went down Tom went for the gun but he misjudged the other guy as his head copped a fierce kick that caught him in the side of the neck sending him off balance onto the floor. The next thing he saw was the young girl jumping onto the man's back as he bent down to get the gun. She dug her fingers into his eyes. This chick had some balls was all Tom could think.

Tom recovered from his floor position as the girl; still clawing at the man's eyes was pummelled back against the wall sandwiched by the big guy which knocked the wind out of her sails. She slid down the wall to the ground winded and the man spun round taking a shot at her. The thud was hardly heard but it made contact in the girl's shoulder and she let out one almighty scream.

Tom had by this point got himself close enough to the man to be able to grab the firing arm, levering it back and over in what looked like a contortionist move. A sharp jerk and the room suddenly filled with firstly what sounded like a ball and socket disconnection pop, as the shoulder of the big guy had obviously come out of its normal position in the sudden swift move. There was a loud scream from the man as his arm fell limp beside him. The gun hit the floor for the second time.

Tom stooped, grabbed the gun firmly this time and spun around to face both men. "Role reversal I think now. Who the hell are you two and who is your boss?"

Both the men were in agony as they stumbled to get themselves together now standing side by side each other they just glared at Tom as he moved around so he could hold them at bay but also be able to see if the girl was OK.

"He shot me. The arsehole shot me." The girl screamed. "Shoot the bastard. Shoot the bastard."

Tom tried to quieten the girl down but the searing pain that had gone through her shoulder had now turned numb and all she wanted was to get her own back on these two perps.

"Calm down sweetheart. Just place this handkerchief over the wound and hold it firm. It's alright it is clean." Tom leant over her handing her the clean white handkerchief he had taken from his trouser pocket. She did as she was told and slowly started to sob with the effects of the numbness that was going through her shoulder now.

"I won't ask again. Who are you and who sent you?" Tom pointed the weapon to the one with the biggest balls, literally.

"Get fucked." The man now holding his dislocated shoulder said. With that Tom had lost his patience and just aimed the gun at the man who had received the kick to his family jewels, let the trigger pull back gently which caused a thud sound and immediately the man hit the floor with a bullet now lodged in his knee. This knee capping was becoming all too familiar now with Tom.

"Now that's his football career over, what about you? Last chance my friend."

The other guy was shocked as he stood still clutching his floppy arm. He looked at his partner then back at Tom. "We were sent to detain the two men who work here." He was panicking a bit now as he saw by Tom's actions that he was not going to mess about any.

"Detain where?" Tom asks.

"Our boss wanted us to get some information from them off their computer. They have some money tied up for him and he wants it released now. We were to deal with them after we had got the information."

"OK that's good. Now who was it who sent you?"

"It was our Imam. He told us what we needed to do."

"Name? Which mosque are you from?" Tom was beginning to feel a bit uncomfortable that here was a definite connection with possibly a Middle East country. He could only think of Iraq and Ashid. The connection could even be with the I.I.G.

The man was a bit slow in responding but as soon as he saw Tom raise the gun he opened up to him.

"Imam al-Ashari, we are members of a small St Kilda Mosque off Alma Road located in Alma Place." The man was shaking now as the shock of his condition started to set in.

"Both of you lie face down on the ground." Tom saw the hesitation on both their faces. "I'm not going to kill you just get down now." They both struggled one trying to get down in the condition of the dislocated shoulder and the other trying to roll over onto his face with a hole in his knee, balls ballooning and eyes that felt like acid had been poured in them but still they both conformed to Tom's request.

Tom went over to where the telephone points were positioned on the wall and pulled out both leads that were plugged into the wall. Returning to the two men now spreadeagled onto the floor with one having one hand over his eyes and his other securely holding his balls for fear they were about to explode. The other guy was just laying face down with both arms beside him. Tom grabbed the good one of this guy and then lifted the other arm over to screaming protests from the man who now was virtually in tears with the pain. Tom tied the two arms together. Here he noticed the infinity tattoo yet again on the man's right wrist.

The other guy was just laying there as Tom grabbed his feet, pulling him by the ankles which just brought on another flurry of screams and protests about his knee and the bouncing across his genital area. Tom turned him around so his feet were directly in line with the other man's feet. Face down meant they would have one hell of a painful escape if they tried. He proceeded to tie the man's hands together under more extreme protests and again noticing the same infinity tattoo. Leaving both there he quickly went out and into the other office where he found more telephone lines again retrieving them for his use. Returning he tied the two pairs of legs and ankles together.

All the ties were tight so movement would have caused the wires to bite into the skin if they flailed about too much. Now for the girl Tom thought.

"What's your name?" Tom asked as he bent down to inspect the wound.

"Gloria." The girl answered. "Who are these guys and where's Joy? The place looks like it has been emptied over the Easter weekend. What the hell's going on here?"

"Look lovely I wouldn't have a clue, all I wanted was to be able to catch up with my old mates here while in town. Look I will get an ambulance for you and call the police but I would like to ask you a favour."

"What's that?" she quizzically looked at Tom.

"I don't want to be here when the authorities come. I work for the Government and it could put me in a sticky position if I am seen here with these jerks. Can you not give a description of me to them when they arrive."

"You on the run or something?"

"No nothing as bold as that but I do need some anonymity." As Tom spoke his mobile burst into life. He pulled it from his pocket and answered it.

"Tom, Gary, have you been able to get to Asia Pac yet?"

"Here now mate but again there were a couple of guys here waiting also."

"Please don't tell me they are dead Tom."

"No you're ok Gary they are just a little tied up at the moment but they did shoot the receptionist from next door, she has a shoulder wound."

"What about Welsh and co?"

"Nothing, they seem to have emptied the place out and disappeared. Just as a sweetener for you Gary these jerk offs here have that favourite tattoo on their right wrists, seems we have a real link now."

After a few short curses Gary came back to the phone conversation. "Either they know you are near them or this Ashid thing you have is closer to the truth than we thought. I have had a conversation with Aspalson and I must admit after we had talked when I told him about his friend Ryder he clammed up and went into some kind of shock.

I've had Crisp checking up on things surrounding him and she has come up with some pretty useful information we may be able to use. It seems he is tied up quite closely to Ashid, more so than would normally be expected of a man in his position. Rumours also have been heard that it appears that our friend Ashid is about to resign his position in the Iraqi Government because of some major disagreements with his seniors in Cabinet. He is a Sunni amongst most of the Cabinet which are Shia which doesn't go for a good mix anyway."

"All I can say Gary is keep a close eye on him; if he is involved with the others then we need to keep him in our sights at all times."

"Crisp has already thought that one through for us Tom. Now how can we get this present situation resolved for you."

"Got anyone here who could vouch for me if I remain and try to explain what has happened here?"

"Leave it with me Tom; we have contacts of course within ASIO there. Just make sure the girl is OK and the men are taken into custody. I'll get the ball rolling from this end immediately."

"Look Gary they did give me some information you may be able to use here. They told me that their Imam at the St Kilda Mosque had given them the order to come here and get information from Welsh off his computer. Any chance we can trace the IPs or something?"

"See what we can do. Sit tight mate be back to you soon."

Tom closed down the call and turned back to Gloria who was trying to listen to as much as possible perhaps to make some sense out of what had happened.

"Sccms like I will be staying with you till you are safely in the hands of the paramedics, Gloria."

"Oh I'm glad. Didn't want to be left alone with these two wankers anyway." Gloria smiled at Tom, her face looking a brighter shade of pale.

Tom was on the mobile again calling both police and ambulance for assistance. The two men trussed up on the floor were motionless but still moaning from their various injuries. While Tom was here he had the gun which neither wanted to try to upset this man as he had already shown a willingness to use it.

Fifteen minutes passed before there was movement in the office as a police SWAT team came racing in firearms raised and calling for everyone to get down on the floor. This was the Victoria Police and their equivalent of a SWAT team called Special Operations Group or SOG. Tom complied with their requests lying down with hands on his head after placing the gun on the floor. The team sealed off the office space pretty quickly collecting the silenced weapon placing it in a plastic evidence bag.

Two members of the team gave immediate assistance to Gloria who pleaded with them that the man who was not trussed up had also been a victim of this outrage.

Tom felt a tap on his shoulder. He looked up at the officer standing above him. He nodded at Tom and asked that he come with him out into the corridor. As Tom stood and followed the officer two paramedics came rushing in with a trolley immediately taking over from the police officers attending to Gloria. One of the officers that had been attending her spoke into his handpiece clipped to his shoulder strap asking for another medic team to come up to deal with the bleeding suspect on the floor not taking any notice of the other man's injury. They had made absolutely no effort to untie the two who were virtually frozen to the floor both moaning in some sort of pain.

Outside in the corridor Tom stopped and turned towards the Officer who had walked him out.

"Tom, I'm Senior Sergeant Carl Bishop." He held out his hand to Tom. "We have someone coming down from ASIO who will be taking over here and wants to speak to you personally. If you could wait in the main reception area with my officers I shouldn't think it will be too long before he arrives."

"Thank you." Answered Tom as he turned and continued down the corridor towards the reception where more of the SOG team were positioned. As he got to the counter from behind him came the sound of the trolley being pushed up the corridor. A bag of saline was hanging above the front of the gurney and a rather pale looking Gloria was laying on the gurney now covered in a blanket.

Tom stopped the paramedics as they got to the door and looked down at Gloria. "You were very brave in there. I've never seen a girl think as quickly as you did. Thank you for your help, hope all goes well and good luck."

Gloria looked up into Tom's eyes. "Thank you for being there or else I may have been just a statistic. Hope all goes well for you, suppose I won't see you again eh?"

"Possibly not. You're a real hero Gloria. Bye." And off went the paramedics towards the lift with other members of the offices on the floor clambering around to get a good view of the action going on. Like vultures awaiting the pickings of the dead.

As the lift door opened, a middle aged man stepped out dressed in a suit covered by a raincoat. Tom thought straight away that this was yet another spook. He stepped aside to allow the gurney to be pushed into the lift with Gloria's head still partially raised for her to try and get a final glimpse of Tom. Unfortunately she was crowded out with the onlookers and didn't see Tom standing looking in her direction from the doorway.

In came the spook going directly to Tom. What is it Tom thought 'have I got that look or did they have a photo sent over of him to peruse?' "Mr W or Tom is it?" the man extended his hand towards Tom which was taken welcomingly and a vibrant shake took place. "My name's Brian Cox, ASIO. Your people got in touch with us earlier. Can you give me the details of what happened in here."

Tom went through what had happened after he had come out of the office next door finding the men at the door of Asia Pac. He was unsure how much information to give to Brian so kept it short and sweet. Brian asked for the information on the St Kilda mosque that he had given Gary.

"Gary told me about the Imam and we can take that side of it from here for you." Brian was trying to reassure Tom that he already had a clearance from Gary to take part stand in this affair.

Tom didn't say too much else waiting while Brian held a conversation with the senior sergeant who had come back down the corridor.

After a few minutes and another gurney coming into the office heading for the man with the knee wound Brian turned around to Tom again. "It seems we have some home grown terrorists causing some problems for you. Those two have been known to Melbourne police for a while and their associates at the St Kilda Mosque have been under some scrutiny for a while now. We will keep these two in custody without any release to the media at the moment.

What else can I help you with Tom? Gary asked for me specifically on this as we go back a way."

"The only thing I need to know right now is the whereabouts of Tony Welsh and Peter Caulfield aka John Scholfield. Is there any chance you can get their addresses for me or even their registrations or even car makes will help?"

"I'm sure I can do that for you my friend. Gary has asked that I take only the part about the Mosque and its associates including any connection with a Mr Ashid in Iraq." He looked at Tom with questioning expressions shrugging his shoulders. "Seems you have uncovered quite a little hornets' nest for your masters' young man."

"Let's just hope it is not something that blows up in all our faces eh." Tom smiled at Brian as one of the men from the back office was led out with handcuffs and his protesting about his shoulder which was being conveniently ignored.

Brian asked for Tom's mobile number which was given without any thought and then the two of them walked back down to the end office where paramedics were treating the man on the gurney. His face around the eyes area was red as. There was evidence of something being poured over his face to perhaps clear the pepper spray from his eyes as his upper body was drenched and there was a small towel over his shoulders and neck. His knee had been patched up now but the area of his family jewels which was covered by a blanket had what looked like a large ice pack on it.

"Handled yourself well here Tom. Lucky they didn't just blow you away in here."

"If it hadn't been for that young lass on the gurney that was here I would have been. She deserves a medal for what she did."

"I take it you are not carrying then. It may cause a few problems if you are."

"No I'm clean Brian, just my hands for company. If that's all can I get away as the guys I am trying catch for the boss have a heads start by the look of this place."

"Sure thing Tom. I'll keep you in touch with the addresses etc you asked for." With that Tom turned to walk away while Brian turned to his SOG team leader bleeping something about Pommy Bastard. Tom took no notice and just continued out to the landing where he had to jostle through the little crowd that had been there since the police arrived. He finally got to the stairwell stepping down three at a time to quickly get out of this building.

Outside the blue building was a row of police cars, vans and a couple of ambulances. Tom turned away from the building and started off back towards his accommodation putting all the information gained today through the brain matter that was trying to analyse all the stuff from before. It made no sense at the moment.

Again he had been outwitted by someone. He tried as hard as he could to put the pieces of this bloody big puzzle together but his efforts were in vain.

CHAPTER 36

By late that afternoon Brian had got back to Tom with both addresses and the makes and numbers of their respective vehicles. Tom took the opportunity to try and get over to the Albert Park address of Caulfield {Scholfield} before it got too dark. The best way in this town at this time of night would be by taxi which he ordered from his room before going down to meet it.

He had had instructions from Gary not to take on too much. i.e. not to go it alone. He had told Tom that he could trust Brian explicitly but Tom wasn't having a bar of anyone else knowing what he was up to. He was determined to go it alone as his past experience had shown him that the more people you trust the more shit hits the fan.

The journey the taxi took Tom lasted about twenty minutes in the traffic of home goers finally placing him down near the address he had at 73 Queens Road. He had instructed the taxi driver to drop him at the Albert park raceway on the southern end of the lake on the Queens Road side. The turbaned driver did as instructed wishing him a pleasant evening as he drove off well rewarded for such a short ride.

Tom walked the park side of Queens Road till he was opposite number 73. Here he waited scanning the building from top to bottom. Another security nightmare if he was to get in and surprise his friend. That was if he was even there.

He had been told that Caulfield had the penthouse apartment which took the whole of the upper floor of the building. Tom casually crossed the road till he was able to get to what looked like the underground car park. Here he looked at the grilled entrance gate hoping to be able to suss out an easy entry point. Not finding any easy way in he decided to hang around in this position till hopefully someone came in by car, whereby he could then sneak into the complex without being seen.

He didn't have to wait long as he saw headlights curve around from the main road and slowly come down the ramp to the garage space. He hid behind the wall that was the start of the garage drive while pulling out some medical gloves he had lifted from the paramedics' bag back at the office. No finger prints to incriminate him if there was anything upstairs of interest.

As the car came to a halt in front of the grill Tom heard the squealing of the roller cage door slowly lift till the car had enough space to be able to go in underneath it. As it moved forward Tom came out from his little hidey hole and slowly, keeping his back to the wall slid into the garage area without the occupants of the car seeing him.

He slid down behind a large gold coloured Lexus waiting for the car doors on the recent entry car to eventually close and the signal of the doors being locked by the vehicles flashing lights. The overhead lights had come on triggered by either the doors or movement beneath them. For Tom that might be a problem if he chose to move while they were out. He peered over the window ledge of the Lexus catching sight of the car that had entered which was now parked. Only one door opened with a male about middle age getting out shutting his door then opening the rear to remove his briefcase. After closing that he must have pressed his lock button as the vehicle's hazard lights flashed to signal it was all locked.

The man made his way to a door off to his right and away from Tom meaning he had his back to him. Tom took the opportunity to creep as quietly as possible towards the door. As the man approached the door he just placed his hand onto the handle and flicked it open. With relief at what he saw Tom slowed just stopping short of the door waiting to hopefully let the man disappear ahead of him. He could not hear anything as the door was a steel fire door and even pressing his ear to the damn thing he heard nothing.

Giving it a few minutes he slowly opened the door slightly to peer in. As the space ahead of him came into focus the lights in the garage clicked off. This gave Tom better vision ahead of him as the lights on the other side of the door were on meaning a possible foyer entrance. He pulled the door further open not hearing any movement ahead of him and saw that there was a flight of well lit stairs to tackle.

Not just one flight but two got him up to the ground floor which had yet another fire proof type of door. This time though Tom was unable to open it. It was possible to open it from the inside but not the outside which meant that the stairs were used as the main fire escape in event of a fire leading out to the garage with a push button on the wall he had seen would automatically lift the cage wire door in an emergency.

He didn't try to open the door as he needed to go to the top of the building anyway so continued till he got to the top of the whole stairwell. He counted the flights to make sure he was actually at the top floor apartment so that he didn't create any unnecessary surprises by jumping into a place that he wasn't expecting. Getting his breath he tried the door first but as with the others in the stairwell it was unable to be opened from the well.

Tom removed his trusty six inch metal rule which he had used so many times before. Slowly pushing the rule in between the door and the jamb he pulled it down till it came into contact with the locking mechanism. He waited listening intently. Still silent, so uncanny for Tom. He flicked his trusty tool and the door clicked and started to open. He held it in position as now he could hear through the crack that had been created. Nothing was evident so he opened it a touch more. Now he could see inside through about an inch gap. He heard nothing but just saw what looked like a small garden area. He could feel the draft coming through the door and he then started to hear the sound of traffic, faintly but definitely there.

He slid the door open to enable his body to slide through the opening, when he got through he found himself on the balcony garden of the penthouse apartment. He kept close to the walled exit till he came to the low wall that surrounded the gardens where he crouched making his way around to the rear door of the apartment.

There were no lights on inside and no sign of any habitation in the apartment. Tom peered through the windows scanning for any movement at all. There was none. Slowly he made his way back to the rear door of the apartment to again do his little trick with his steel rule. Inside the apartment it was absolutely spotless, not the sort of clean you would expect from a bachelor even one such as Caulfield. Soldiers were usually very tidy keeping things in place but that was sort of regimental for them but usually when one leaves the services it went partially out the window like a rebellion but not this place it was absolutely spotless and smelt that way.

There were no ornaments, no pictures just furniture exquisitely placed with not a speck of dust to be seen anywhere. Tom went through the apartment without turning on the lights as the screens were open and the night sky was now clear and bright with plenty of outside light complete with a three-quarter moon glowing in the night sky overhead.

In the bedrooms there was not a piece of clothing anywhere to be seen, no grooming materials and no evidence that anyone was living or had even lived here. It was immaculate. Out in the lounge there was a large flat screen TV and radio that again didn't look as if it had ever been used. There was none of the usual evidence like TV magazines or papers on the side. The lounge was leather and smelt new, the coffee table showed no sign of ring marks from cups or mugs and there weren't even any place mats out of place. The kitchen was the last area Tom was to check; it was where the rear door of the apartment had opened into and was huge. You could have cooked a feast for the Royals in here with a team of chefs without any of them getting in each other's way. All the equipment around the kitchen was top of the range with the cupboards being two pack white glowing brightly in the reflected light.

He had checked every cupboard, drawer in the place and now stood in the kitchen wondering when Caulfield had decided to disappear into thin air. Then he saw on the side of the kitchen cabinet a pamphlet. Picking it up it showed a group of pictures of this apartment and what was available in it. Strikingly at the top was the notice 'For Sale offers welcomed'. Owner had given the reason for the sale as having to move interstate for business. It was dated only today 10 April. Tom, after reading through, took the pamphlet and folded it into his pocket. It had the address of the real estate which might mean they had a contact number or forwarding address for him.

Tom slid out of the apartment the same way he had entered closing the door securely behind him. Getting to the fire exit door he had come through previously he slowly opened it to make sure no one was using the stairwell. All quiet so Tom proceeded down the stairs and back into the garage where he found the lights came on as he entered the large area. He made his way over to the button he had seen on the wall about three metres from the cage rollerdoor and pushed on it. The door started to open up and as soon as he could he slid underneath and disappeared out onto Queens Road.

Tom looked at the little map he had taken from his own room, seeing that he was only a couple of kilometres from St Kilda decided he would take an evening stroll to check out the Mosque on Alma Place. He just hoped that Gary and his ASIO friends wouldn't get too upset if they saw him in the vicinity.

The walk was a pleasant one for Tom as he was most impressed with the houses that he passed and the care the owners took in their gardens. Lots of new developments were being started along the way with new businesses moving into the area. Low level small office blocks were being developed wherever there was some vacant land. This town was still growing rapidly unlike London which was spreading.

Arriving at Alma Place Tom slowly sauntered along the narrow side street till he saw in front of him a cluster of blue flashing lights. All blue but it wasn't a disco that was for sure. Tom stopped where he was viewing what was up ahead. There were some other bystanders around him but they took no notice of Tom standing gazing down at the commotion ahead of them.

SWAT team members were going in and out of what looked like a large house just up to his left. Tom thought he would try and get a closer look at what was going on so started to walk towards the confusion. As he approached there was a group of Australian Lebanese youngsters standing yelling abuse at the officers that were going into the house empty handed and coming out with computers, boxes full of gear and also some handcuffed people protesting angrily.

"What's going on?" Tom asked one of the young boys if front of him."

"Those pigs are invading our Masjid." One of the younger men of the group answered back to Tom.

"When did this all start?" Tom asked further.

"About an hour or so ago. They stormed in here as if they were some kind of invasion force. They have taken our Imam away in a police car in handcuffs."

"I'm sorry to hear that." Replied Tom sounding quite empathetic. "I'm sure it will all sort itself out in the wash and he will be back teaching again soon." Tom looked at the young guys and nodded to them getting a nod in return.

"It must be time for Jihad" the young man shouted at the top of his voice which brought a yell of agreement from all the others standing around them. Tom turned around and headed back in the direction he had come before any further actions started. The last thing he wanted now was to be caught up in some kind of racist riot.

As he was about to turn into Alma Road a car screeched to a halt at the end of the junction and a rear window opened with a familiar face looking out.

"Want a lift Tom?" Brian's familiar voice called over. Tom was slightly startled at first hoping that he would not be noticed in this area after this morning's efforts. He faced the vehicle then stepped over to the opposite door to where Brian's head was poking out of and got in. In the rear of the car he looked at Brian and smiled. "Didn't waste any time then did you?"

"Mate the information we got from those two reprobates you caught was gold star quality. They gave us everything we needed to be able close down this little haven of activity and lock up the Imam for a long time.

You would not believe what was in that place. They had enough gear to start a war of their own."

"Anything that might be useful for me as who the contact was in communication with?" Tom asked hoping in some way that Ashid's little lifestyle might at last be spoiled.

"Nothing yet mate but we have all their computers so will be slowly going through them over the next couple of days to see what transpires. I'll let you or Gary know if we find anything useful."

Tom thanked Brian for his honesty; he still had problems on the trust issue even now. Vicki was a kick in the guts that set him back miles in the trust department. The car made its way into Collins Street just as Tom finished thanking Brian. Within seconds he was dropped outside his accommodation and the car had driven off.

CHAPTER 37

Wednesday 11 April

This morning was just going to be a big fishing expedition for Tom. As before he caught a taxi to Queens Road where going by the information on the pamphlet he had picked up last night from Caulfield's apartment the property dealer was located just a short walk just up the road.

Icon Properties was located in one of the Tower Blocks just five minutes' walk from Caulfield's place and when Tom arrived there he could see that this was where only the rich boys came for their property deals. Inside this vast office space were rows of larger than life desks, floors that looked like they had been destined for someone's palace, with marble facades adorning the perimeter of the whole of the internal space.

Tom was met at the lift entrance as he exited it, something like the big stores when you walk in the salesman pounce on you straightaway. This time though it was a slinky looking woman about Tom's age but just a tad shorter than he. She wore a very short dress that hugged all the right places showing all the right things including two very bulbous, plastic looking breasts. They say sex sells and now Tom could see why. If he was buying today he was already sold without even looking at the property he wanted to buy.

"My names Alisha. What can I do for you Sir?" The sexy voice matched the near perfect body in front of him.

"Thank you Alisha, I have just arrived in town, tried to visit a friend of mine in actual fact and found that he has put his property on the market with your company. Seems he has moved and I was wondering if you could give me his forwarding address. I only have a couple of days in Melbourne on this trip and would very much like to catch up with him."

Tom's little white lies were becoming much too common for him these days but as always they sounded quite convincing to whom he spoke to.

"Well Sir I may be able to help if you would like to follow me." As Tom followed Alisha sashaying along he was thinking things that would have got him arrested if it were known. The arse on this babe was so inviting. He had to stop himself from staring at it as she swayed her way towards her desk then there was the problem of keeping his desperate eyes from undressing her as she sat there or just the fact that he kept ogling her boobs.

"Now Sir what address is it your friend has on the market?" she smiled at him knowing full well his thoughts as his eyes had given him away big time.

Tom held out the pamphlet he had taken from the kitchen top the night before. "I found this at the front door when I called this morning." "Oh Yes I remember Mr Scholfield's penthouse suite, charming man." She stopped at that and got up to go to the rear of the office space. "Just one moment Sir I will check it out for you." She sashayed off to a filing cabinet at the rear returning with a small folder held closely to her stomach. Placing it on the table she resumed her seat much to Tom's pleasure.

On the top of the folder was written Scholfield's name complete with the property address along with the price they were hoping for, $1.2 Million. Boy this arsehole has done himself proud Tom thought to himself.

"Hmmm." Alisha went through the folder. "I'm afraid there isn't a forwarding address. It seems Mr Scholfield has gone interstate and all we have is his mobile number to be able to contact him with. I'm sorry but he has specifically written here that it is not to be handed out to anyone." "Well it was worth a try Alisha, it has been years since we spoke to each other, we were in Iraq together in the military." Tom was hoping by playing on the old soldier at twenty three he might rattle a bit of leverage in sympathy.

"Just hold on Sir while I check with my manager." Alisha again got up and did her thing but this time Tom did not watch her luscious movements just spun the folder around quickly looking into the pages within. He found what he wanted the mobile number which he memorized spinning the folder back to where it was originally. As he scanned the area around him he saw that no one had seen him turning the file peering then into it.

Alisha returned bending forward so far over the table that Tom thought the plastic boobs were about to fall out if they had the chance. She scooped up the folder looking directly at Tom, there was absolutely no embarrassment on her face. She knew what she was displaying and worked it well. Tom thought that she would have a very high sales commission each month if she approached all her customers this way.

"I'm very sorry Sir my manager says we have to follow our customer's wishes to the letter, confidentiality and all that. Perhaps if you give me your number we can pass it onto Mr Scholfield when next we speak to him."

"I don't have a mobile with me on this trip but you can tell him Derek Sweetman called in town to see him if you like." Tom didn't hesitate to give that name knowing it was still secreted away by the Brits from the papers about his downfall.

He thanked Alisha, leaving this exquisitely furnished office and returning via taxi back to his accommodation. When he was behind closed doors he fired up the mobile to Gary giving him the number hoping they could put a trace on it and then be able to give him some idea of his whereabouts. Gary said to Tom that he would also have Brian do it as it would be quicker overall by someone in house so to speak and that he would get back to him ASAP.

Tom packed up his things booked out of the apartment he had been in for the past few days. His next stop was going to be Mt Evelyn to try and pin down Welsh if he could.

Leaving the city just after lunchtime Tom had a good drive out to the north east towards Mt Evelyn. The total drive distance was a pleasant 50 kms getting Tom into the quaint little village about 1430hrs. Stopping in the village he was able to top up on a hot coffee while enquiring the route to Wattle Valley Road where he hoped he would find Welsh hiding out.

The drive from the village found him navigating through to Wattle Valley road which turned into a narrow bitumen road whose width wise would have held only a single car at any one time. The houses along this road were on the larger executive scale than the rest of the village that he had seen driving in. Negotiating through tree lined areas of the road he finally came to the end of this long Cul De Sac. Just off to the right was the house he was seeking sitting down below the curvature of the hills to its left but in itself standing in a prominent position overlooking the next valley.

This was not what Tom had expected after all the other living arrangements these crooks had had amongst themselves. This was a house standing on four acres of rolling green space. He didn't hesitate as to whether to take the car in just continuing along the driveway to the circular parking frontage by the house. The house was three levels of meticulous design overlooking an American barn and field which would be the perfect area for any horse enthusiasts. Just by the garage was a small purple coloured Hyundai parked with its windows still open. The garage looked large enough for three cars but it was closed at this point so Tom deliberately parked in a position by the Hyundai which would stop anything from leaving if the garage were opened.

Getting out of his car he chose to just walk direct to the front door around to the left of the building. He knew Welsh was an older man about mid fifties and after serving his country had retired moving out to Australia where his daughter had decided to live. She was married to some high flyer in Sydney and had a couple of children a boy and girl.

Reaching the main front door Tom rang the bell. Within a couple of minutes the door opened and standing at the door was an elderly lady in her sixties dressed like Sadie the cleaning lady.

"Yes, what can I do for you?"

"Mr Welsh please."

"Sorry but Mr Welsh is away at the moment."

"Can you tell me when he is to return then?"

"At this stage no. He has gone to see his daughter in Sydney and didn't say when he would be returning. I think he was hoping he would be able to stay there for a while."

Tom didn't pursue the matter any further and thanked the woman for her help. He had to make plans now to be able to get into the house to search for any relevant information that may come in useful but was unsure if the old girl was a resident in the house or just the local cleaning lady. He would have to watch, wait and see. Jumping into his car he left the property and drove a short way up the road where he parked off into the trees out of sight.

It was times like this Tom wanted to be able to talk to someone special but that had passed since Vicki's betrayal to him. He kept telling himself he should get a good book and keep it handy for these types of occasions. He didn't have to wait that long though, about an hour or so later the purple, a sickly purple at that, Hyundai drove past him going fairly fast for the older driver perched behind the wheel. Tom waited till it was out of sight then turned his car around driving back to the property.

This time he left the car outside the neighbouring property behind some trees making his way into Welsh's place on foot.

A quick look around the buildings outside calmed his fears of a possible burglar alarm being there but he would still have to be careful as some of the larger properties were hardwired with a direct link via the phone lines with security companies. He estimated if that was the case he would have around fifteen minutes by the time he entered to do what he had to do. There were no stickers or other warnings that people sometimes put on their glass frontage to discourage people from breaking in.

With his usual plastic gloves on he ventured forward with his old faithful steel ruler which got him in through the door easily yet again. Opening the door he scanned the door frame to check for trip switches. Nothing found so he went into the hallway looking around the ceiling level for signs of any movement sensors. Not finding anything he made his way slowly to the garage to see what was there. Inside there were no cars just a large ride on mower and racks along two walls filled with cans containing liquids which would be possibly for the gardens and of course fuel for the mower.

Up to the top of the house he found what would have been three bedrooms all of which were unused. At the next level he found the master bedroom and ensuite which had been used complete with a large walk-in wardrobe housing a large range of very expensive suits. Tom spent time going through all the jackets and trouser pockets to get anything that might be useful. His search continued through to the dresser and bedside tables. All he found was a note to pick up some dry cleaning from in the city.

There was a study as well on this level where he found a printer but no computer. Welsh must have worked using a laptop for convenience as he could just unplug taking it where ever he went. There was a filing cabinet in the corner which was totally empty and no paper evidence of any kind was to be found anywhere, this guy had cleaned up his entire show before he had left. A diary in the desk top drawer caught Tom's eye though so he picked it out and went through it rather quickly seeing that there was lots of entries of associates' addresses. Perhaps Welsh had left it by mistake Tom thought as he pocketed it thinking he would look through it later when he had more time.

He had been in the house now for about thirty minutes without interruption and it was already getting dark outside. Suddenly there was a flash of light through the windows as he ventured into the lounge area.

Ducking down quickly he automatically went over to the window where he could see directly down at the drive, there in the drive was a medium sized white van with Scripts Security sign written on the side of it. Tom froze, had he tripped something or was this just a routine check.

He waited listening intently for the door to open at the front of the house. Two men had climbed out from the van with torches in their hands they had walked in different directions around the house. It must have taken them about fifteen minutes to complete their rounds as they did not appear together again till they were back beside the van. Tom hadn't moved for fear that he could be heard walking across the polished wooden floors. They boards did creak a little as he had already found out. Wishing these two would just get back into their van and piss off he stood silent against the wall by the window, patiently waiting.

The two guys opened the side sliding door and proceeded to lift out a flask complete with cups from inside. This was not time to have a damn picnic Tom wanted to yell at them. His legs were getting stiff with not moving. Another ten minutes before the cups and flask went back into the van and the sliding side door was again shut. Some jocular bantering started up before the two got back into the van and drove away. Tom waited a little longer till he saw the lights of the van disappear up the road beyond the trees.

Thankfully that was it Tom thought continuing his search around the house. There were a number of sides in the lounge and rummaging through the drawers of each uncovered very little. Tom was beginning to think that these guys were the secret service with the way that they had left nothing around any of their residences that he had searched recently.

In the kitchen he checked every cupboard and drawer with again little to find. As he was about to leave he noticed the small stainless steel bin in the corner of the kitchen. Pressing the pedal with his right foot the lid flew open and he peered inside. There was nothing but a screwed up piece of paper. Lifting it out he unravelled it to reveal a message that Welsh had left for his cleaner. It read:

Have gone to visit Michelle.
Will be away for a few weeks.
Will call when I am due to return.
Don't change your routine as the dust builds up so keep to your usual call times.
Regards
Tony Welsh

Tom folded the paper placing it in the diary he had found in the study. At least he had a name but only the first not her married name. He hoped when he looked at the diary later that night he might find the next clue he was looking for to be able to find the man.

Suddenly as he was leaving the building there was another flash of lights from a vehicle coming down the driveway. Tom went straight out from where he had come through the door dropping behind some bushes where he could observe who had now ventured into this little domain.

He lay quiet waiting for any movement. Mouth slightly open, with his head tilted towards the place where he had seen the lights to enhance his hearing. He heard doors opening and closing on a car, then voices. The voices were Australian and they were in no way trying to be quiet. As he lay there three guys of varying height came around from where they had parked and walked towards the front door. They tried the bell but didn't wait too long before the leader as it seemed told the other two to belt down the door.

These guys had absolutely no etiquette in entering premises that didn't belong to them. The door frame splintered and they all rushed in, two pulling what looked like knives or some other type of offensive weapons from their jackets. Lights went on in the house as they went from room to room. Tom remained still in the bushes wondering why the security company couldn't have come now instead of earlier unless of course these creeps had also been watching from a distance. Mind you if they had done then someone, more than likely the security boys, would have been hurt or killed.

The whole house was ablaze with lights within five minutes with the light filtering down towards where Tom lay. He couldn't move now for fear of someone seeing him. He waited. The noises coming from the house were a mixture of shouts, swearing, breaking glass and furniture. They were ransacking the damn place.

Tom wanted to try and get around to the garage area so he could get the number plate of their vehicle. He was aware that there may also be another person in the vehicle, a driver ready to make haste away from here. He looked about him, light was blazing everywhere around him from the house. He slowly crawled across bush to bush scurrying quickly where the light hit the ground. The noise in the house hadn't declined one iota as Tom finally got to a position where he could see the car that the thugs had arrived in.

A large dark blue Suburban stood facing away from the garage waiting patiently for its passengers to return so it could transport them at a rapid pace away from here. Tom looked at the number plate but failed to be able to work out the letters from the distance he was. The lights of the Suburban were off at this point.

Suddenly there was a flash from the gap above the garage doors then a red glow suddenly appeared. The bastards had fired the place. Shit this was going to make it hard to get out of here as it was sure to bring every Tom, Dick and Harry from all points around. They would surely see his car where he had left it and would probably take its number being not one they recognised as a local. He had to do something quickly and possibly delay these louts from leaving before him.

The driver of the Suburban was closest to him so the best he could do would be to crawl back a touch, then come around on him from the garage wall. The noises in the house were now growing louder as he saw more flashes and red glows appearing at the windows in other areas of the place. He made his move dashing across to the garage wall where he clung to the wall around the side away from the vehicle.

Taking a deep breath he slid to the corner edge and peered around. The driver had his door closed but was shaking his head in time to the music he was listening to on the radio. Another deep breath and Tom rushed around the corner taking three steps to get to the driver's door where he instantly pulled up the handle pulling it open. It wasn't till the door actually opened that the driver realized there was someone there which put Tom with the advantage. He grabbed the guy's collar and pulled him hard but as he did so the seat belt snapped into action. What bloody getaway driver wears a seatbelt Tom thought to himself?

Tom had grabbed the man with his right so was slightly off balance but before the guy could either yell or hit back Tom had lifted his left fist punching the driver fair in the side of the head directly at ear level. It sent bells ringing through the man's brain and his eyes started to roll. Tom released his right then quickly brought it back and with an open hand planted a well place chop to the Adam's apple area. The driver bent forward gasping for breath beginning to choke. Tom then went for the ignition keys turning them anti clockwise before puling them out of their little orifice.

Tom pulled back out of the cab just as one of the others was coming around the corner. He yelled to the rest as he lurched himself at Tom. Sidestepping the guy who was about the same height as himself but a thicker set man Tom let him continue his motion forward where he hit the driver side on. Tom placed all his weight behind the door of the Suburban slamming it into the man now recovering from hitting his mate. There was a crunch heard followed by a yell of pain as the door connected and the man instantly went to the ground in pain.

Tom started to leg it away from the vehicle not bothering to get the registration number now before the rest came out. He had taken about ten paces or so when he heard the others clambering around the corner of the garage yelling for the driver to get them out of here. The keys were still in Tom's hand but not for long because as he turned to exit from the way he had entered he threw them into the darkness. He could now hear feet trampling heavily in hot pursuit after him.

Over the fence of the perimeter Tom legged it up the road towards his car having his keys out ready to open the door. He had made sure he had it pointing in the right direction to make a quick getaway himself. Starting the car he shoved it into gear and moved off spinning the wheels just as one of the pursuers came within range throwing himself at the boot of Tom's car. Looking into the mirror he smiled as he hit the throttle harder spinning the wheels as he went. He saw that the man who had actually nearly caught him was now on the ground with his mate standing alongside him.

In the distance behind him he could see the glow of the fire looming high into the sky. The red glow in the sky showed how intense the fire was. Tom just hoped that the men behind would be caught in the act so to speak and would have to face the authorities for the damage they had done to such a nice place. He never thought for one minute that they were doing the same as him looking for Welsh. He never even ventured down that road not tonight anyway.

The next few hours Tom just kept motoring towards Sydney till he managed to find a Service area that was open where he could grab a bite to eat and more coffee. Just outside of Albury Wodonga on the NSW—Victoria Border he managed to get his chance. Settling back into his car after thoroughly nourishing himself he started to go through the diary page by page that he had retrieved from Welsh's place. Tom was beginning to feel sorry for the cleaner as when she made her way back to the house on her next call, there was going to be someone else on the unemployment list.

The diary proved to be a positive find. In it he found the address and phone numbers of Michelle and her husband John who lived up in the Blue Mountains just west of Sydney. There were also marked on certain dates some sort of code listings but were difficult to comprehend and for which he had no clue about, codes were not his thing. Some dates were also marked with times when certain people rang him including the guys in Athens, Nassau and also a large letter A which Tom could only pin onto a coincidence for Ashid. At some stage he would have to let Gary have this piece of evidence, all he wanted at this point was the address of Welsh's daughter.

Tom continued on his journey the following morning leaving Albury heading up towards the Blue Mountains. He was amazed at the countryside he passed as he drove through the undulating hills between Albury and Lithgow. Passing Cowra he was tempted to go to the old Japanese World War 2 prison camp as he had read about it in his history interests in college but decided he needed to get to where he needed to be to get a hold of Welsh before he took it on himself to disappear again.

He drove through Bathurst along what he thought was part of the V8 track used in the big race they had there each October. It was a bit of a kick as he came down over the mountain and hit the straight pushing his hire car to the max. He wondered how he had ended up on that road as it wasn't part of the main highway he had been travelling on. He thought he must have had a grey moment by detouring unknowingly off the highway. It made a pleasant break for him though taking his mind off the task ahead which was in fact now giving him headaches.

The last stop of the day was Lithgow where Tom found a motel called the Bowen Inn off the main Great Western Highway positioned off the listed road behind a housing estate and medical centre. This would be ideal as it was only a short way to Blackheath where Welsh's daughter lived with her family and it was also out of the way to prying eyes.

Tom settled for the night here knowing that the following day was Friday 13, lucky for some though, not lucky for most, would give him time to look at local maps and make plans to tackle Welsh if he was still in the area.

CHAPTER 38

Vauxhall Cross Thursday 12 April

The conference room on Gary's floor today was a hive of activity. There were papers strewn across the massive table and the TV on the wall was showing some of the video that was taken of Aspalson over the past few days.

Sitting at the larger than life table were only two people Gary Warlock and Sandra Crisp. In front of Sandra sat a pile of folders which she was lazily tapping her fingers on while giving Gary a brief summary of the video on the screen.

"Since you spoke to Aspalson he has been a very busy man. He has visited more people these last few weeks than he has done over his term at the Foreign Office the past two years." Sandra started to open her files as the video paused. "You have seen by our tail on him that he has been not only at work but spent a considerable amount of times at his bank. You might think it normal for some but for Aspalson it isn't. He has never visited the branch before in years but recently he has been there five times."

"Do we know what he has been doing at the bank branch Sandra?" a questioning Gary asked rubbing his chin.

"Without throwing up a flag of warning to him, no Sir. We have someone inside whenever he goes in but he is seen only by the branch manager whenever he arrives."

"Can we approach the manager about it without stirring up too much?"

"I have someone going in today on the proviso that it is a matter of National Security which will mean the manager has to be open with us but also not give any warning to Aspalson. That is the worry of it at present as we are unsure how close he is to Aspalson."

"What checks have been made to clear the manager from it?" Gary had now turned to face Sandra Crisp as she slowly filtered through her files.

"At present to date we have no real connection between the two but are checking things like clubs, pubs etc to make sure." She removed a couple of sheets from her file. "This is our biggest concern, Sir, this shows that Aspalson has an overseas account which has been used recently and has funds in it that far outweigh his salary he earns from the Government."

"I remember you telling me about these from your man inside the Cayman Island Bank, isn't it?"

"Yes, we have double checked every entry and it also coincides with times he has met Ashid either here in London or in Baghdad when he has visited there for various Government meetings. But we still do not know if the payments going into his account are from Ashid, that information is a bit harder to get at present. It is very coincidental though."

"With all the information we have on both Aspalson and Ryder what can you surmise for me Sandra?"

"I really do not want to stick my neck out on this but at a guess I'd say our friend Aspalson is getting some sort of payoff from an outside source. The reason I say that is because we have been able to isolate Ryder's accounts now he is deceased and they show very similar payment times but with lesser amounts. On his salary he would have had to work the next hundred or so years with free board to acquire the amounts he has in his accounts."

"On the Video he seems to be covering himself with solicitors, real estates and his bank, so what do you think he is up to with this?"

"This makes it easier for us. The real estate has told us they are being commissioned to sell his properties, not just his residence. They have been asked to carry that out over the coming weeks.

As far as the solicitor goes well he was not too keen to co-operate which is the usual for those jerks. Client confidentiality and so forth. Even the threat that if there was a problem with National Security we would drag his name through the coals as well as Aspalson didn't open him up. That just clammed him right up. We warned him not to alert Aspalson of our enquiries as he would find himself somewhere special in the world listening to a language he did not understand.

If you join the dots it very much looks like he is about to fly the coop. Insiders have said he has been a bit introverted of late but that might be because Tom dropped his loved one out of circulation. Some say he is getting restless and they fear he is about to have a nervous breakdown."

"Great that just about gives me an out, Sandra. How about we go over to the Foreign Office tomorrow and hit him up with what we have so far. It is a bit of a stab in the dark but it may be the thing that throws him over the edge and pulls the skeletons out of the closet."

Just then Sandra's mobile played a waltz. Both burst out laughing as she fumbled with it to answer.

"Boyfriend???" Gary asked with a wink.

Sandra laughed louder, shook her head before she pressed the answer button she replied. "Not a chance. The last fella I had dumped me because of my job. What time do I ever have to myself since you got me working alongside you guys?"

She held the phone to her ear giving off noises of understanding as the sender was relaying their message. She started to show signs of a broad smile of confidence and reassurance as she thanked the sender shutting down the phone.

"Well there you are. We have the proof now. It seems that the manager at Aspalson's bank rolled over for us and has given us some details which now give us reasonable proof of his past dealings.

Some of the payments are now confirmed to have come from Asia Pac in Athens, Nassau and Melbourne. The best bit though is that the last payment was made through a third party in Basra. It seems our little friend is in cahoots with Ashid on something other than Government business. Just a moment Gary." Sandra stopped talking and started to frantically go through another file she had in front of her. Pulling a complete folder over to look at, she hurriedly went through it jotting down some dates and figures from different pieces of paper.

"What have you got?"

"I just remembered some of the Government deals we have been placing with Iraq following our involvement there. Here are the dates and who was responsible for some of the contracts that were placed over there. It seems that nearly 90% of the deals for contracts were originally approved by Aspalson which is against the initial policy set out by the Prime Minister.

He wanted clear and concise contracts that were completely transparent to avoid any fraudulent dealings taking place. By asking for this transparency it meant that all contracts had to be dealt with by a group of people with not one heading more than two contracts of similar content.

When you look at the dates, times and contents you will see that that hasn't been happening, Aspalson has been dipping into more than he was intended to have been allowed. If the PM gets hold of this he is up the creek without a paddle and the Government will undoubtedly be placed in an embarrassing position of cover up and lies."

"That's it then Sandra we face up to Aspalson first thing tomorrow morning in his office. I want you to itemise all you have there, briefly but make sure we have the actual dates of funds transfers, what their totals are and where they were placed. It seems Mr Aspalson has some explaining to do not only for him but also his sidekick Ryder.

Last thing, Sandra can we freeze all of his accounts as of today? That should put the bullet up the barrel for him."

"I'll get it in motion now Sir." She got up from the large conference table ejected the video and then started to gather the papers that were strewn everywhere. Seemed like Sandra Crisp was about to work a late one to prepare for Friday 13.

Next morning at 1000 hrs Gary along with Sandra left Vauxhall Cross for the short trip across the river to the Foreign office. They had placed a call early to ensure that Aspalson would be there asking for an immediate meeting to discuss events that had taken place in Australia over night. Even though Aspalson asked questions, Gary said it was a delicate point and he needed Aspalson's expertise to resolve the issue face to face.

Aspalson had no idea about what Gary was on his way to do that morning. He sat patiently waiting for his arrival not realizing that the fuse for his demise had already been lit. Gary had given him the sprat to catch the Mackerel in asking for his expertise which he always rose to the occasion for.

It was close to 1100hrs when Gary was shepherded into Aspalson's office closely followed by Sandra Crisp dressed formally in her captain's uniform being badged as an Intelligence officer.

"Take a seat Gary." Aspalson suddenly stopped as Sandra followed closely in behind. "Oh er Captain Crisp isn't it?"

Sandra just nodded taking a seat without even being asked. The door to the office was closed by the secretary that had showed them in and the three of them sat looking at each other with Aspalson suddenly showing signs of nerves as beads of sweat started forming on his brow.

"Well what is it that needs my attention so urgently Gary?"

"I am going to come directly to the point Reginald my friend, it seems we have uncovered a bit of a fraud or coercion between Asia Pac, Ashid at the Iraq Interior Ministry and yourself."

"I beg your pardon. How dare you? What nonsense is this?"

Gary looked at Sandra who drew out a brief list of deals with Iraq complete with dates, times and names. Also she produced the banking details she had obtained only the afternoon before. She placed these on the desk with the wording facing Aspalson. He bent his head to read the pages shaking it frantically at the read.

"This is preposterous, it cannot be correct, these figures have been manufactured by someone surely."

"No, Sir." Sandra was firm in her reply. "All these figures for the contracts I have spent hours going over and I must confirm they are all correct. There are no mistakes.

As far as the bank figures go on this list." She pointed to it. "They are also correct and have been confirmed by your own bank manager as of yesterday. It seems your assistant Lieutenant Ryder was also a benefactor of this so called scheme. I must point out that at this stage we have frozen all your financial dealings till we have spoken to the Prime Minister to avoid the possibility of embarrassment between ourselves, Iraq and the British public."

Aspalson went completely white with shock before burying his head in his hands which were close enough to the desk making his head bang on the top of it. "This is not what it seems Gary believe me. There is some mistake here. I need to speak to the Foreign Secretary immediately. Something isn't right here."

"Look Reginald we can give you till close of play today to speak to the PM about this problem before we have to contact him but we cannot hold this back any further. Speaking to your boss upstairs will only make the matter worse by bringing it to the fore within your Department, we need to cut this rot out before it gets out I'm afraid. Do you understand?"

"There has been some mistake but please leave it with me and I will try and see the PM at lunch today to talk this through and clear it up. Thank you Gary for highlighting this problem to me."

The meeting was now at an obvious end and the sheets Sandra had placed on the table were left there for Reginald Aspalson to ponder over. He knew he was in a tight corner and had only one option and that was to plead with the PM trying somehow to cover his arse as much as possible.

He looked at the figures trying to see if he could lay the blame firmly on Ryder seeing as he couldn't defend himself but there were so many entries for both of them that it would not look very realistic. He had little option but to face up to his undoing. The best he could think of was possibly resign and collect all that he could that wasn't frozen and bugger off out the country which he was planning to do soon anyway.

He made a call to Ashid getting him up to date on the matter but received no sympathy from him whatsoever. Ashid had other things on his plate at the present and was not interested at all in the floundering Aspalson's request for help.

Aspalson sat staring into oblivion while he tried to see if there was any way he could come out of this safely. The bastards had frozen his bank accounts which was a bitter disappointment. He had tried to get Ashid to fund him so far as spirit him away out of the country and away from pointing fingers but Ashid had just cursed him for being so stupid followed by an immediate slamming down of the phone.

Ringing the PM on this Friday wasn't the best. He was a bit superstitious about Friday thirteenth but told Aspalson he could give him an hour or so at one o'clock which he hurriedly got himself ready for. He shredded the papers Sandra had given him while also checking his diary for entries of any incrimination. Within the hour he left his office not wanting to return to it ever again. He had made his mind up and would fall on his sword to a point anyway, he would just resign saying he had inadvertently taken shortcuts with the contracts to try and speed them along.

After a very intense meeting with the PM in which his boss threatened to string him up in the Tower by his balls Aspalson had laid his resignation down on the table which was duly accepted by the PM followed by him being expressly dismissed from No 10.

The world had collapsed around Reginald Aspalson of late. Friday the thirteenth was to be remembered for his day of disloyalty to the British Government and its public. He would be absolutely disgraced and sent to Coventry by all that knew him.

His lover Phil Ryder had been killed by that little shit Warburton who was definitely on some kind of vendetta against him. Life was looking greyer and greyer when his car finally stopped outside his lush country residence. He was politely wished good afternoon by his driver whom he thanked for all he had done for him in the past. The driver was at a bit of a loss as he had no idea what had transpired inside No 10 that afternoon. He would not know anything till he read his Sunday paper over breakfast that weekend.

Aspalson went into his home asking his butler to just take the rest of the day off as he wanted to be left alone for the remainder of the day. In his office was an unopened bottle of single malt which he thought he would have saved for a special occasion but now it seemed appropriate to open it which he did pouring a beaker full. This didn't touch the sides at all as it passed his lips so mellow, sliding down his throat warming his very centre.

Reginald sat thinking through what he could do to overcome the present problems. The money was not there for him as he had planned due to the diligent efforts of GCHQ and Six to freeze him out. He was now alone, rejected and lost. His associate in all this trouble, Ashid had also rejected him that day not wanting to help him when he needed it most. It was getting to be all too much but there was a way out, the only one he could think of. Another couple of glass full's of the single malt and his brain was saying to him 'I don't really give a shit'

Within two hours the sky outside had darkened over for the night with Aspalson's brain also darkened over from his drinking, he had run out of ideas. In front of him was a note pad which he started to scribble on. His writing wasn't the best after downing the bottle of scotch in such a short time but he managed to put down all he could to explain his forage into the evil that had overtaken him. He headed up to the top floor of his residence rather unsteadily nearly falling back down the stairs on three occasions; it took him thrice as long to get to the top of the stairs as it would normally have done.

In the bedroom he found his robe placed on the bed and pulled the cord out from the waist hoops. It wasn't that long so he searched his wardrobe finding two others even after stumbling over a couple of times inside. Getting the cords he had tied together and he was no boy scout to be assure, he went out onto the landing where he tied the end to the top of the balustrade.

With tears forming in his eyes he made a slip knot looping it over his head. Climbing over the balustrade he was now finding that the whole world around him was spinning uncontrollably. Could he turn back possibly repair what had happened in the past, he never would find out as he slipped with his left foot which sent his body over the small ledge then plummeting down to meet the floor below. It never made the floor as the robe cords became taut held causing a sudden snap sound that reverberated around the foyer of his splendid abode, as Aspalson's neck broke throwing his head off to one side. His eyes just gazed staring ahead, blank, wet with tears, he was now at peace, not having to worry what anyone thought of him or not even worrying about what might happen to him. He had joined his great love Phil in the unknown realm of death. The coward's way out for him most would say.

Reginald Aspalson's body was not found till the following morning by his butler. The authorities were called in immediately but all were intercepted by MI5 who had been brought up to date by the PM the night before. The press would not be having a field day over this suicide at least.

His note was handed to Five's chief who called Gary over to look at it:—

To who finds this message.

Life sometimes gives us opportunities which we take without really thinking about them.

I took chances myself which were wrong and I have now been placed in a world of darkness, alone. I miss my friend Phil knowing I will never meet anyone as loving as him ever again.

I hope I can be forgiven for what I have done but like all Governments we are placed in positions that lead us to some kind of temptation.

I cannot face the pain anymore.
Signed Reginald Aspalson

Neither Gary nor his counterpart in Five could see the sense in the writing but Gary knew that this was possibly the only way out he had left to be able to take. Not even a mention of Ashid as he had hoped would have been the case when he drove over to the building where Five was housed.

The Sunday papers came out with a story that the Undersecretary at the Foreign Office with responsibility for the Middle East had resigned due to ill health. There was no mention of any death which would not be reported on till the following month when it would be announced that Reginald Aspalson had passed away after a short illness involving pancreatic cancer. The Government can and will cover whatever they need to, to keep their own validity with the Public. The butler was sworn to the Official Secrets Act and was fortunate enough to gain another post with an increase in remuneration to keep him quiet. Oh how the SYSTEM works so well.

CHAPTER 39

Baghdad Friday 13 April.

A meeting of urgency had been called by the Prime Minister this morning after the disaster that had befallen the Government Building the day before. On Thursday while the Council of Ministers had been having their meeting they had adjourned for lunch but during that lunch a suicide bomber had entered the building detonating himself killing one Minister and injuring many others. This building being Baghdad's Convention Centre houses the Parliament of Iraq. It is situated inside the Green Zone which is reputably the most secure area in Iraq and still guarded by the Americans but individual building security was being enforced by Iraqi police and troops themselves.

When the lunch had been called Jamal Ashid had conveniently excused himself from the lunch date to deal, as he had told others with some pressing matters at his Ministry. Just another delusional citizen that had become a bomber was the feeling amongst the survivors, no one even thought it strange that only one member of the Council would be excused as the explosion happened.

Ashid was making his plans to exit his public life in Government and the bombing was just another diversion for his plan to succeed. He was only disappointed at the fact that the bomber did not claim more lives. Also he was enraged by the fact that there should have been two other suicide bombers that would have caused even more death and casualties. They had backed out at the last minute which was an unthinkable act for Ashid, it was a broken honour and he was determined to enact his revenge on those two people when he eventually found them. The two unexploded vests were eventually found near the canteen which led to a vigorous investigation within the centre to find the culprits. Ashid was more concerned that he might be uncovered by his two weak mules that had bolted but they were the chances you took when you paralyse a brain to do the unthinkable.

This morning's meeting comprised the remaining Council of Ministers. The only ones absent were those that had been injured the day before and of course the poor soul that had died. Headed by the Prime Minister Nouri al Maliki the room where they were meeting today had already been checked and double checked by specially trained sniffer dogs which meant that the Government were feeling they were under permanent attack at the present. Dogs in the Islamic world were normally viewed as unclean animals and were not the sort of thing you would rely on for a friendly use so the Council Of Ministers must have felt really threatened to have had the dogs scan the meeting room they were now in.

Along with the PM were two Deputy Prime Ministers, ministers from Defence, Finance, Foreign Affairs, Oil, Agriculture, Works and Planning, Communications, Construction and Housing, Education, Industry and Minerals, Justice, Science and technology, Trades, Water resources and of course Jamal Ashid as Minister of Interior.

When the meeting got underway there were some heated shouts and arguments around the table between what seemed cultural differences. Shiites, Kurds and a minority of Sunni were throwing accusations at each other for the events of the previous day. The blame game where ever you are in the world is always the first card played in this type of arena.

Being in the Sunni minority, Ashid was also the most vocal of the Sunni members. Disliked by the PM for the way he had tackled many of the major projects around the country because he should not have been involved in them at all in the first place. He greatly influenced many of the other Ministries because he controlled the police and anti terrorist groups using them indiscreetly to deal with Ministers who would not conform to his ideas.

The meeting went for around two hours of bantering back and forth without really achieving anything of importance. Ashid saw his opportunity to be able to cut and run before he himself was possibly found out. He was concerned that the two cowards, as he called them, might be detained by the Allies instead of his own Police and if that be the case he would be uncovered as a traitor to the State then executed.

Better leave and do your own thing from a good hiding place than be executed as then your ideas will normally die with you. He had so many things he wanted to be able to do, one being the total disruption of Iraq and also the Allies themselves. He had a distinct dislike of the British and Americans constantly declaring them as the destroyers of a once proud and robust nation.

As the meeting started to wind down Ashid stood up holding his hand up to gain silence around the table. Some looked in surprise at him as he had actually interrupted the PM in his final address to the Council which was not the best protocol to have. Silence immediately swept around the table including the PM who stared at Ashid angrily and sat down totally rejected.

Ashid stood and glanced around the table at his contemporaries. He produced a broad smile and then held his index finger of his right hand up directing it insultingly at the PM. "You are the cause of the lack of security at this place no one else. You must take the ultimate responsibility of this cursed situation. May Allah have mercy on you for your incompetence?"

All around the table faces started to turn red some with rage, others with embarrassment. How could anyone speak to the PM in this manner? Shock was on the face of Maliki as he sat staring at Ashid in disgust. He did not respond to the comments as he should have, he was lost for words, but sat with his friends close at hand who were murmuring their disgust at Ashid.

"I cannot any longer sit on this Council with such insular and stupid lackeys to the Western world. You are all a disgrace to Islam and the Prophet. You sit here day after day talking but there is never any positive action. You are the invention of Satan's Army."

With that he turned and walked towards the exit leaving behind a room that had now broken into turmoil. Yelling for Ashid's head had begun by his enemies around the table which were many. His once allies on the Council sat keeping quiet not wanting to feel the wrath of the majority as they had once supported this man in the past. Ashid took no notice of any of the calls thrown at him leaving the room and then fleeing to his office where he had already started making arrangements to destroy many of his notes and files.

In his office were two men who were totally loyal to him but was it loyalty or they were frightened of him and never wanted to upset this man of steel. They apologised for the fact that they had not found the two default bombers as yet but were busily looking trying to locate their relatives to take vengeance on them.

Ashid asked both men to leave and to make their way to the secret hiding place in Mosul to the Northwest of Baghdad that had been previously arranged. The city of Mosul sat astride the Tigris River and was now the home for Ashid and his new band of followers that he had recruited over the past two years or so. As the two left a third man entered the room, carrying a large box, signalling his allegiance to Ashid with a salute. Anan Sadam Wahli was a thirty year old ex revolutionary guard of the ousted President Saddam Hussein. He was broad shouldered, about six foot tall and with arms and legs that looked like they had been sculptured.

"Sir there is rumours you are to be arrested for your outburst at the Meeting of the Council this morning." Anan was not at all in any form of panic, as cool as a cucumber as you could be.

"I expected that recourse." Ashid responded with a broad silly grin he had used to offset his colleagues many times in discussions. "We leave for Mosul now but we will leave behind a gift for our friends when they come searching Anan."

As Ashid cleared the final remnants from his huge desk checking for anything that could incriminate him in any way, he turned to Anan and nodded. At the signal he had just received from Ashid, Anan lowered the box onto the desk and opened the lid. Inside was a pack of C4 with trailing multiple wires of all colours. Anan was an expert in bomb making and when he made these types of gifts up he made sure that no Bomb Disposal experts could defuse the thing at all easily. There were at least three anti tampering devices wired into it and sitting taped on the top of the explosives was a mobile phone. He started to remove the phone as they had found out that the previous day's bomb had forced the Government to take the unusual action of shutting down the mobile network in Bagdad.

Anan fiddled with the wires drawing out two which he then, after disconnecting one of the phones on the desk, connected in his wires. Ashid looked on totally amazed at the speed with which Anan completed his actions.

"Are you sure this is going to work as we want and not by error?" Ashid asked hoping that no one would ring the special blue phone Anan had used.

"Sir, this is the phone from my office direct to here and no one can use it without first pressing the code to unlock the dialling mechanism.

When we leave here we go via my office from where we will be able to set this off at the time of our choosing."

As he completed the task he had started he cleaned the mess on the table and pocketed the mobile. With smiles all round the two men finally left the office and descended the stairs to the outer main door. Here there was a car waiting to whisk them away to Mosul but firstly they needed to go to Anan's office where they would wait to detonate the bomb. Anan had already asked that Ashid's secretary ring them when his office was housing the arresting officers that were on their way.

Driving away Ashid looked one last time at the building he had called home for quite a while trying to visualize the mess that they would be leaving behind in just a few more minutes.

Two minutes later they were sitting in Anan's office in the building of the Directorate of Military Survey about half a kilometre away to the north. They patiently waited.

At Ashid's office sirens were heard as a convoy of Military and Police vehicles pulled up to the front entrance escorted by American Marines to ensure the PM's wishes were carried out correctly. It seemed strange to many as the Ministry of Interior was the controller of Police and Anti terrorism. No one inside the building had any idea what was going on as the action had been instigated by the PM and his cronies to shut Ashid down after his inglorious outburst at the morning meeting.

As senior officers raced into the building they stormed directly up to Ashid's office where the secretary sat gob smacked at the amount of senior brass that had suddenly appeared in front of her. They did not wait for any comment from her just bursting into the office to find it empty. They began going through drawers and cabinets as the secretary rang the number she had been given by Anan.

On the desk stood the box that Anan had brought in looking just part of the furniture being very ornately carved and not one of the men looked at the ornate object as it sat close to the telephone it was connected to. By now there were about ten senior officers and six high ranking Government officials in the office by the time Anan had put the phone down after thanking the secretary for her call.

As police and American Marines stood guard outside the building stopping people leaving or entering the blue phone on the desk started to ring. All in the office began to turn as all of a suddenly there was one almighty bang and a flash that lit up the office and street outside even in the daylight. The damage was catastrophic as windows blew out from surrounding offices and rubble fell from the Interior ministry walls as parts of the wall of Ashid's office fell onto the pavement below showering those standing there. The smoke that was so prolific following the blast was spiralling up into the clear blue sky above.

Not one person survived inside the office, the secretary also wore the brunt of the exploding internal walls of the office and died instantly, so much for her co-operation and loyalty with Anan's request. She had just become another collateral statistic. Three police in the cordon below died as a result of falling debris along with two Marines. There were also many other casualties both inside the Ministry and outside that had now to be cared for. The whole place was one big chaotic mess.

In Anan's office both men had looked out from the window to see the flash and bang that had even at this distance shook their building. The smoke spiral was large and black showing there was an obvious fire now enveloping the top half of the Interior Ministry as both Ashid and Anan looked at each other and smiled. They had achieved more this Friday than the suicide bombers had done on the previous day.

They both left Anan's building casually and departed the area by car heading north towards their safe stronghold in Mosul. Scheming was now the priority of the day for Ashid and it was to be the future he was always dreaming of to bring down the present Iraq Government because of their close allegiance to the Americans and British. But also for Ashid he was now on his ultimate journey of trying to also destroy the calm and coolness that was always shown on the streets of their allies overseas. He was surely going to disrupt them as much as he could in the future because he had the manpower, tools and equipment to do it being brought in through the backdoors of his enemy.

However, what he hadn't banked on was the fact that he was also being watched from a distance. All the actions of the past few days were even now being transmitted back to GCHQ and analysed by Captain Sandra Crisp. What she would make of it all was to be seen but at least someone had eyes on Ashid.

CHAPTER 40

Friday 13 April 2007

Whether lucky for some or not, today was to be a busy day for Tom, having to filter through all the maps of the local area checking the Blackheath spot for the location of Welsh's daughter who under her married name of Waller was living with husband and two children, a boy and girl aged 11 and 9 respectively. Spending the morning checking and double checking he decided to take his belongings with him as a precaution in case he had to move from Blackheath in the other direction. He never checked out of the motel having paid for three nights in it so no one was the wiser for his driving out that day they would think he was just sightseeing. As he made his way from his accommodation at Lithgow to Blackheath to find Welsh he just hoped he was one of the lucky ones on this Friday.

The drive from Lithgow took him about half an hour through leafy tree lined roads and over rolling hills where the views were absolutely outstanding. This was surely one of the nicest places to live in this State. Down into Blackheath on past the railway station Tom had to take the next left which took him onto Govetts Leap Road. Tom had done his homework well finding the address of the Waller's in Romaine Street fairly easily.

This was a narrow country lane with no where to park other than someone's driveway. That would be out of the question for Tom, not wanting to spark any observations on himself just yet.

Driving back up onto Govetts leap he decided to call into Blackheath cabins to check for a vacancy. It was about a kilometre from the house so a good brisk walk pace would see him there in no time.

With the evening sky darkening over he settled into one of the cabins which he had booked again making it for three days in advance. Grabbing a bite to eat was his next move which was simple as he had driven past a pub called the New Ivanhoe on the main turn off. They had a bistro there and it was there that he made his way to eat. Spending a couple of hours at the pub he retired back to his cabin where he turned on the TV making sure the sound was acceptable for his neighbours, if there were any. This park was quiet really but then again April wasn't really the holiday season this side of the world.

Making sure that there was no one around Tom exited the cabin and made his way on foot to the address he had viewed a few hours earlier. Once into Romaine St there was no street lighting which eased Tom's mind of being seen.

As he approached the address he got more and more confident with himself. On the gate was a sign with the name of the property as Macarthur Park, which gave Tom a bit of delight as he remembered a song with the same name sung by the Small Faces from back in his Dad's era and he had heard it played so many times by the old feller. Whether or not this one would melt as in the song was to be seen.

This elevation of spirits led to him venturing down the driveway in the shade of trees till he reached what looked like the garage which was built in under the main house. From the window above a light shone through the blinds that had been pulled closed. The garage doors were shut and there were no cars in the drive.

The only lights here were some along a pathway that led to the front door of the main house. Tom avoided them making his way around the darkest side of the building till he came to what seemed a fence that separated the house area from the valley drop over to one side. Looking along the wall of the house he could plainly see a huge bay shaped window wall or atrium that overlooked the valley on the other side of what appeared to be a balcony. On the upper storey was another smaller style bay window which was in darkness.

Tom crept cautiously around the wall of the balcony so he would be able to see into the large bay window. Above his head was a row of windows that had the lights blazing out highlighting anything that moved close to the house. The light was a fluorescent style light which Tom assumed would be the kitchen.

Coming to the Bay window the lights were on and there was movement inside. He edged his way further on and outwards till he could see into the room from the good cover of low lying bushes. It looked like a family room with the log fire burning away on one wall and the TV blasting out one of those reality shows.

From where he could see there were two children sitting on the sofa laughing and staring at the TV. On a reclining chair to the side of the sofa sat a large man about 35 resembling Norm, the Aussie character who found it difficult to exercise. He was just reading what looked like a novel. To his right was an attractive blonde woman who looked like she was talking to someone in the kitchen.

Tom waited for a while in the hope that the person in the other room would come into the family room. He was rewarded pretty quickly when there was a man slowly walking out of the kitchen clutching a mug of hot drink. There he was Welsh in all his glory spending time with his family. He didn't sit down but looked like he was excusing himself for the night. He turned and walked to the other end of the room where it looked like a lobby of some description.

Tom saw the door open and the night outside on the other side of the house. He immediately moved to the end of the house and along the wall till he could get to the front of the house. Here he found yet another building. It was two storeys high and there were lights on in the upper storey. He heard footsteps coming down a path heading towards the building. He pushed himself hard against the wall into the shadows. As the footsteps neared he heard a young boy's voice call out.

"Grandfather, are you going to come to my softball match tomorrow, it is the last week and we are in the finals?"

"Sure will Brodie, wouldn't miss it for quids, what time is it?" "We leave at 8 o'clock, Good night Grandfather." "Good night son."

The door behind Welsh shut and he continued towards the other building. Tom would let him move to where he could better take any advantage. Going in through the side door he shut it behind him and Tom heard him climbing what seemed to be stairs. After a few moments the lights dimmed above and the TV in the room came on.

Tom moved to the front of the building hoping to be able to see a car there but when he got to the front of this barn type building it had two doors which were shut and locked after an unsuccessful attempt by him to open them. Above the door was the usual basketball ring found above most garages in this country.

Tom abandoned his plight for tonight going back to his room till the following morning. He would follow Welsh tomorrow checking out his movements for anything strange. Hoping he would be in contact with Caulfield at some stage.

Saturday morning was a chilly affair but at least it was dry. Tom left his cabin at 6.30 taking his car he waited at the end of Romaine Street as it was the only way to exit it. He sat patiently waiting till about ten past eight when a large Toyota four wheel drive pulled up at the end of the street. Sitting inside was the attractive blonde driving with Welsh sitting next to her laughing and chatting. The children were both in the back seat. Waller must have remained at home Tom thought, but that theory was blown out when behind the Toyota came a convertible Morgan Plus 4 with its hood up. Filling the windscreen was Norm and he was hot on the tail of his family.

Tom slipped in behind Norm as they headed off towards the main highway. Driving down through Katoomba Tom nearly lost his goal as Norm pulled off to go in a different direction. Tom caught sight of the Toyota as he pulled up at some traffic lights. They were still moving along the main highway. He chased after them once the lights changed and got comfortably to within three cars lengths.

Further down the highway they drove through Wentworth Falls then on towards Springwood. This journey took them all of fifty minutes which is some ride to take your kids to a sports meet in any man's language, they must be dedicated softballers.

Pulling off the highway into Springwood proper they finally stopped at a park called Lomantia where the fields were set up as diamonds for the kids' softball games.

Welsh and the family disembarked their vehicle carrying fold up chairs they made their way to one of the playing areas. Tom waited till they were settled down before he moved from his vehicle to a spot nearby where he could watch Welsh closely.

During the next hour he saw Norm arrive to watch his son and also a couple of friends of his daughters whom Welsh obviously knew. Tom used his phone camera to take some pictures as he watched them all getting involved in the game. Young Brodie was beaming he had the entire spotlight today, it was his special day and his family was watching him.

Brodie was not bad either at his game. He was catcher for part of the game which brought many cheers from his Grandfather who was obviously so proud of him. While batting Brodie hit a Homer at one point when all the bases were full which brought home all the runners and caused such a commotion in the Welsh Waller camp that you couldn't hear anyone else except that lot. Vocal as you could get.

After the game the family left the grounds in their two vehicles with the daughter tagging along with Dad in the Morgan while the other three went in the Toyota. Stopping on the way they treated themselves to MacDonald's before they headed for home. Tom followed till they reached their street then wandered off back to his cabin.

That night Tom again went to the Waller household. There was little difference around the house than the day before. When Tom got there they were all out on the balcony celebrating Brodie's team win having a bar-b-que. They laughed and joked about the day with plenty of talk of a planned day out for Sunday to Penrith Water Park, some kind of kayak course. Tom couldn't see Norm doing anything like that but then again surprises were always on the menu with the larger size men.

Retiring for the night Tom slept well that night, it was getting close to challenging Welsh time.

On Sunday morning he arose to a bright blue sky knowing he needed to give Gary a call.

"Gary I have located Welsh, he is with his daughter and her family. I am going in today to see if I can get to him, perhaps bring him in without any trouble."

"Well that would be a distinct change from bodies being left everywhere mate."

"Bollocks Gary. I'll leave the phone on just for you. Hopefully I will call when I have finished for you to clean up the pieces eh?"

"Tom you are such a comic at times. I'll see if I can get someone to assist you."

"No Gary, I need to do this alone mate. I'll call you if I need anything."

"OK Mate will wait for your call. Take care."

And with that Tom hung up hoping Gary would stick to his plane then walked down towards the Waller house. He waited for a short while till within an hour he saw the Toyota pull up out of the drive and head out. In it was Norm driving this time with the blonde by his side. In the back were the two kids. Welsh was not in the car with them, which caused Tom to freeze hoping he hadn't missed an opportunity with Welsh fleeing the area overnight. Damn he thought to himself, should have kept eyes on the place overnight.

During the day the house being privately located at the end of this quiet country lane now showed its magnificence being perched high looking over park like gardens and World Heritage National Park. It would have had views from every room. It was a classic mountains design with exposed timber beams as Tom found out as he climbed over fences to get a broader prospective of the property.

From his vantage point near the barn building he managed to see inside the lower section as the doors were open. In the right hand space was the silver grey Mercedes that belonged to Welsh and alongside it the Morgan. Further inside he could see a tractor and ride on mower. The car was still here but where was Welsh. He moved closer to the building keeping as low as he could.

On reaching the doors of the barn he slide inside to look at the Mercedes to see if he could immobilise it in some way thus delay any departure that may crop up. In the ignition were the keys which after careful opening of the door with little noise Tom was able to remove them and shove them into his pocket.

Moving further to the rear of the building where he could see some stairs that led to the upstairs loft he listened for any movement or talk. These were the stairs he had heard Welsh ascend on the Friday.

There was no noise at all coming from upstairs so he backed himself out of the barn and headed for the main house rear. Here he tried to see from his previous nights hiding spots into the windows of the house. He saw nothing and no one.

Slowly he came about the house to the front garage where again the doors were open and inside was another car, a Holden Commodore Caprice in black refinery and grey interior, an executive style car possibly Norm's business vehicle. Tom crept into the garage to check it out and saw there was a stair well towards the rear of the garage. He slowly went to the stair but suddenly he felt two hands on his shoulders, then he felt himself lifted and he was thrown to one side bashing his head and shoulder up against the wall.

That sent ringing through his ears once again, this was becoming a habit and he stumbled only to find a giant fist land squarely on his face missing his chin by millimetres. His head flew back with the whiplash of the punch on his cheek which again belted his head against the wall.

Dropping to his knees he did what he learnt from training and rolled out of the firing line over against the other wall.

As he did so he heard curses and stamping noises as whoever had given him the thump turned then moved close to him again. Tom sprang to his feet bringing his hands up to defend himself.

There in front of him was Welsh fists up and advancing onto him rapidly. Tom took evasive action giving himself plenty of room to be able to counter any attack he was open to. Welsh moved in quicker now throwing punch after punch but missing as Tom parried and ducked. Welsh wasn't going to ease up any time soon either. He kept coming at Tom so Tom had to do something and that was a sharp fist to the sternum which blew the drive from Welsh. Tom followed it with a sharp kick into the side of Welsh's torso which sent the fifty year old something careering into the Caprice side pillar.

Tom moved into the attack as Welsh regained his feet but as he did so Tom gave him one hell of a punch to the jaw that put out Welsh's lights. He hit the deck hard and just lay still but at least breathing.

Tom looked around for something to neutralise him with finding some convenient zip ties in a packet on the bench at the rear of the garage. Zipping up Welsh's hands he had him laid on his front hands to the rear. Walking over to the sink that was in the corner he splashed cold water on his face to clear his mind then picked up a small container filling it with cold water. Going back over to the still prostrate Welsh he poured the water over his head which caused him to stir pretty violently.

"Who the fuck are and what do you want?" Welsh belted out still facing the floor.

"You don't know me but I sure as hell know you. Your mate Caulfield set me up back in Iraq and I really need to pay him back."

"That's fuck all to do with me son."

"Oh I think it does have something to do with you as you and your dear cousin were into thieving off the Government then. Remember the dead men that once were your comrades in arms. Someone wants justice at least for those guys."

"Look pal surely we can talk about this eh?"

Tom lifted Welsh up and started to walk him to his room above the barn. Getting him up the stairs was a bit hectic as they were so narrow but eventually they were in the loft of the barn which was set up like a bachelor pad. Tom threw Welsh into a chair still zipped up which caused him a bit of anguish as he sat crushing his arms behind him.

"Now I just need to know where my friend and yours Caulfield is." "If I knew I would tell you believe me but I don't. He told me he was heading up towards Queensland and that's about it. If I had known what he was planning with the men back in Iraq I would have stopped him."

"Yeh right. I bet you would. You're as cheap and as transparent as the rest of them. You lie to protect your own well being and you know full well that the game is now up and therefore you need to come clean before the authorities slap you in irons."

"Listen I can give you whatever you need but I need to be able to get to my phone."

"You have to be kidding me. I don't trust you as far as I can throw you. Now where is Caulfield."

"I really don't know. He hasn't been in touch since we left Melbourne. I just want my family to be left out of this please."

"That's fine but you are going to have to face the consequences of your actions you know that."

Welsh started to talk about what had been happening since Athens and the way his men disappeared. He went onto Nassau and the death of Forbes, who he guessed now Tom was the one who had eliminated him, which Tom confirmed. What he could not fathom was the fact that the other man in Nassau, Sweetman, had just disappeared off the face of the earth.

Tom put him straight on Sweetman giving him details of how he found him and the two Arabs who had chased after him. He also gave details of the Arab involvement in Athens and London. Welsh sat and shook his head at hearing this news. He knew that something weird was going on and now he had it confirmed by the man standing in front of him.

"That bastard Ashid is behind my men dying you've just confirmed that. He is gearing up for something but what I couldn't tell you. He came over the entire friend thing before and now he has proven the fact that he has turned on us."

"Well you know what they say my friend you can never trust an Arab they will steal your shirt off your back without you even feeling it is gone."

Welsh was starting to look rather dejected now, head down while shaking his head going from side to side. All he had was now on the verge of collapse, he could feel it.

Suddenly Tom heard a vehicle coming rapidly down the driveway. He ran over to the window to peer out. It wasn't the family but a large van that screamed to a halt in front of the barn area. Out jumped four big Middle Eastern looking guys.

"Shit not again." Tom let out. "Looks like your friends have found you as well."

"Ashid's men?" Welsh questioned.

"Looks that way from here." Tom came over to Welsh after he saw the men head off towards the house. "I think for a while we are going to be partners Mr Welsh." Tom cut off the zip ties. "Remember that they killed your mates and that is probably your destiny with them on this visit so don't think they will get you out of this fix with me."

"Look, after my men got shafted I have little trust in Ashid let alone the general Arab populace."

Tom looked around for a weapon of some description but saw nothing of any use. Welsh had moved to his storage cupboard he was using as a wardrobe where he pulled out what looked like a walking stick. Well thought Tom we are so well armed two against one and we have a bloody walking stick.

Slowly they moved down the stairs to get outside where they might stand a better chance in the open. As Tom came down the stairs he looked to the far end of the barn at the van that was parked there. There was no one inside that he could see from the mirrors so he told Welsh to remain where he was while he went to the van to immobilise it.

Slowly making his way through the garage Tom found a crow bar and a box of six inch nails, probably used for fencing around the property. He crept to the open door peering out as far as he dare. He saw nothing and no one so he quickly went across to the van where he wedged some nails under each tyre that would penetrate when they reversed away to turn.

Coming back to the garage he made his way back to Welsh who was trying to see what was going on through the side door. One of the men from the van had come out and was looking around the gardens for any form of life. He wasn't taking his time either, running from cover to cover in the hope he would find Welsh or someone who knew where he was.

Tom grabbed Welsh's arm "Wait till he comes this way then we can perhaps lure him in." Welsh nodded and waited. Tom signalled Welsh that he would go out through the doors and come back around the side to deal with the guy in the garden if he chose to stay out there.

As Tom went out the doors and made his way around the barn walls he heard some shouts coming from the house all were shouting in English. As he passed the window on this side of the barn he peered in to see Welsh waiting patiently still by the door.

Tom got to the corner, looked around it and saw the man in the garden still pouncing from one spot to another. Tom bent down and picked up a stone, he aimed it at the bin that was near to the door where Welsh was standing. He threw the stone hitting the bin which automatically made the man spin around to see what the noise was. He looked at the barn deciding to make his way towards it. As he came towards the barn Tom could see that he was carrying a gun in his hand. Boy, were they at a BIG disadvantage, especially with weaponry like that.

The man got close to the door of the barn disappearing out of Tom's sight for a second. Tom went as quickly and as quietly as possible along the back wall to be able to pin the man somehow, either him or Welsh.

There was a sharp bang, not from a gun though which made Tom speed up. He came around the corner to find the door wide open and the man sprawled across the floor with blood coming from a wound upon the top of his head. Tom went in closing the door behind him. Welsh was just standing over his new found friend chuckling to himself.

Tom bent down picking up the gun, a Glock 17, checked it out and finding a full magazine which he then placed it firmly in his trouser waistband.

Welsh looked on as Tom went about checking the man for life, finding him still breathing asked Welsh to get something to tie him up with plus a rag to gag him. Welsh came back with zip ties, the best quality ones, which were hastily zipped around wrists and ankles virtually shutting off the man's circulation. That would send his limbs numb if he woke up too soon.

The rag was rolled, tied in a knot in the centre and placed inside his mouth where it was kept in place by gaffer tape wrapped around his head. Both Welsh and Tom then lifted the man and placed him inside the boot of the Mercedes shutting the lid quietly before they both exited the barn through the front open doors.

Sticking together, Tom followed by Welsh made their way around to the rear of the main house. Sticking close to the walls they made their way to the front garage which lay underneath the lounge room giving good access to the house through it from a direction other than the front door.

The noise upstairs as they got near the top of the stairs was becoming angry with curses but the language used although glowingly abusive was in clear English. These guys were Australian or well educated in Australia.

At the top of the stairs it opened up into the formal dining room where they could hear the voices of the three men clearly upstairs in the master bedroom above them ripping things out searching for something.

They did not attempt to venture up those stairs instead choosing to move down through the house to the bedrooms at the other end. These doors were open wide displaying the mess inside which showed Tom that the men had already done their thing in them. With Tom moving into one room and Welsh into the other they both did the same when in their respective rooms, both lent against the wall behind the door waiting in the hope that the men would move in separate directions giving them the opportunity to pick them off one at a time.

There was some more crashing happening above their heads in the space above. Then silence before the thundering stomps of boots coming down the stairs to the level of the main floor which they were on.

Then loud voices could be heard. "Sandy you go and check the barn. Jake you try the garage down below. Now where the fuck is Dan?"

That answered Tom's question as to the name of the poor blighter that they had stuffed into the trunk of the Mercedes. Tom hoped he was still out for the count not being able to alert his mate Sandy who was now heading his way.

There was movement in all directions as they went about their various orders. Tom waited but Welsh had become increasingly angry, he was damned if he was going to let Ashid's crew stuff up the lives of his daughter's family by wrecking their home. He moved slowly towards the door peering around it to try and locate the one who had issued the orders to the others. He couldn't see anyone at first so moved out further into the Family room. As he did Tom heard a man yell "There you are you prick. We have been looking for you my friend"

Before Tom could come out from his hiding place he heard a rush of steps made by someone running forward then a loud bang as a gun went off. Someone hit the floor and he knew who that would be, Welsh. He spun out of the door rolled on the floor aiming the Glock at the other end of the room where the noises had come from bringing its sights clearly onto the man now standing over Welsh.

The gun went off with the bullet hitting the man cleanly in the chest. He just looked down for a split second then with eyes spread wide apart he fell forward onto his face over the top of a bleeding Welsh who was lying nursing a stomach wound. The mess in the family room had just become worse with pools of blood on the lush carpet that adorned it.

The noise from the shots would surely bring the others running as it had reverberated around the house like a stone in a metal box. Sure enough yelling at the top of his voice Jake came belting up the stairs from the garage below. As he did he was holding his gun down by his side very unprofessionally. Tom didn't hesitate taking aim and letting a round pin Jake fair between the eyes. His eyes did not react at all just stayed open but went blank. He dropped down to the floor oozing more blood but this time over the formal dining room carpet.

Tom collected both guns from the deceased then tried to help Welsh up onto a chair. As he did so Sandy came running in from the front of the house holding his gun up ready to do battle. He must have heard how many shots went off realising that there must be someone else about with a gun.

He fired off two shots as he came in on the move sending both shots to the right and above Tom's head. Unfortunately for him Tom was in no mood to miss bringing the Glock up and pumping two quick shot at the head of Sandy. His head exploded at the rear with the impact of two rounds hitting it, jolting it back but his feet were still in motion going forward which lifted his body slapping it down on its back with one almighty thud.

Knowing that all the occupants of the van were now accounted for with only one survivor Tom tore up a shirt on the victim in the lounge and rolled it up getting Welsh to hold it as tight as possible to his wound to slow blood loss. He then rang the only person he knew in Australia and that was Brian Cox at ASIO. After a brief summing up over the phone Tom hung up turning to Welsh and saying. "Seems everything will be ok we have people on their way. They are arranging an ambulance for you and a cleanup squad for the house. How long is your daughter going to be out for?"

"Till late today I think. Look pal I need to thank you, you didn't have to do what you've done."

"I did mate believe me; my bosses are fed up with the shit I keep leaving behind me. You sure you don't want to share Caulfield's whereabouts with me?"

"If I knew I would but he is I know heading to Queensland. That's all I know sorry." Tom didn't pursue it any further. He had Welsh which meant there was only one more ex British squaddie to go.

Before anyone arrived Tom made a point of checking the dead right wrists finding the usual tattoo that he witnessed so often during his travels. How did they find Welsh? Again unanswered questions. He had only spoken to Gary but he was sure Gary was OK.

Tom waited for the ambulance to arrive which was accompanied by officers from ASIO and the Federal Police. The boot man, Dan, was taken into custody, which meant he would be answering a lot of awkward questions over the coming days.

For Welsh he was sorted by the paramedics then being hushed away by ambulance to a secure hospital under guard. Tom guessed that he would be spirited away to the UK before he recovered to complete more questioning back in Old Blighty and then face the consequences of his past actions.

Before Tom left he went to the loft above the barn where Welsh had been staying taking the opportunity to have a good look around.

What he found was a small note book of times, dates, numbers with some kind of code which he pocketed. Also in the robe was a laptop which he discreetly placed under his arm as he left the room and using the keys he had for the Mercedes still in his pocket he went to the car to undo the door where he placed his find in there locking it again afterwards.

Back in the house Tom met Brian Cox who was just standing in the Family room shaking his head at the mess that was there in front of him. Tom walked slowly up to him and said "There you are Brian more home grown terrorists for you no longer a threat." And laughed aloud.

"Gary told me you had a reputation of leaving a trail of bodies wherever you went. Boy he was underestimating you I think." Brian smiled back at Tom.

"You need me any more mate as I've really got to get a move on." "Anything you want to share with us Tom."

"Not at this stage Brian, I think I will leave that to Gary if I may." "Ok Tom, stay safe eh!" Brian just laughed at the indication he made to Tom.

Cleared by the ASIO people now onsite, Tom walked out to the front of the barn where the van was removed the nails from the tyres under it, then reversing it out of the way. Getting inside the Mercedes he started it up and drove it out of the garage giving a quick wave to the men on the ground now busily searching for clues about anything of interest.

Tom realized he had left them with a bit of a bombshell to sort out but in this case he was sure they were being paid well for their efforts. Sitting in the Mercedes, this was luxury plus without any dings to it. He was sure no one would complain if he handed over his hire car while using this beauty on wheels.

Back at the cabins Tom went through the computer finding list of banks, accounts, files for various transactions and deals not yet completed. He had absolutely no idea what the codes or figures were in the note book. He knew he would have to get this somehow to Gary. He also wondered how Ashid had got hold of Welsh's location.

Tom thought about Welsh's family and how they would react to what had happened at their home while they had been away having fun for the day. They were about to lose the one man who cared for them the most in this world, Tony Welsh. They would not see him again unless they made a trip to the UK for his trial.

CHAPTER 41

Tom had had the mobile switched to silent during his incursion into the Waller property, now late on the Sunday evening he switched it back up to be greeted by a string of messages from Gary to call him urgently.

After dialling Gary's number a sombre voice answered it. Gary sounded as if he was a bit down and worried about what he had received from Brian via phone earlier. He went through what had happened at the house that day and sighed with relief that at least there were two people they would be able to question.

He congratulated Tom on saving Welsh from his own demons of so called friends and also that he had given their friends at ASIO a firm member of a gang associated with Jihad movements in Australia that they could eventually follow up with.

The next message was to tell Tom what had happened at home and in Iraq the past few days. He highlighted the bomb attack at the dinner for the Council members of the Iraq government saying that Ashid had conveniently excused himself that day but the following day had launched a major verbal attack on the country's Prime Minister and the rest of the Council of Ministers. Then how Ashid had left with the PM then giving orders for his immediate arrest.

The biggest surprise was the explosion at the Interior Ministry that had taken so many lives, then with the disappearance of Ashid and some of his closest people just after it. Originally the Government thought that Ashid had been killed in the explosion but after Sandra Crisp got answers from her people on the ground it was plain that he had had some involvement in the blast. She had reported back that her people had followed Ashid from the Government building after his verbal onslaught with the Council, gone to his office followed by many of his closest colleagues leaving the building by various cars and he went off with a man named Anan to the Directorate of Military Survey where he was when the explosion on his own office went off. Shortly after that he left with Anan in a car with two others for Mosul where he was now.

Unfortunately Crisp's people had lost him when he entered Mosul but they were certain that is where he had remained since arriving. There had been no contact by anyone of his cronies at the Borders either with Jordan or Syria. Crisp had now given orders for her people to search as far and wide as possible for Ashid or any of his immediate followers. All the information she had on Ashid was given to Gary who then filtered what was necessary to the Iraqi Government.

Gary was now in full agreement that Tom was correct all along in his assumption of Ashid that he was also linked to the money convoy when it disappeared.

Tom told Gary about the package he now had and asked that someone call to collect at some time to get it back to him in the UK while he went after the last man standing.

"I suppose Tom you want to finish this operation off yourself then?" Gary knew what the answer was going to be before he even asked the question.

"Bloody right I do Gary. Have you been able to get a location on his mobile phone position yet?"

"We did but as you know with such a vast country as Australia the signal drops in and out quicker than you might think."

"I understand that Gary but if you can give me a rough idea of direction I can possibly get close enough to be able to judge where he is going."

"Well Tom it is a certain thing that he is travelling North as his signal has been showing through Victoria and then into NSW but we have lost it since. The last location we had was a place called Dubbo about two days ago."

"He's virtually running parallel to me Gary. Look let me get near to him as much as I can without any help from the locals. The last thing I want is to warn him in any way. I don't know what sort of friendships he might have with local police and you know being one himself he would have geared up many associations over the years he has been around. If I need further help I will ask you to get it but till then just give me the coordinates of his location over the coming two to three days. I should be close to him by then."

"If it isn't too much to ask, Tom is there any chance that we might get him back in one piece?"

"I won't promise anything Gary but I will try, that I promise." Tom sat with the phone still to his ear for a couple of seconds then continued. "Oh Gary." He said

"Yes Tom."

"Gary thanks for all your help eh. It is much appreciated."

"No problems my friend, a pleasure and Tom keep safe we want you back in one piece as well. You have a permanent job here if you want it."

Tom never answered Gary's statement just turned off the phone retrieving his map to see where the town of Dubbo was as far as highways went with the best and fastest way to get there.

CHAPTER 42

Monday 16 April

At the crack of dawn Tom was out and raring to go. He could see the light at the end of the tunnel at long last. He had closed off his stop at the cabins the night before so he could leave as early as he wished this morning. Time was just after 0530 hrs with the sun not quite awake yet. To drive at this time risked the possible collision with one of many of the local inhabitants. Oversize rabbits they called kangaroos on this continent. To hit one of those caused more damage than you could cope with. Another problem animal was the large flightless bird they had in these parts, the emu. Both were an absolute pain in the arse while driving in twilight conditions.

Tom pulled into a service centre where he could top up on his usual coffee and food to keep him going for the day ahead. Sugar fix was also a mainstay for Tom so he bought packets of sweet lollies and peppermints to refresh on while tackling the long haul to Dubbo.

Tom was all but into his drive by an hour and a half when the mobile kicked in beside him on the passenger seat. Holding it to his ear while driving, not the best thing to do on the country or any roads come to that, he answered it being greeted by Gary who was eating his dinner 12000 miles away in London.

"Tom, hope I have caught you early enough, I have someone who can pick up Welsh's gear from you today OK?" Gary was garbling some of his words as he was chewing at something on the other end of the call.

"Great, where and when?" Tom was just overtaking a large truck while holding and talking on the mobile at the same time.

"Just north of Sydney, a place called Mount Kuring-Gai. I know it is in the opposite direction for Caulfield but he is going north anyway and the roads on the coast would be faster for you to cut him off before the Queensland border." Gary started to sound somewhat apologetic as if he had realized Tom was already on the road going the other way.

"Shit." Tom blurted out as he indicated to pull over onto the hard shoulder of the road he was speeding along. "I started off this morning Gary; I'm about half way between Orange and Bathurst about a hundred and fifty kilometres from where I was in the Blue bloody mountains."

"Sorry Pal but I couldn't be sure about the pick up till about fifteen minutes ago. I had someone fly out Sunday to be able to give you some back up. He arrived early this morning your time."

"He?" Tom asked the question.

"Yes, he, Gerry from Sofia was free and I thought what better than for someone you knew. I know what you are like with the trust factor Tom."

"Ok Gary stop rubbing it in eh. What time is he expecting me?"
"Doesn't matter as he will be running to your time schedule. He has your mobile number which I told him to call at 0800 your time."

That gave Tom about half hour as he manoeuvred the Mercedes around in a 'U' turn heading back the way he had come. Traffic was starting to build now but Tom wasn't going to let that stop him from his final hurdle. He was speeding between 100 and 130 kph as he still hung onto the mobile waiting for some good news from Gary, if there was going to be any.

"The other thing Tom is that Caulfield's phone hadn't moved the past few days from Dubbo till yesterday afternoon your time when it started to show he was heading further North. Just one thing bothers me though Tom, it seemed rather strange that he started to move shortly after we found out about Welsh in Blackheath. Don't know if its coincidental or what but, Tom, take care, keep watch behind and just keep your intentions to me and me alone."

"Will do Gary, I'll get to Gerry give him the stuff but I don't want any help at this stage."

"He's there if you want him, just keep it in mind. And Tom he is a trusted colleague of mine, I will vouch for it."

Tom thanked Gary for his efforts but cursed the shit out of him once he had closed off the call. Three hours wasted in his mind and Caulfield could do just about anything without him being able to get anywhere near close. The Mercedes was moving well as he overtook many a surprised driver to re-enter Bathurst, this time not taking any diversions off the track to get through the town.

Gerry rang just as he exited Bathurst to confirm he was on his way to the meeting point. There was no definite meet point as yet but after the Hi's and greets Tom said he would call Gerry once he got near to the spot and arrange a definite.

The traffic was starting to build heavily now, with people trying to fumble their way to their work places, as he rushed through the towns on the Blue Mountains road. He got back to Blackheath but time was getting the better of him and he was starting to get frustrated with the slow moving cars that had now got huddled around him. He had got back to his original start point but it had taken a fair while extra to do it.

The main rush to work was on now as he tackled the highway that led down towards Sydney. Even though this part of the State had a good network of freeways he was unsure of them as the names were just as foreign to him as anywhere else in the world where he hadn't been before. After a couple of near disasters of taking the wrong way on a couple of the Toll roads Tom finally got to the Northern side of Sydney heading out on the F3 Freeway towards Newcastle.

Tom was making sure he could account for any vehicle that stuck close to him for any amount of time. What if someone was following him? Perhaps he should have left the Mercedes behind, perhaps someone had a fix on this particular car being it was Welsh's. He would deal with it as soon as he could but till then the urgency was dropping off the gear for Gary then getting on his way after Caulfield.

Time was creeping on and it wasn't till around lunchtime that he took the turnoff to Mt Kuring-Gai. Sticking now to the speed limits through this area because of the increased presence of police patrols he finally got to the centre of Kuring-Gai where he pulled over and called Gerry.

Not too much was needed as Gerry had found a quiet place which was not too quiet in the Industrial area just after the town centre. He gave Tom the directions which were simple enough. As you went further along the old pacific Highway you reached what looked like a slice of the road that had been cut into the hard rock as the sides were there either side of it. At the Traffic lights just past this point was a turn to the left called Beaumont Road which Tom was told to follow and then on the right just a few hundred yards or so was a turn to the right called Hamley which was a dead end street where Gerry said he was waiting at the end in a white Ford sedan.

Although Tom trusted Gerry to some extent after he had helped him to get out of Sofia he felt that he was being pulled into a tight corner.

He could see as he drove that there were many businesses along these roads and they were busy. Plenty of eyes around which was fair enough. He was constantly looking around to check on cars following or just stationary with eyes that followed him as he went past. There was nothing he could see so he continued on into Hamley and slowly down the road where he could see a white sedan parked facing him.

As he drove closer the Ford's lights flashed and the driver got out of the car. Tom was close enough to see the figure breathing a sigh of relief as he fixed his eyes on the man from Sofia. Not stopping in front of the Ford Tom chose to circle around and come up alongside so they were both facing towards the exit from the road. He stopped the car but left it running as he got out shaking Gerry's hand.

"Great to see you again Tom. Gary told me the hassles you have been having."

"Great to see you again Gerry. Didn't leave you holding the can when I left I hope?"

"Nothing I can't handle. Now what have you got for us." Both men walked to the back of the Mercedes where Tom opened the boot to reveal the laptop and notebook plus some other papers he had chosen to take that might be of help. Handing them over to Gerry who immediately took them to the boot of the Ford which he opened placing the loot into it.

Just then Tom peered up the street to see two black cars that had just pulled into Hamley and had parked one on each side of the road. He looked at Gerry and back to the cars. No one had got out of them but he could see that there was at least two in each in the front seats.

Tom nudged Gerry and bent his head down so they could not be seen behind the Ford boot lid. He removed the Gun that he had retained from his last exploit at Blackheath. Gerry looked at him with slight shock and his eyes stared at the gun now firmly in his hand and readied for action.

"Two cars have just pulled in. Perhaps I am being paranoid but it looks a bit sus to me Gerry. Are you armed?"

"Haven't had time to I'm afraid. Thought you were going to turn on me then. Gave me the fright of my life."

They both stayed put just peering separately at the road ahead. Tom shook his head as he asked Gerry if he had told anyone else of the meet.

"No one Tom. That was made clear to me by Gary. Only Gary, you and I know about this."

Both boot lids were closed down as Gerry moved to get behind the wheel of his car again. "You want me to drive out first Tom?"

"No mate, I'll go but stick close to me. If there is anything going to happen I will deal with it using this car. I was only thinking that someone might have a tag on this one. It was after all Welsh's car."

Gerry smiled as Tom with the gun tucked under his T shirt walked back around the Mercedes to the driver's seat and clicked on the seat belt. He started to move forward but as he did so the cars ahead moved out to block the road. Here we go again thought Tom as he eyed both drivers and passengers ahead of him.

Gerry held back just a touch so as to be able to drive around any obstacle if he needed to. Tom moved forward some more then stopped as the two cars in front turned into each other totally blocking the way out. Either side there was pedestrian walkways but not enough to accommodate a car the size of the two he and Gerry had.

Tom dialled the mobile and started to speak to Gerry. "I will try and push them out of the way, just hold back a bit to give yourself a chance to get through. Can't see if they are armed as yet but at a guess I'd say they are." Gerry acknowledged Tom and waited as Tom revved the engine of the Mercedes then slammed it into Drive spinning the wheels creating smoke that stunk to high heaven. The Mercedes lurched forward gaining momentum as it went till by the time it had reached the two cars blocking its way it was up to seventy kph. Tom steered the car to the point between the fronts on the two cars bracing himself for the impact.

As he got within five metres of the cars panic must have set in to the drivers as one on them tried desperately to reverse out the way of the big limousine that was barrelling towards them. One of the passengers jumped out of the car on Tom's left producing a handgun which he then spun around pointing it towards Tom in the car over the top of his own.

Tom hit the two front ends of the cars virtually lifting both shunting them back up the road and out the way. His bonnet folded up very ugly from the front and noises began almost instantly as if metal was contacting with metal in the engine bay.

The one who had tried to reverse out of the way actually spun around with the impact and slammed against the kerb side from whence he was parked moments earlier. Tom could see both the heads in the front seats move violently from side to side as impact from him then the kerb jolted them in different ways.

The other car moved violently off to Tom's left but not as far as the other one had. Unfortunately for the passenger that had got out, for him the game he had played proved fatal as before he could even get his sights fixed on Tom the car had moved so hard against him it threw him to the floor then slid over the top of him trapping him below it producing screams of pain from the culprit.

Tom looked in his rear view mirror to see if there was enough room for Gerry. He saw him coming forward aiming for the gap that had been created for him. The driver and passenger in the other car had started to get out both holding firearms firmly in their hands. Tom slammed his handbrake on while still in motion causing the car to start to spin off to the right. He didn't quite manage a full 180 but with the revs over the limit he spun the wheels completing the movement. This brought him about facing back the way he had come. One of the men was taking aim at the Ford while the other was turning towards Tom.

Without thinking about it Tom just kept the throttle high and again smacked into the car he had spun out of the way. As he did so he gave no time for the man pointing the gun at him to jump clear pinning him between both cars causing his broken body to flop over the jagged Mercedes bonnet that was now even worse than the first hit. His gun went from his hand as his body flopped and buckled under the impact. He would give no further problems to the two in this fracas.

Two shots rang out as the man on the other side of the car took aim at Gerry but with the jolt that Tom had made it put him out of his aim and the shots went through the passenger side of the windscreen. Tom leapt out of the now crippled Mercedes to see the other driver also now out of his car with yet another gun in play. He brought up his weapon letting off a shot at the one aiming at Gerry. It caught the man in the shoulder and he spun around falling to the ground in pain. The man on the other side of the road let off a couple of shots which hit his partner's car as Tom was now crouched down behind its shattered wing.

While the shot rang out Gerry had ducted down but kept the wheels in motion. By the time Tom had dropped one of the men Gerry was through the blockade and moving fast up the road where after a hundred yards he pulled off to the left and opened his door so he could at least peer down at the mayhem in the hope that Tom would find his way out.

Tom waited, saw what Gerry was doing then tried to move out from the tangled mess he had created. As he tried to there were more shots fired. None made contact thank goodness. Tom was able to roll and move away from the front of the cars and managed to get down behind the Mercedes boot. Two more shots rang out hitting the back right wing of the Mercedes.

It was turning into a standoff as the two weren't willing to lift their profiles up for the other to take a good aim at. Tom finally made his mind up and started to move back away from his car towards the side of the pedestrian walk where there was a low fence leading into the business alongside.

The furore that had erupted had brought a few prying eyes out of some of the buildings lining Hamley Street but when more shots rang out they soon disappeared accompanied by shouts and screams all round.

Tom leapt over the fence and ran towards the gate where he would be able to be in line with Gerry. As he reached it he saw his opposite number running along the opposite side pedestrian walk towards Gerry. Tom lifted his gun and took aim letting go two shots in succession. He made contact with both and the man hit the deck staining the dusty surface with red that was pouring from his torso.

Tom raced over to Gerry who had seen him coming driving the car to parallel with the kerb. Still moving along the kerb Tom opened the passenger door and jumped into the seat which Gerry took as his signal to get the hell out of there. They drove hard out of the Industrial area and back out onto the freeway heading north.

Tom immediately they were on the freeway got hold of Gary who answered very sleepily. Giving details of what had gone down Tom wondered again how the hell someone knew where he was. He questioned Gary who much to his anger at the implication of deceit tried feverishly to calm Tom's anger down. By the time Tom had calmed himself he was almost saying how stupid he was to have taken Welsh's car with the possibility that someone had it tagged.

By that night they had reached Newcastle where they holed up for the night. Before close of play that day though they had hired two more cars so they could continue their journeys separately hopefully unknown to anyone. Tom made sure that he would be notified when the stuff he had given to Gerry reached Gary in London.

On the TV news that night was a mention of some kind of a gangland shooting in Mount Kuring-Gai without any pictures of the incident. There was absolutely no mention of any suspicious vehicles which had left the scene or even being there. The government whichever it might be was surely trying their hardest to keep a cover on the scenario which Tom had found himself deeply involved in.

CHAPTER 43

Tuesday 17 April.

This morning bright and early saw the two colleagues shake hands then depart in different directions. Gerry headed south towards the Capital Canberra where the British High Commission was situated. He was to deliver the package that Tom had given him to the Commission.

Gerry's journey was to take him the majority of the day but on arrival he received a further message from Gary asking that he head back to Tom's location to give him any help he may need. Gerry was able to get himself refreshed for the trip back but was still extremely tired by the trip he had made from Sydney to Canberra after his flight out from Europe.

For Tom he was to continue north in the direction of Caulfield who was still being monitored by UK satellite resources. He finally made his way to the turn off to the Hunter valley where he headed inland on the New England Highway hoping he would be able to intercept Caulfield soon ending this torment of a task.

Pulling into Rutherford Tom made his way to the BCF store there where he was able to rekit himself to the conditions he was now seeing. Rain and cold were the order of the day in NSW and Tom's gear was more summer attire than autumn/winter.

Gore Tex materials were the required attire needed in jacket, gloves and boots. Just as he was leaving the store he received a call from Gary telling him Caulfield's signal had become stationary in a place called Dunadoo, a small town about three hundred kilometres west of Tom's present position. Tom located the small township on his map estimating he was about three and a half hours away.

Returning to his car he checked the Glock magazine counting five rounds left in the clip. He was sure he had enough back up to deal with the last of his demons.

The drive from Rutherford took him into the Hunter valley proper and off inland further when he reached Branxton onto the Golden Highway. Past what must have been the biggest open cut mines he had ever seen before in his short life. He arrived in Denman where he eventually stopped to get some food and drink.

His mobile chimed in again as he was about to leave. Gary on the other end had more news for him. The signal they had was beginning to fade at times in and out of reception. He was concerned they might lose it before nightfall and thought he had better update sooner rather than later.

Tom found the message interesting as it indicated that Caulfield had left the highway he was on and was heading towards Tamworth. The signal had failed at times due to the large area of National Park which he was travelling across. Communications in these areas constantly dropped out because of the distance between towers and the lack of said towers.

Tom again checked his map and found fortunately he would be able to take a turn that would lead him back up to Muswellbrook and back onto the New England. He estimated he could beat Caulfield into Tamworth if he tried hard enough as the roads he was about to travel were much better for speed than the ones through the National Park area that Caulfield was taking.

By nightfall Tom had reached a small place called Willow Tree where he crashed for the night. Messages between him and Gary were frequent and indicated that the signal from Caulfield was getting more pronounced as he made his way into the more populated areas. By the middle of the night it was estimated that Caulfield had got through to Tamworth where the signal now sat stationary again. They could only assume that he was resting his weary head as well.

Next morning Tom was ready to take the final step to confront Caulfield. He was about to leave when Gary messaged him that Caulfield's signal had returned west to a place called Quirindi, they were still tracking.

This for Tom was great news as he was only a matter of fifteen minutes from Quirindi. With excitement growing in his belly he waited patiently for news that would then give him the opportunity to set out for the town of Quirindi positive that today,18 April, was going to be the day of resolution for him and those that had died at the hands of Caulfield and his cronies.

CHAPTER 44

April 18 Quirindi

As he sat thinking about what has gone before and what might suddenly arrive at his doorstep Caulfield had what he thought was the upper hand in this whole affair. The young soldier he had used and set up to take the can back in Iraq to offset the investigation in the hope it would have taken the highlight off him and his mates was like a little English bulldog. He had a grip of something and just wouldn't let it go no matter what happened.

Caulfield fortunately had help now from an old associate policeman he had known for many years. He definitely had the upper hand in this one for sure in his mind's eye. He had found out that the Brits had been tracking him since he left Victoria through his contact and they had been passing that information to the little shit now fixated on his tail.

It was now time to end this pursuit for ever but to do it he would need to bury the bull dog, Tom Warburton for good.

What was his plan going to be? That was easy as he had found about 200 acres of steep rocky paths and dense forest area which led into what the locals in this region called Hidden Valley. A place that was rarely visited even remained remote to the locals. Here he would lure Tom and deal the final blow to his escapades. He would never be found in this place not in a million years in this remote little area. His police colleague now in the State was going to assist him for a price of course which he had no problems with. The man had been tracking Tom for Caulfield since he had last seen him in the Blue Mountains when he had tracked down his cousin Tony.

Caulfield had tried to end it all in Kuring-Gai with the help from a few bikie friends he had been given by contacts overseas but that had ended up a complete cock up to say the least. To lure him here was going to be difficult as well but at the same time he had an ace card up his sleeve in the help being given him by the ASIO officer he had paid off. They would be flying in a chopper with three men to be able to close Warburton off completely once inside this remote area. This would be the final fling leaving Caulfield to be able to disappear into Queensland where he really wanted to be.

His companion on his trip at the moment was a thirty year old bar maid he had picked up in Melbourne months back, she had been his constant companion for the trip not asking any questions and just enjoying the lifestyle he had laid upon her. All she had to do was keep him happy which was for her as easy as being twenty years his younger she had the time of her life during many nights of orgy like sessions with this man who always managed to give her the ultimate prize of sexual accomplishment. This man was one hell of a stud in her eyes.

Being in Quirindi the two were equipping themselves for a short camping expedition into the bush. She asked no questions, Caulfield gave no explanation just made sure she was always truly satisfied. He didn't care how long this partnership went for because when he became fed up with it he would just dump her as he had so many times before and replace her with another model who wanted what he wanted.

They stocked up at the Supa IGA in town and with the boot of his BMW full of camping gear they headed off towards the Quipolly dam some 12 kilometres north from town. Here he would take a right heading up the rough dusty track towards an old farm now abandoned but up for sale.

He had purchased a pre paid mobile while in Tamworth which he had loaded all the numbers he needed into it before disposing of the mobile he had always carried. He dumped that in the bin at the side of the Shell garage just before the turn off to Quipolly still switched on to confuse those that were tracking him. He was just hopeful that it would lead Tom to him quickly.

Before the night set in Caulfield was determined to be in the area of the Hidden valley but he knew that was going to be difficult as they had to hike from the old farmhouse up into the rocky expanse behind where the tracks were not the best especially in the dark.

After talking to some of the locals he was assured that the trail to Hidden Valley would take nearly a whole day to accomplish without having to set up camp as well. Not being familiar with the area, although carrying a good map similar to an Ordnance Survey he made the decision to heed their advice of timeframe so decided to sleep over in the farmhouse then tracking up to Hidden Valley the next morning. His companion was excited at the prospect of being alone with her stud for another night. They were settled in the farmhouse by mid day having hidden the car inside an old shed that lay to the rear of the house.

The weather was also starting to close in with rain forecast for the area over the coming few days. The nights were cold but for Caulfield he had body warmth from his companion, he wasn't fazed at all.

In his head he just had visions of being able to culminate the ventures of Warburton for good. This was going to be his final fling before he would be able to at last disappear from the world to enjoy life without worry.

CHAPTER 45

Quirindi 18 April

Tom sat waiting for about three hours before he received a message from Gary. Caulfield's signal had gone off for a while then back on but it was definitely located in Quirindi. That was all Tom needed for him to jump into the car setting off for the town with its 2500 residents. Surely Caulfield couldn't hide amongst so few.

Pulling into the town by mid day he was surprised at the layout of this small town. It was spread quite sparingly over quite a distance. Mainly an agricultural hub the town centre of just one main street that ran from south to north with the residential areas being spread around. The street was lined with trader shops of all descriptions.

Tom went up and down the main street a couple of times after which he ventured through the side streets of the place trying to pinpoint Caulfield's BMW which he knew from his feeds in Australia he would still be driving. Perhaps he had changed his car as well just recently but that was not what he was led to believe. Tom was persistent having travelled every road and track within a couple of kilometres of the centre. He found absolutely nothing.

A desperate call was made to Gary in the hope he could really pinpoint the signal from Caulfield's phone. Gary apologised with just an assurance that the signal was still within the town area. He would get GCHQ to try to zero in on it somehow but that would take time.

Tom needed to relax for what he was expecting ahead of him so decided to book into the Terminus Hotel just opposite the railway Station. Waiting is always the nervous time of any operation, it was time to think, time to worry. He just had to be patient. He could always think of a Plan

B as they always did in the Army, something he was not too good at doing lately.

He had no idea that following him was his old pal Gerry who under orders from Vauxhall Cross was to keep a low profile but be there in case he was needed. Gerry was to be available but needed to stay at a distance because of the implications that it would lead to if he became involved in any untoward actions which might cause problems between the British and Australian Governments. Allies or not being on station without the knowledge of the host country could always cause some niggly hiccup.

By the time Tom had settled himself into his room, Gerry had travelled up to Willow Tree which put him only fifteen minutes from Tom if he was needed.

19 April

It was the early hours of the morning that Tom finally got a call from Gary which gave him a reference point for Caulfield's signal. Tom didn't try to understand how they managed to get such a precise location technology was advancing so rapidly it was leaving most people way behind anyway.

At three o'clock in the morning it looked quite suspicious for someone to start walking the streets of this quaint little town but that is what Tom did. He was even more determined to find the fix of this signal.

By the time he was near the Shell garage he knew he was getting close. He circled across the road to be able to see but not be seen. From the school side of the road he watched the Shell garage with keenness and some internal excitement. There were no lights on at all and the forecourt was empty. There was one car down the side but with the mist on the windows it didn't look as if anybody was in it. Tom carefully crossed the street to the garage side. Rain had started to fall and the temperature was down low. The rain droplets stung Tom's face as he closed in on the vehicle in the garage.

Slowly he crept up on it till he could make out the inside. He peered into the windows but there was nothing inside just a mess of empty coke bottles and food wrappers.

Damn he thought to himself. He checked again the co-ordinates of his message from Gary. He was within ten meters of the damn signal. He moved in a circular motion giving him the ten meters he was estimating.

One side took him to the start of the forecourt which was totally empty. The other side was to a fence which separated the Shell forecourt with an engineering company next door. There was nothing near that company's side of the fence.

The only possibility would be inside the shop area but with no lights on it seemed strange that Caulfield would be in there at all. To his left Tom noticed the bin, a large metal wheelie bin about two metres square. He shook his head not really wanting to venture in there. But worst comes to the worst he thought, as he lifted the lid and with the torch he had in his pocket looked inside.

He couldn't see much for the muck and papers that were strewn inside. Suddenly an idea hit him which might help him not having to delve through the rubbish. He messaged Gary to ring the mobile they were tracking. If anything by Gary ringing it Caulfield wouldn't have any idea he was near at hand as it would show an overseas number on the screen.

Patiently he waited, then, all of a sudden he heard the faint ringing of a mobile tune. It was a sound that he recognised as the Pink Panther theme. It was coming from inside the bin. He reluctantly lifted the lid again greeted by a volume increase. To the side of the bin was a crate which he pulled over to enable him to climb into the bin. This was what he really did not want to have to do he thought as he dropped down onto the waste material inside. The tune was still going when he finally lifted a load of old newspapers to find the glow of the mobile playing the Pink Panther theme.

He grabbed the phone immediately removing himself from the mess and stench inside the bin. He felt at that moment that someone was having a lend of him especially with the tune the damn phone had been playing. He immediately messaged Gary with the information of what he had found which was greeted with disappointment; they had been out foxed by Caulfield.

Tom went through the mobile but everything in its memory had been erased. No contacts, no recent calls, no text messages. Tom was devastated with the find. He felt all was lost as he made his way back to the hotel room to again ponder what to do. The weather was deteriorating with the rain falling fairly heavily now.

As the morning sun rose trying its hardest to brighten the day it was as Tom felt dismal and depressed. He had lost track of the man he desperately wanted to get to. Now he would have to try another approach. He spoke to Gary as soon as he could during the morning going over options as to try to find the man. He wanted to find him, he needed to find him and it would have to be done now with possibly help from the local authorities which they all wanted to avoid if they could. Gary was sceptical about asking anyone in Australia for help knowing he would be pulled back a few pegs if he attempted to get help from above to try.

Tom asked if they could just try to locate the car, possibly a registration check, traffic cams on the highway, anything, he was desperate. They had the details of it perhaps they could try and find it under the guise of someone in Europe wanting to get in touch with the owner, Scholfield. Gary humoured Tom saying he would see what he could do but while he waited to just sit tight where he was and not do anything drastic.

During the course of this day his anger grew as he felt he had failed in his attempt to bring Caulfield to justice. He tried hard to think of ways around the diplomacy angle but each time he thought of something there was that scary diplomatic angle looming up on him. Exhausted he collapsed on his bed mid afternoon falling into a deep sleep.

While Tom was desperately trying to find different ways to find Caulfield, only 15 kilometres away Caulfield himself was trekking through the undergrowth towards his destination of the Hidden Valley. By nightfall he had reached the point of the Valley he was looking for finding the perfect position under some thick bushes where he and his companion could pitch their tent and would be hidden from view in any direction.

Making camp was a breeze for them even in the wet and mud as they had had to contend with it for the whole day so far. They had enough supplies of clean and dry gear to get by and the night ahead was to be a memorable one for Caulfield as he became the rampant stallion he had always thought himself as. He knew that he would get plenty of warning of the presence of Warburton from his colleague anyway.

CHAPTER 46

Friday 20 April.

At 0600 Tom was awoken by his mobile ringing. Looking at the screen it didn't display anyone he knew but just indicated blocked number. He was still dressed in the gear he had been wearing the afternoon before when he collapsed on to his bed exhausted. He fumbled the mobile before he eventually got the green button pressed.

"Hello?" he quizzically spoke into the mouthpiece.

"Believe you have been looking for a friend of mine Mr Warburton." Came a distinct tone that Tom recognised as an Australian accent and one that was familiar to him from a while ago but he could not quite pin point it.

"Who is it?" Tom asked.

"Oh come on surely you're not that stupid. You've been travelling the globe taking out people to get to a certain Mr Caulfield I believe for reasons only you can justify. I think it is time we got the two of you together to sort this out once and for all don't you agree?"

"This isn't Caulfield so who and what is your interest in all of this?" Tom asked trying to figure out the face behind the voice.

"It doesn't matter who I am but my friend Peter is desperate to get together with you to sort out what has been bugging you so much."

"OK when and where?" Tom was keen to get to the point.

"I will text you some co-ordinates which I'm sure you will be able to follow seeing as you are military trained. I suggest you go to a camping shop or the like to get yourself a good enough map of the area around the Quipolly dam. My friend is keen to sort this all out Tommy boy as soon as possible."

"When then?"

"By the time you get organized perhaps tomorrow will be OK for both of you."

"Ok send the co-ordinates and I will get out to wherever tomorrow." Tom was keen to get the location but was not willing to wait for another day to be able to get to Caulfield.

The phone went dead as Tom stared at it in his hand. Come on, come on. That was all that went through his head as he waited for the text message to come in. It was all of ten minutes before the text noise sounded and again the blocked number print appeared with the text following immediately. Tom quickly wrote the co-ordinates down and rang Gary.

"You say a private blocked number rang you Tom?" Gary was overly suspicious at the call.

"Yes Gary. What I don't understand is how the hell they got my number. Remember I told you it was to be given to no one you can't fully trust well it seems that Caulfield has a friend here somewhere and he is the one passing on messages between him and me. It's got to be someone close to our investigation Gary; I don't care what you think. Who would know my mobile number?"

"Tom believe me I have given it to no one except Gerry. The voice you heard is it someone you recognise?"

"It does seem familiar. An Aussie accent. Let me th . . ." Tom stopped dead in the middle of his conversation. "I do recognise the bloody voice, its Brian's. That guy you said was a close associate of yours, someone you could trust. What the fucks going on Gary?"

"Tom I don't understand. If its Brian's then what the hell is he doing helping Caulfield anyway?"

"He must be closer than you think Gary. Did you give him my number from this mobile?"

"Only in case of an emergency, that's all. Tom please don't do anything drastic, I'll get Gerry to get to you so you can fathom this out together."

"Gary I told you trust is the thing I don't care much about. Every time I have trusted someone they have stabbed me in the back. I don't want help now, I can do this myself. Sorry Gary but trust is the one thing that I just can't get to accept of anybody, especially now this has happened"

"Tom please let me help you." Gary never got to finish the conversation as the mobile was shut down and within the next ten minutes it was reported to be dead with the signal lost. Gary shook his head hoping that he could still give some assistance to Tom; he frantically called Gerry to get him in motion to head to Quirindi.

He called Sandra Crisp at her apartment giving her the details he had to date asking that she immediately try to set up a satellite cover over the area surrounding the co-ordinates that he had got from Tom. It was a matter of urgency he felt Tom's life was now in danger.

Gary had been a field agent once knowing that going into an area alone with the odds stacked against you normally ended up with you on the Mortician's slab. He did not want that to happen to Tom, not now.

CHAPTER 47

Tom never waited around for anything else. He made his way to the local shops trying in vain to get a map of the area he had the coordinates for. No one had anything he could use in town other than just a suggestion to try the Council Offices which was located just along the road heading towards Tamworth. That was a welcomed suggestion from the newsagent.

Tom immediately ran the length of the road to the Council offices where he found a young girl at reception who was keen to assist him as he had told her he was looking at buying in the area. She had come up with a map which she said actually showed the area he was looking at. She also told him she knew that particular farm was also on the market she believed if he wanted to go to the agents by the side of the pub where he was staying.

Tom thanked her for her help and with a copy of the map went back to his room to pack the gear he needed into a backpack he had purchased. He then loaded his car for what would be his insurgence into the bush area by the Quipolly Dam.

Before finally starting off he made his way to the hardware shop where he purchased a large knife similar in shape and design to a K Bar. With this, a small pair of binoculars and a compass he got into the car heading off towards Quipolly Dam, a drive on a narrow bitumen road of around 12 kilometres. He was unaware of Gerry being within eyeshot of him as he drove because all he could think about was finally confronting Caulfield. Gerry did hold back till he was sure that Tom would not be able to pin him down as a watcher.

The rain had eased some but the sky was starting to look really threatening above them as they both separately headed to the dam. Tom just hoped he would have the element of surprise now as he thought that Caulfield would not be expecting him anywhere near till the following day.

The roads speed limit was 100 kph and Tom used it plus some to get to the Dam area. Within minutes he was at the turn off which would lead him up into the bush area then finally on to the place on the map he had fixed with the coordinates, Hidden valley.

Cautiously Tom entered the old farm's land through a rickety gate that had seen better days. The drive was dirt and stone but with the rain that had preceded today it was worse for wear making it at some points difficult to get traction on the rear wheel drive vehicle Tom was using. The ruts either side of the track were also a problem trying to ride the high spots so he didn't tear out the underside or the sump.

Finally he came up to the farmhouse where he saw for himself the abandonment that was evidence of non habitation. Grass was knee high, growing ever stronger by the day being encouraged by the present rainfall. He motored around to the far side of the house where he saw a steel double garaged shed sitting with both roller doors closed. Slipping and sliding even more he finally pulled up at the front of the garage where he disembarked his vehicle preparing himself with gun, knife and backpack before trying the roller doors. The first he tried opened with ease and when he was able to peer inside he saw Caulfield's BMW sitting there, muddy and with all windows closed.

Tom now focused away from the garage towards the house which he now felt he should really check first. Dropping his backpack in the garage doorway out of the rain he slowly made his way to the rear sliding door of the house. Trying it luckily again he found he was fortunate as it was unlocked. Pulling the Glock from his jacket he slowly opened the sliding glass door trying to see inside.

When finally inside the room that he had accessed he found what looked like a lounge area with a wood burner in it. It was slightly warm but when he opened the door he found just ash inside. He knew that there had been someone here in the past couple of days. Turning away from the fire he saw to his left an arch which led to the front door and to his right an arch which led to the kitchen. The right was his choice as it was more open. Entering the kitchen he found leftover food on the side which didn't look too old. At least there was no green mould growing on it yet.

If someone was hanging out here then you would expect them to keep the place clean at least to prevent any possible food contamination like E coli.

As he went further passing the front door to his left and another door that led out to the grass behind the house he saw there were a number of doors down along the passageway. The first opened to a bare room. The second at the end to the left was also a bare room. The third opposite was also bare and the one to the right of it, the last of what were the bedrooms, had smells of deodorant still recognizable. There was also that smell you get when two lovers have been at it for a while. It takes a while for that smell to disappear.

Satisfied that the house hadn't been used for a day or so Tom went back to the garage where he checked out the BMW. It was unlocked but he could not locate the keys anywhere.

Lifting the bonnet of the car Tom was determined he was going to make it bloody difficult for anyone to use it before he got back; he removed the control cable to the injector system placing it in his backpack for safe keeping.

It had been a while since he had done any serious hunting in forests or bushland so he would have to search his memory for all the tricks the old man had taught him as well as his own Army training. Coming back through his mind was that old statement one of the other recruits had been reminded of 'Soldier first, tradesman second'

Closing the roller door behind him Tom made his way to the track that was still visible to the left hand side of the house past some rather large trees which looked rather sickly, bent and buggered. Here he found what was the path used by someone earlier as he could make out two sets of footprints, one size nine like his and another rather smaller, possibly female by the size, width and length.

Looking back to where he had come from he saw the landscape laid out in front of him with the dam centre stage of the view. This place would surely be one of the most beautiful places to set up home he thought. These were million dollar views here.

If anyone was watching he would be out in the open trekking up the hill on this track so he decided to go further left where what looked like an old fence line was running parallel to the track under the cover of the trees. He made his way slowly to the top of the first hill stopping every few meters to listen for any unusual sounds.

What Tom didn't know was that Gerry was observing him from the bitumen road just before the dam through powerful binoculars that he had. He was going to watch his back as much as possible. He had a lot of respect for this young lad, the determination he had, the persistence to get the job done, he was family.

At the top of the first rise Tom followed around to the left going down and then up again through a gully. The rain had started to fall again but this time harder than he had seen before. Hood up he made his way to what looked like a small dam off to the right. The water was starting to flow over the edge running down the small valley here towards the house below but off to its left.

Opposite the small Dam was a boulder about three meters high and two meters square. It looked like it had a flat top to it. Tom went around the boulder where he found a large bush which gave him some shelter, after placing a poncho he had in his backpack over it, from the teeming rain now cascading down onto him. He decided to hold here for a while in the hope that the rain would ease a bit. The ground around was becoming very slippery as it turned to mud. There was no use pushing too hard as he would lose the advantage by trying to go on in the mud sodden ground.

The time was starting to creep on with Tom thinking he might just start to lose the advantage he thought he had. The rain started to ease to a drizzle again which gave Tom the opportunity to continue but just as he came out of the bushes he heard what seemed like a low flying helicopter. The sound was definite as he was used to the noise they made when he was in Iraq surrounded by them coming in and going out all day and night.

He retreated back into the bush holding his head to one side trying to pin point the direction the chopper was coming from. He finally heard it to his left coming up over the rise which was pretty steep. It came into view about hundred meters to his rear where it hovered a while. Tom suspected it was trying to find a landing spot as it turned, moved slowly in one direction then turned again moving slowly back. It was an Australian Blackhawk he recognised but there were no markings on the sides which was strange.

As it moved further away from his hiding spot he saw the side doors open and then saw what looked like ropes being thrown out either side. It was now about two hundred and fifty meters away when Tom saw the first of three black clad figures abseiling down the ropes. Once all three were on the ground the ropes were pulled back on board and the chopper banked away to its right disappearing back over the rise. The noise of the Blackhawk soon disappeared out of earshot as Tom decided to climb the large boulder to get a better view of the guys that had just arrived. He packed up the poncho and threw the backpack up onto the boulder.

Once on top of the boulder he produced the small binoculars to scan the area where he had seen the men drop. Sure enough there they were making their way towards the garage where he had left his car. On reaching it he viewed one of the figures lift what looked like a silenced MP3 pumping a round in each of the tyres.

Well yet again Tom thought to himself another hirer is going to be decided pissed off with him on the way he looked after their cars. Tom couldn't even think who these black clad figures could be. All three were wearing black gear with full face balaclavas but what was obvious they were not any friends of his. Could they be Ashid's men again? This was becoming a bit of a farce as he didn't know if they were after Caulfield as well or were they just turning the hunter into the hunted as was his case.

Tom stayed put, silent as he saw the three dark figures start to make their way up the track in full view of anyone who wanted to see. They didn't seem to be bothered about being seen at all but then again they were armed with some serious fire power. All Tom had was a Glock with five rounds left in it and a knife.

Within five minutes the three figures had made their way to the boulder and were standing just below where Tom was lying on the top. He could hear their voices quite clearly as they came to a stop close by the boulder. The rain had slowed right down now drizzling then stopping, then drizzling again, a persistent drenching over time Tom thought.

Voices started to become clearer so Tom strained his ears to get as much of what was said as he could.

"Troy you stay here to keep an eye on the track anyone in and out." Tom recognised the voice speaking, it was Brian Cox. But why would he have destroyed the tyres on the car? This was beginning to confirm he was in cahoots with Caulfield meaning he had known most of Tom's movements and was passing them on.

"Roger that." Came the reply from the one designated as Troy.

"Steve and I will go up to where our friend is and check if Warburton is anywhere on the track or near. I will use the radio to check between each of us, my call sign is Alpha, you Troy are Bravo and Steve, Delta. If you see anything out of character then we call it Charlie OK which will give us time to get to where the caller is?" Brian Cox was definitely in control. "I will be calling at fifteen minute intervals to check so synchronize watches now." There was a slight silence as they must have checked to make sure they were all on the same time. They confirmed the check together.

The other two acknowledged the order as Brian along with Steve set off towards the end of the first dam where they then crossed over to the other side of it. Tom could see now that there was another dam above and beyond the first which was gushing water down a small waterfall into the first.

Shit Tom just couldn't move at the movement. Troy below would hear if he tried, he was pinned and just hoped that no one could see him on the top of the boulder from further up the hill. He had lost sight of the two traipsing upwards after they got around the second dam. The trees there were denser than any he had passed earlier thank God.

Time drifted on, another thirty minutes further and as he lay there Tom heard Troy speak into the radio "Bravo, clear, out." For the second time Tom heard. They certainly were going to keep in touch every fifteen minutes that was obvious.

As the clock came around there was another call from Troy repeating what he had said before. Tom had to do something or seriously be compromised here. He slowly moved to the edge of the boulder where he caught a glimpse of Troy who had relaxed somewhat lifting his balaclava up onto his head exposing an earpiece in his left ear which protruded about two inches down the side of his face, the microphone. Tom had seen this type of radio communication before and knew at the edge of the ear piece was a small button with voice pick up. This was confirmed as on the next check he saw Troy repeat the words again with his left hand rising to press the pretzel.

The rain had come in dribs and drabs; Tom was soaked on the outside but still dry inside with the good choice of gear he had bought. Watching for any opportunity he kept his eyes pinned on Troy as he walked away from the boulder to take a leak by a bush on the other side of the path. He dropped his MP3 over his shoulder on its strap and juggled with his appendage to get the required result. He didn't seem at all perturbed by the scenario he was in possibly thinking four to one was good enough odds for anyone.

Troy was just fixing himself up as Tom ceased on the opportunity to have a go. Troy was about three metres from the boulder as he was starting to back up to the rock as Tom rose to his feet with knife in hand. As Troy got to the half way mark backing towards the boulder Tom dropped from the rock slipping in behind Troy who didn't hear a thing till he felt the wind gust of Tom falling in behind him.

By then he was too late because as Tom Landed he threw his left arm around Troy's head pulling it to the left and with his right brought the knife up then across the throat area finally dragging it across the skin left to right of the neck. Troy felt nothing but a cold feeling going through his body as the blood oozed out from the cut made which had torn both the carotid arteries. Troy couldn't yell or say boo as the throat opened up to the elements. Tom held him for a couple of minutes before dragging him back to his original position at the base of the boulder.

Propping Troy up against the boulder he removed the balaclava, radio and MP3 from the dead body. He removed Troy's watch as it was calibrated to the others. The next call was to be in a few moments and Tom had to be ready. He pushed the earpiece in and waited. The balaclava he held about his mouth as all of a sudden the call started with 'Alpha clear'

Tom answered holding the balaclava to his mouth. "Bravo, clear out." He then heard Steve repeat his call sign. All seemed good so he carried on placing a load of broken bushes by Troy propping him up but also covering him just partially.

Retrieving his gear from the top of the boulder Tom started to make his way up the hill again but staying the opposite side of the dams rather than following the track where Brian and Steve had gone. The odds had shortened now to three to one. He had the map marked and he knew he was on track to be able to circumnavigate this Hidden Valley area with the skills he had.

CHAPTER 48

As Tom had done before the ex SAS man Gerry made his way around the fence line coming up towards the boulder where Tom had been some fifteen minutes earlier. He slowly came to the boulder stopping when he noticed there was someone sitting there in dark gear similar to what he had seen from the road when the chopper had come over.

Gerry withdrew a touch and went around the long way till he was sure that the man sitting there couldn't hear him or see him. He slunk up to the sitting man with his own firearm trained directly on the guy. When he was within jumping range he lurched forward dropping down directly on the man's position smacking his gun across the poor sods head. He didn't feel a thing anyway.

That was easier than I thought it would be, Gerry thought to himself as he felt no movement beneath him. Must still have it in me old man he proudly said to himself. As he pulled up away from the silent figure it was then that he saw the open neck wound that had been concealed by the dark jumper as he approached. Gerry bent down to see if there was any pulse even though he knew that this man was as dead as because he could see at closer looking the blood that was down the front of the man's gear. He grinned to himself thinking Tom was on top of it still and must have seen the men come down from the Blackhawk earlier.

Checking to make sure he put Troy back into the same position as Tom had done he then checked the footprints that led away from the boulder.

The rain was starting to come down heavily again. Gerry found there were multiple footprints going around between the two dams that were there but there was only one set going alongside the second dam in the parallel to those on the opposite side of the dam. Gerry was going to follow Tom as he would be able to help him better if he was near at hand now there were other players on the field.

It wasn't long before he heard the voice repeating 'Bravo clear out' every fifteen minutes. He held back as he did not recognise the muffled voice that was speaking.

Two hours further along the light was beginning to fade and it was getting harder to see in the drizzle that was still coming down around the area. Gerry knew he would upset Tom if he got too close to him but at the same time he needed to be able to assist if he was needed.

As they ventured further it was then that he heard the man in front of him drop to the ground. Before he could he felt the sharp pain of something sharp hit him in the thigh. He did not yell just stopped and dropped as he placed his hand along the thigh that was now burning from the inside. Blood was pouring out; he had been shot but hadn't heard a damn thing. There was no bang, no thud that he was aware of but it may have happened when the man ahead dropped to the ground. He lay still, waiting for the perpetrator to appear in the hope that he would think he had taken the man out.

Up in front what had made Tom hit the deck was the radio barking in his ear. "Delta, Charlie spotted will take shot." That was all it needed for Tom to hit the deck as he thought that Delta or Steve had spotted him. He also never saw a flash or heard a shot or thud from a silenced weapon but did hear something fall from about twenty meters behind him.

Tom turned to see if he could make out anything from the rear but saw nothing in the dark watery mist. All of a sudden he spotted a dark shadow move to a line directly behind him but facing away in the opposite direction. He pulled the MP3 up and waited as the shadow moved further away from him. Then he heard what was an unsilenced weapon discharge. Who the hell was it back there, someone out hunting or something?

Tom went off to the right and around to where he had heard the falling object. In his earpiece were hurried words asking for updates from Delta. Tom ignored it all as he came around to find one dead dark clothed figure and a rather strained looking face of a man he knew well enough.

"What the fuck are you doing here Gerry?" he asked bending down to inspect what he saw as a bullet hole oozing blood from his leg.

"Gary asked me to be available in case you needed me pal." Gerry was angry with himself at being seen by the shadow man. "I think I am getting too old for this shit."

"I told Gary I was fine and wanted to do this alone you dickhead. Look at you bleeding all over the place."

"Talking of bleeding I caught some of your handy work back there my boy." Gerry grinned at Tom.

The radio kicked in yet again. "Alpha, what was that shot delta? Come in Delta." Brian was beginning to get anxious by the sound of his voice. "Bravo did you hear anything?"

"Bravo, negative out." Tom answered looking down at a still grinning face of Gerry.

"I'm just too old for this shit any more." Gerry came back with. "Lost the old skills I think Tom, sorry for that."

"You're alright Gerry now let's get you patched up." Tom looked at the body sprawled at their feet and saw that the man had a battle dressing on his belt which Tom rapidly removed and proceeded to place on the wound to Gerry's leg. He also ripped up some of the dead man's clothing to strap up the leg so Gerry wouldn't lose too much blood. As he finished he looked at the old goat and said. "You stay here while I sort out the rest. The MP3 is fully loaded other than the one through your thigh. You going to be ok?"

"Yea sure Tom go and finish this shit will you, I'll stay put till I can get some energy to return down the hill and get reception on the mobile." With that Tom left Gerry on his own making sure he was hidden under some cover away from the rain as much as possible. He set up his poncho as further protection from the rain. As Tom left his supposed help he turned back to him, laughed saying "Do you realize who we really are

Gerry?"

"No what do you mean?"

"Mate, think about it eh! Just look at our names, Tom and Gerry. Get the drift, you just stay and be the good little mouse you are while I go off scratching for clues."

Both he and Gerry burst out laughing with Gerry adding. "Never occurred to me but eh those guys never got themselves killed so why should we."

"Right on Gerry." Tom turned still smiling at the similarities of the cartoon characters and them. That smile never left his face for quite a while that night. He had a lot of time for his old mate and perhaps he was starting to trust him as well, about time he said to himself.

CHAPTER 49

The night had closed in now with the rain being more consistent than before. The track became slippery than ever with areas washing away all the evidence of any footprints that were there previously. Tom still had the radio bleating into his ear with questions being asked about Delta who for some unknown reason, to Brian anyway, had gone silent after an exchange of gunfire.

"Bravo, make your way up the track, something's up. I will meet you where Delta was last about twenty minutes from your location."

Tom just gave a 'roger that' and then set about planning for the arrival of Brian Cox. This was going to make it a balanced one on one after this little foray. He pulled some thick lengths of branch back to one side of the path and started to sharpen the edges of them to a point. A trap was formulating in his plan just in case Cox wasn't alone. He was about 250 meters away from Gerry so had no worries about him being in a compromised position. The other thing he would be thankful for was the fact that Gerry had a powerful weapon if needed to back him up.

Tom hastily sharpened ten branches each one over an inch thick and about a metre long. He placed five either side of the path at a point where there was bushes but no trees to hinder someone who had to get off the path quickly. With the ground getting softer by the minute with the rain he had no problem in driving the branches spike up into the ground and securing them at an angle with loose rocks and mud, covering them by pulling the bushes across their spike tips. The trap was finally set.

Waiting for the enemy is always the time where you feel your heart beat harder than normal in anticipation of the confrontation. Tom could hear his beating loudly in his ears wondering if the beat was that strong it might send vibrating waves across the ground to the opposition. No chance of that, silly thought.

The rain was still coming down as Tom got off the path just after the trap he had set between the trap and where his mate was covered. He moved under the cover of a large tree surrounded by bushes. He listened intently for movement coming towards him. For ten minutes he waited wondering if Cox was coming along this particular track but as he was about to move out to check he suddenly heard a sloshing noise just ahead of him. Time had come to enter the next phase.

The radio burst into action again in his ear as Cox tried to locate the position of what he believed to be Troy but this time Tom never responded. He waited patiently for Cox to come into view lifting the silenced MP3 ready to hit the path and make Cox dive for cover. Rather that he impale himself than for Tom to notch up yet another shot person.

The radio kept on but Tom refused to respond listening to what was a single movement ahead of him. Through the raindrops he caught a glimpse of what appeared to be a shadow moving cautiously. It came stealthily along the track towards him. As the shadowy figure got to the trap area Tom let off a couple of rounds into the ground just ahead of the figure. Cox immediately stopped calling out to Troy to hold his fire. Tom had hoped Cox would have dived to either his left or right directly into the path of the sharp spikes that were there but he didn't, he just stood still staring forward shouting abusive comments to Troy.

Tom heard the start of the radio comment which Cox, thinking Bravo was shooting, went in to say it was him but he never finished as Tom appeared before him pointing the MP3 at his chest.

"Drop your weapon Cox, its over." Tom called out at him.

"Clever little pommy shit, thought you would have been caught by now." Cox answered as he lowered his weapon finally dropping it by his side. "They warned me you were like a bulldog not letting go."

"Kick it over to the side." Tom called out to Cox indicating the MP3, with Cox responding positively and kicking it into the side of the track.

Tom walked over to Cox who now had his hands down by his side. "How about you put the hands on your head and stand just still." Tom waved the MP3 in Cox's face as he spoke.

Cox slowly lifted his hands to his head staring blankly at Tom. Tom came close enough for Cox who let out one hell of a cry and slammed his hand firmly onto the barrel of the gun. With his other hand he came round with a closed fist into Tom's neck region.

Tom was caught out totally, pulled back on the trigger which let off a couple of thuds into the dark sky while stumbling backwards till he was able to plant his feet firmly on the ground again. He went forward with his fist turned to hit Cox in the solar plexus but Cox shepherded the blow away. Both of them still had one hand on the MP3. Blow after blow came from each with both being able to palm the other away.

Tom suddenly let a kick go which landed firmly in the groin of Cox catching him totally unawares. He still refused to let go of the weapon though and pulled hard in a twisting motion which brought Tom to within his fist range. He let go another blow towards Tom's head. Tom ducked placing his left leg behind Cox's and giving him a gentle shove with his open hand. Cox went over but again still refused to let go of the gun. Tom had to go with him but by doing that he gave Cox the advantage in the fact he was on top with Cox placing a foot under him hoying him over the top of his head as he lay on the floor.

Tom refused this time to give up the gun and they both ended up twisting around to try to stand. Cox was first up which caused Tom to have to spin himself around without taking his hand away from the gun. He managed to get his feet in the right position enabling him to spin in the air in quick motion landing on both feet and throwing a sharp deadly open chop to the throat of Cox.

There was nothing Cox could do. He wore the chop about his Adam's apple which made him release the gun barrel falling backward and to his right. He was right in the area of the trap falling face first into the spikes. As he hit them his breath went out of his lungs as well as the fire feeling that went through his stomach in three places from the impact of the spikes. He had become impaled there on the three spikes struggling to bring his hands into a position to assist himself because his lungs were still fighting to overcome the closure of his throat from Tom's blow to his throat.

Tom rushed to where he lay holding the weapon he had close to the back of Cox's head. He didn't want Cox to die just yet as he wanted information from him about Caulfield if he could. As he stood over him he saw the damage he had created to his fellow combatant. Through the back of Cox poked two of the three spikes he had dived upon. The third had broken off in his gut which was causing him excruciating pain. Tom kicked Cox's hand away from the weapon he had kicked earlier then grabbed his collar pulling him up upwards off the spikes and over onto his back.

We all know that if something penetrates your body you should leave it there and just donut the entrance and exit points but Tom wasn't about to be First Aider of the month, not today. He knew he had very little time before Cox bled out so he immediately threw him a question.

"Who else is with Caulfield?" Tom asked looking down at what was once a serious looking copper but now all he saw was a screwed up face in lots of pain.

"Who?" Cox asked back at him.

"OK Scholfield, who else is with him?"

"Just some Sheila." Cox was starting to cough up blood as he spoke. "Get me some medical help pleaseee." Pleaded Cox running his hands over the spike points of entry that he was desperately trying to stem the flow of blood from.

"Haven't got time you arsehole. What has he got up there weapon wise?" Tom needed this information in the hope he could outwit him when he eventually arrived at his camp.

"I need help Tom Please. He has his Sheila and a rifle, now please for Christ sake." He coughed again wincing in pain and spitting out blood at the same time.

"It's all about trust in life Coxie." Tom looked down on him still with the sickly looking smile he had since leaving Gerry back up the track. He lifted his MP3 pointed it at Cox's head and pulled on the trigger. There was a thud and Cox's head blew out the rear spreading what little brains he had onto the wet muddy undergrowth. One on one now thought Tom turning and moving up the track now knowing he was about twenty minutes from his final objective.

Tom started to feel a bit repentant about the killing he had done over the past few months but the feeling never lasted long as his adrenalin was flowing so fast through his body he was focused totally on finishing this whole saga today.

During the time of the scuffle, while Tom dealt with Cox and then left heading up the track to meet Caulfield, Gerry had recovered his composure a touch and was trying to pull himself up to be able to get back down the track towards the house where he knew he could get reception for his mobile. It was a painful effort but he made it all being slow as it may have been. He did eventually make it back down to the house where he was able to get in touch once again with Gary reporting what he had witnessed so far.

Gary immediately started the proceedings to get help to both Gerry and Tom as soon as possible. His only dilemma was who to trust as the one he had trusted was now he believed under the pay of the other side.

CHAPTER 50

The rain again eased off as Tom made his way further along the track towards Hidden valley. He was now caked all over in mud from his little scuffle with Cox as he strove to climb some of the more steep areas rather than go via an exposed track. The dark cloudy sky had given him all the cover he really needed but had also hampered him in his quest to get to Caulfield before the night had really set in. The smells around him now were pleasant like fresh grass and flowers. A bit of rain certainly brightens up the bush.

He was about ten minutes from his ultimate destination when he felt he needed to rest to prepare for the final onslaught. He hid under a large bush throwing a large plastic bag he had over his head suspended in the bush. He sat under it and went through the gear he had in his backpack. Here were the knife, compass, map, cans of deodorant and shaving foam. He wondered whether it was worth carrying such crap but kept it together anyway. Soap, shaver dry clothes were all in the bag as he had always learnt, there is no better preparation than being dry.

He changed some of his gear which had got wet, rolling up the removed stuff and placing in a hole he dug with his knife which he would leave in under the bush as he left. He had taken about ten minutes to get himself ready and with a chew at a Mars bar put the sugar rush into him he wanted so desperately. Always carry chocolate the old man had said it does wonders in the cold and the wet.

Tom sat wondering what his father would do if he were in the position he was now. He had always listened to the advice he had given him over the few years he had known him. His Dad had become his hero with the way he had fought his way to justice along with his mother and accepted his responsibilities when he had finally found them out. He had the patience of a saint, always kept calm in stress situations and thought his way through any obstacle that faced him. If only I could just have a little of him in me then I would be pleased he thought.

The thoughts of his parents brought his confidence levels up again and he prepared to move out to meet his nemesis. Leaving behind in the bush what he no longer needed he threw on the backpack after rolling up the plastic bag, picked up the MP3 and returned to his compass and map to complete the final meters ahead.

It wasn't too long before he finally heard some movement up ahead of him. The sky with its cloud cover was still dark and with no moon visible it was almost impossible to see anything. But as he came around what appeared to be the crest of the Valley he saw to his right a glow of what was a fire. How it had kept burning in the weather that had come previously that evening was baffling till he got closer to it. His curiosity was answered by the time he was within fifty meters. There in front of him was a ledge hanging over the fire and under the ledge was a tent with a light on inside.

If only Caulfield could see what was silhouetted by the light to those outside he would have been truly embarrassed. As Tom got closer he could pick out the outline of a naked women positioned on what would have been all fours with behind the figure of a flat chest male moving in and out from the rear of the female. It tended to bring a smile to Tom's face as he thought he might just catch Caulfield as he reached his goal.

It did not look at all flattering as the female was throwing back her head and moaning while her breasts slapped back and forth under the momentum of the male picking up a fair pace as he must be nearing his ultimate destination. Tom thought he could now take them both in total surprise while they were on their ride of pleasure so he slipped off the back pack and fumbled inside the top pulling out the can of deodorant. He knew he had brought it for a reason.

He slowly crept nearer the tent and the fire at its front. The noise coming from within the canvas was gaining in momentum as he got closer. Tom's face lit up as he thought he would catch Caulfield right on his vinegar stroke spoiling perhaps his last ride of freedom. He grabbed the can just tossing it to the middle of the fire where the flames started to lick at it.

It wasn't long before the noises of sexual accomplishment and a loud explosion caused by the can being ignited by the fire both rang out. The silhouette movement stopped dead and the male withdrew from his position to grab what looked like a rifle that would have been lying beside his legs. The poor woman left without satisfaction just crumbled onto her front in distress. The cover of the tent lifted and the outline of a man stood stark naked except for the MP3 he waved around.

Tom had after tossing the can on the fire withdrawn back to cover behind a rock. He was just peering over trying to stop himself from laughing at what was standing before him.

Caulfield looked right then left then down to the fire where he could see the evidence that caused the explosion before he stepped back into the tent to pull on his trousers and a shirt. The woman was pleading with him to finish what he had started but he tried to explain to her that there was something amiss outside and he would have to sort it out first then come back and finish her off. She sighed and pulled the sleeping bag up over her body.

Their generated heat must have made them both immune to the cold now evident outside as Caulfield returned to the outside of the tent in only a shirt, trousers and boots which were untied. He moved to the right of Tom holding a torch to his barrel to light up ahead. He moved around the hanging rock he was under and peered into the light he was shedding out over the ground. Nothing was in the light.

Caulfield came back to the tent proceeding to move to the other side. As he did so Tom moved stealthily out from his cover and round behind where Caulfield was.

Tom wanted to take this guy alive as he had done with Welsh. They needed to face their own justice for what they had done back in Iraq. He placed the MP3 he had by the rock out of sight, a chance to take but he felt confident enough to make it.

Caulfield was close to the rocky edge of a drop off point when Tom came close behind him. The rain had stopped now so any movement made was not hidden by the falling droplets. As Tom got within a couple of meters Caulfield either felt the hairs on his neck go up or heard a slight movement as he spun around to face what was there.

Tom was quick enough to be able to grab the barrel of the MP3 before Caulfield could let off any rounds. Pushing the weapon to his right while at the same time bringing his left boot hard down onto Caulfield's right knee which sent Caulfield falling backwards onto the ground followed by a yell of pain from the knee.

Caulfield kept hold of the MP3 as his face screwed up as he stared at the serious but smiling face of Tom as he landed on top of him. This last effort knocked the wind out of Caulfield but he still wasn't prepared to let go of his weapon.

The pair began rolling around in the mud neither letting go of the MP3 but with Caulfield's finger on the trigger there were a couple of thuds as the mechanism released the shots as it felt the finger pull back on it as they rolled. Neither was caught by the bullets as they exited the barrel travelling out harmlessly over the Valley below.

Tom finally got the advantage having the weapon pressed between him and Caulfield. He pushed hard on to it finally being able to close the distance between the gun and Caulfield's throat. He lifted his weight onto it in the hope he would be able to render Caulfield out of puff but it wasn't to be as just as he had the gun at the throat a leg came crashing up into his groin which threw him off the top of Caulfield. The role had changed and now Caulfield was on the top of the pile.

Tom frantically tried all he could to reverse what was happening but Caulfield was still good, not like the others, he was still fit and well trained to deal with this type of argument. The frustration showed as both pulled, pushed and rolled as much as possible to change the advantage to themselves.

Finally Tom got the momentum he needed by twisting one way then reversing his movement rapidly in the other direction which threw Caulfield off balance slightly. His finger now no longer on the trigger Tom was able to throw him over to the left of his body where he released a hand before bringing it down squarely onto the jaw of Caulfield. The weapon was finally released and became free for Tom to grasp by the barrel then throw behind him.

Caulfield looked up now with fear in his eyes as he had no way of dealing with the younger man now pinning him down. Tom gave him another crack at the jaw which sent Caulfield's eyes rolling in his head and then his lights went out for a short while. Tom released his grip on Caulfield stood up bringing out the Glock he had tucked into his jacket pocket. The commotion outside had frightened the woman in the tent leading her to pull on some clothing so not to get embarrassed if anyone new was to see her.

Tom took no notice of what the woman was doing in the tent; his only concern was Caulfield at the present. He needed to be able to tie him up and find a way to get him to people he could trust. Tom found some short ropes that were just sitting by the side of the tent which he could use. He trussed up Caulfield's wrists as tight as he could in front of him which was not the norm as he would find out soon.

He didn't notice the woman exiting the tent with a pistol in her hands shaking violently with inexperience. She pointed the pistol at Tom before saying. "Let him go and stand to one side or I will shoot you."

"Look this isn't your fight. You don't know what this man has done in the past that has brought me here after him."

"I don't care just untie him and get over against the wall."

Tom turned slowly not complying with the orders she had given him. As he turned he saw for himself how nervous the woman was. She was standing with both hands on the gun but they were waving around as if she was trying to pinpoint a moving object.

"The best thing you can do is put the gun down before someone gets hurt eh?" Tom kept his cool as he tried to calm her down. He moved slightly forward to see her reaction but all that did was make her fingers pull back on the trigger and a shot rang out which echoed around the Valley. Tom felt the pain then in his left shoulder. The bitch had shot him; the fire in his shoulder was burning like shit. He looked at her grabbing his own arm. His weapon was back in his pocket so he was out of the reactive mix. Below him Caulfield was slowly coming to with a moan here and there.

Tom could only try one thing and that was to leave Caulfield trussed up and move to the wall where she had told him. That way he may have a chance to get to his gun. He moved away from Caulfield hoping she would go to him and try to undo the knots there. He was right, as he planted his back against the wall trying hard not to think about the bullet now lodged in his shoulder the woman moved over to Caulfield where she knelt down beside him but still holding the waving gun out front of her and still pointing at Tom.

"You Ok Hun." She said down to Caulfield.

"Yea I'm fine, just a little sore from his damn knuckles." His voice was a touch unstable as he spoke. Tom just starred at the two of them as they exchanged eye expressions to each other.

"What do I do with him?" the woman was a trite confused now as Caulfield suddenly gained his domineering personality again.

"Undo these damn knots will you. I'll deal with the youngster." The woman acknowledged him by immediately placing the gun by the side of them both and got both her hands moving as quickly as she could to the knots. It was the only chance Tom felt he had so he took it. He pulled out the Glock with his right hand shouting at the two in front of him.

"Just hold your horses you two." Tom was holding the Glock firmly in his right hand but his left arm was now dangling beside him numb from the pain in the shoulder. "Move away from him now or I'll blow his brains out in front of you."

The woman was shaking profusely now as she stood and moved away from her man. Caulfield was still trussed up as no success had been made on the knots Tom had tied. Caulfield's eyes showed signs of hate as the daggers that could have been sent via them mystically penetrated into Tom.

The woman had moved to near the edge of the rocks and was still shaking badly wondering what kind of a mess she had got herself involved in. She obviously knew some of the story to have been here anyway but love or lust really leads the blind at times. Caulfield got to his feet wrists still tied in front of him as Tom came closer to his prey to speak.

"In all this time I have no need to kill you Caulfield just to make sure you face what you have to for your past misdemeanours. You sacrificed your own men, new boys to the corps and then Mahmoud a decent Iraqi proud of his country and seeking to bring it to what it needed in democratic terms." Tom stood about a meter and a half from him staring intently at the sorrowful looking man wondering now why he was even lecturing him.

"Who cares about collateral damage, I for sure don't. Mahmoud just got in the way after finding out about me from one of his contacts, he had to go. How much would it cost for you to forget it all Warburton?" Caulfield never ever had any qualms about trying to bribe his way out of any situation.

"Didn't you try that before when you set me up you bastard?" Tom moved forward smacking Caulfield fair across the face with the Glock. That made him bend slightly down as he took it full force across one cheek. He righted himself ready to reply to Tom.

"When I first picked you as the stool pigeon I wasn't sure who you were, you know. I already had you played for the one to use, new boy on the block and all that. It wasn't till afterwards that I found out who your old man was. Thought he would be the one to come after me and I think I could have taken him easy now because of his age.

Didn't expect you to survive the Iraqi prison you were in anyway. Still can't get my head around to the fact that you were rescued by our own boys."

"What about Ashid's involvement in all of this?"

"Ashid, that slimy little Arab. You don't know just how powerful he really is. If it wasn't for him though, we would have had problems getting our haul out the country back then.

Don't underestimate the man Warburton he will come after you eventually, you know that don't you?" Tom felt Caulfield was trying to put the frighteners on him to unnerve him but he wasn't playing.

"His turn will come Caulfield mark my words."

"You really haven't a clue who or what that man can do have you?" Caulfield laughed into Tom's face.

Tom ignored the remark and shirked off the possibility that Ashid would come after him at all.

As they talked the woman was moving behind both the men. She had her eyes on the gun lying on the floor near to her. Perhaps if she could get to it then she and Caulfield could continue on with what they had started with their travels to Queensland.

Tom's eyes caught a glimpse of her movement but as he did so did Caulfield who took the opportunity to try again to free himself. He kicked out at Tom connecting with Tom's left thigh which threw him off balance sending him stumbling to his rear. When this took off the woman raced towards the weapon she had her eyes on and Caulfield turned sharply towards the same objective.

Tom regained his feet just as he saw Caulfield and the woman accidentally collide near the handgun. Smacking both their heads together sending both in different directions. Caulfield fell forward onto his face but the woman took the brunt and being smaller than Caulfield the knock sent her careering towards the edge of the rock face.

Tom saw to his horror where she was heading and tried in vain to get himself to where she was but it was a lost exercise as he got near to her she had already overcompensated for her movement and with fear in her eyes she started to slowly fall over the edge.

There was an almighty scream as if it was in slow motion the woman clawing at the air around her started her decent to the bottom of the Valley below. Her scream was heard till she hit the bottom. It was pointless looking over the top as the visibility was next to nothing. Tom stopped near the edge but soon turned around to see Caulfield running full pelt away into the darkness beyond. Having to give chase was not what Tom wanted, his shoulder was aching and he was beginning to feel drained with the loss of blood from it.

He set off after Caulfield without a further thought listening as he went to make sure he was going in the right direction. He heard the curses as he was sure he heard Caulfield fall a couple of time ahead of him. Breathless and drained he continued after the man who had caused so much pain to him and his colleagues.

Tom knew he was possibly running around the brim of the Valley roof as he was not aware of any uphill or downhill motion. Caulfield managed to position himself in a way to be able to spring back a large branch onto his opponent. Difficult as it was with his hands tied in front but Tom's mistake as he would not have been able to do it if his hands were tied behind as they should have been.

Suddenly Tom was stopped by a branch that came crashing down onto his back. Tom went barrelling spreadeagled into the mud of the track he was on. The wind knocked out of him and worse still the Glock had been lose in his hand was sent out of his grasp now was lost in the bush. The next thing he felt was a boot in the ribs, then another. He pulled his right arm up over his head for protection. His left was slow to respond and only came up as far as his chest. He curled himself into the foetal position to protect his family jewels just as a kick was placed close to that region.

"Your turn you little shit." Caulfield was heard saying as he threw another giant kick to Tom's back. "You had your chance now it's my turn. You may find out what it's like to perish in the bush in this vast country." And with that he planted another kick to the head which was fended off by Tom's hand and arm.

Caulfield was breathless as he tried to kick over and over again. Finally succumbing to empty lungs he planted his arse onto a rock near at hand. Tom became thankful the guy was older and needed more of a break between his kicks. He peered from his position to see Caulfield sitting with his head down and his chest expanding and retracting rapidly.

Tom hurt but the adrenalin running high within his system perhaps had been kicked in by Caulfield. He sprung to his feet barrelled into Caulfield knocking the old sod off the rock and onto the muddy floor. It was Tom's turn now as he went hell for leather with one boot following another into the ribs and head area of Caulfield. At one stage he thought he heard a crack as he lashed into Caulfield's ribs. Then with a quick kick to the head area he caught Caulfield off his guard and buried his boot just below the chin area which sent Caulfield flying amongst the stars.

Tom was knackered not wanting any more of this pummelling exercise. He checked Caulfield's ties and dragged his sorry arse towards the rock he was once sitting on.

It was a few minutes later that Caulfield came back to the world of the living. His face was black with mud covering what was underneath that mud skin beginning to blue over with the bruises that would be evident once he was washed down.

Caulfield now felt the age he really was, old. He was regretting ever getting into a stoush with this young bull dog in the first place. What was the end result, which he was unsure of as he lay propped against the rock thinking about his life before he had turned evil? Through his mind flashed the faces of the men he had killed, men that had served like him for Queen and country. His head was drooped whether in shame or just fatigue it didn't matter; all had been lost now as he pondered to himself what would the outcome be in the end.

Suddenly the sound of a chopper could be heard coming from the South. Tom shook his head as if in despair. The last chopper he had seen brought an extra three men for him to have to deal with. He was not feeling the best to have to deal with anymore somehow he would have to find his gun or get Caulfield back to the tent area where he knew there were weapons.

Caulfield's head rose and a smile came over his face. "Cavalry on the way, perhaps it's your last chance to get the fuck out of here."

Tom didn't answer but just grabbed Caulfield by the neck dragging him to his feet. He was keen to get back to the tent area before anyone else joined the game.

The chopper got louder then drifted off a touch before Tom just heard it humming in the distance. They weren't far from the tent when he heard it slowly gain in volume as it moved closer towards their position. Urgency came over Tom as he forced the issue with Caulfield who was trying his hardest slow down the pace. He had guessed why Tom wanted to get back to the tent. Tom called on every piece of energy in his system to push on managing to reach the tent before the loud chopper suddenly came overhead.

Tom was now armed again with Caulfield face down on the ground. Tom stepped under the ledge as the chopper with its bright light came into view at the open side where the Valley sat. Bringing the MP3 up into aim he waited till he could see for sure what was happening. The night around him was dark and dreary except for the search light strung beneath the chopper trying to locate them.

The Blackhawk moved slowly towards the edge of the valley wall training the light around to catch a glimpse of the people on the top. Tom pulled back further under the ledge as the Blackhawk hovered close to the campsite. The light was moved around the area finally pinning the tent in its beam.

Tom was estimating the distance of the beam to be able to shoot out the light and remove the eyes they had on the ground. He moved slowly out training his weapon onto the beam area and the source of it. As he came out of the ledge he was caught by the edge of the beam highlighted with weapon pointing up towards the chopper.

Suddenly a voice rang out from a loud speaker on the chopper. "Tom it's the little mouse Gerry, this one's friendly mate." Tom recognised the voice and burst out laughing at the Tom and Gerry bit. He lowered his weapon thankful that perhaps this was all over.

"Someone's coming down to give you a hand Tom."

Tom looked up at the beam stepping back slightly under the cover of the ledge so not to be blinded. He stared into the brightly lit night seeing suddenly a crewman being lowered on a hoist complete with rescue cradle. A sort of stretcher unit came into view which was good to be able to strap his captive into. As the crewman came within the last few feet, Tom came out to meet him grabbing Caulfield by the scruff of the neck as he went.

"Seems it was the Cavalry after all Caulfield but definitely not yours." You could see the disappointment on Caulfield's face as the crewman and Tom strapped him into the stretcher unit and hoisted him up to the cabin above. Still tied he was no problem for the Army guys waiting there for him.

With a few more minutes passing by the cradle came down again with the crewman and stretcher. Tom got on board this time taking the weapons he could find with him. He knew he would have to report the loss of gear that was in the area but that would be up to the local boys to find it as he just wanted to be out of here. As he lay in the stretcher on its way up to the cabin he thought about the months that had gone before and the problems he had to overcome in the process. He closed his eyes as he heard the friendly voice of Gerry when he was pulled into the cabin.

"Told you eh, Tom and Gerry never die, they are the good guys." Spread about him Tom could see a couple of heavily equipped Squaddies and the crew guys all were laughing alongside Gerry. The only one who never got the joke was Caulfield who was now handcuffed to a rail near the far door.

The Blackhawk banked away as Tom closed his eyes dropping into a deep sleep. He wouldn't wake till after the chopper landed and he was sped off along with Gerry to hospital to have the bullets removed that they had collected that evening.

As for the mess that was left behind the local Army boys were already on site removing all traceable objects plus the retrieval of the four bodies spread along the track and in the Valley. Tom needn't worry anymore, his job was done now. All he needed now was to repair himself and return to his home in UK to grieve properly for his mother.

EPILOGUE

Ho Chi Minh City
16 May 2007

After an arduous 19 hour flight the Austrian airlines plane touched down at Tan Son Nhat Airport once the centre of the American and South Vietnam Air defence of South Vietnam in the 70s. It would have been a haven then during the war for service personnel swanking their stuff around the place but now it was a tourist entry point for the Southern part of the Republic of Vietnam. Just to one side there was frantic construction going on building what was a new terminal to compliment the one already in place and the hurry was to finish for an opening in September this year.

Who'd have thought that between 1968 and 1974 this place was the busiest military airbase in the world? During those last days of the war, Pan Am was operating Boeing 747 services four times a week to San Francisco via Guam and Manila. Military charters operated by Continental used 30 Boeing 707 per week throughout 1968-1974. Now that's what you could call a busy place, now it was just a normal airport shifting tourists in and out of the Southern part of the country.

There were four people walking off the plane together here today. Coming via business class they were amongst the first to disembark. At the front was a male and female looking very official, Gary Warlock and Sandra Crisp strutted towards the immigration desks followed by two males one in his fifties and the other a younger twenty three year old version. Both followed closely behind the other two. The fifty year old was holding a small box which contained an urn which carried the ashes of his dear wife. He was returning her to her roots where she requested she wanted to rest for her eternity.

The twenty three year old was sporting a shoulder brace holding his left arm close to his chest. He had just recently received a bullet wound to the shoulder and undergone an operation to remove the fragments in April. It was still sore and it showed as he winched whenever anyone came close enough to brush up against him. Tom Snr and Tom Jnr walked comfortably side by side to the Immigration desk where they stopped and handed their passports to the official behind the screen and patiently waited.

A strange look came over the official as he scrutinised the passports onc at a time then returning to the faces in front of him. He pressed a button on his desk which immediately brought two armed airport guards with machine pistols out to the counter. Neither men at the counter moved or showed any concern about the move as did most of those now queuing up behind them.

You could see the faces of those behind trying their hardest to guess what the problem was. Drugs, wanted men, the faces showed it all.

"Can you please come with us gentlemen?" The senior guard nodded at Tom Snr. Tom returned the nod with a smile.

Both men followed the leader with the other guard coming up the rear. They weren't being marched as such just a polite escort out and into a secure lounge where both Gary and Sandra were sat waiting for them surrounded by about five or so Government Officials, some in suits, some in uniform.

"That was interesting." Tom Snr looked at Gary. "The poor sod thought he was seeing double."

"Dream on old feller." Tom Jnr piped in smiling at Sandra as she stood to introduce the officials now congregated in the private lounge before them.

Amongst the dignitaries were two Government Ministers who had flown down from Hanoi earlier in the day, the local District Commander of Ho chi Minh and a couple of senior military personnel. It looked like the President of the US had just touched down for the first time in Vietnam. There were smiles all around, handshakes that again confirmed to Tom Jnr that his shoulder wasn't healing that fast.

After some diplomatic soul searching amongst those gathered, the four guests from the UK were driven by limousine to the Hotel Continental Saigon which was conveniently located in the city centre within walking distance of most major attractions.

Once booked in the four visitors met in Gary's room to chat about the coming days.

"It seems we are honoured guests today but in 1972 you Tom would have been hung, drawn and quartered for your operation here to sneak out Sam. The Minister of Internal Affairs Nyhong said he was aware of the operation from papers he had come across later. It seems they followed your progress till the culmination of the apology given by the US. You are some sort of hero here now however.

Your rescue and subsequent marriage to one of their own has put you in the high rankings of the place. Lucky sod if you decided to stay here I reckon you would live like a king for the rest of your life."

"Well that's not going to happen. My little piece of heaven is in England. I just want to complete Sue Lin's wishes. She wanted desperately to be laid to rest where her parents were slaughtered back on the dreadful day in 1972.

I am just glad the authorities here have been so helpful towards us, Gary."

"It took a while but after a bit of explaining from Sandra here they fell over themselves to help. They feel you had the same enemy as they did at the time."

Tom Snr looked at Sandra and smiled his appreciation. She however was too focused on the young Tom to offer any further statements for Tom's benefit.

"We have quite a full itinerary ahead guys so I suggest we get our heads down and wake tomorrow with refreshed minds as we are to be given the Royal tour before we go north." With that they all separated to their individual rooms to rest.

For the younger Tom his head was still swimming from the months that had preceded this journey.

The closure of the money scam that had claimed so many lives was still not clear enough in his mind to shut it down once and for all. The UK Government had returned some $70 million US to the Iraqi Government which was the original amount but they did not disclose the fact they had actually recovered some $200 million which was only about 75% of the haul so far. They were not about to disclose the money trail they had uncovered that led to Ashid. That investigation was still ongoing.

As for Aspalson well his memory was just allowed to dwindle into the wind. He had been uncovered by the Firm as dishonest with the subsequent consequences, his demise under his own hand. He would only be remembered as the man who had to resign because of ill health but died just weeks after his resignation unfortunately.

As for Welsh, he lost everything including his lush pension from the Military. He no longer had need for money as his home was now in the Military prison in Colchester, affectionately known as the Glasshouse, where he would be spending some time before being transferred to one of Her Majesties Prisons where he would while away the rest of his days locked away from everything he knew and loved.

Caulfield was grilled so much he would have wondered whether it would have been easier for him to have jumped along with his girlfriend back in the NSW town of Quirindi. He gave little away in reference to Ashid who he had grown to despise after he found out it was actually his plan to eliminate the British participants of the scam and take control of the whole business finances. But still he kept quiet about some of the stuff he knew.

His temporary resting place was the same prison as Welsh where they would never be allowed to communicate or be seen in the same area at the same time. Life was decidedly changed for him. After a short stay in Colchester he also would transfer to one of the civilian prisons, no doubt a different one than his cousin.

In Tom's mind he was fixated on Ashid, there was something not quite right with this man he had that figured but the blighter had disappeared out of sight since the fracas he had created in Baghdad. Perhaps one day that would also come to rest and he could have closure.

For a couple of weeks now he had talked and talked to his father trying to find solutions to what was now a major distrust towards humans of every description. One of the conversations he had with his father was about Vicki. How he had thought that that was his destiny and how she had lied and deceived him so. It was the hardest thing to overcome for him and still he had problems letting it go.

His father had come forth with a statement to him about trust. "Trust is the ability to bank on, believe in, be sure of, confide in, count on, depend on, have confidence in, have faith in, pin your hopes on, and rely on. Sometimes there can be total coverage of these but sometimes there are only a few. Sometimes our trust in others is destroyed by things out of our control. We must never let it stop our trust in everyone we meet for out there are people that are to be trusted and it just needs that step forward on our part.

There will always be disappointments in life but you have to take the good bits and run with those for they are the building blocks of your happiness, son."

With all his father had gone through he was always the positive one these days. With Mum he was so happy and even now he was positive as he knew he could not stop what has happened already, it was a spent cheque he'd say, just look to what you can change and head that way.

Over the coming days they were treated to what was the most interesting tour for those relishing in old war wounds. Places such as the Reunification Palace which was as a government building significant for its role in the Vietnam conflict preserved almost exactly as it was in 1966, Notre Dame cathedral, Municipal Theatre and museums displaying the leftovers of the US war they had won so brilliantly. The majority of the displays in the museums were a major put down on the Americans and what they perceived as their war crimes.

Sunday 20 May

The four were taken early this morning back to the airport where a military plane awaited them. When on board they were flown the hour or so up to Da Nang. Here they transferred to a helicopter for the remaining part of their trip to the area near the border of Cambodia, Laos and Vietnam. This was the most uncomfortable part of the journey but one they knew was bringing closure for them and Sue Lin.

Here in the sombre grounds of what once was the thriving village of Kham Linh a memorial had been erected to the lost villagers slaughtered by the Americans in 1972. The grass was lush and green and there was now a road that led here from the highway not far away.

The small obelisk that had been put there in the centre of the green seemed strange for such a country of Vietnam but it was stunning to say the least protruding up with small plagues placed around it complete with family names. They were told that a similar one had been placed at Xa Cha Duk the other village Tom and his friends had found in 72.

As Tom knelt along with his son at the obelisk he pulled out a plague which he handed it to the official standing alongside him. On the plague it read '*Sue Lin Warburton once of this village, now returned for all eternity.*' It was underwritten in Vietnamese dialect. The official moved to one side and proceeded to fix the plaque to the obelisk while the two Toms prayed silently beside each other.

Suddenly to their right a familiar voice spoke. "Eh Gov you can't do this without the rest of the team." There standing proud stood Geordie looking down at the pair smiling. Tom Snr stood and threw his arms around his old pal. Tom Jnr just smiled and nodded at Gary as he knew that he had organized this little reunion the week before.

"Geordie you look great. Thanks for this."

“Do you think I could miss out on a team member being finally rested? She was our little team member after all Tom.”

There were tears in the eyes of all the grown men standing there even as Sandra had put her arms around young Tom to stop herself from weeping. He didn’t try to shirk them off like he would normally have done, perhaps Dad’s talk had done some good after all.

Just as they composed themselves Geordie pulled out another little plague from his pocket, it read. *‘Somewhere near this mark lies the body of John Weatherhead {J Dub}, friend, colleague and hero to Sue Lin. May his death never be in vain.’* He handed it to the official who placed it below Sue Lin’s plague.

“There at last we have been able to close the pages Tom.” Geordie turned and he and Tom Snr hugged once again, cried and smiled together looked on by the others there.

Mosul Iraq 26 May

Ashid stood in front of the many men and women he had recruited over many years smiling, preaching to them about the greater good they would achieve in the future. He had them all psyched up by the time he placed his right hand in the air to bring silence to the babbling throng assembled.

“It is time for our final Jihad against the infidels and those that have succumbed to their bribes. We now go against the Great Satan, Little Satan and the blind follower in the Southern Cross.”

There were yells of great joy heralding through the hall and everyone in that hall had one distinct thing the same, on the right wrist at the top was a tattooed infinity mark that went across it side to side.

CPSIA information can be obtained
at www.ICGtesting.com
Printed in the USA
LVHW032144161121
703501LV00006B/47

9 781638 716747